PRAISE FOR *APOCALYPSE TACO*

"WEIRD, FREAKY FUN."

—PUBLISHERS WEEKLY

"HALE POSITIVELY REVELS IN THE WEIRDNESS OF HIS PREMISE . . .
A WELL–BALANCED MIX OF SCI–FI, HORROR, AND HUMOR."

—KIRKUS REVIEWS

"HALE HAS DONE IT AGAIN—ANOTHER GRAPHIC NOVEL THAT OFFERS
A TERRIFIC BLEND OF THE EERIE AND THE HUMOROUS."

—SCHOOL LIBRARY JOURNAL

"PERFECT FOR FANS OF WEIRD FICTION, WITH A VISUAL STYLE
THAT WILL APPEAL TO FANS OF HORROR COMICS."

—BOOKLIST

APOCALYPSE

A GRAPHIC NOVEL BY

NATHAN HALE

AMULET BOOKS
NEW YORK

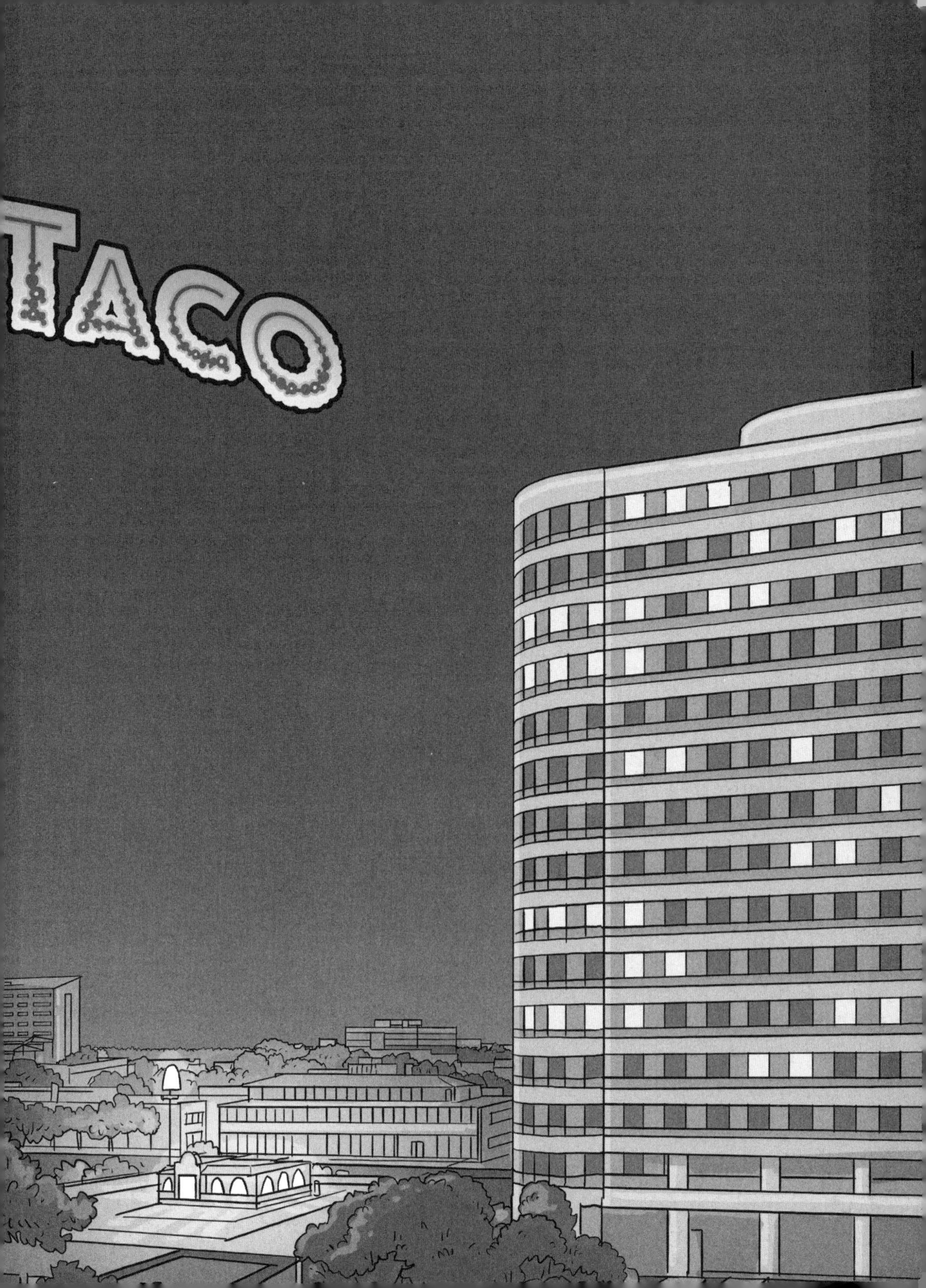
TACO

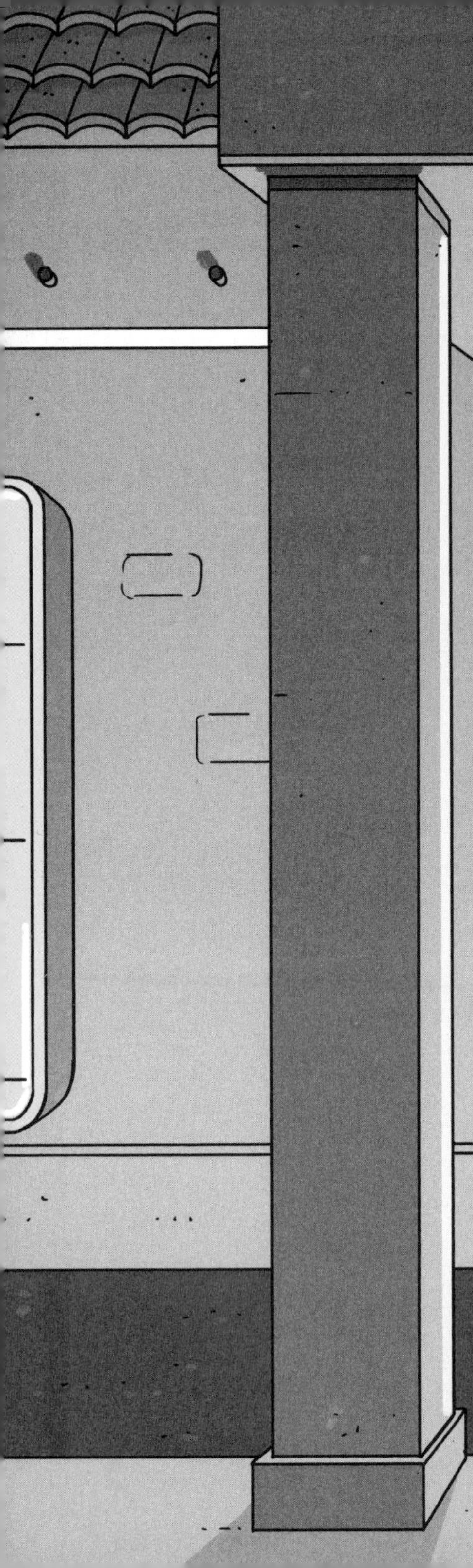

PUBLISHER'S NOTE: THIS IS A WORK OF FICTION. NAMES, CHARACTERS, PLACES, AND INCIDENTS ARE EITHER THE PRODUCT OF THE AUTHOR'S IMAGINATION OR USED FICTITIOUSLY, AND ANY RESEMBLANCE TO ACTUAL PERSONS, LIVING OR DEAD, BUSINESS ESTABLISHMENTS, EVENTS, OR LOCALES IS ENTIRELY COINCIDENTAL.

THE LIBRARY OF CONGRESS HAS CATALOGED THE HARDCOVER EDITION AS FOLLOWS:
NAMES: HALE, NATHAN, 1976– AUTHOR, ILLUSTRATOR.
TITLE: APOCALYPSE TACO / NATHAN HALE.
DESCRIPTION: NEW YORK : AMULET BOOKS, 2019. SUMMARY: TWINS AXL AND IVAN, WITH SID AS THEIR DRIVER, MAKE A LATE--NIGHT FAST--FOOD RUN FOR A HIGH SCHOOL THEATER CREW BUT RETURN TO DISCOVER THAT ALIENS HAVE MADE COPIES OF EVERYTHING. IDENTIFIERS: LCCN 2018047718 ISBN 9781419733734 (HARDBACK)
SUBJECTS: CYAC: GRAPHIC NOVELS. EXTRATERRESTRIAL BEINGS--FICTION. IMPERSONATION--FICTION. BROTHERS--FICTION. TWINS--FICTION. THEATER--FICTION. GRAPHIC NOVELS.
CLASSIFICATION: LCC PZ7.7.H345 APO 2019 DDC 741.5/973--DC23

PAPERBACK ISBN 978-1-4197-3913-2

BOOK DESIGN BY CHAD W. BECKERMAN

PUBLISHED IN PAPERBACK IN 2020 BY AMULET BOOKS, AN IMPRINT OF ABRAMS. ORIGINALLY PUBLISHED IN HARDCOVER BY AMULET BOOKS IN 2019.

PRINTED AND BOUND IN USA
10 9 8 7 6 5 4 3 2

AMULET BOOKS ARE AVAILABLE AT SPECIAL DISCOUNTS WHEN PURCHASED IN QUANTITY FOR PREMIUMS AND PROMOTIONS AS WELL AS FUNDRAISING OR EDUCATIONAL USE. SPECIAL EDITIONS CAN ALSO BE CREATED TO SPECIFICATION. FOR DETAILS, CONTACT SPECIALSALES@ABRAMSBOOKS.COM OR THE ADDRESS BELOW.

ABRAMS The Art of Books
195 Broadway, New York, NY 10007
abramsbooks.com

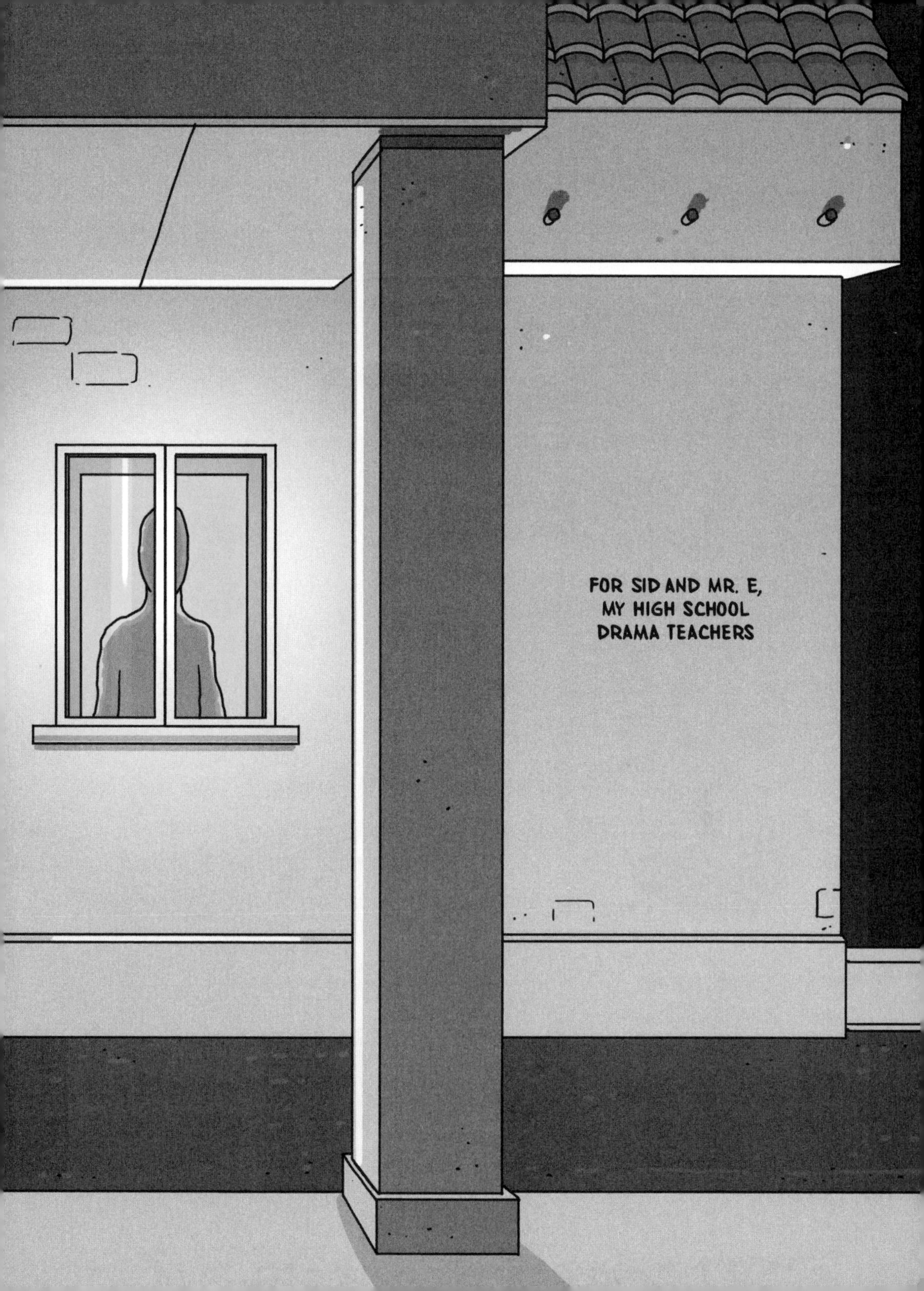
FOR SID AND MR. E,
MY HIGH SCHOOL
DRAMA TEACHERS

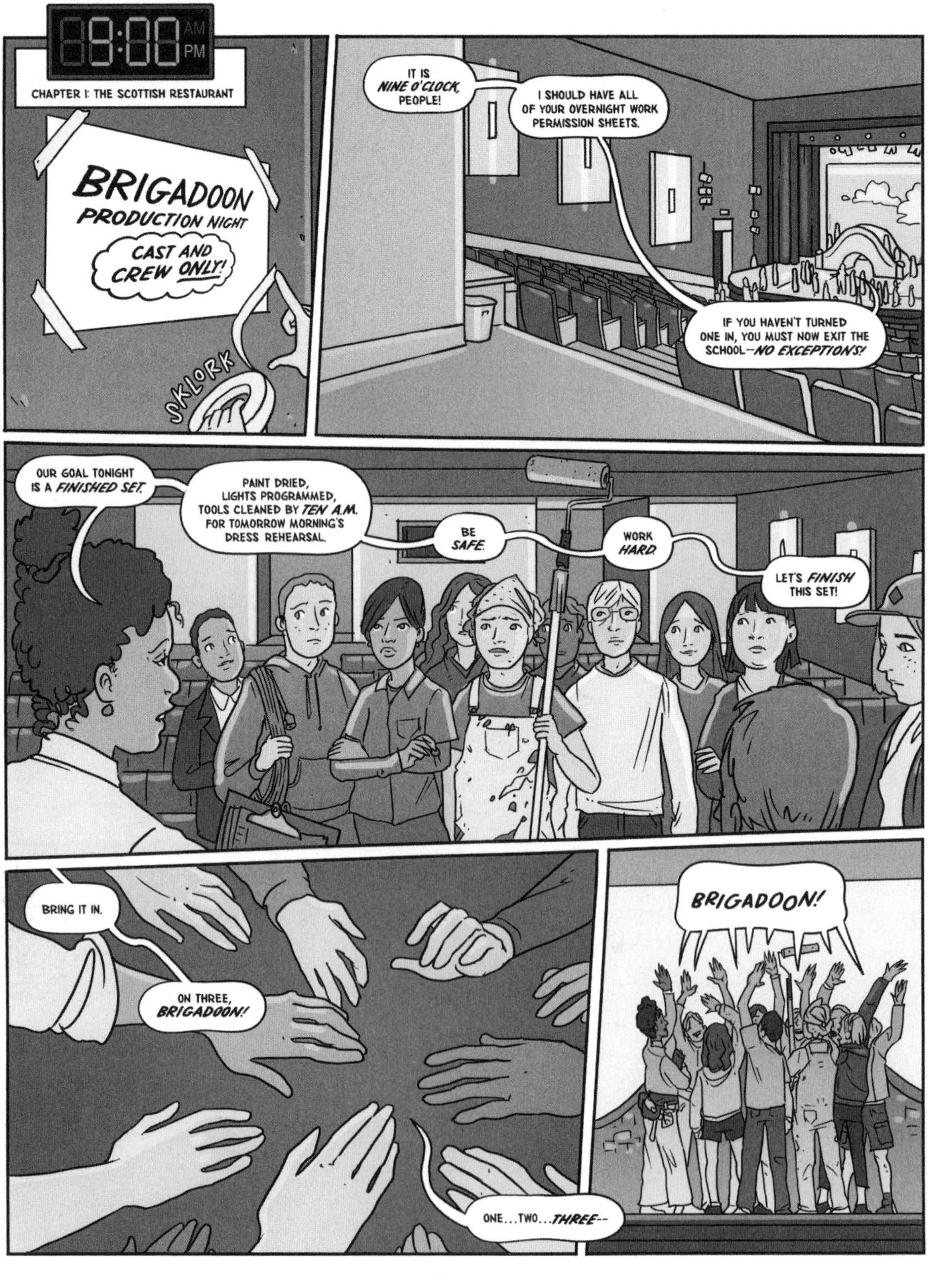
9:00 AM PM
CHAPTER 1: THE SCOTTISH RESTAURANT
BRIGADOON PRODUCTION NIGHT
CAST AND CREW ONLY!
SKLORK
IT IS NINE O'CLOCK, PEOPLE!
I SHOULD HAVE ALL OF YOUR OVERNIGHT WORK PERMISSION SHEETS.
IF YOU HAVEN'T TURNED ONE IN, YOU MUST NOW EXIT THE SCHOOL--NO EXCEPTIONS!
OUR GOAL TONIGHT IS A FINISHED SET.
PAINT DRIED, LIGHTS PROGRAMMED, TOOLS CLEANED BY TEN A.M. FOR TOMORROW MORNING'S DRESS REHEARSAL.
BE SAFE.
WORK HARD.
LET'S FINISH THIS SET!
BRING IT IN.
ON THREE, BRIGADOON!
ONE...TWO...THREE--
BRIGADOON!

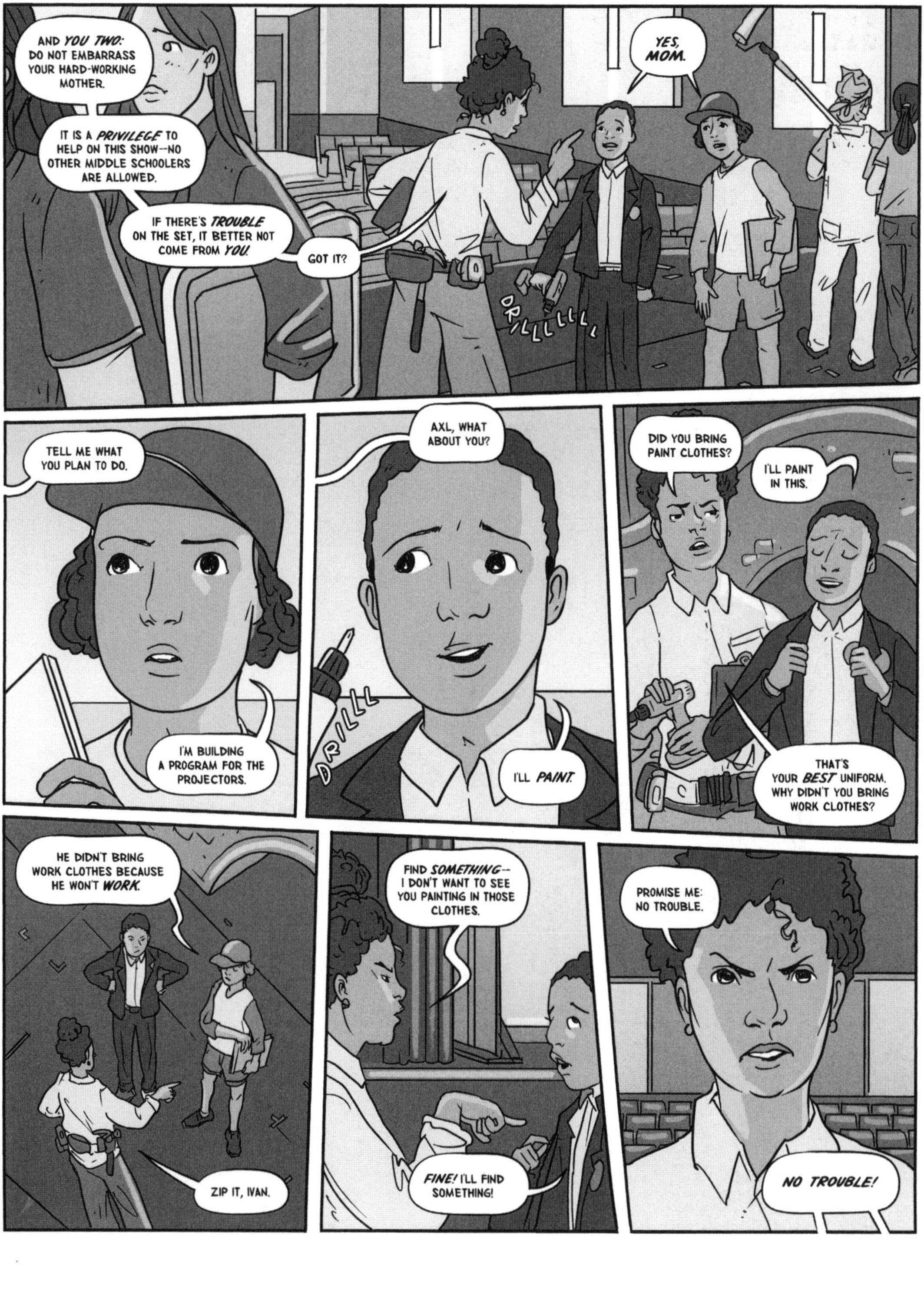
AND YOU TWO: DO NOT EMBARRASS YOUR HARD-WORKING MOTHER.
IT IS A PRIVILEGE TO HELP ON THIS SHOW--NO OTHER MIDDLE SCHOOLERS ARE ALLOWED.
IF THERE'S TROUBLE ON THE SET, IT BETTER NOT COME FROM YOU.
GOT IT?
YES, MOM.
DRILLLLLL
TELL ME WHAT YOU PLAN TO DO.
I'M BUILDING A PROGRAM FOR THE PROJECTORS.
AXL, WHAT ABOUT YOU?
DRILLL
I'LL PAINT.
DID YOU BRING PAINT CLOTHES?
I'LL PAINT IN THIS.
THAT'S YOUR BEST UNIFORM. WHY DIDN'T YOU BRING WORK CLOTHES?
HE DIDN'T BRING WORK CLOTHES BECAUSE HE WON'T WORK.
ZIP IT, IVAN.
FIND SOMETHING-- I DON'T WANT TO SEE YOU PAINTING IN THOSE CLOTHES.
FINE! I'LL FIND SOMETHING!
PROMISE ME: NO TROUBLE.
NO TROUBLE!

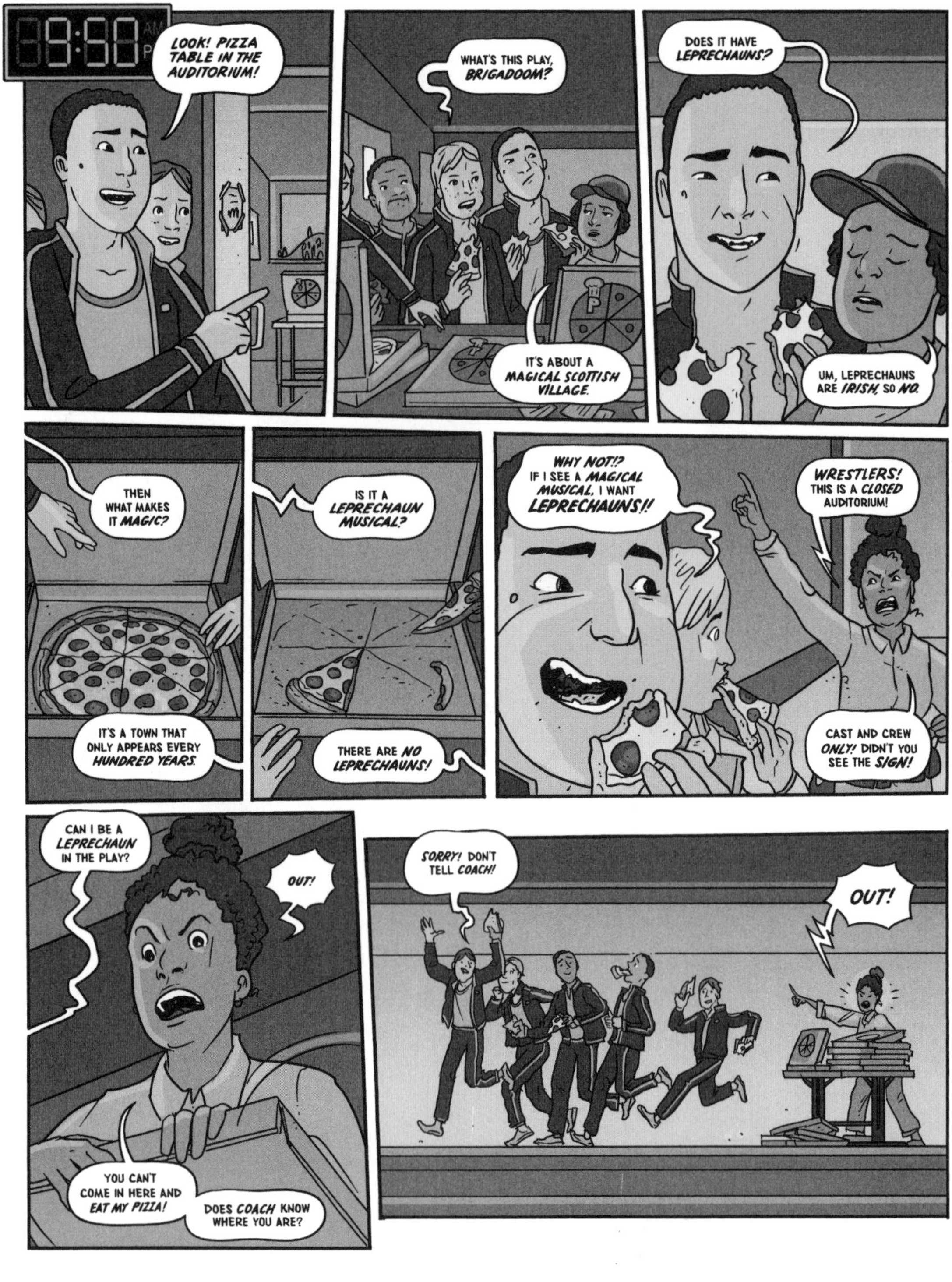
9:50 AM PM
LOOK! PIZZA TABLE IN THE AUDITORIUM!
WHAT'S THIS PLAY, BRIGADOOM?
IT'S ABOUT A MAGICAL SCOTTISH VILLAGE.
DOES IT HAVE LEPRECHAUNS?
UM, LEPRECHAUNS ARE IRISH, SO NO.
THEN WHAT MAKES IT MAGIC?
IT'S A TOWN THAT ONLY APPEARS EVERY HUNDRED YEARS.
IS IT A LEPRECHAUN MUSICAL?
THERE ARE NO LEPRECHAUNS!
WHY NOT!? IF I SEE A MAGICAL MUSICAL, I WANT LEPRECHAUNS!!
WRESTLERS! THIS IS A CLOSED AUDITORIUM!
CAST AND CREW ONLY! DIDN'T YOU SEE THE SIGN!
CAN I BE A LEPRECHAUN IN THE PLAY?
OUT!
YOU CAN'T COME IN HERE AND EAT MY PIZZA!
DOES COACH KNOW WHERE YOU ARE?
SORRY! DON'T TELL COACH!
OUT!

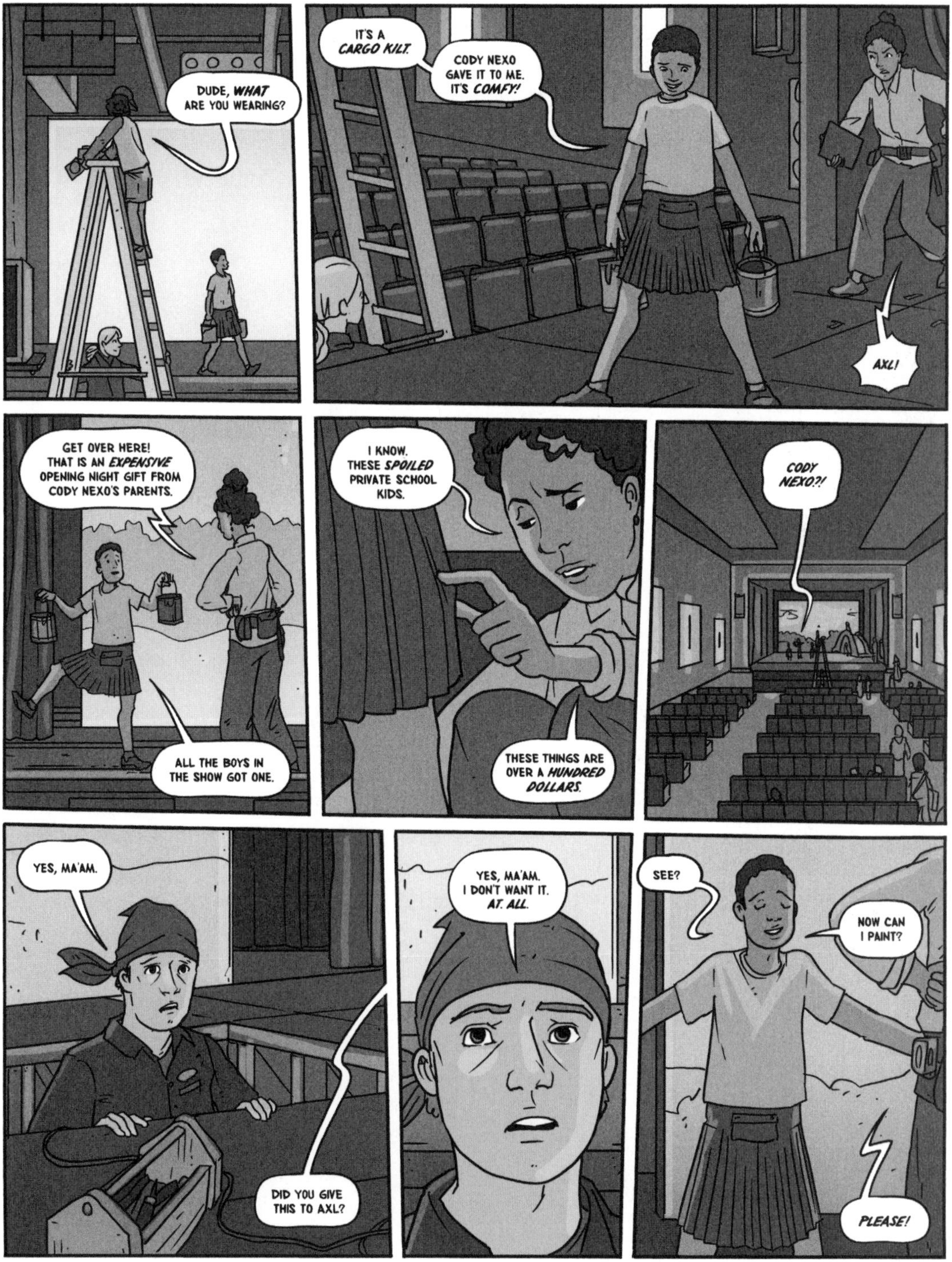
DUDE, WHAT ARE YOU WEARING?
IT'S A CARGO KILT.
CODY NEXO GAVE IT TO ME. IT'S COMFY!
AXL!
GET OVER HERE! THAT IS AN EXPENSIVE OPENING NIGHT GIFT FROM CODY NEXO'S PARENTS.
ALL THE BOYS IN THE SHOW GOT ONE.
I KNOW. THESE SPOILED PRIVATE SCHOOL KIDS.
THESE THINGS ARE OVER A HUNDRED DOLLARS.
CODY NEXO?!
YES, MA'AM.
DID YOU GIVE THIS TO AXL?
YES, MA'AM. I DON'T WANT IT. AT. ALL.
SEE?
NOW CAN I PAINT?
PLEASE!

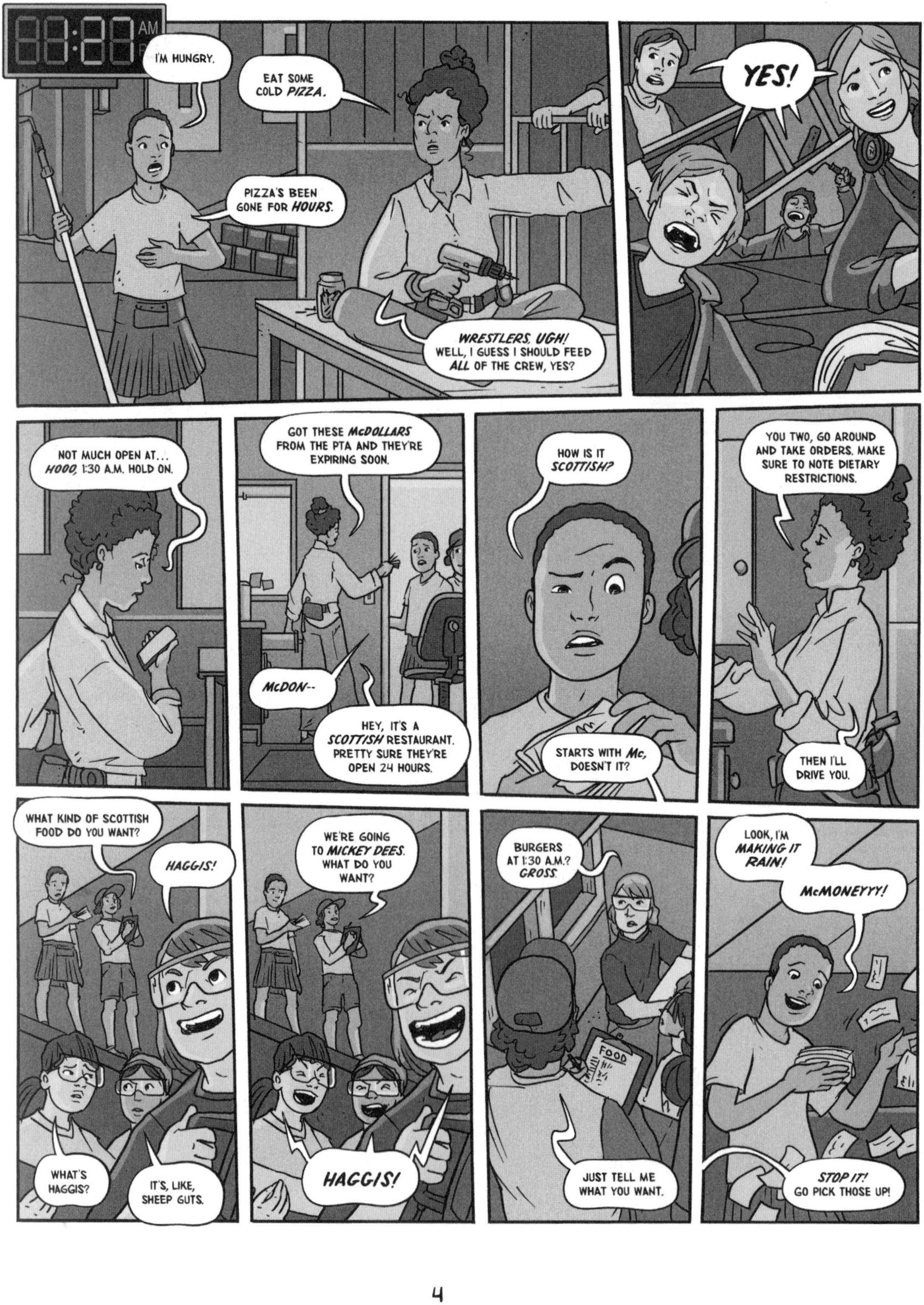
AM
I'M HUNGRY.
EAT SOME COLD PIZZA.
PIZZA'S BEEN GONE FOR HOURS.
WRESTLERS, UGH! WELL, I GUESS I SHOULD FEED ALL OF THE CREW, YES?
YES!
NOT MUCH OPEN AT... HOOO, 1:30 A.M. HOLD ON.
GOT THESE McDOLLARS FROM THE PTA AND THEY'RE EXPIRING SOON.
McDON--
HEY, IT'S A SCOTTISH RESTAURANT. PRETTY SURE THEY'RE OPEN 24 HOURS.
HOW IS IT SCOTTISH?
STARTS WITH Mc, DOESN'T IT?
YOU TWO, GO AROUND AND TAKE ORDERS. MAKE SURE TO NOTE DIETARY RESTRICTIONS.
THEN I'LL DRIVE YOU.
WHAT KIND OF SCOTTISH FOOD DO YOU WANT?
HAGGIS!
WHAT'S HAGGIS?
IT'S, LIKE, SHEEP GUTS.
WE'RE GOING TO MICKEY DEES. WHAT DO YOU WANT?
HAGGIS!
BURGERS AT 1:30 A.M.? GROSS.
FOOD
JUST TELL ME WHAT YOU WANT.
LOOK, I'M MAKING IT RAIN!
McMONEYYY!
STOP IT! GO PICK THOSE UP!

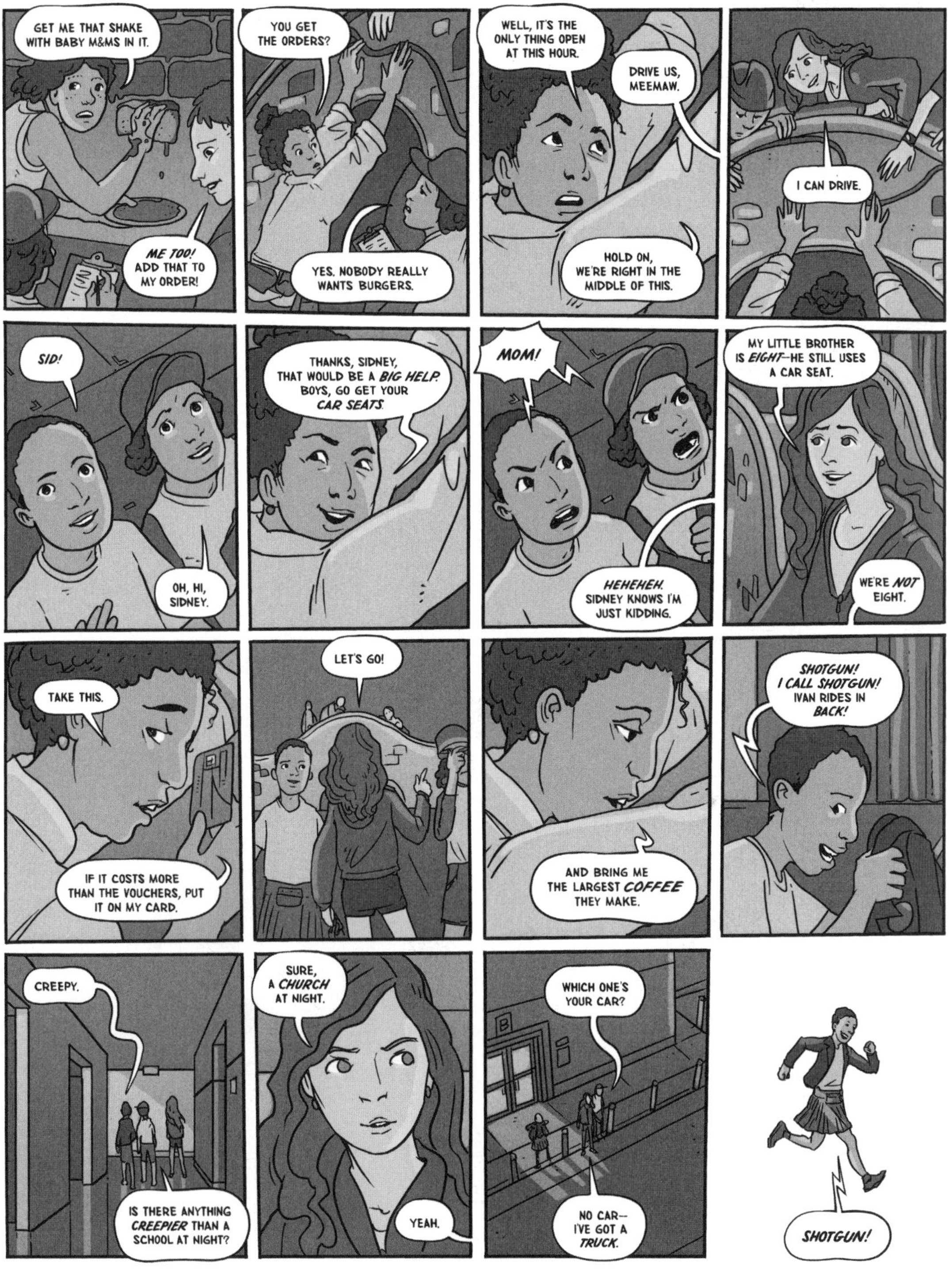
GET ME THAT SHAKE WITH BABY M&MS IN IT.
ME TOO! ADD THAT TO MY ORDER!
YOU GET THE ORDERS?
YES. NOBODY REALLY WANTS BURGERS.
WELL, IT'S THE ONLY THING OPEN AT THIS HOUR.
DRIVE US, MEEMAW.
HOLD ON, WE'RE RIGHT IN THE MIDDLE OF THIS.
I CAN DRIVE.
SID!
OH, HI, SIDNEY.
THANKS, SIDNEY, THAT WOULD BE A BIG HELP. BOYS, GO GET YOUR CAR SEATS.
MOM!
HEHEHEH. SIDNEY KNOWS I'M JUST KIDDING.
MY LITTLE BROTHER IS EIGHT—HE STILL USES A CAR SEAT.
WE'RE NOT EIGHT.
TAKE THIS.
IF IT COSTS MORE THAN THE VOUCHERS, PUT IT ON MY CARD.
LET'S GO!
AND BRING ME THE LARGEST COFFEE THEY MAKE.
SHOTGUN! I CALL SHOTGUN! IVAN RIDES IN BACK!
CREEPY.
IS THERE ANYTHING CREEPIER THAN A SCHOOL AT NIGHT?
SURE, A CHURCH AT NIGHT.
YEAH.
WHICH ONE'S YOUR CAR?
NO CAR— I'VE GOT A TRUCK.
SHOTGUN!

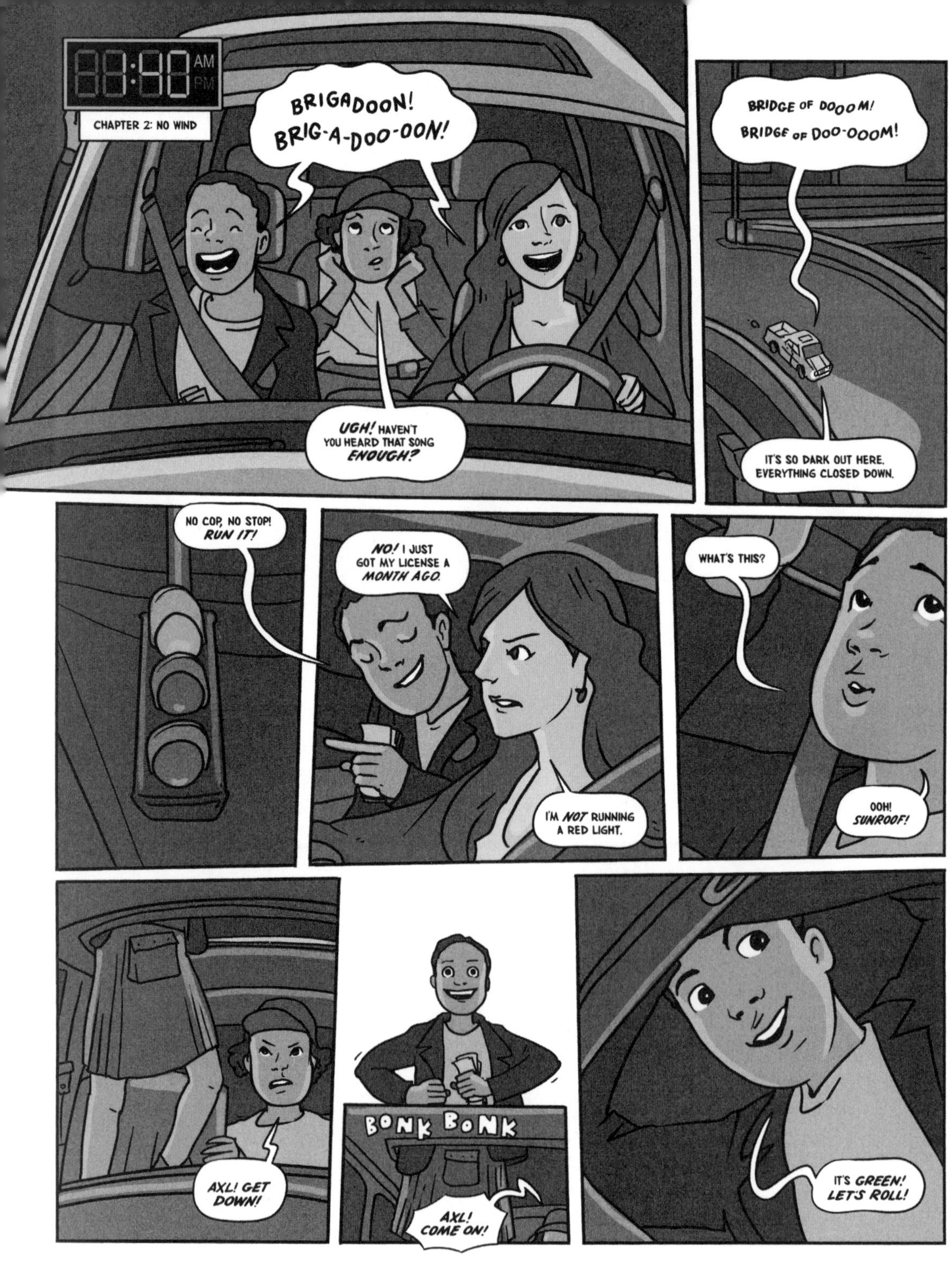
11:40 AM PM
CHAPTER 2: NO WIND
BRIGADOON!
BRIG-A-DOO-OON!
UGH! HAVEN'T YOU HEARD THAT SONG ENOUGH?
BRIDGE OF DOOOM!
BRIDGE OF DOO-OOOM!
IT'S SO DARK OUT HERE. EVERYTHING CLOSED DOWN.
NO COP, NO STOP! RUN IT!
NO! I JUST GOT MY LICENSE A MONTH AGO.
I'M NOT RUNNING A RED LIGHT.
WHAT'S THIS?
OOH! SUNROOF!
AXL! GET DOWN!
BONK BONK
AXL! COME ON!
IT'S GREEN! LET'S ROLL!

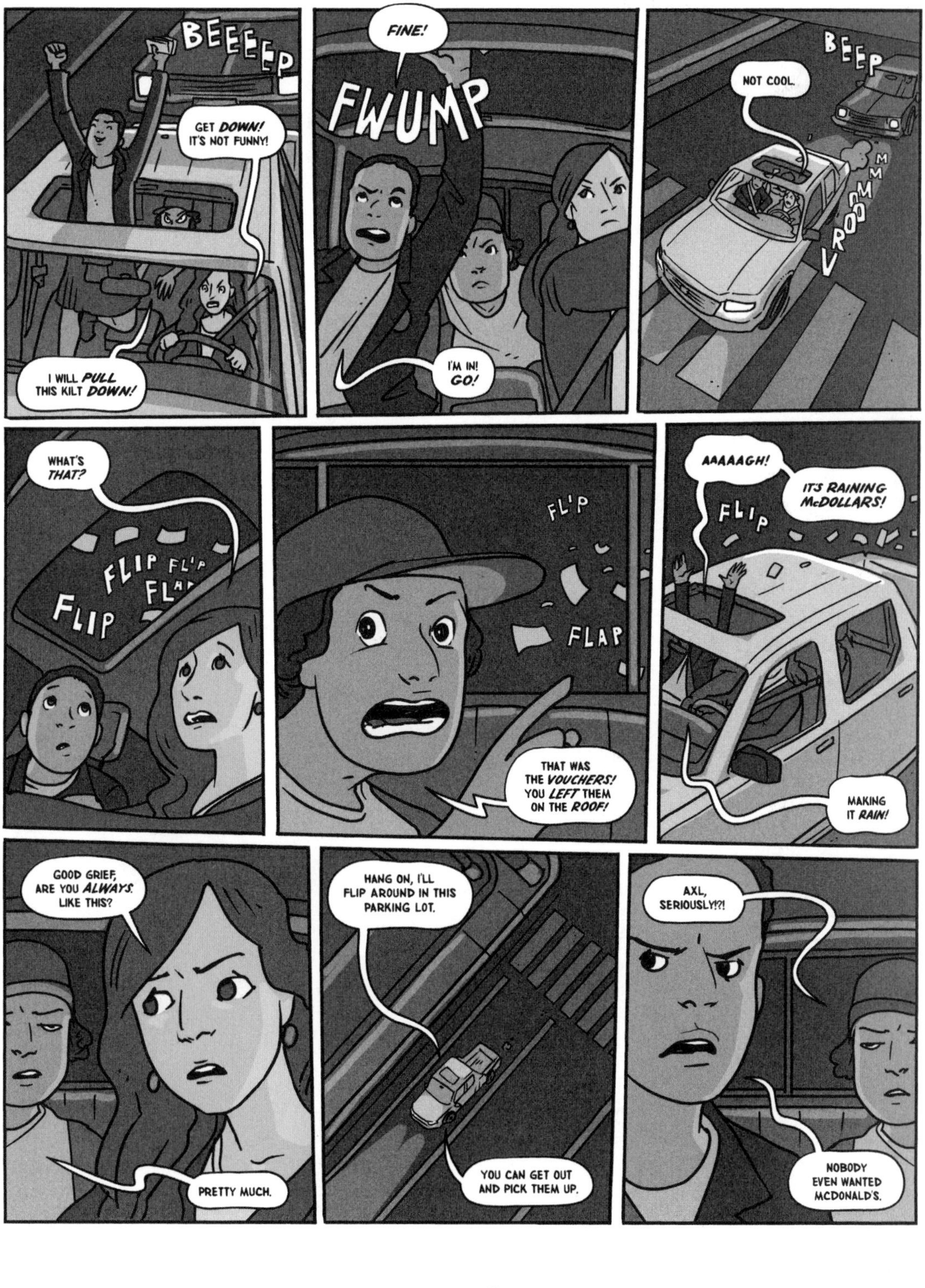
BEEEEEP
GET *DOWN!* IT'S NOT FUNNY!
I WILL *PULL* THIS KILT *DOWN!*
FINE!
FWUMP
I'M IN! *GO!*
BEEP
NOT COOL.
VROOMMMM
WHAT'S *THAT?*
FLIP FLIP FLIP FLAP
FLIP
FLAP
THAT WAS THE *VOUCHERS!* YOU *LEFT* THEM ON THE *ROOF!*
AAAAAGH!
IT'S RAINING McDOLLARS!
FLIP
MAKING IT *RAIN!*
GOOD GRIEF, ARE YOU *ALWAYS* LIKE THIS?
PRETTY MUCH.
HANG ON, I'LL FLIP AROUND IN THIS PARKING LOT.
YOU CAN GET OUT AND PICK THEM UP.
AXL, SERIOUSLY!?!
NOBODY EVEN WANTED MCDONALD'S.

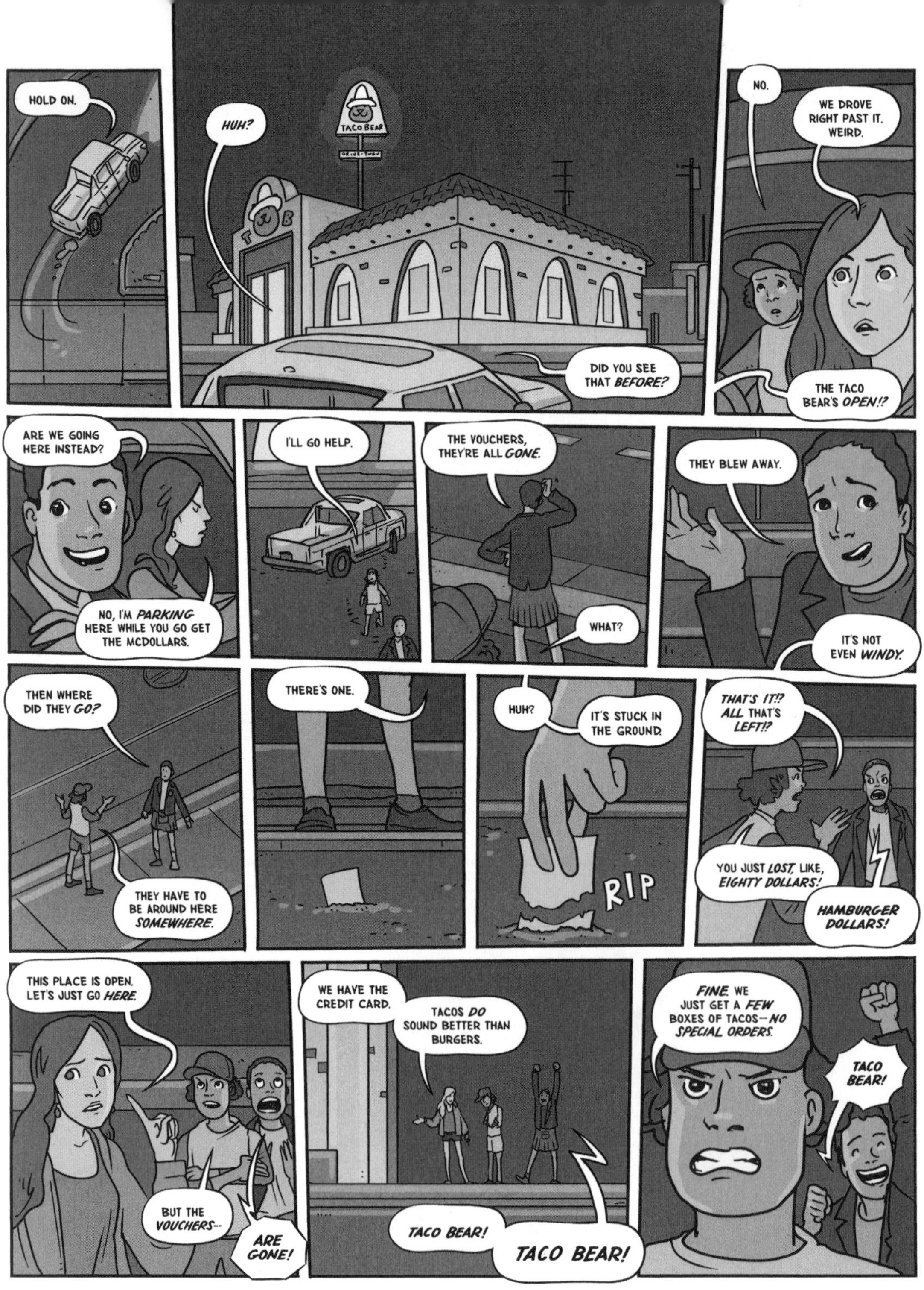
HOLD ON.
HUH?
TACO BEAR
DRIVE-THRU
DID YOU SEE THAT BEFORE?
NO.
WE DROVE RIGHT PAST IT. WEIRD.
THE TACO BEAR'S OPEN!?
ARE WE GOING HERE INSTEAD?
NO, I'M PARKING HERE WHILE YOU GO GET THE MCDOLLARS.
I'LL GO HELP.
THE VOUCHERS, THEY'RE ALL GONE.
WHAT?
THEY BLEW AWAY.
IT'S NOT EVEN WINDY.
THEN WHERE DID THEY GO?
THEY HAVE TO BE AROUND HERE SOMEWHERE.
THERE'S ONE.
HUH?
IT'S STUCK IN THE GROUND.
RIP
THAT'S IT!? ALL THAT'S LEFT!?
YOU JUST LOST, LIKE, EIGHTY DOLLARS!
HAMBURGER DOLLARS!
THIS PLACE IS OPEN. LET'S JUST GO HERE.
BUT THE VOUCHERS--
ARE GONE!
WE HAVE THE CREDIT CARD.
TACOS DO SOUND BETTER THAN BURGERS.
TACO BEAR!
TACO BEAR!
FINE. WE JUST GET A FEW BOXES OF TACOS--NO SPECIAL ORDERS.
TACO BEAR!

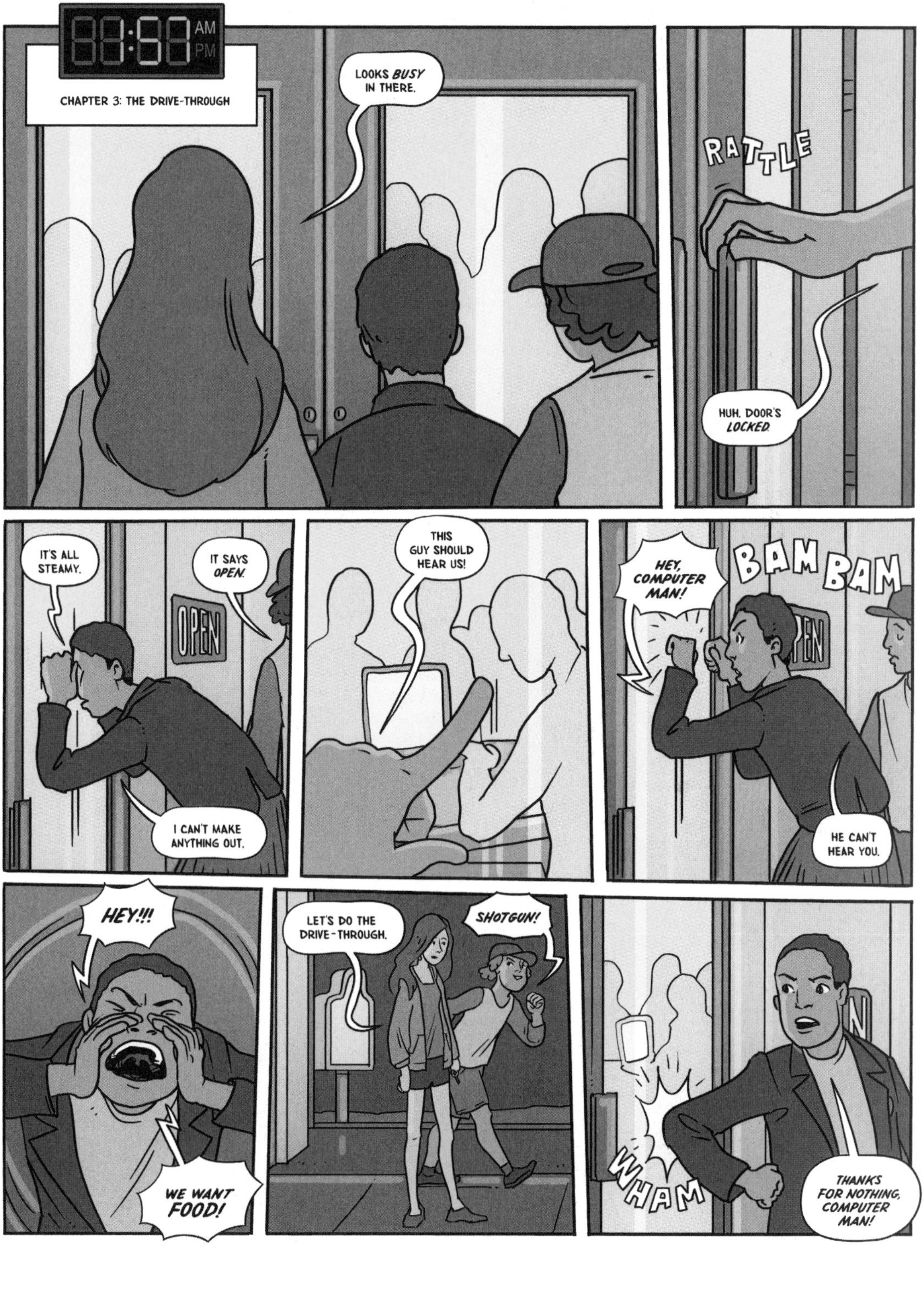

AM
PM
CHAPTER 3: THE DRIVE-THROUGH
LOOKS BUSY IN THERE.
RATTLE
HUH. DOOR'S LOCKED.
IT'S ALL STEAMY.
IT SAYS OPEN.
OPEN
I CAN'T MAKE ANYTHING OUT.
THIS GUY SHOULD HEAR US!
HEY, COMPUTER MAN!
BAM BAM
HE CAN'T HEAR YOU.
HEY!!!
WE WANT FOOD!
LET'S DO THE DRIVE-THROUGH.
SHOTGUN!
WHAM
THANKS FOR NOTHING, COMPUTER MAN!

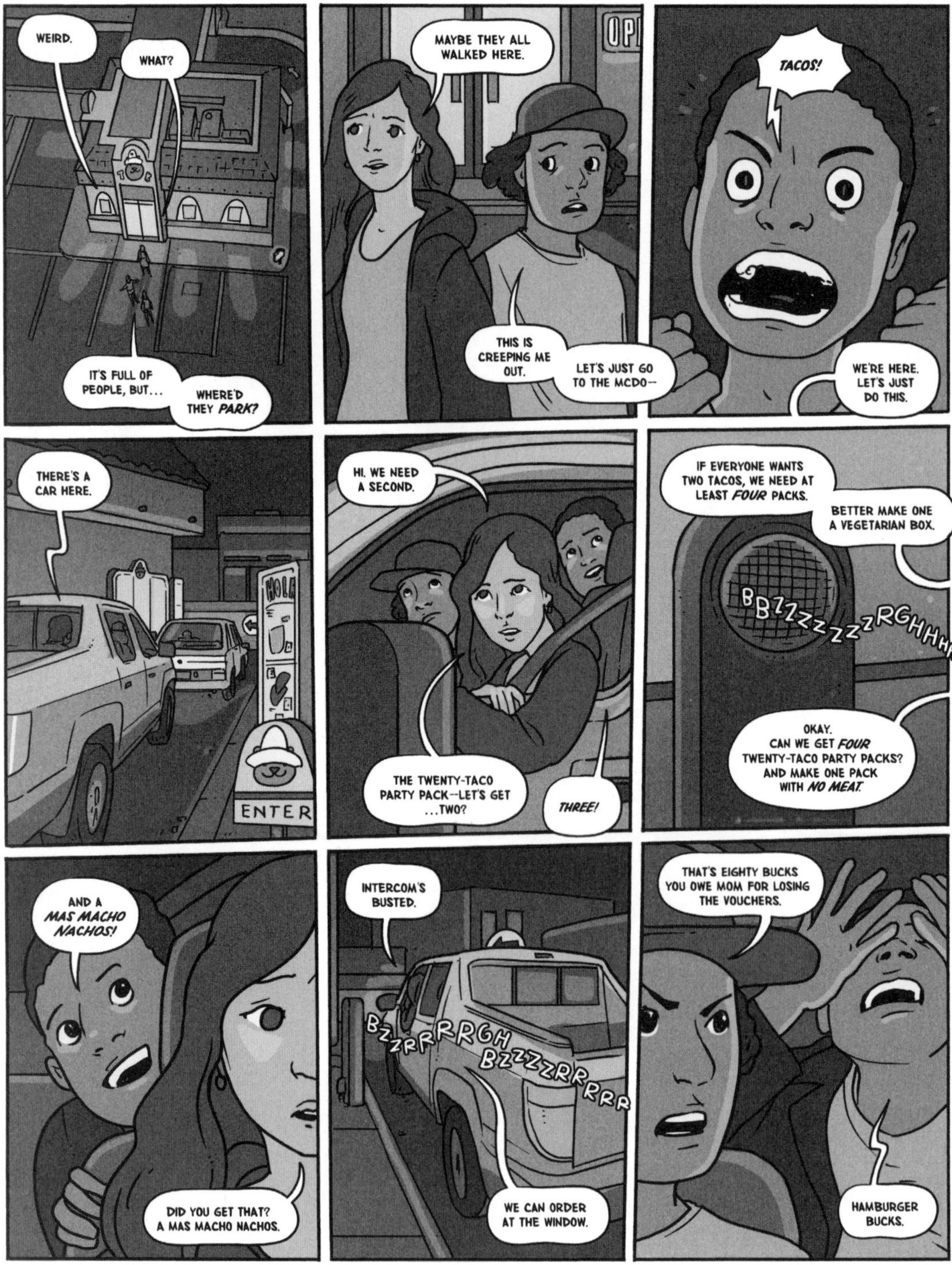
WEIRD.
WHAT?
IT'S FULL OF PEOPLE, BUT...
WHERE'D THEY PARK?
MAYBE THEY ALL WALKED HERE.
THIS IS CREEPING ME OUT.
LET'S JUST GO TO THE MCDO--
TACOS!
WE'RE HERE. LET'S JUST DO THIS.
THERE'S A CAR HERE.
HOLA
ENTER
HI. WE NEED A SECOND.
THE TWENTY-TACO PARTY PACK--LET'S GET ...TWO?
THREE!
IF EVERYONE WANTS TWO TACOS, WE NEED AT LEAST FOUR PACKS.
BETTER MAKE ONE A VEGETARIAN BOX.
BBZZZZZZZZRGHHHH
OKAY. CAN WE GET FOUR TWENTY-TACO PARTY PACKS? AND MAKE ONE PACK WITH NO MEAT.
AND A MAS MACHO NACHOS!
DID YOU GET THAT? A MAS MACHO NACHOS.
INTERCOM'S BUSTED.
BZZRRRRGH BZZZZRRRRRR
WE CAN ORDER AT THE WINDOW.
THAT'S EIGHTY BUCKS YOU OWE MOM FOR LOSING THE VOUCHERS.
HAMBURGER BUCKS.

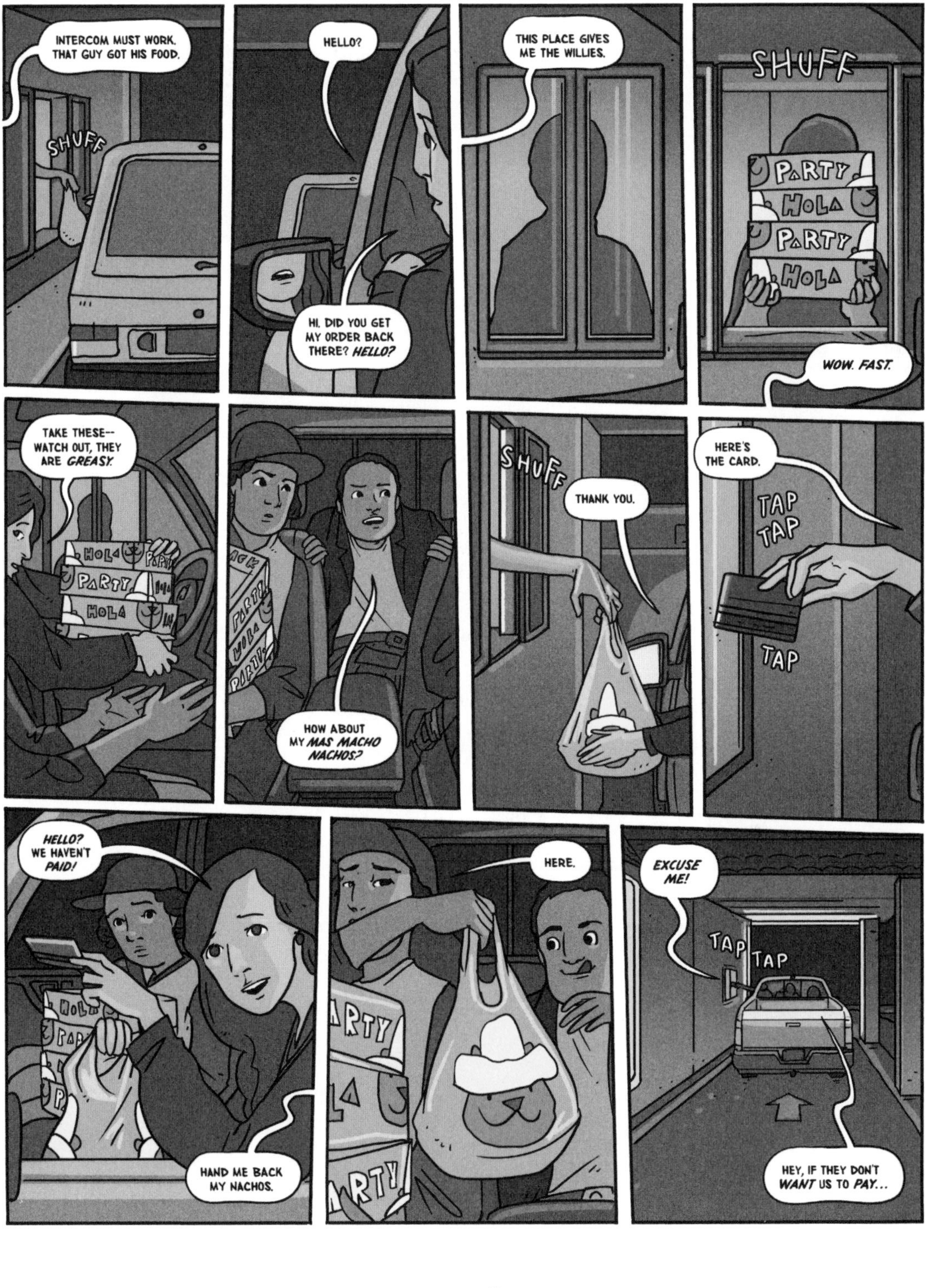

INTERCOM MUST WORK. THAT GUY GOT HIS FOOD.
SHUFF
HELLO?
HI, DID YOU GET MY ORDER BACK THERE? HELLO?
THIS PLACE GIVES ME THE WILLIES.
SHUFF
PARTY HOLA PARTY HOLA
WOW. FAST.
TAKE THESE-- WATCH OUT, THEY ARE GREASY.
HOW ABOUT MY MAS MACHO NACHOS?
SHUFF
THANK YOU.
HERE'S THE CARD.
TAP TAP
TAP
HELLO? WE HAVEN'T PAID!
HAND ME BACK MY NACHOS.
HERE.
EXCUSE ME!
TAP TAP
HEY, IF THEY DON'T WANT US TO PAY...

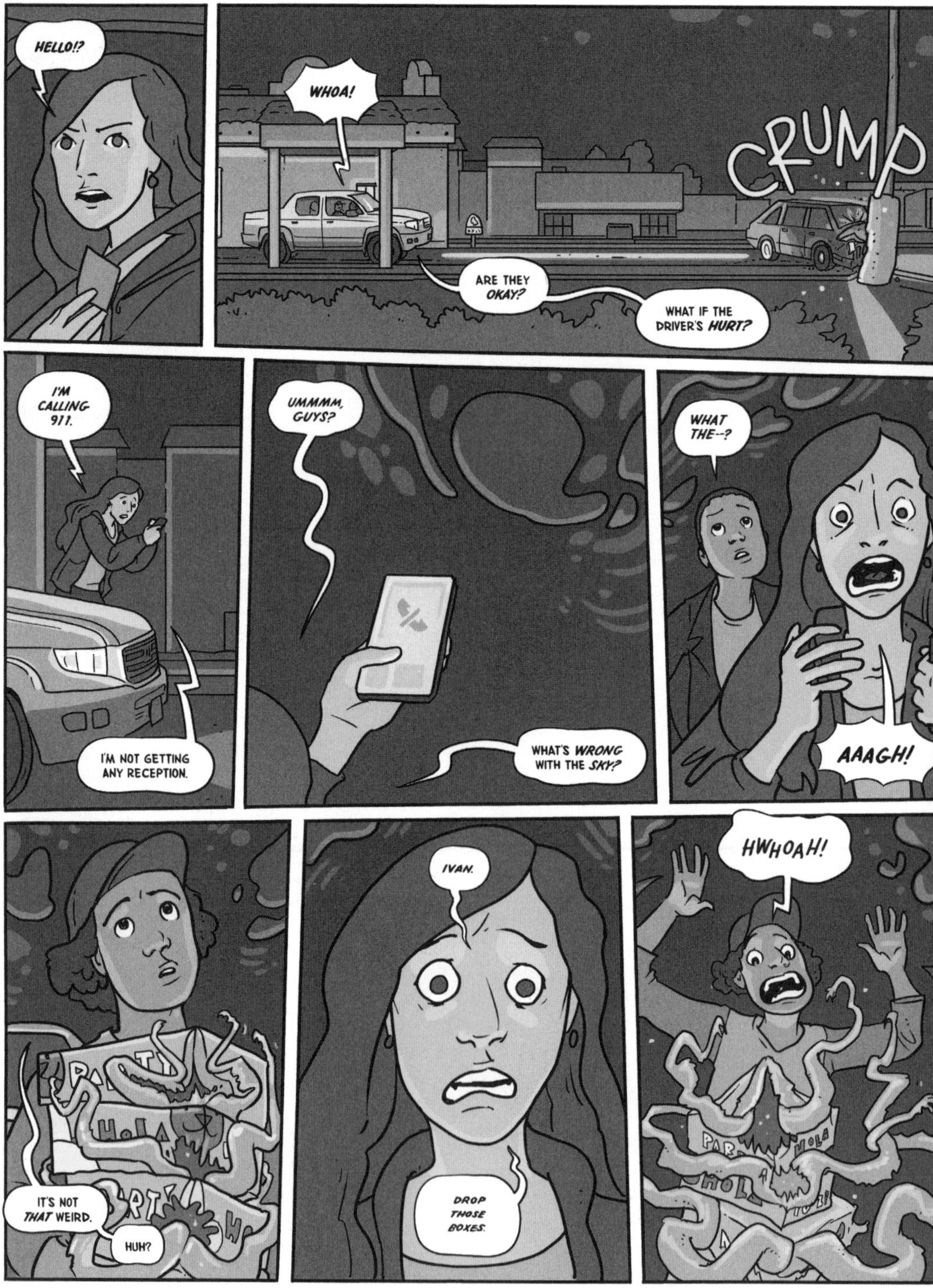
HELLO!?
WHOA!
CRUMP
ARE THEY OKAY?
WHAT IF THE DRIVER'S HURT?
I'M CALLING 911.
I'M NOT GETTING ANY RECEPTION.
UMMMM, GUYS?
WHAT'S WRONG WITH THE SKY?
WHAT THE--?
AAAGH!
IT'S NOT THAT WEIRD.
HUH?
IVAN.
DROP THOSE BOXES.
HWHOAH!

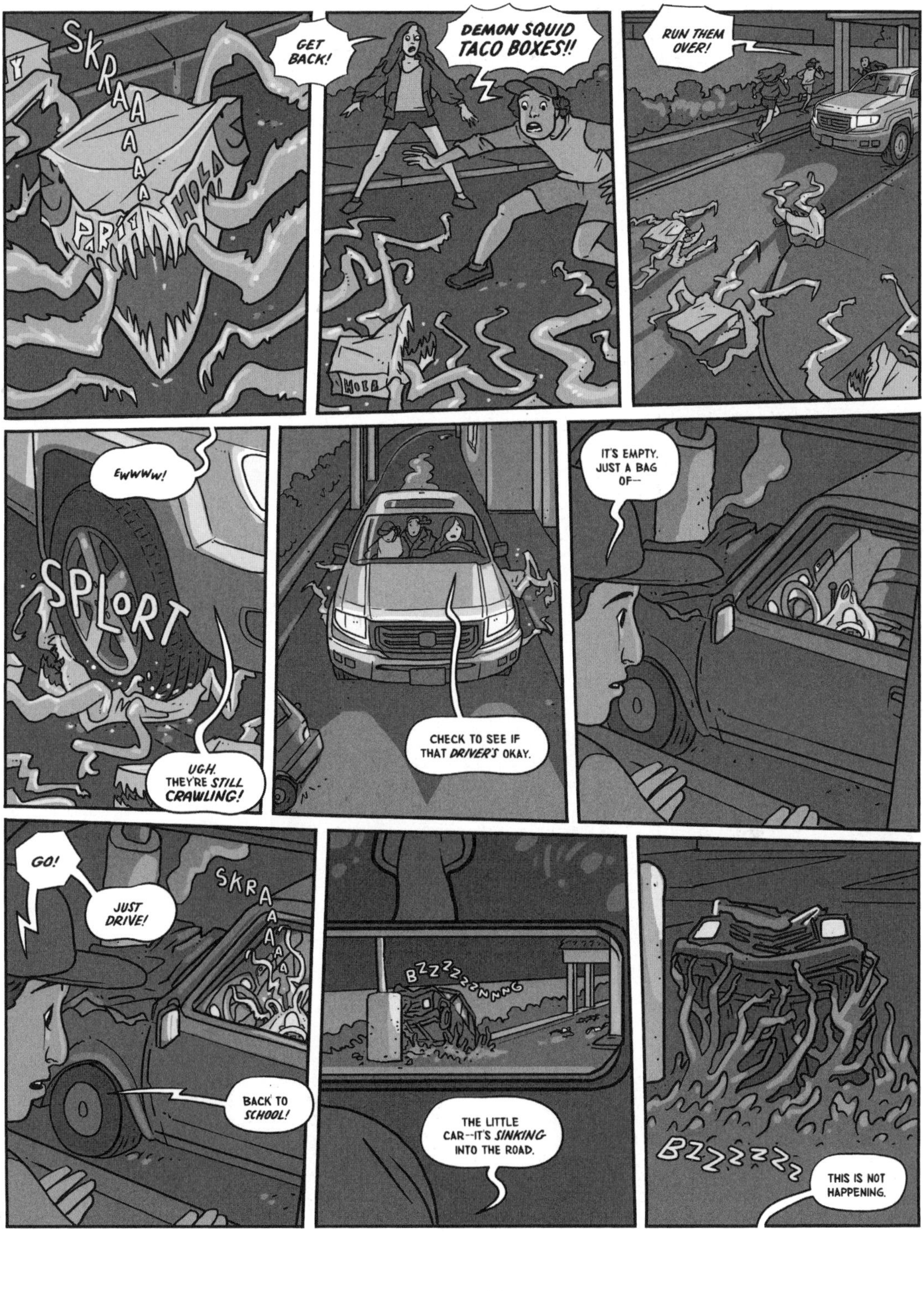
SKRAAAAAAA
PRÍÍ
HOLA
GET BACK!
DEMON SQUID TACO BOXES!!
HOLA
RUN THEM OVER!
EWWWW!
SPLORT
UGH. THEY'RE STILL CRAWLING!
CHECK TO SEE IF THAT DRIVER'S OKAY.
IT'S EMPTY. JUST A BAG OF--
GO!
JUST DRIVE!
SKRAAAAA
BACK TO SCHOOL!
BZZZZZZNNNG
THE LITTLE CAR--IT'S SINKING INTO THE ROAD.
BZZZZZZ
THIS IS NOT HAPPENING.

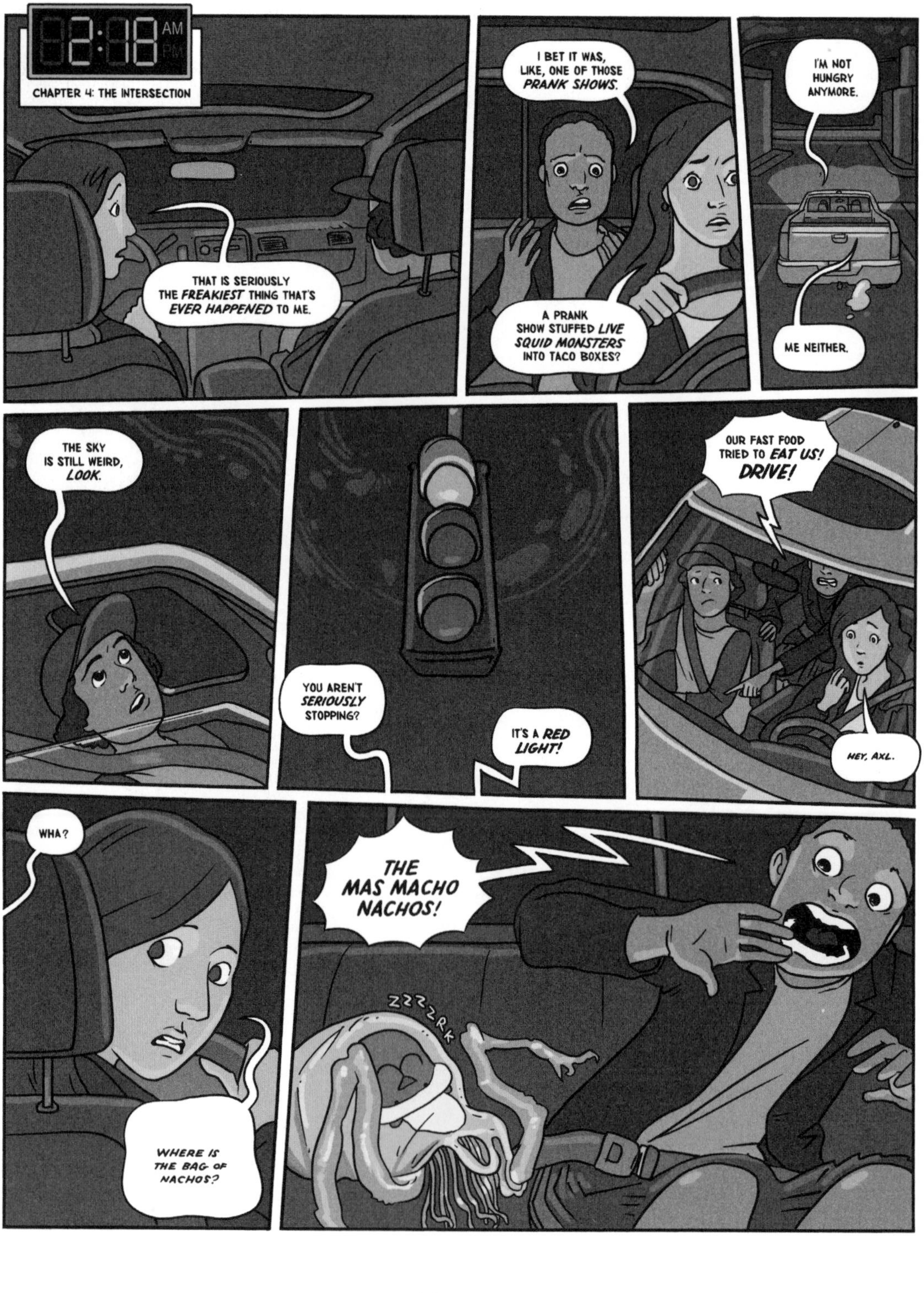
2:18 AM PM
CHAPTER 4: THE INTERSECTION
THAT IS SERIOUSLY THE FREAKIEST THING THAT'S EVER HAPPENED TO ME.
I BET IT WAS, LIKE, ONE OF THOSE PRANK SHOWS.
A PRANK SHOW STUFFED LIVE SQUID MONSTERS INTO TACO BOXES?
I'M NOT HUNGRY ANYMORE.
ME NEITHER.
THE SKY IS STILL WEIRD, LOOK.
YOU AREN'T SERIOUSLY STOPPING?
IT'S A RED LIGHT!
OUR FAST FOOD TRIED TO EAT US! DRIVE!
HEY, AXL.
WHA?
WHERE IS THE BAG OF NACHOS?
THE MAS MACHO NACHOS!
ZZZZRK

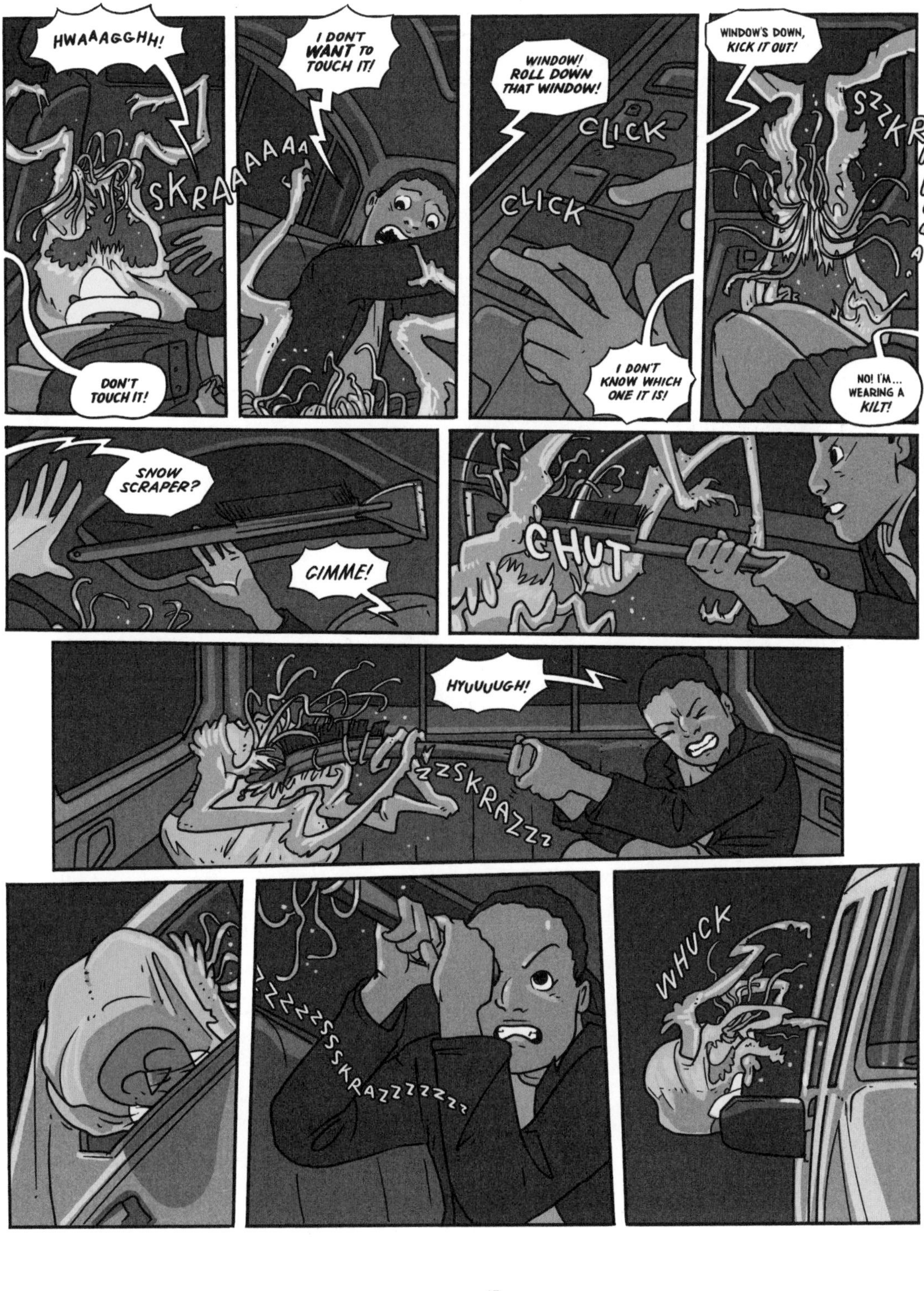

HWAAAAGGHH!
SKRAAAAAAA
DON'T TOUCH IT!
I DON'T WANT TO TOUCH IT!
WINDOW! ROLL DOWN THAT WINDOW!
CLICK
CLICK
I DON'T KNOW WHICH ONE IT IS!
WINDOW'S DOWN, KICK IT OUT!
SZZKRAAAAAA
NO! I'M... WEARING A KILT!
SNOW SCRAPER?
GIMME!
CHUT
HYUUUUGH!
ZZSKRAZZZZ
ZZZZZZSSSSKRAZZZZZZZZ
WHUCK

IT'S OUT! *GO!*

THE *LIGHT* HASN'T *CHANGED!*

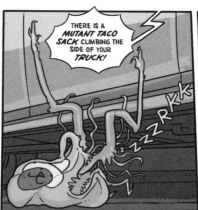

THERE IS A *MUTANT TACO SACK* CLIMBING THE SIDE OF YOUR *TRUCK!*

ZZZRKK

GOOOO!

LOOK, *GREEN!*

SKLORK

STILL THINK IT'S A *PRANK SHOW!?*

GET US TO THE SCHOOL, DON'T STOP FOR *ANYTHING!*

I'M NEVER VOLUN- TEERING FOR A LATE-NIGHT FOOD RUN AGAIN.

SKRAAA..

WE NEED TO CALL 911.

STILL NO COVERAGE.

THERE'S THE SCHOOL.

MOM WILL KNOW WHAT TO DO!

THE LOT'S EMPTY. WHERE ARE EVERYONE'S CARS?

EVERYONE LEFT?

WHAT IS GOING ON?

WE'RE NOT GONNA BE READY FOR DRESS REHEARSAL.

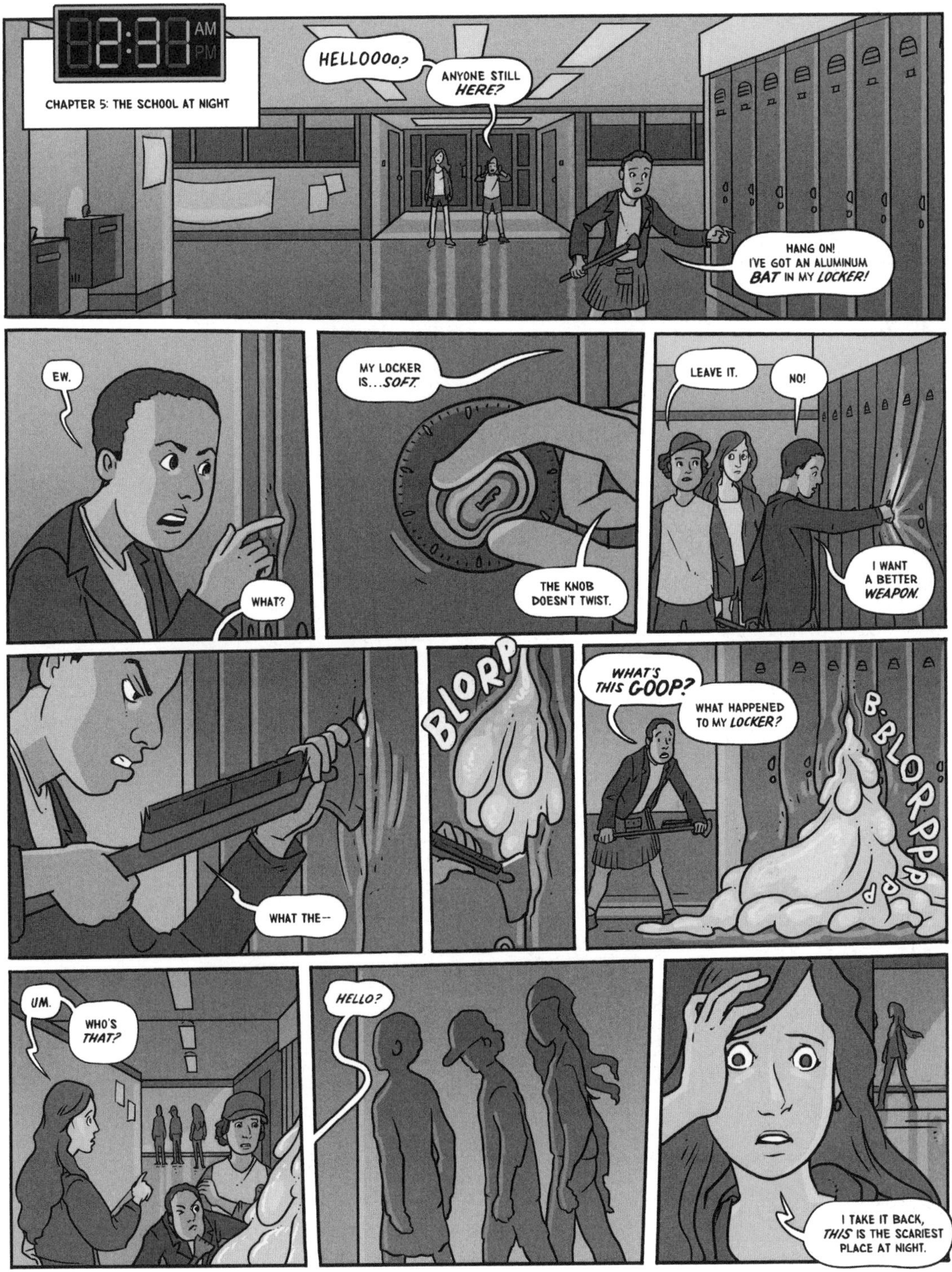
12:31 AM PM
CHAPTER 5: THE SCHOOL AT NIGHT
HELLOOOo?
ANYONE STILL HERE?
HANG ON! I'VE GOT AN ALUMINUM BAT IN MY LOCKER!
EW.
WHAT?
MY LOCKER IS...SOFT.
THE KNOB DOESN'T TWIST.
LEAVE IT.
NO!
I WANT A BETTER WEAPON.
WHAT THE--
BLORP
WHAT'S THIS GOOP?
WHAT HAPPENED TO MY LOCKER?
B-BLORPPPP
UM.
WHO'S THAT?
HELLO?
I TAKE IT BACK, THIS IS THE SCARIEST PLACE AT NIGHT.

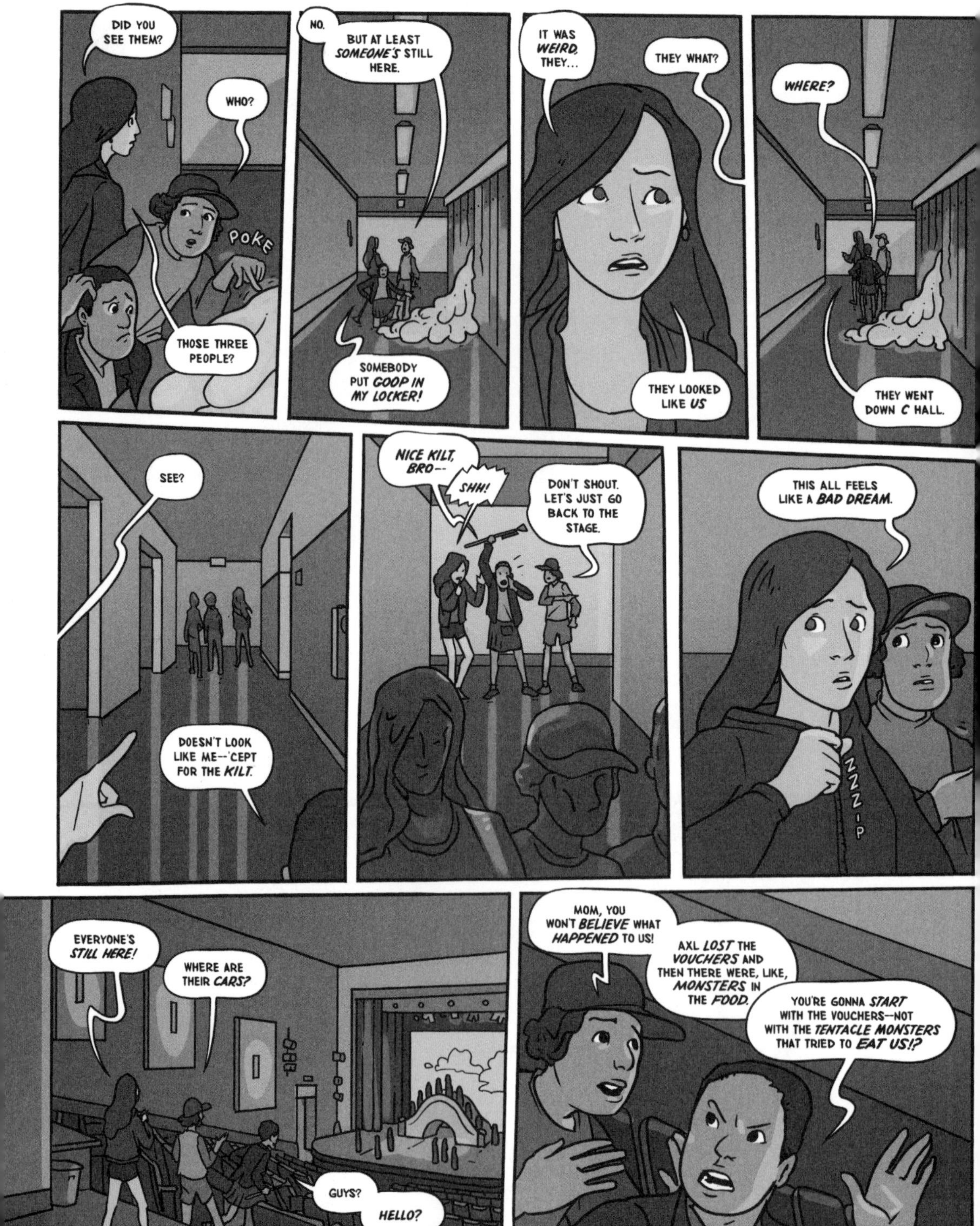
DID YOU SEE THEM?
WHO?
POKE
THOSE THREE PEOPLE?
NO.
BUT AT LEAST SOMEONE'S STILL HERE.
SOMEBODY PUT GOOP IN MY LOCKER!
IT WAS WEIRD, THEY...
THEY WHAT?
THEY LOOKED LIKE US
WHERE?
THEY WENT DOWN C HALL.
SEE?
DOESN'T LOOK LIKE ME--'CEPT FOR THE KILT.
NICE KILT, BRO--
SHH!
DON'T SHOUT. LET'S JUST GO BACK TO THE STAGE.
THIS ALL FEELS LIKE A BAD DREAM.
ZZZIP
EVERYONE'S STILL HERE!
WHERE ARE THEIR CARS?
GUYS?
HELLO?
MOM, YOU WON'T BELIEVE WHAT HAPPENED TO US!
AXL LOST THE VOUCHERS AND THEN THERE WERE, LIKE, MONSTERS IN THE FOOD.
YOU'RE GONNA START WITH THE VOUCHERS--NOT WITH THE TENTACLE MONSTERS THAT TRIED TO EAT US!?

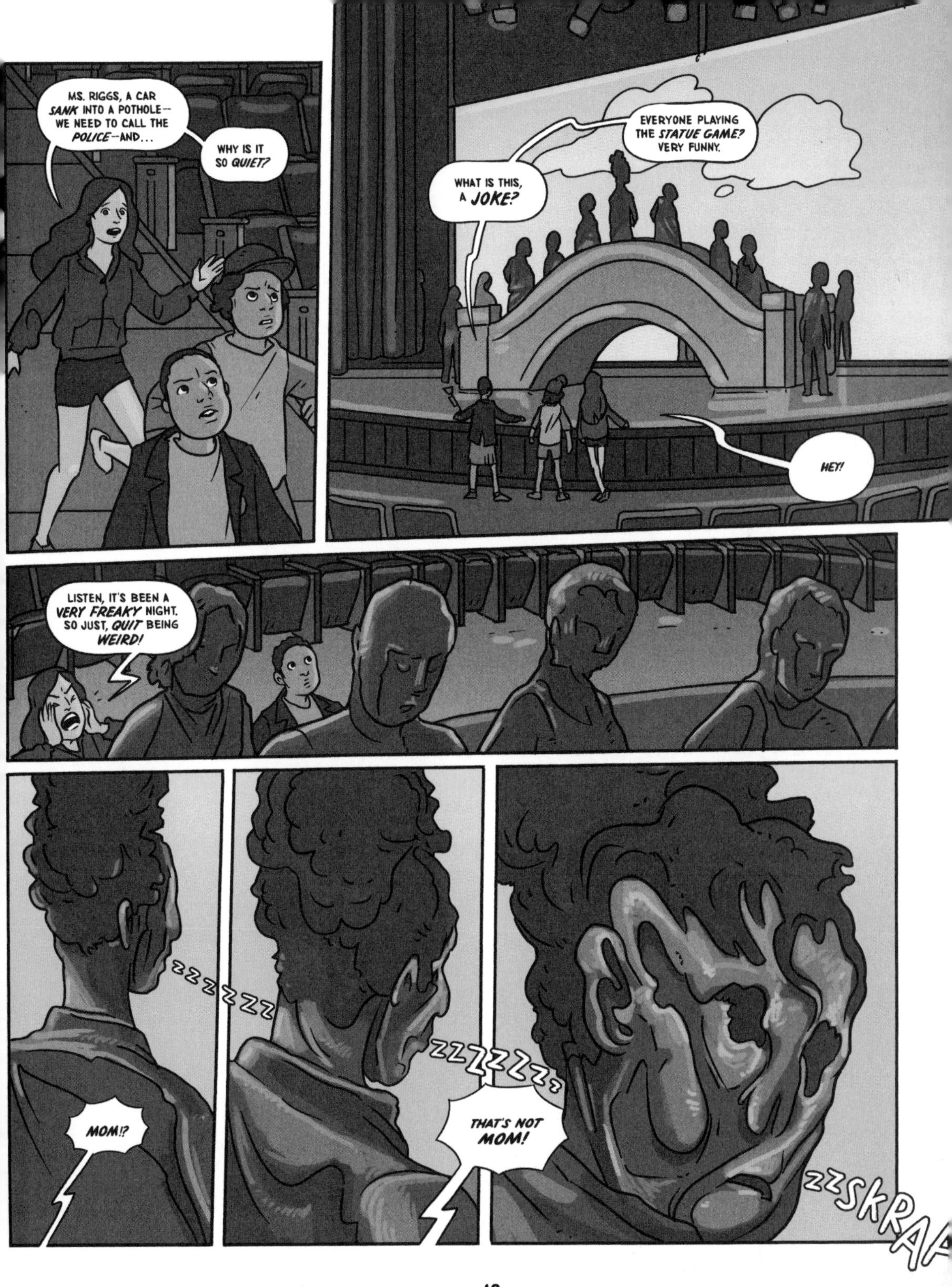
MS. RIGGS, A CAR SANK INTO A POTHOLE-- WE NEED TO CALL THE POLICE--AND...
WHY IS IT SO QUIET?
WHAT IS THIS, A JOKE?
EVERYONE PLAYING THE STATUE GAME? VERY FUNNY.
HEY!
LISTEN, IT'S BEEN A VERY FREAKY NIGHT. SO JUST, QUIT BEING WEIRD!
ZZZZZZ
MOM!?
ZZZZZZZ
THAT'S NOT MOM!
ZZSKRAA

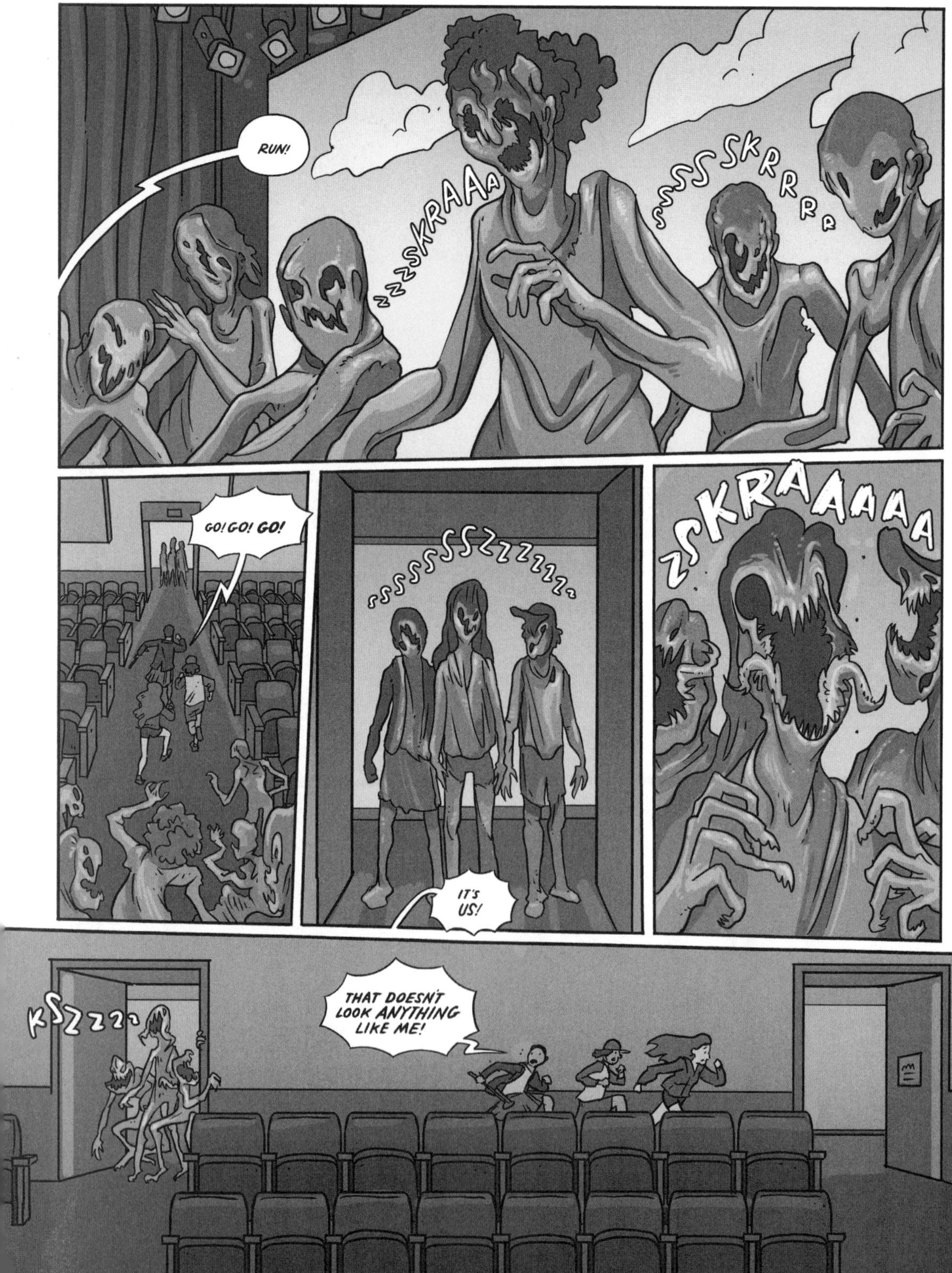
RUN!
zzzSKRAAAa
sssSSKRRRRR
GO! GO! GO!
sssSSSSZZZZZzz
IT'S US!
zzSKRAAAAAA
KSZZZzz
THAT DOESN'T LOOK ANYTHING LIKE ME!

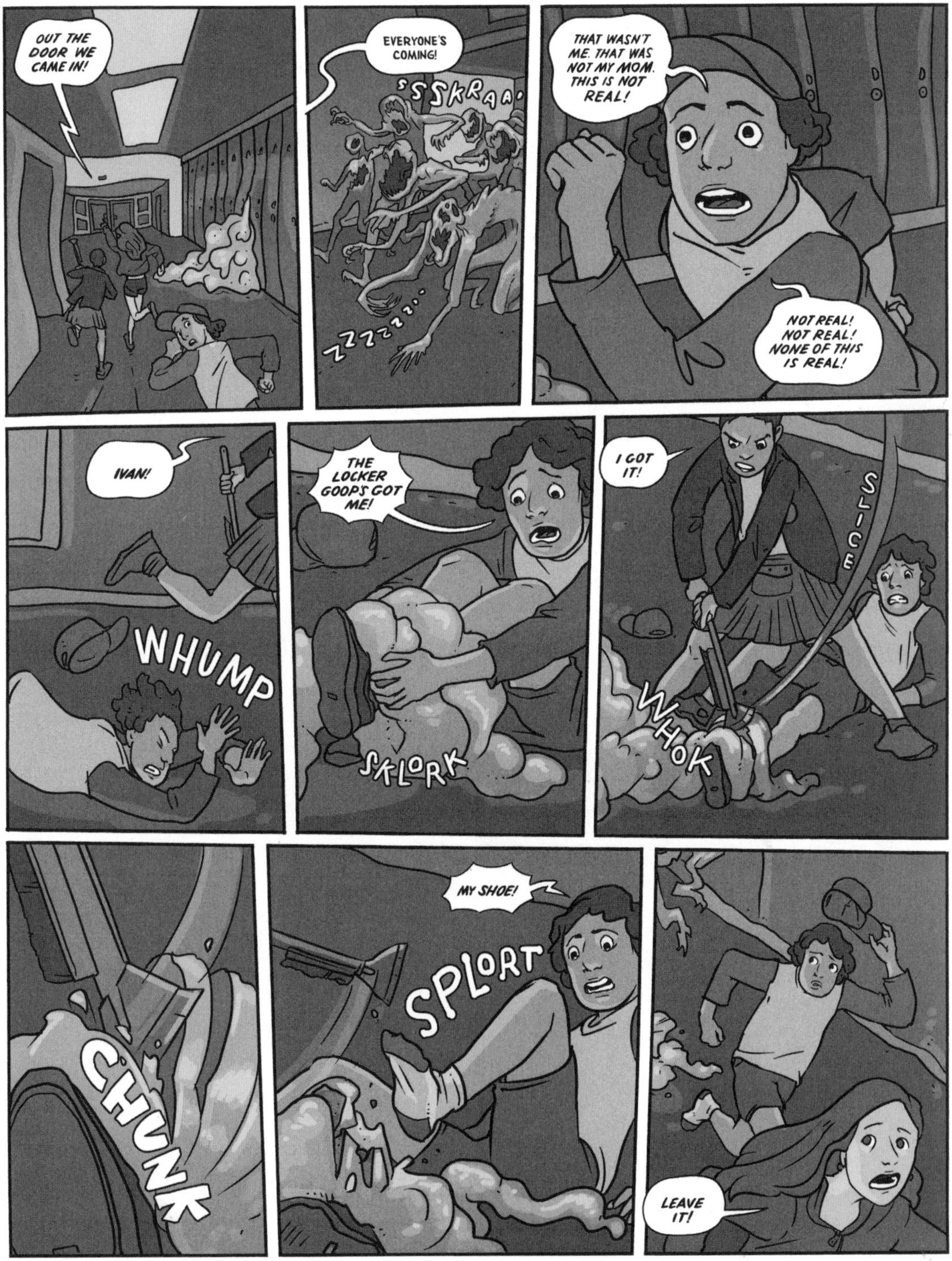
OUT THE DOOR WE CAME IN!
EVERYONE'S COMING!
SSSKRAAA
ZZZZZZZ
THAT WASN'T ME. THAT WAS NOT MY MOM. THIS IS NOT REAL!
NOT REAL! NOT REAL! NONE OF THIS IS REAL!
IVAN!
WHUMP
THE LOCKER GOOP'S GOT ME!
SKLORK
I GOT IT!
SLICE
WHOK
CHUNK
MY SHOE!
SPLORT
LEAVE IT!

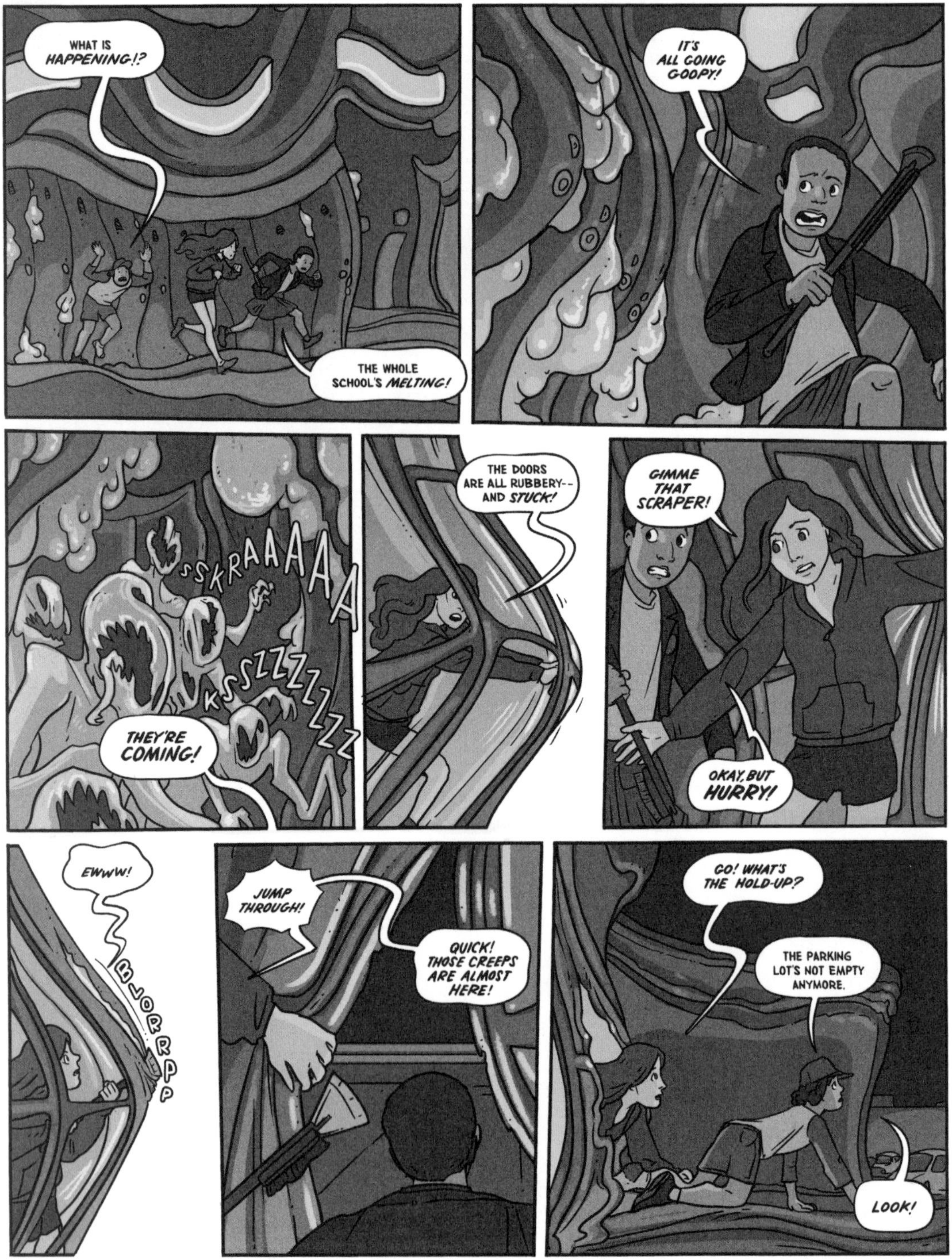
WHAT IS HAPPENING!?
THE WHOLE SCHOOL'S MELTING!
IT'S ALL GOING GOOPY!
SSKRAAAAAA
KSSZZZZZZZ
THEY'RE COMING!
THE DOORS ARE ALL RUBBERY--AND STUCK!
GIMME THAT SCRAPER!
OKAY, BUT HURRY!
EWWW!
BLORRRPP
JUMP THROUGH!
QUICK! THOSE CREEPS ARE ALMOST HERE!
GO! WHAT'S THE HOLD-UP?
THE PARKING LOT'S NOT EMPTY ANYMORE.
LOOK!

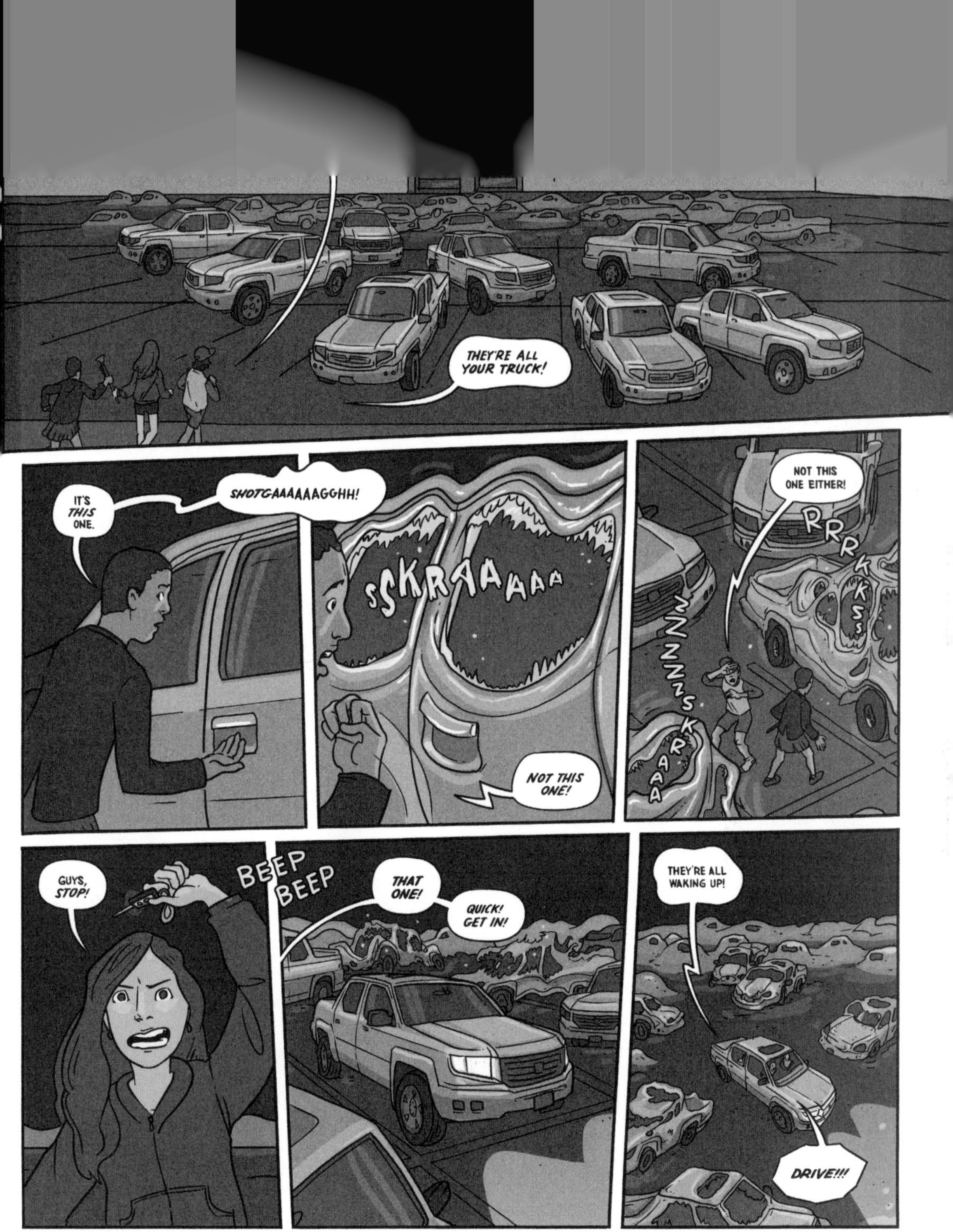
THEY'RE ALL YOUR TRUCK!
IT'S THIS ONE.
SHOTGAAAAAAAGGHH!
SSKRAAAAAA
NOT THIS ONE!
NOT THIS ONE EITHER!
RRRKKSS
ZZZZZSKRAAA
GUYS, STOP!
BEEP BEEP
THAT ONE!
QUICK! GET IN!
THEY'RE ALL WAKING UP!
DRIVE!!!

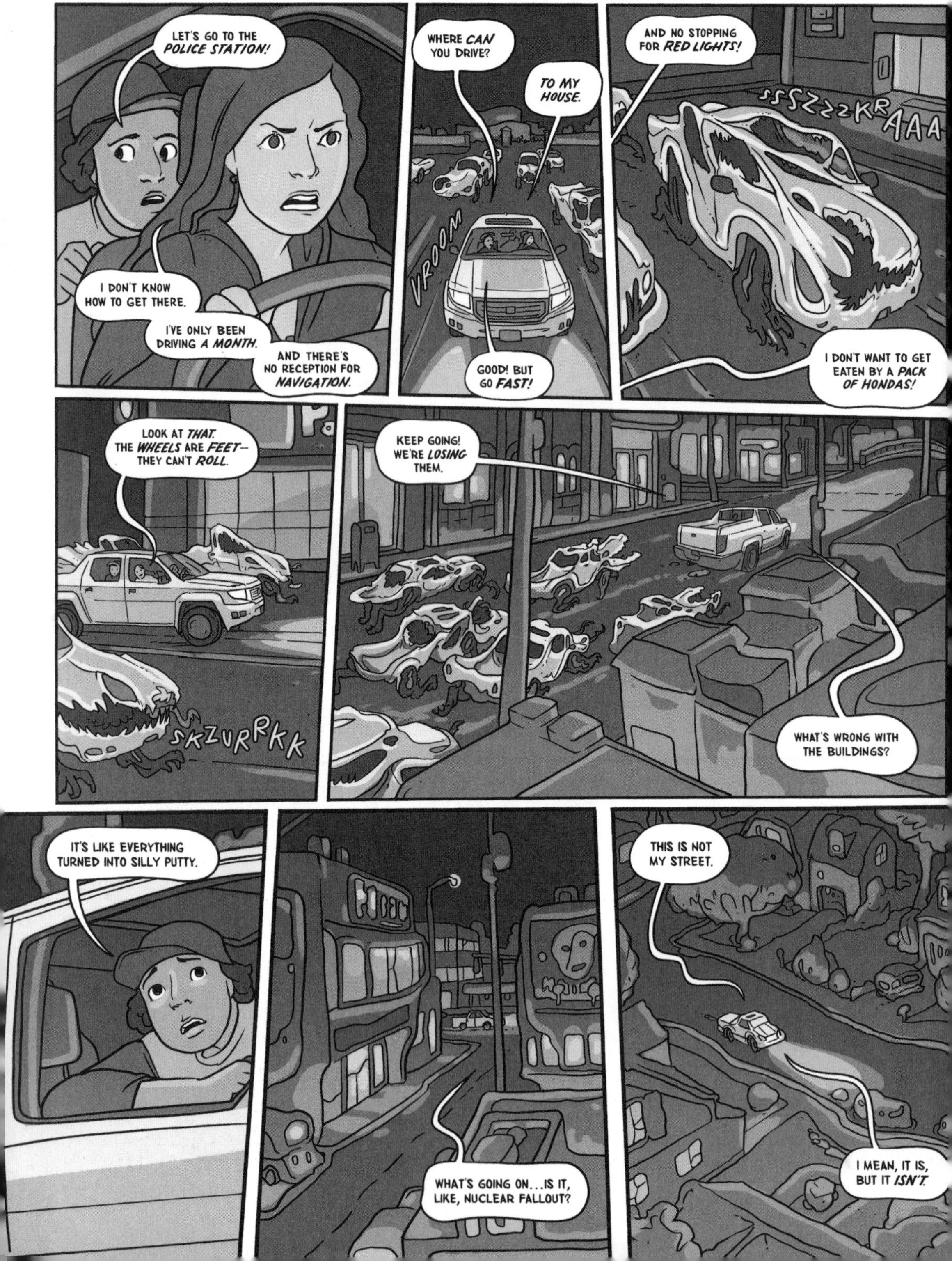
LET'S GO TO THE POLICE STATION!
I DON'T KNOW HOW TO GET THERE.
I'VE ONLY BEEN DRIVING A MONTH.
AND THERE'S NO RECEPTION FOR NAVIGATION.
WHERE CAN YOU DRIVE?
TO MY HOUSE.
VROOOM
GOOD! BUT GO FAST!
AND NO STOPPING FOR RED LIGHTS!
SSSZZZZKRAAAA
I DON'T WANT TO GET EATEN BY A PACK OF HONDAS!
LOOK AT THAT. THE WHEELS ARE FEET-- THEY CAN'T ROLL.
SKZURRKK
KEEP GOING! WE'RE LOSING THEM.
WHAT'S WRONG WITH THE BUILDINGS?
IT'S LIKE EVERYTHING TURNED INTO SILLY PUTTY.
WHAT'S GOING ON... IS IT, LIKE, NUCLEAR FALLOUT?
THIS IS NOT MY STREET.
I MEAN, IT IS, BUT IT ISN'T.

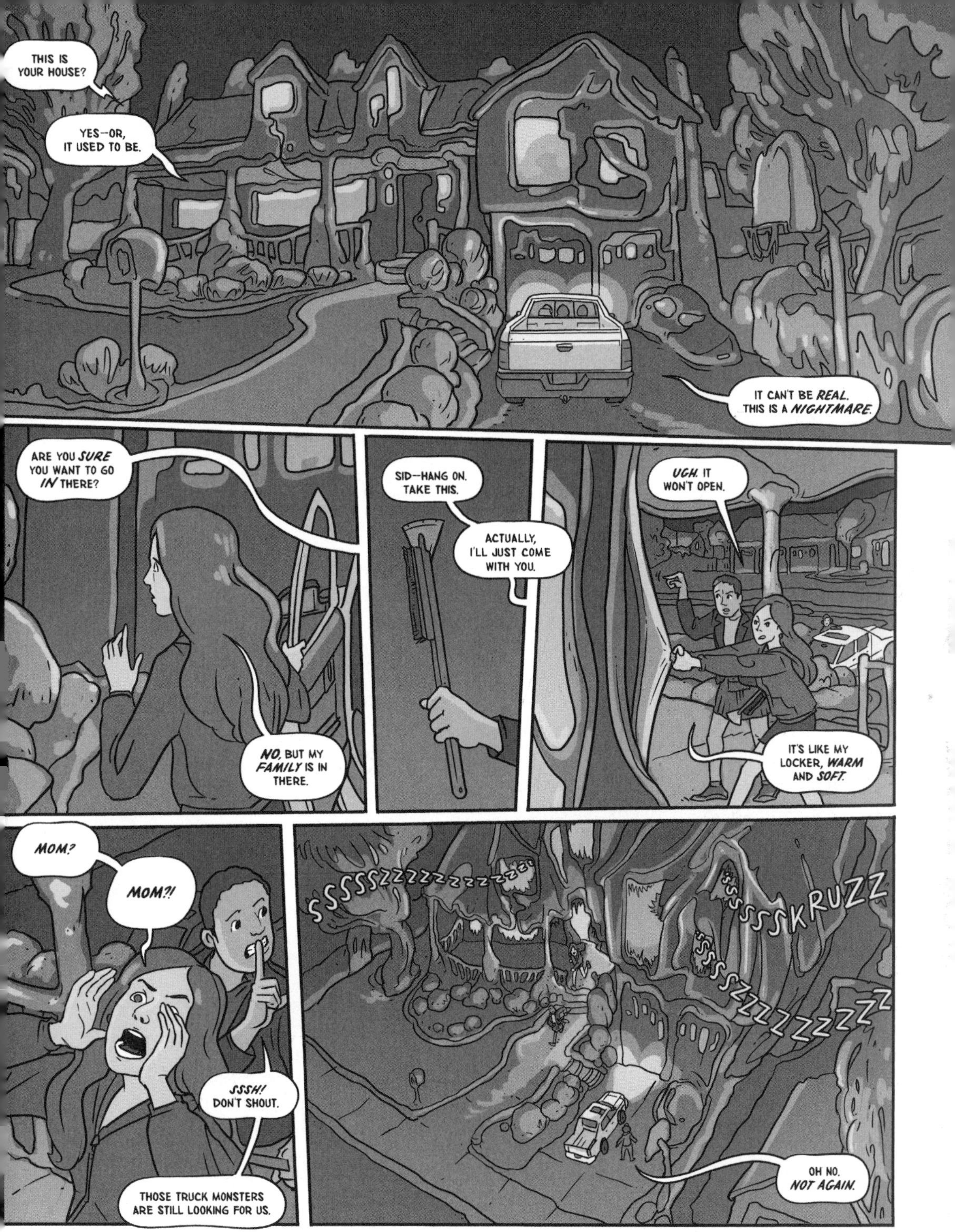
THIS IS YOUR HOUSE?
YES--OR, IT USED TO BE.
IT CAN'T BE REAL. THIS IS A NIGHTMARE.
ARE YOU SURE YOU WANT TO GO IN THERE?
NO, BUT MY FAMILY IS IN THERE.
SID--HANG ON. TAKE THIS.
ACTUALLY, I'LL JUST COME WITH YOU.
UGH. IT WON'T OPEN.
IT'S LIKE MY LOCKER, WARM AND SOFT.
MOM?
MOM?!
SSSH! DON'T SHOUT.
THOSE TRUCK MONSTERS ARE STILL LOOKING FOR US.
SSSSZZZZZZZZZZZZ
SSSSSSKRUZZ
SSSSZZZZZZZZZZ
OH NO. NOT AGAIN.

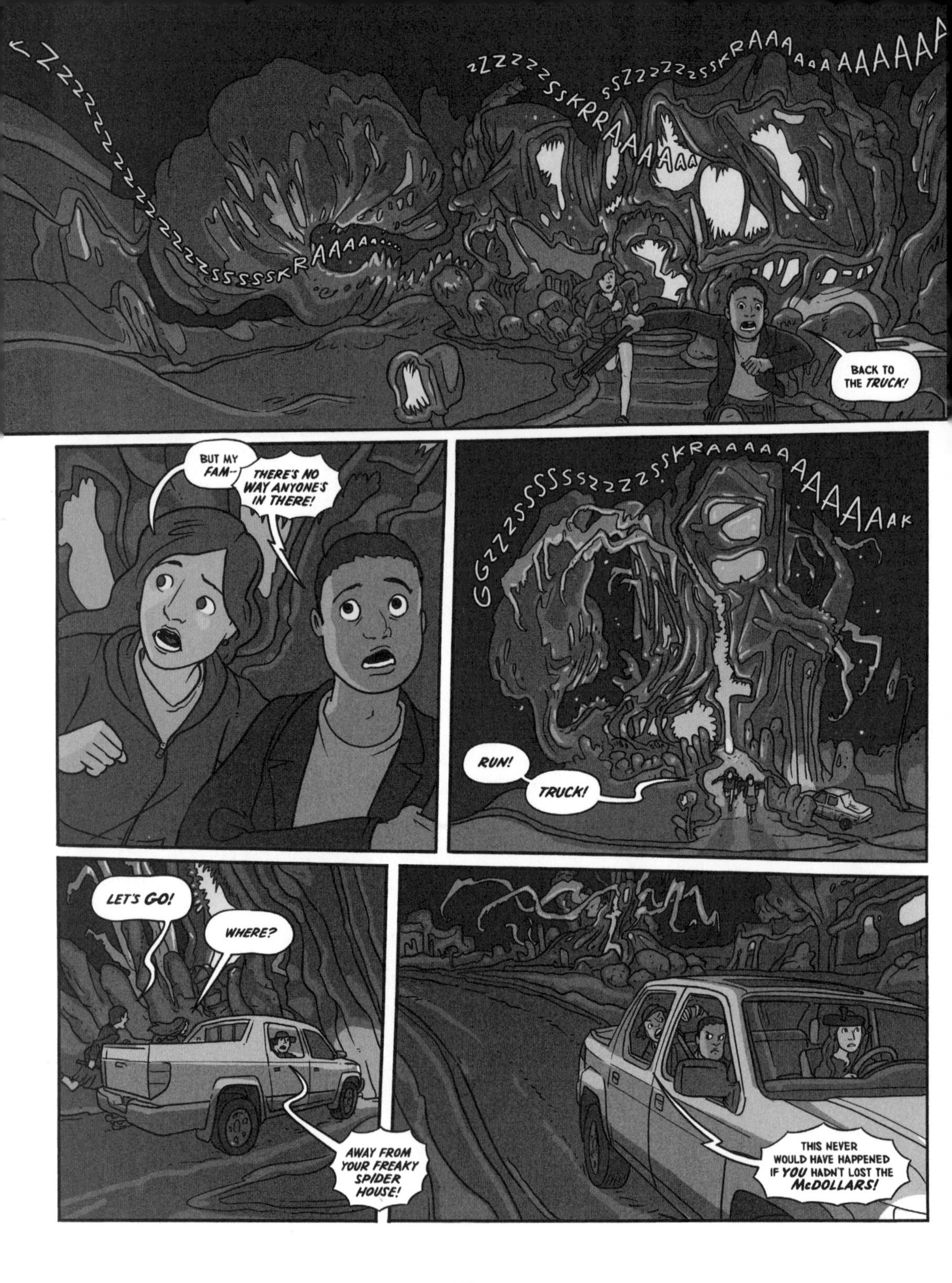

<ZZZZZZZZZZZZZZZZZZSSSSSSKRAAAAA....
zZZZZZSSKRRAAAAAA
sSZZZZZZSSKRAAAAAAAAAAAAA
BACK TO THE TRUCK!
BUT MY FAM--
THERE'S NO WAY ANYONE'S IN THERE!
GGZZSSSSSZZZZSSKRAAAAAAAAAAAAAK
RUN!
TRUCK!
LET'S GO!
WHERE?
AWAY FROM YOUR FREAKY SPIDER HOUSE!
THIS NEVER WOULD HAVE HAPPENED IF YOU HADN'T LOST THE McDOLLARS!

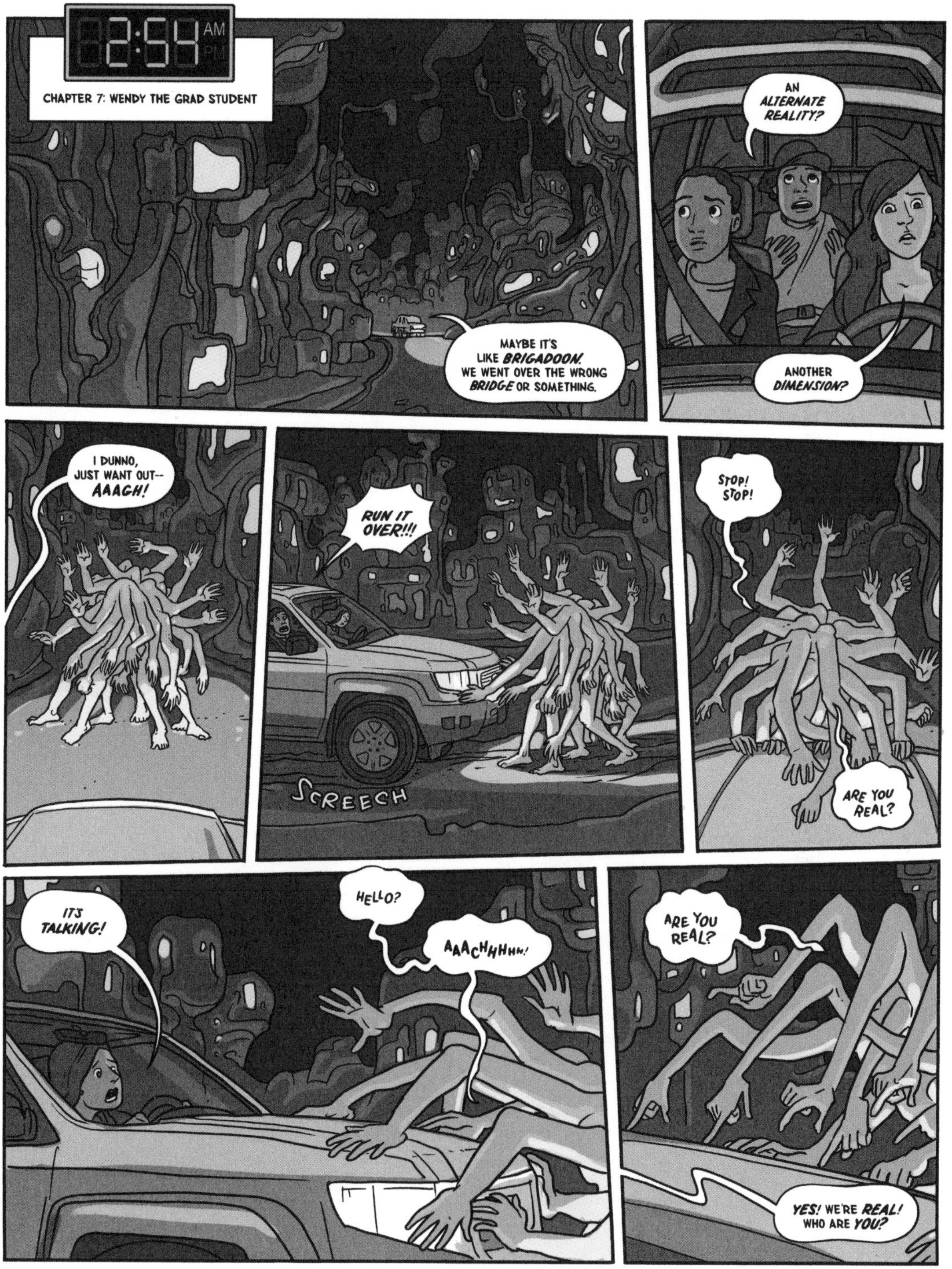
2:54 AM PM
CHAPTER 7: WENDY THE GRAD STUDENT
MAYBE IT'S LIKE BRIGADOON. WE WENT OVER THE WRONG BRIDGE OR SOMETHING.
AN ALTERNATE REALITY?
ANOTHER DIMENSION?
I DUNNO, JUST WANT OUT-- AAAGH!
RUN IT OVER!!!
SCREECH
STOP! STOP!
ARE YOU REAL?
IT'S TALKING!
HELLO?
AAACHHHHH!
ARE YOU REAL?
YES! WE'RE REAL! WHO ARE YOU?

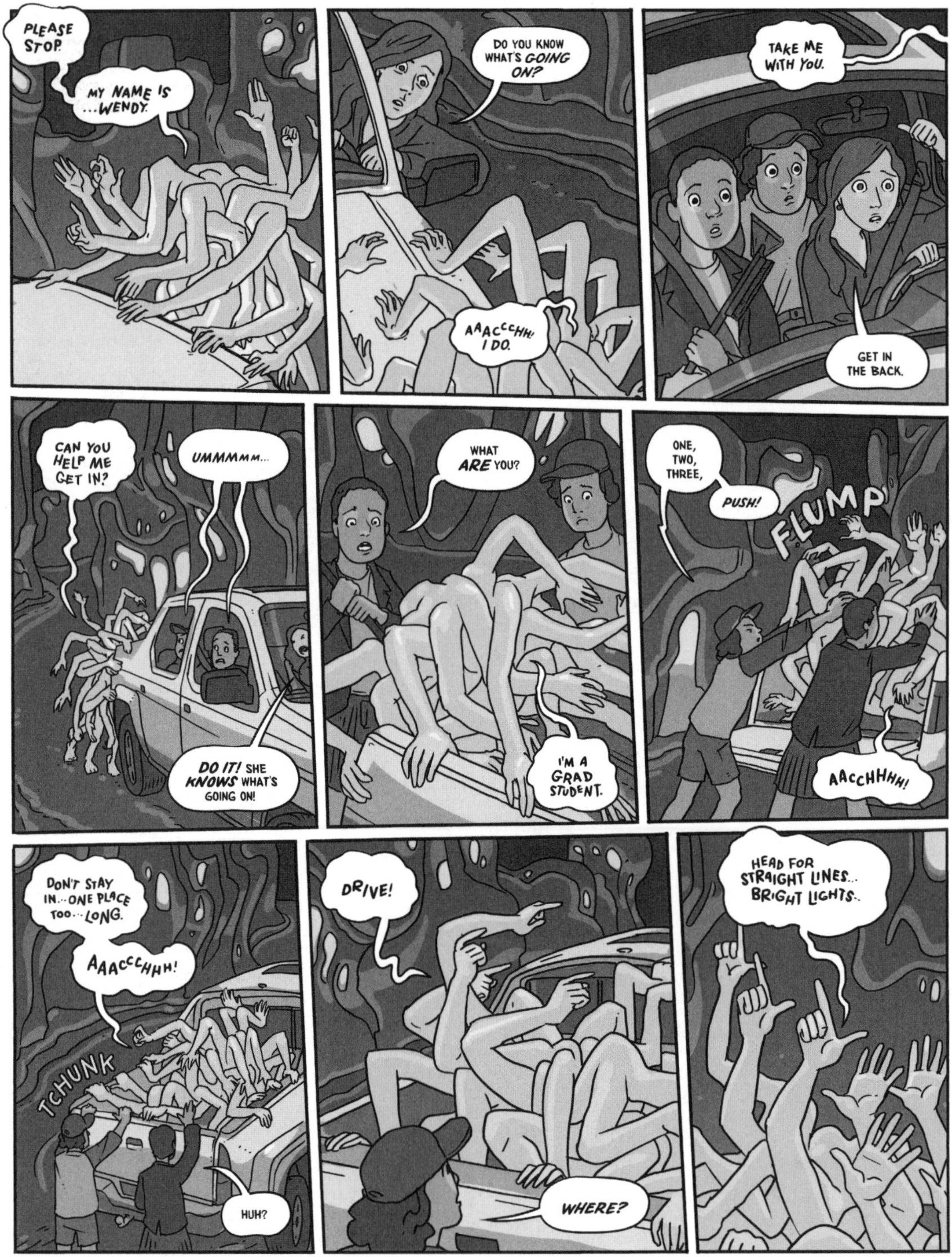

PLEASE STOP.
MY NAME IS ...WENDY.
DO YOU KNOW WHAT'S GOING ON?
AAACCCHH! I DO.
TAKE ME WITH YOU.
GET IN THE BACK.
CAN YOU HELP ME GET IN?
UMMMMM...
DO IT! SHE KNOWS WHAT'S GOING ON!
WHAT ARE YOU?
I'M A GRAD STUDENT.
ONE, TWO, THREE,
PUSH!
FLUMP
AACCHHHH!
DON'T STAY IN... ONE PLACE TOO... LONG.
AAACCCHHH!
TCHUNK
HUH?
DRIVE!
WHERE?
HEAD FOR STRAIGHT LINES... BRIGHT LIGHTS...

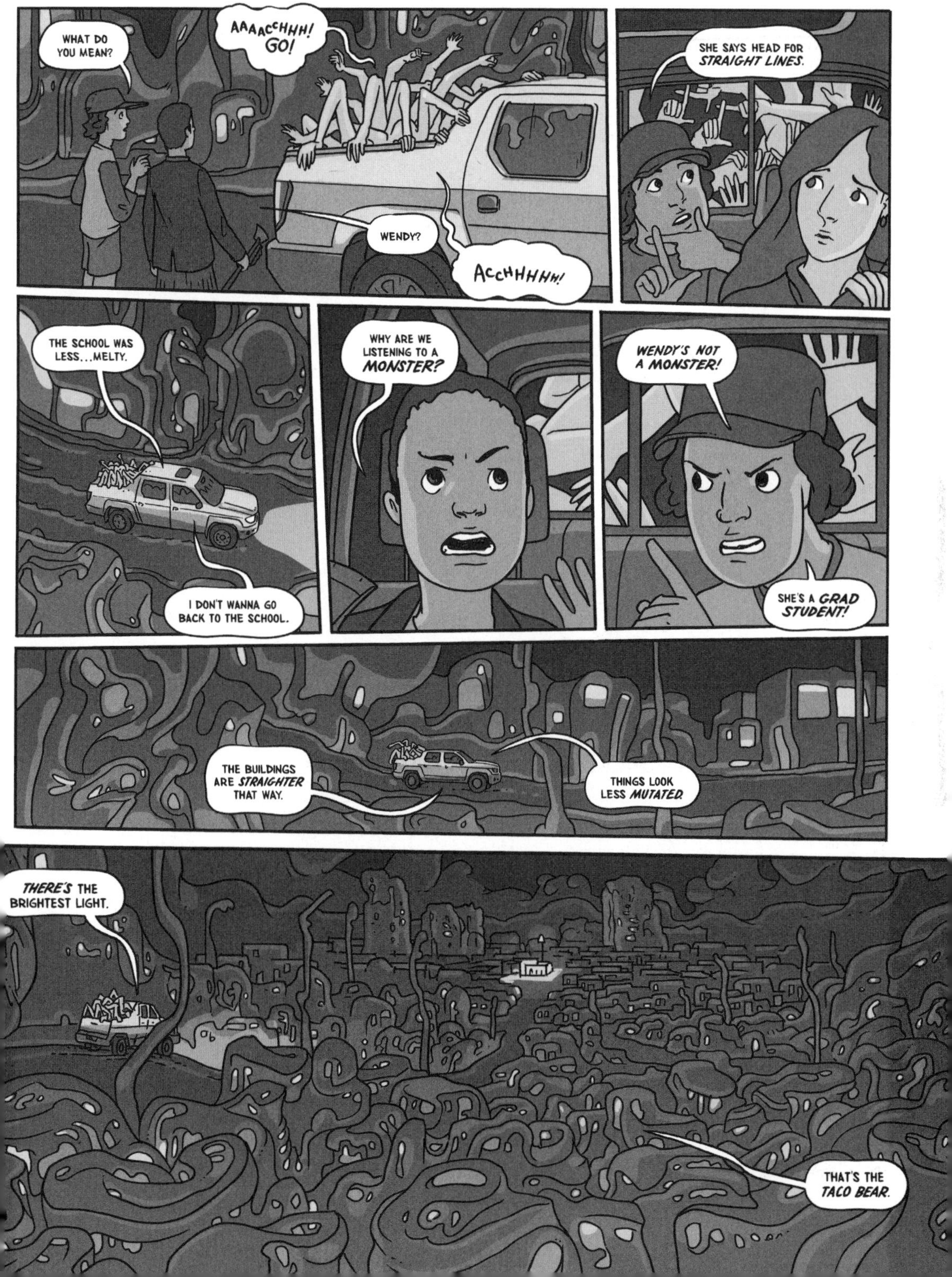
WHAT DO YOU MEAN?
AAAACCHHH! GO!
WENDY?
ACCHHHHH!
SHE SAYS HEAD FOR STRAIGHT LINES.
THE SCHOOL WAS LESS...MELTY.
I DON'T WANNA GO BACK TO THE SCHOOL.
WHY ARE WE LISTENING TO A MONSTER?
WENDY'S NOT A MONSTER!
SHE'S A GRAD STUDENT!
THE BUILDINGS ARE STRAIGHTER THAT WAY.
THINGS LOOK LESS MUTATED.
THERE'S THE BRIGHTEST LIGHT.
THAT'S THE TACO BEAR.

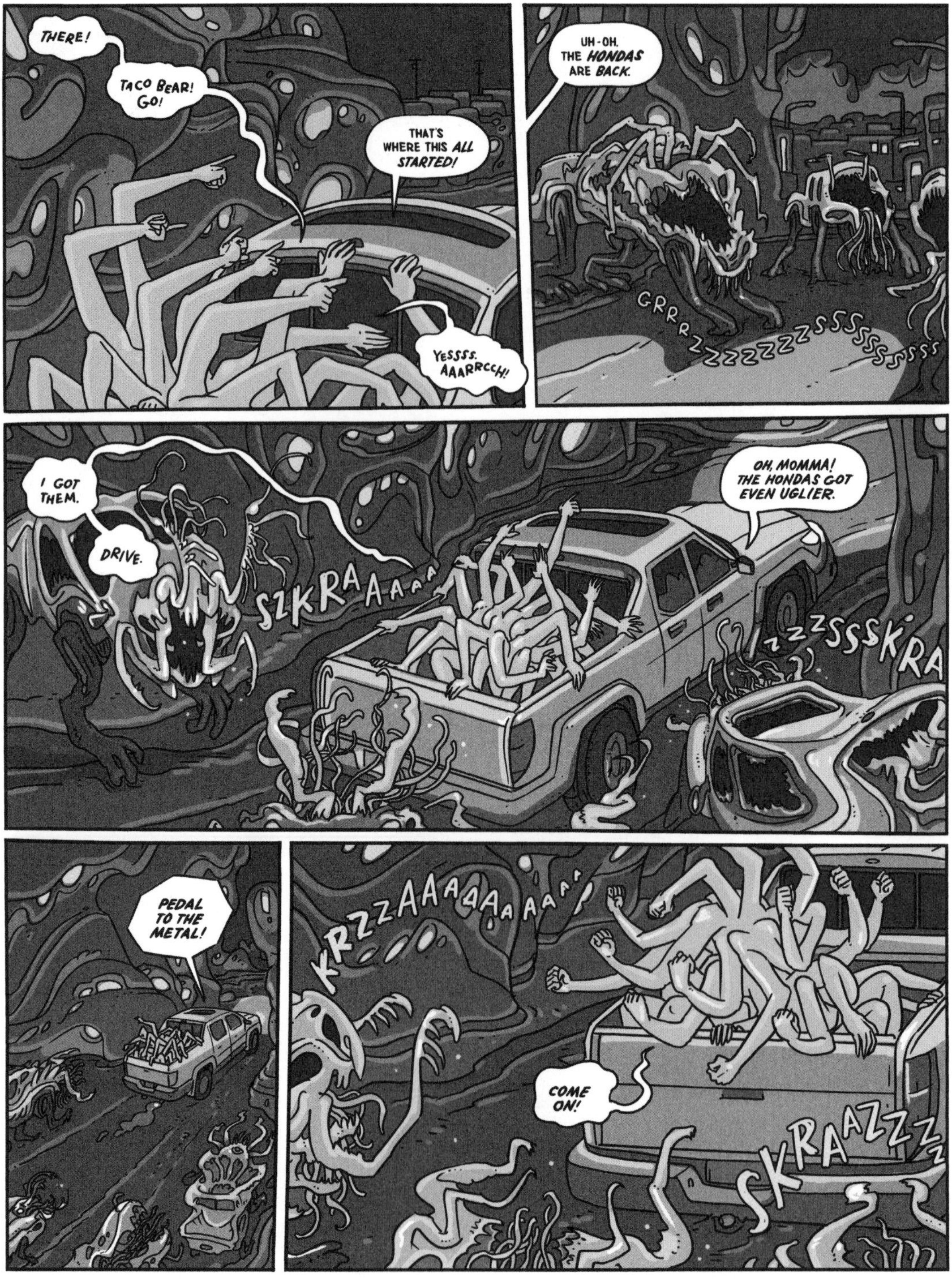
THERE!
TACO BEAR! GO!
THAT'S WHERE THIS ALL STARTED!
YESSSS. AAARRCCH!
UH-OH. THE HONDAS ARE BACK.
GRRRZZZZZZZZSSSSSSSSSS
I GOT THEM.
DRIVE.
SZKRAAAAA
OH, MOMMA! THE HONDAS GOT EVEN UGLIER.
ZZZSSSKRA
PEDAL TO THE METAL!
KRZZAAAAAAAAAA
COME ON!
SKRAAZZZZ

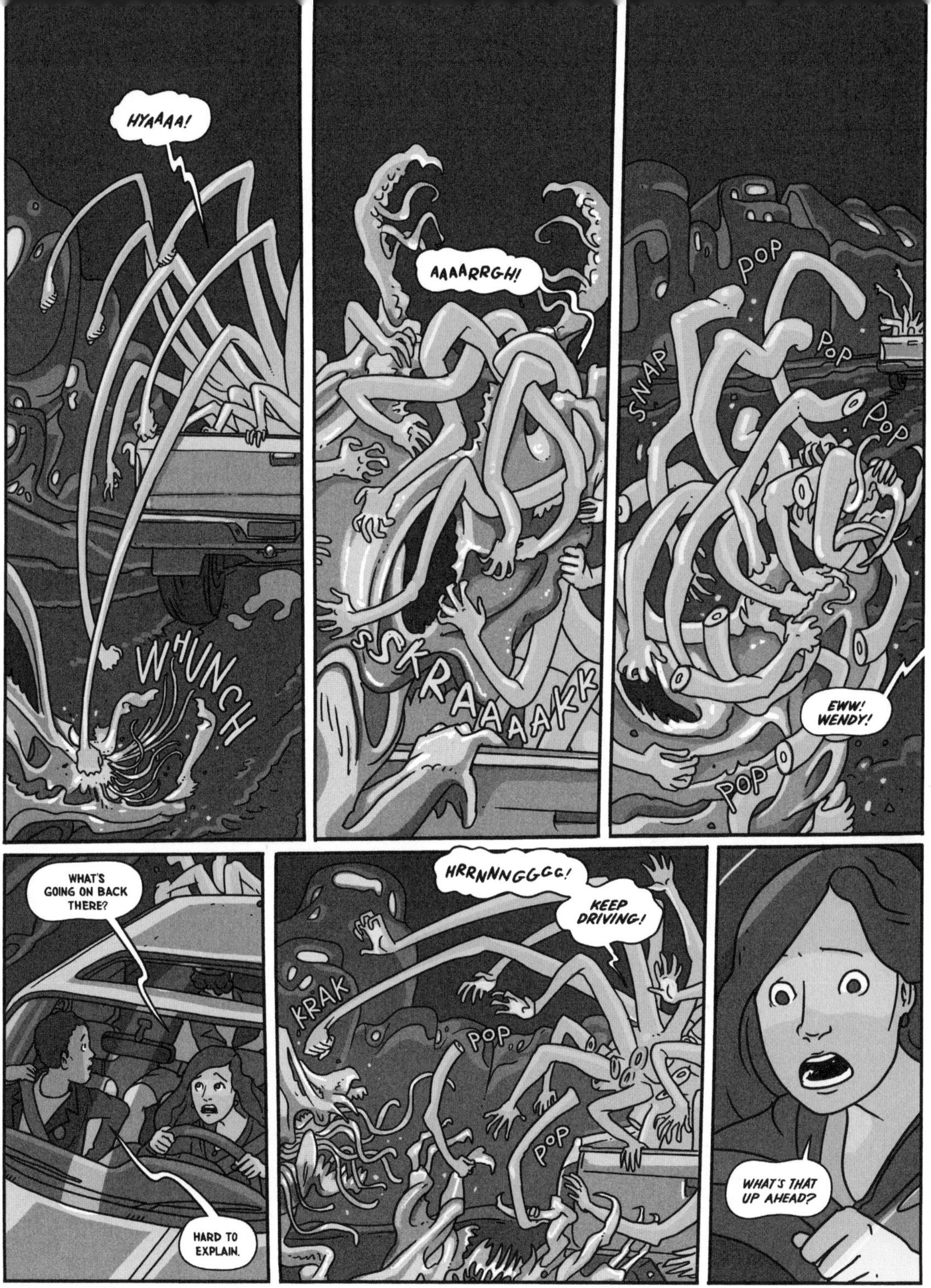
HYAAAA!
WHUNCH
AAAARRGH!
SSKRAAAAAKK
POP
SNAP
POP
POP
EWW! WENDY!
POP
WHAT'S GOING ON BACK THERE?
HARD TO EXPLAIN.
HRRNNNGGGG!
KEEP DRIVING!
KRAK
POP
POP
WHAT'S THAT UP AHEAD?

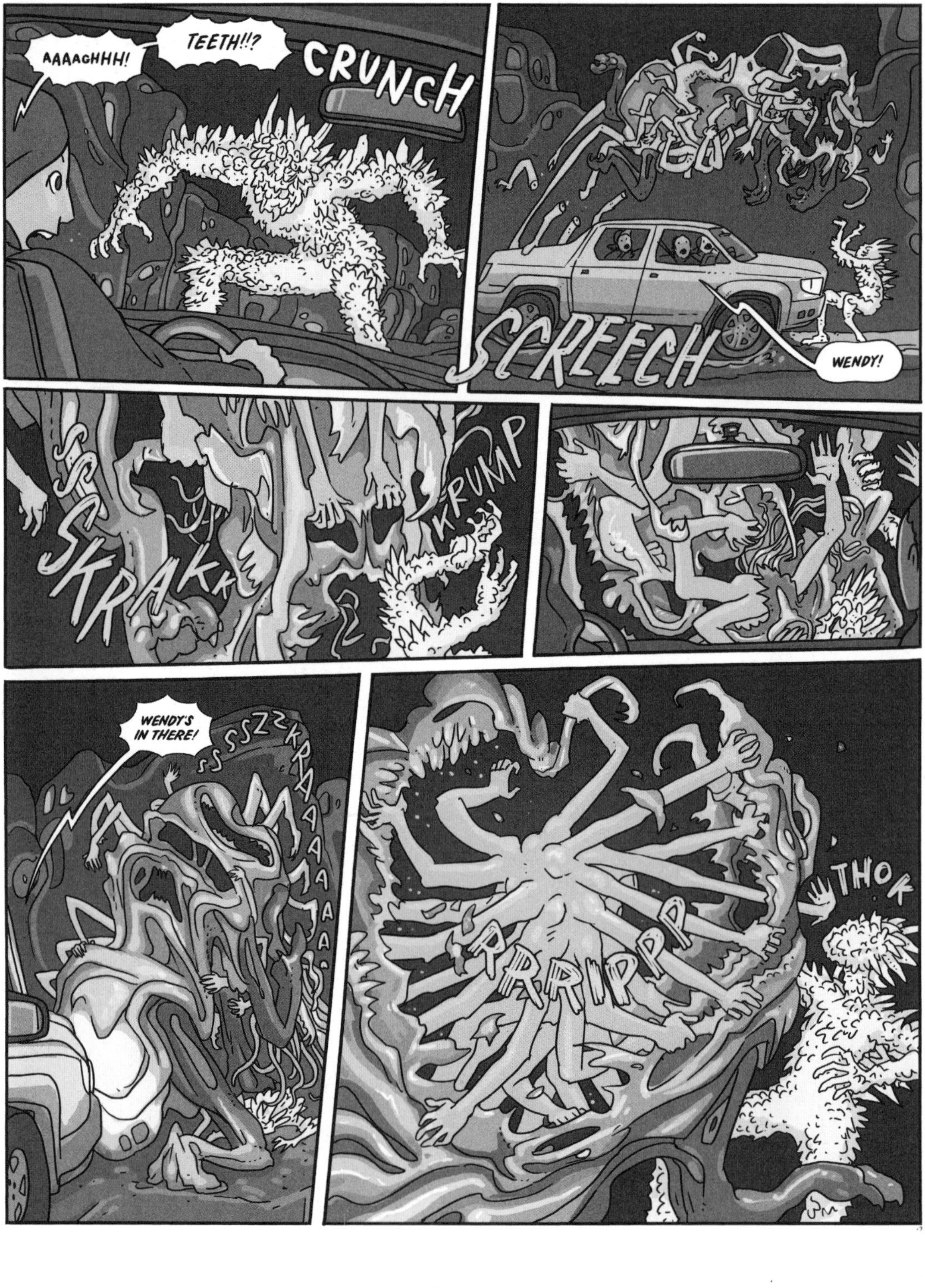
AAAAGHHH!
TEETH!!?
CRUNCH
SCREECH
WENDY!
SKRAKK
KRUMP
WENDY'S IN THERE!
SSSZZKRAAAAAAAA
RRRIPPP
THOK

I'M GLAD WE PICKED HER UP?

YEAH.

SKRUNK

MMMSSSKRAAA...

GULP

WENDY!!

WENDY?

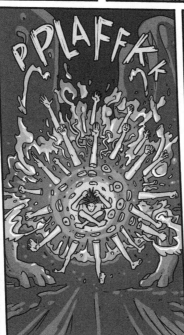

PPLAFFKK

IT'S WENDY! SHE REALLY IS A GRAD STUDENT!

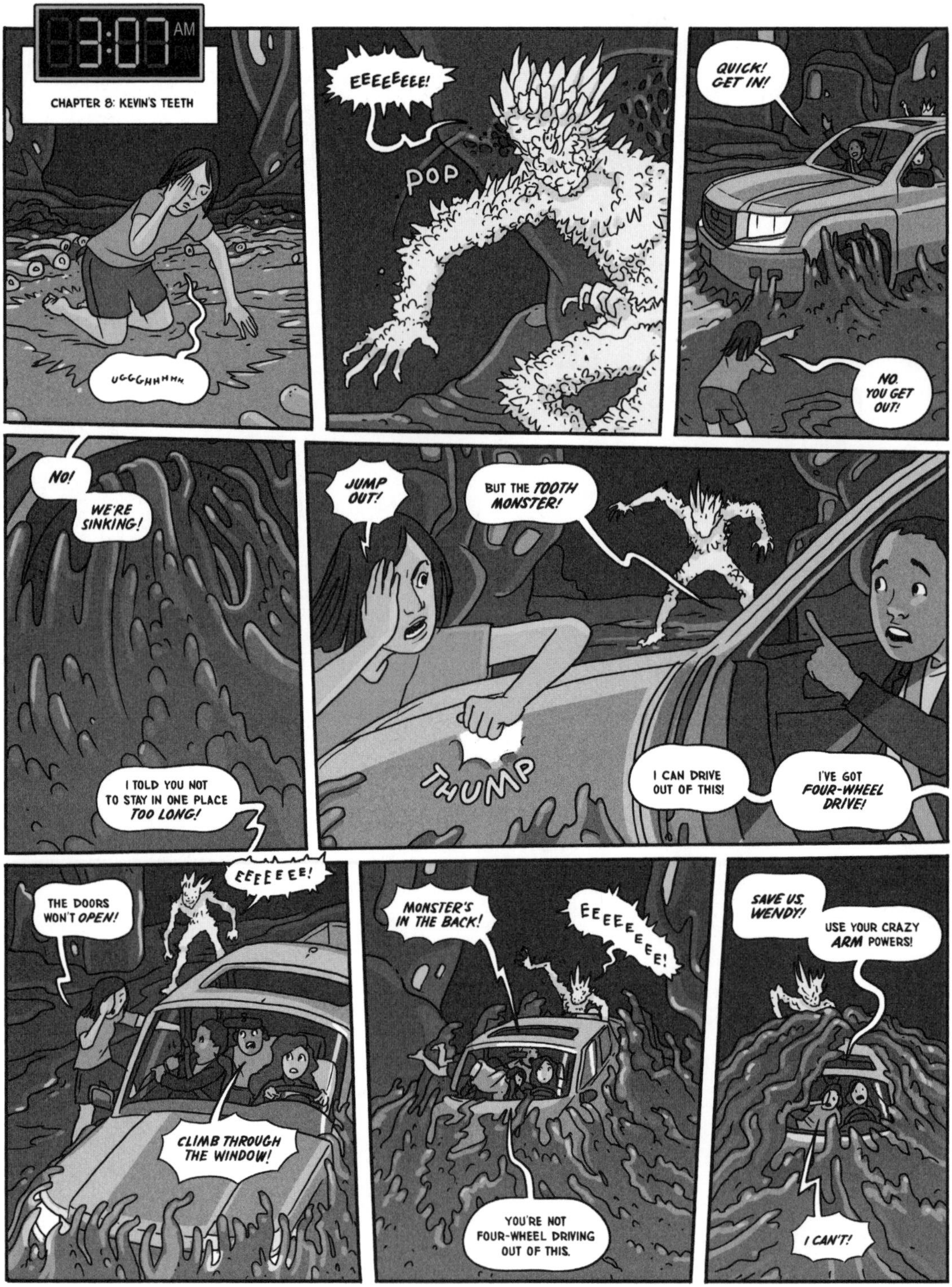
3:07 AM PM
CHAPTER 8: KEVIN'S TEETH
UGGGHHHHH
EEEEEEEE!
POP
QUICK! GET IN!
NO. YOU GET OUT!
NO!
WE'RE SINKING!
I TOLD YOU NOT TO STAY IN ONE PLACE TOO LONG!
JUMP OUT!
BUT THE TOOTH MONSTER!
THUMP
I CAN DRIVE OUT OF THIS!
I'VE GOT FOUR-WHEEL DRIVE!
THE DOORS WON'T OPEN!
EEEEEEE!
CLIMB THROUGH THE WINDOW!
MONSTER'S IN THE BACK!
EEEEEEEEE!
YOU'RE NOT FOUR-WHEEL DRIVING OUT OF THIS.
SAVE US, WENDY!
USE YOUR CRAZY ARM POWERS!
I CAN'T!

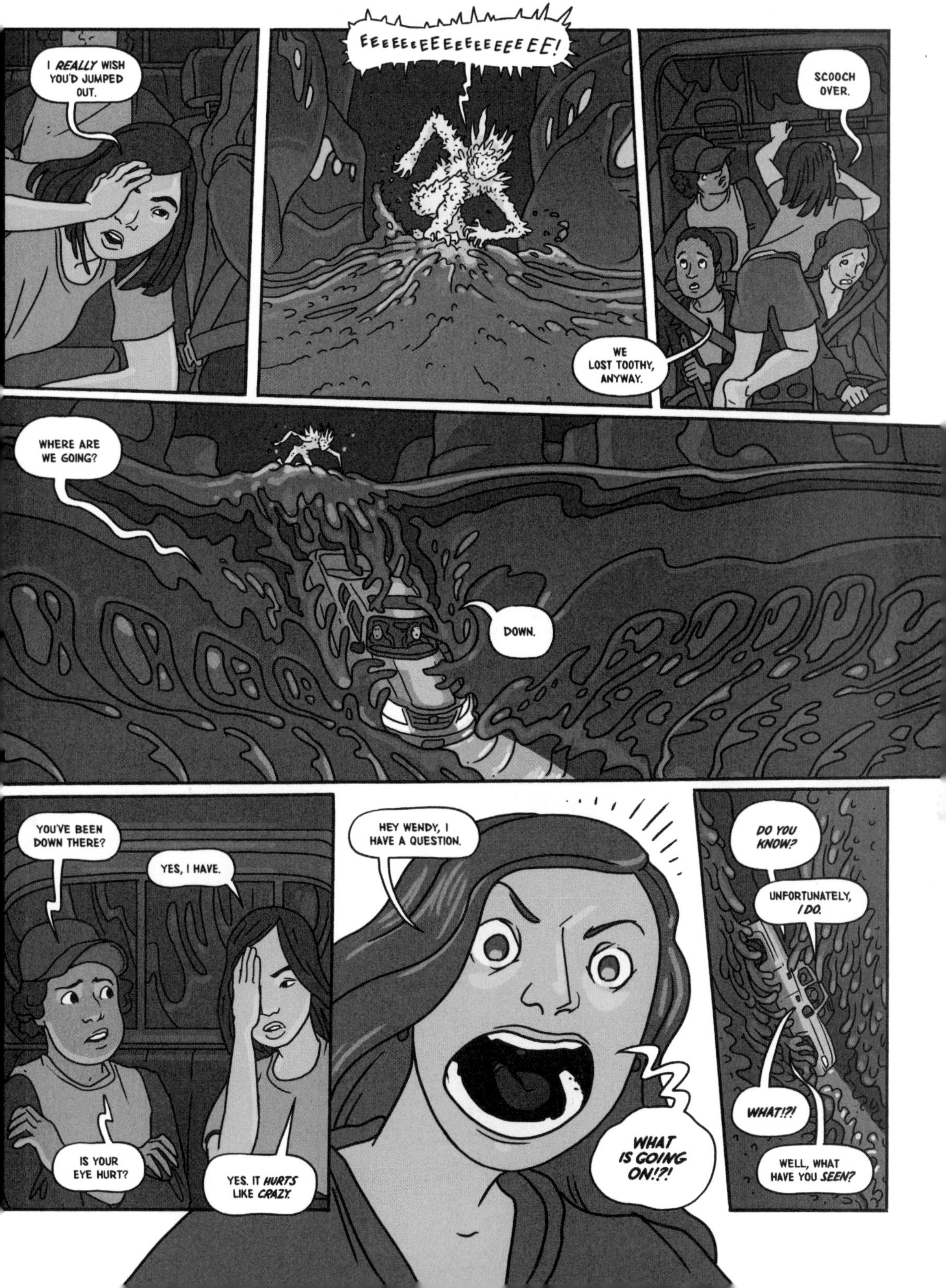
I REALLY WISH YOU'D JUMPED OUT.
EEEEEEEEEEEEEEEEE!
SCOOCH OVER.
WE LOST TOOTHY, ANYWAY.
WHERE ARE WE GOING?
DOWN.
YOU'VE BEEN DOWN THERE?
YES, I HAVE.
IS YOUR EYE HURT?
YES. IT HURTS LIKE CRAZY.
HEY WENDY, I HAVE A QUESTION.
WHAT IS GOING ON!?!
DO YOU KNOW?
UNFORTUNATELY, I DO.
WHAT!?!
WELL, WHAT HAVE YOU SEEN?

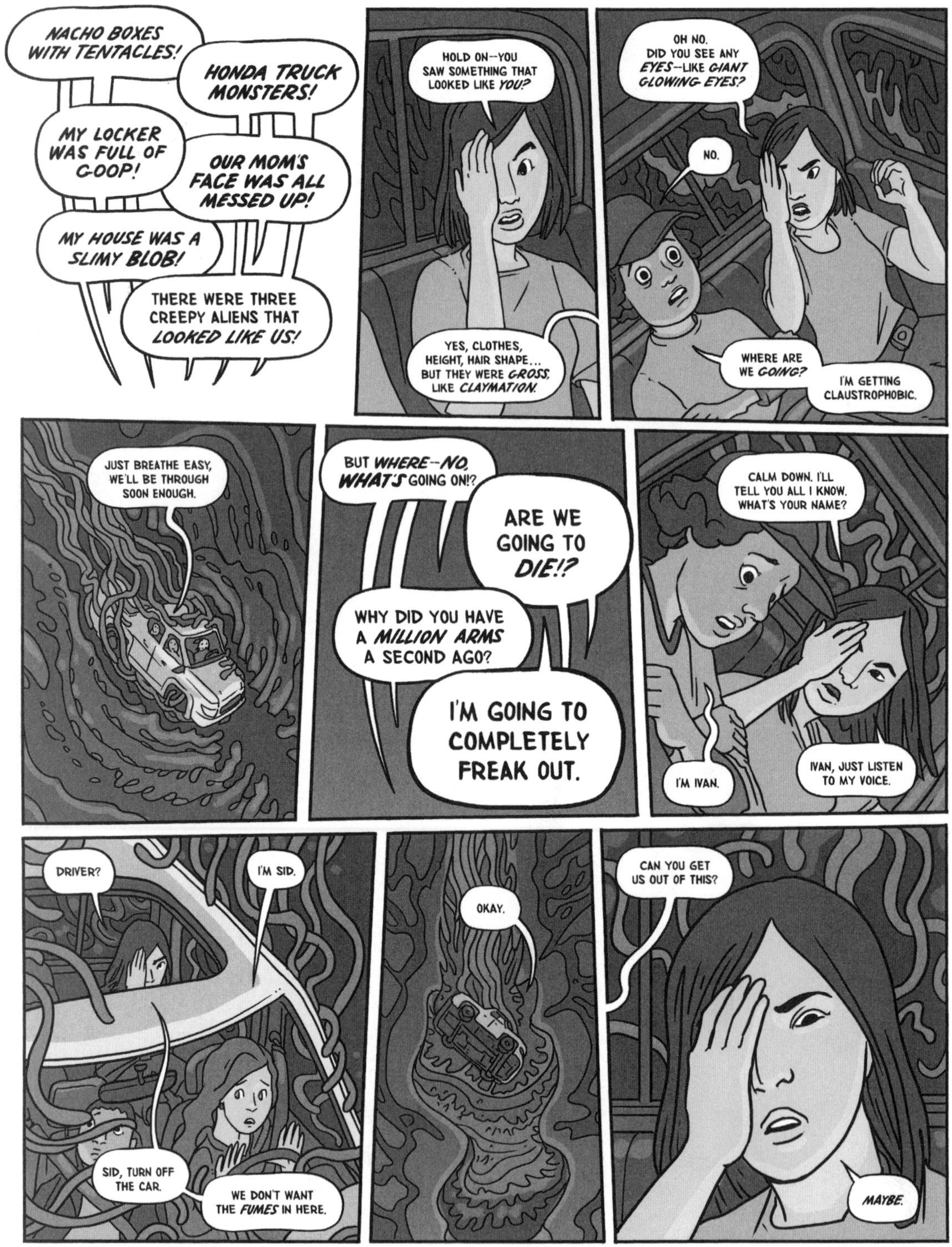
NACHO BOXES WITH TENTACLES!
HONDA TRUCK MONSTERS!
MY LOCKER WAS FULL OF GOOP!
OUR MOM'S FACE WAS ALL MESSED UP!
MY HOUSE WAS A SLIMY BLOB!
THERE WERE THREE CREEPY ALIENS THAT LOOKED LIKE US!
HOLD ON--YOU SAW SOMETHING THAT LOOKED LIKE YOU?
YES, CLOTHES, HEIGHT, HAIR SHAPE... BUT THEY WERE GROSS, LIKE CLAYMATION.
OH NO. DID YOU SEE ANY EYES--LIKE GIANT GLOWING EYES?
NO.
WHERE ARE WE GOING?
I'M GETTING CLAUSTROPHOBIC.
JUST BREATHE EASY, WE'LL BE THROUGH SOON ENOUGH.
BUT WHERE--NO, WHAT'S GOING ON!?
ARE WE GOING TO DIE!?
WHY DID YOU HAVE A MILLION ARMS A SECOND AGO?
I'M GOING TO COMPLETELY FREAK OUT.
CALM DOWN. I'LL TELL YOU ALL I KNOW. WHAT'S YOUR NAME?
I'M IVAN.
IVAN, JUST LISTEN TO MY VOICE.
DRIVER?
I'M SID.
SID, TURN OFF THE CAR.
WE DON'T WANT THE FUMES IN HERE.
OKAY.
CAN YOU GET US OUT OF THIS?
MAYBE.

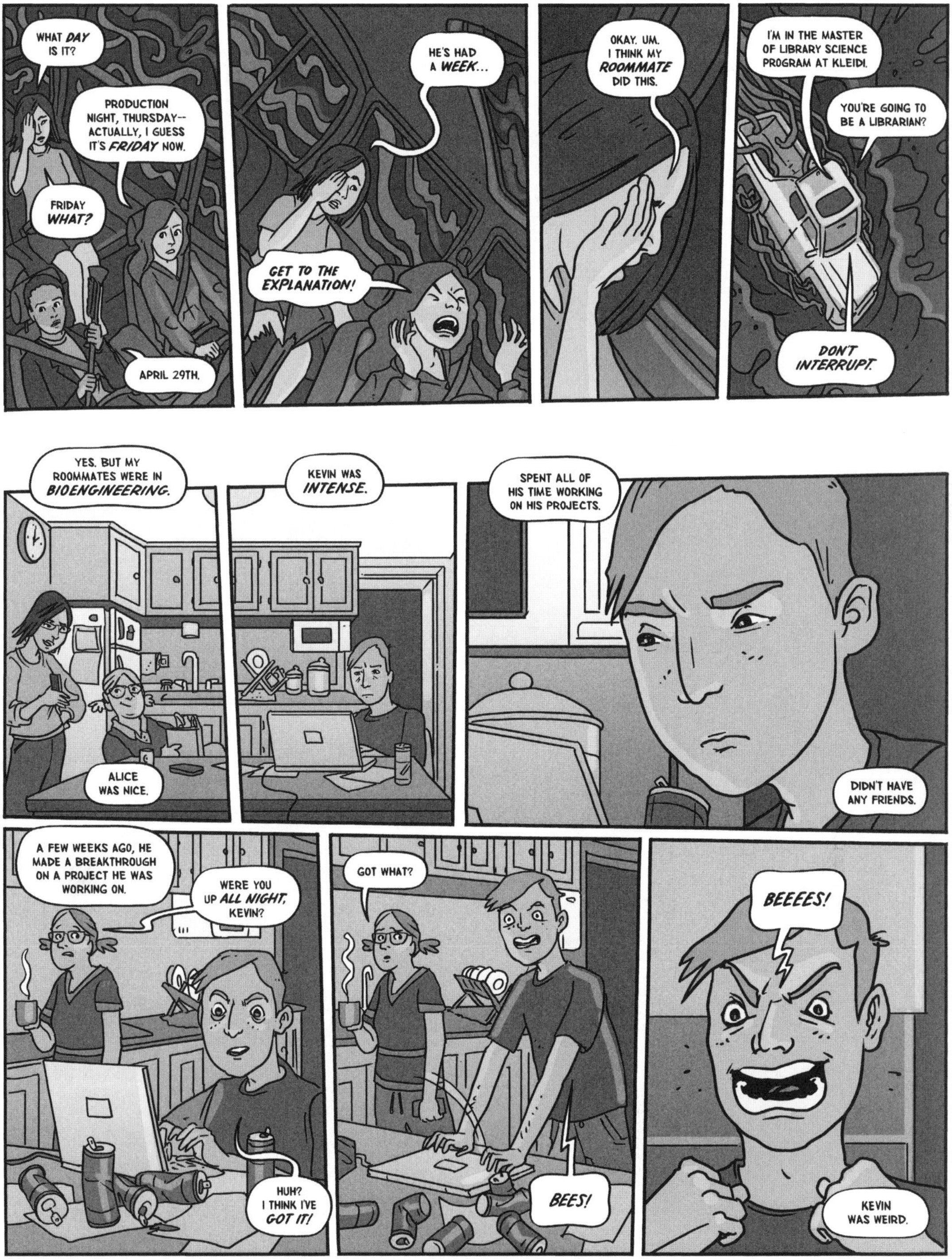

WHAT DAY IS IT?
PRODUCTION NIGHT, THURSDAY-- ACTUALLY, I GUESS IT'S FRIDAY NOW.
FRIDAY WHAT?
APRIL 29TH.
HE'S HAD A WEEK...
GET TO THE EXPLANATION!
OKAY. UM. I THINK MY ROOMMATE DID THIS.
I'M IN THE MASTER OF LIBRARY SCIENCE PROGRAM AT KLEIDI.
YOU'RE GOING TO BE A LIBRARIAN?
DON'T INTERRUPT.
YES. BUT MY ROOMMATES WERE IN BIOENGINEERING.
ALICE WAS NICE.
KEVIN WAS INTENSE.
SPENT ALL OF HIS TIME WORKING ON HIS PROJECTS.
DIDN'T HAVE ANY FRIENDS.
A FEW WEEKS AGO, HE MADE A BREAKTHROUGH ON A PROJECT HE WAS WORKING ON.
WERE YOU UP ALL NIGHT, KEVIN?
HUH? I THINK I'VE GOT IT!
GOT WHAT?
BEES!
BEEEES!
KEVIN WAS WEIRD.

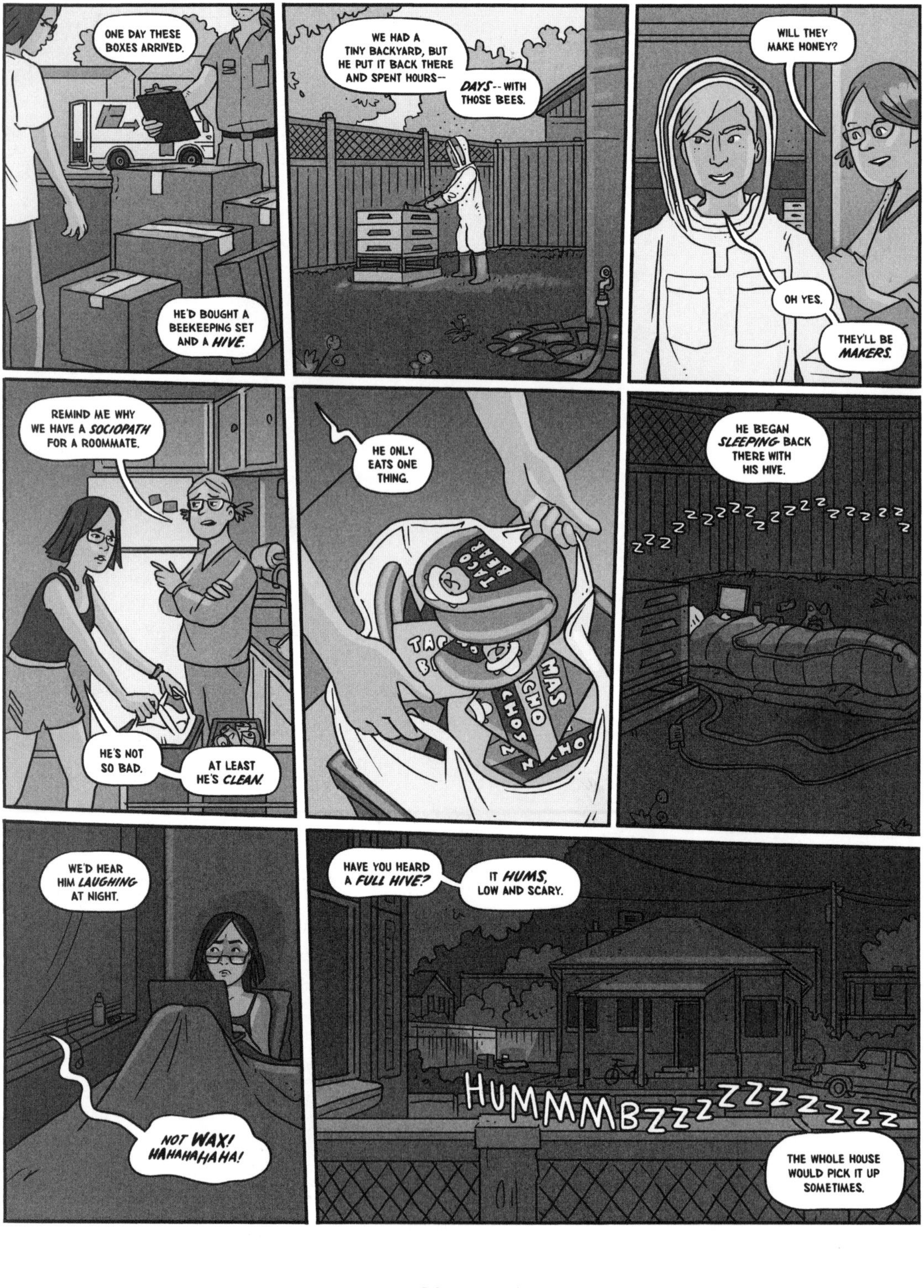
ONE DAY THESE BOXES ARRIVED.
HE'D BOUGHT A BEEKEEPING SET AND A HIVE.
WE HAD A TINY BACKYARD, BUT HE PUT IT BACK THERE AND SPENT HOURS--
DAYS--WITH THOSE BEES.
WILL THEY MAKE HONEY?
OH YES.
THEY'LL BE MAKERS.
REMIND ME WHY WE HAVE A SOCIOPATH FOR A ROOMMATE.
HE'S NOT SO BAD.
AT LEAST HE'S CLEAN.
HE ONLY EATS ONE THING.
TACO BEAR
MAS NACHOS
HE BEGAN SLEEPING BACK THERE WITH HIS HIVE.
ZZZZZZZZZZZZZZZZZZ
WE'D HEAR HIM LAUGHING AT NIGHT.
NOT WAX! HAHAHAHAHA!
HAVE YOU HEARD A FULL HIVE?
IT HUMS, LOW AND SCARY.
HUMMMBZZZZZZZZZZZ
THE WHOLE HOUSE WOULD PICK IT UP SOMETIMES.

HE QUIT GOING TO CLASS.

HE BEGAN RUNNING CABLES AND CORDS BACK THERE.

WE NEED TO GET A NEW ROOMMATE.

THIS ONE'S *LOST HIS MIND.*

HEY, KEVIN, WHAT *EXACTLY* ARE YOU *BUILDING* OUT THERE?

THE FUTURE.

WE'RE MAKING BEEF BULGOGI—YOU DON'T HAVE TO EAT THAT JUNK FOOD.

I *LOVE* TACO BEAR.

AND THESE ARE FOR THE *HIVE.*

SNORT.

I'M PRETTY SURE *BEES* DON'T EAT BEAN BURRITOS.

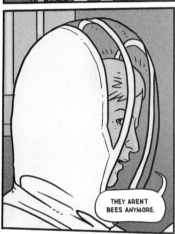

THEY AREN'T BEES ANYMORE.

WHAT WERE THEY!?

IT'S GETTING LIGHTER.

WHAT WAS HE *MAKING?*

HOLD ON. YOU ARE GOING TO GET *DIZZY* IN A SECOND.

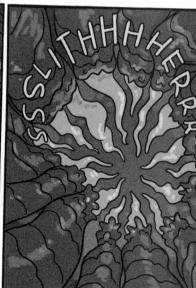

SSSLITHHHHERRR

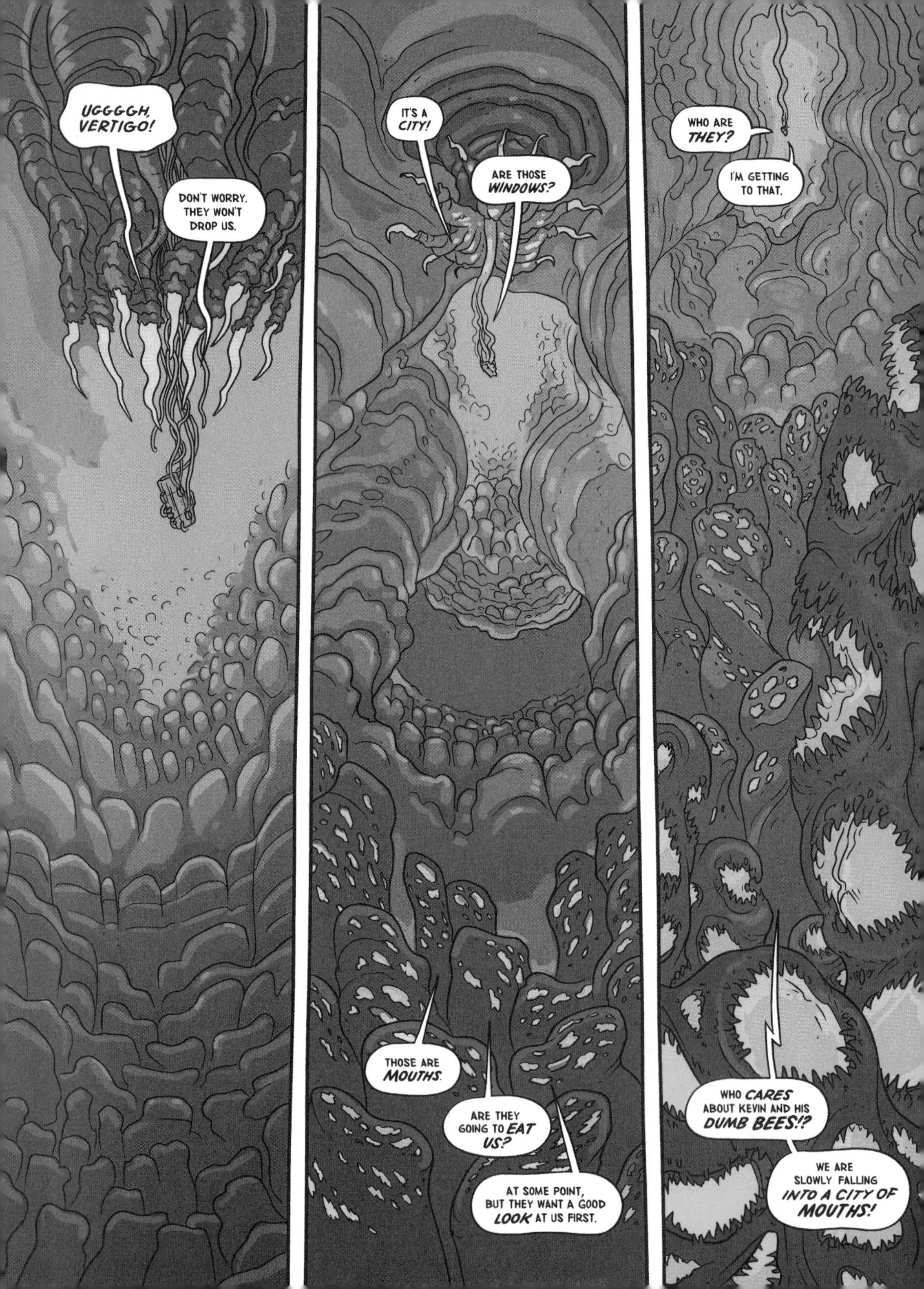
UGGGGH, VERTIGO!
DON'T WORRY. THEY WON'T DROP US.
IT'S A CITY!
ARE THOSE WINDOWS?
THOSE ARE MOUTHS.
ARE THEY GOING TO EAT US?
AT SOME POINT, BUT THEY WANT A GOOD LOOK AT US FIRST.
WHO ARE THEY?
I'M GETTING TO THAT.
WHO CARES ABOUT KEVIN AND HIS DUMB BEES!?
WE ARE SLOWLY FALLING INTO A CITY OF MOUTHS!

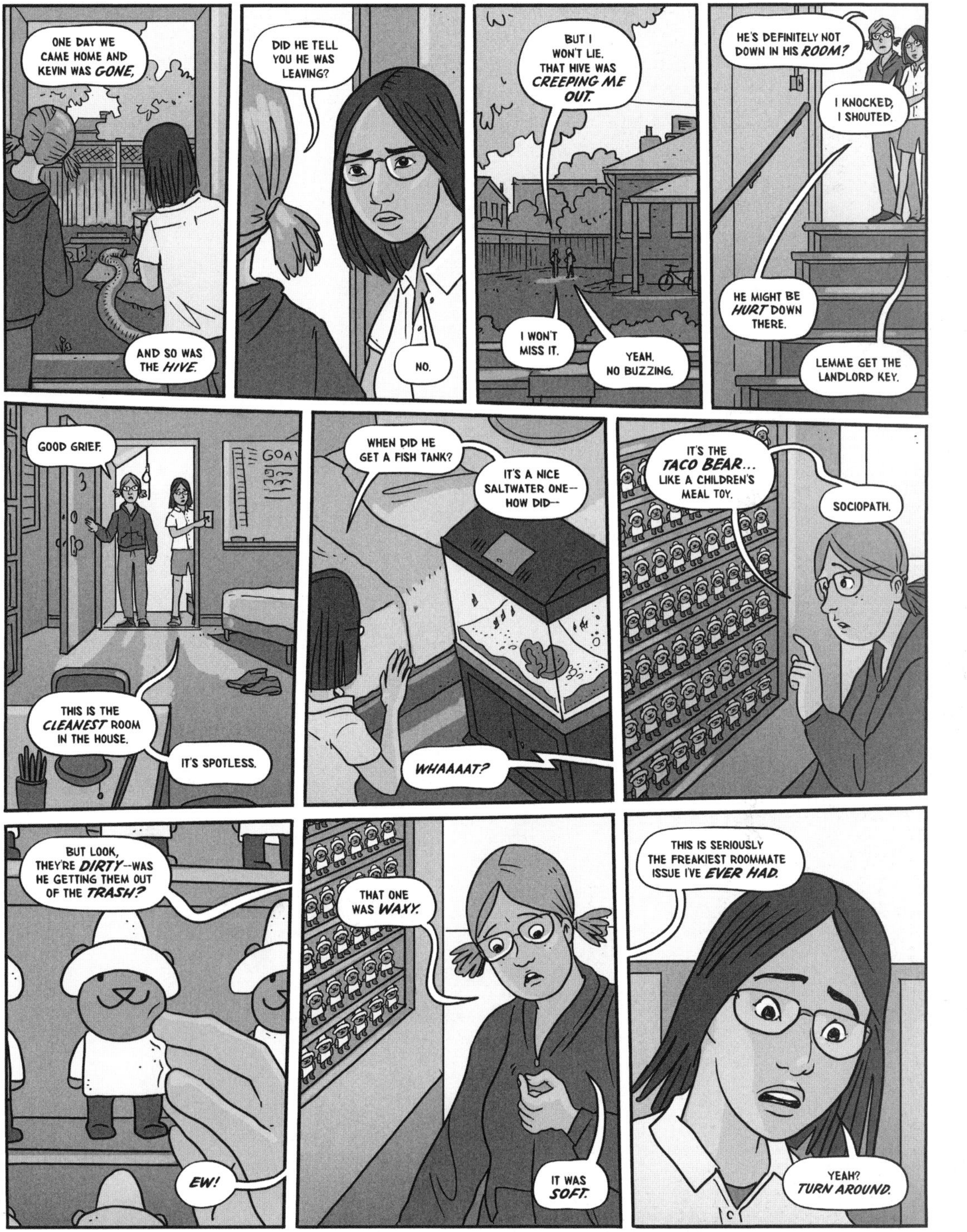
ONE DAY WE CAME HOME AND KEVIN WAS GONE,
AND SO WAS THE HIVE.
DID HE TELL YOU HE WAS LEAVING?
NO.
BUT I WON'T LIE. THAT HIVE WAS CREEPING ME OUT.
I WON'T MISS IT.
YEAH. NO BUZZING.
HE'S DEFINITELY NOT DOWN IN HIS ROOM?
I KNOCKED, I SHOUTED.
HE MIGHT BE HURT DOWN THERE.
LEMME GET THE LANDLORD KEY.
GOOD GRIEF.
THIS IS THE CLEANEST ROOM IN THE HOUSE.
IT'S SPOTLESS.
WHEN DID HE GET A FISH TANK?
IT'S A NICE SALTWATER ONE--HOW DID--
WHAAAAT?
IT'S THE TACO BEAR... LIKE A CHILDREN'S MEAL TOY.
SOCIOPATH.
BUT LOOK, THEY'RE DIRTY--WAS HE GETTING THEM OUT OF THE TRASH?
EW!
THAT ONE WAS WAXY.
IT WAS SOFT.
THIS IS SERIOUSLY THE FREAKIEST ROOMMATE ISSUE I'VE EVER HAD.
YEAH? TURN AROUND.

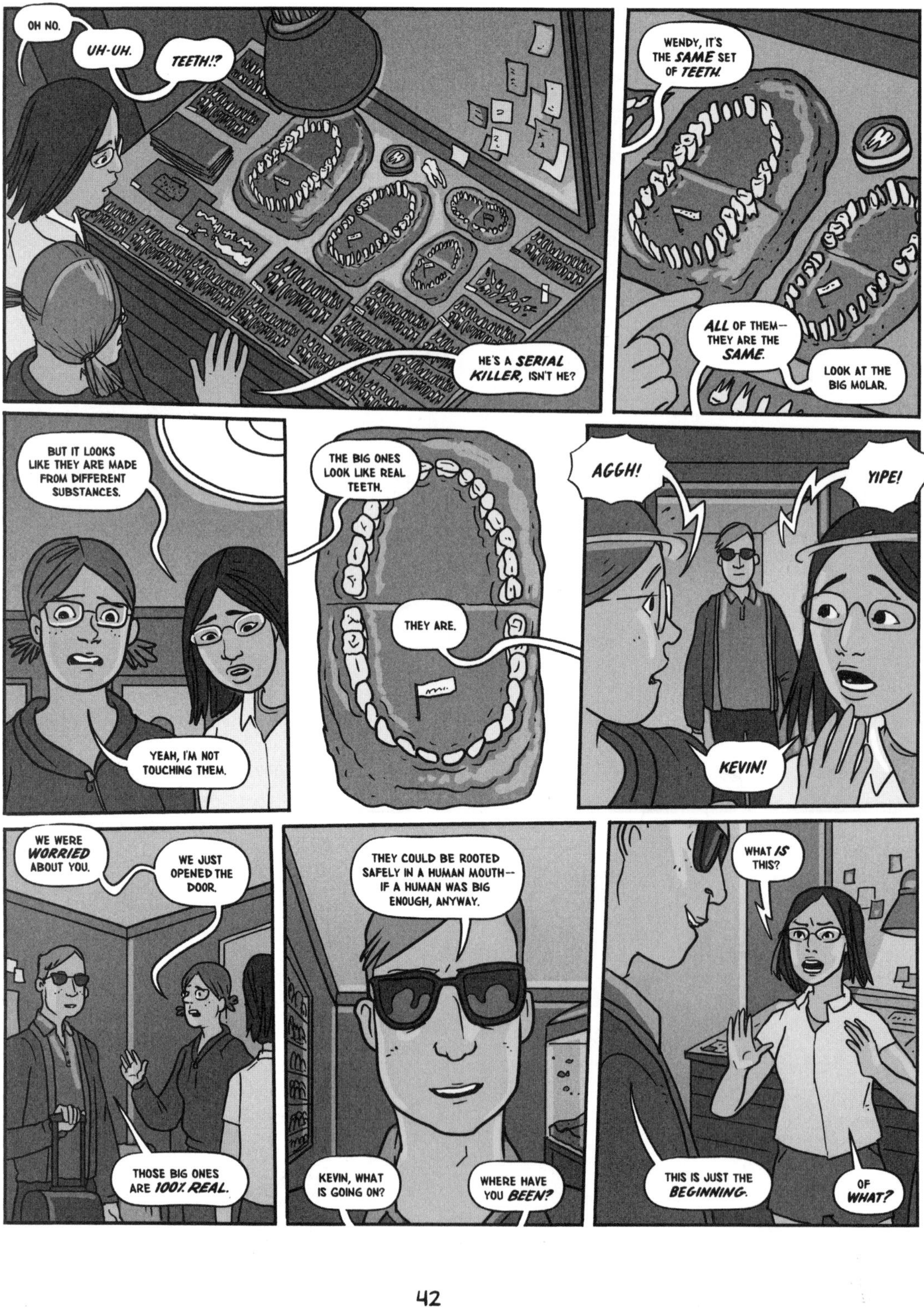
OH NO.
UH-UH.
TEETH!?
HE'S A SERIAL KILLER, ISN'T HE?
WENDY, IT'S THE SAME SET OF TEETH.
ALL OF THEM— THEY ARE THE SAME.
LOOK AT THE BIG MOLAR.
BUT IT LOOKS LIKE THEY ARE MADE FROM DIFFERENT SUBSTANCES.
YEAH, I'M NOT TOUCHING THEM.
THE BIG ONES LOOK LIKE REAL TEETH.
THEY ARE.
AGGH!
YIPE!
KEVIN!
WE WERE WORRIED ABOUT YOU.
WE JUST OPENED THE DOOR.
THOSE BIG ONES ARE 100% REAL.
THEY COULD BE ROOTED SAFELY IN A HUMAN MOUTH-- IF A HUMAN WAS BIG ENOUGH, ANYWAY.
KEVIN, WHAT IS GOING ON?
WHERE HAVE YOU BEEN?
WHAT IS THIS?
THIS IS JUST THE BEGINNING.
OF WHAT?

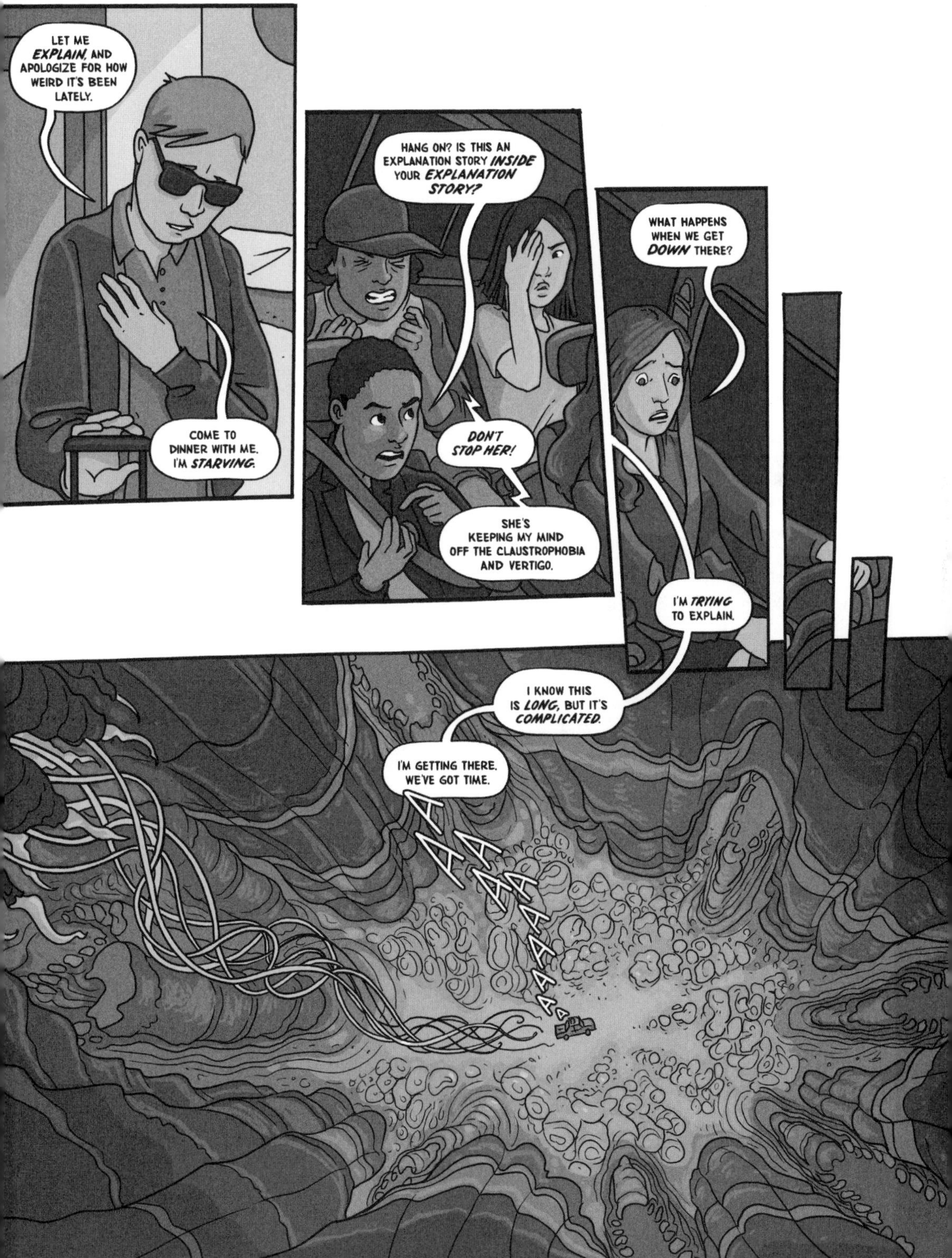
LET ME EXPLAIN, AND APOLOGIZE FOR HOW WEIRD IT'S BEEN LATELY.
COME TO DINNER WITH ME. I'M STARVING.
HANG ON? IS THIS AN EXPLANATION STORY INSIDE YOUR EXPLANATION STORY?
DON'T STOP HER!
SHE'S KEEPING MY MIND OFF THE CLAUSTROPHOBIA AND VERTIGO.
WHAT HAPPENS WHEN WE GET DOWN THERE?
I'M TRYING TO EXPLAIN.
I KNOW THIS IS LONG, BUT IT'S COMPLICATED.
I'M GETTING THERE. WE'VE GOT TIME.
AAAAAAAAAAA

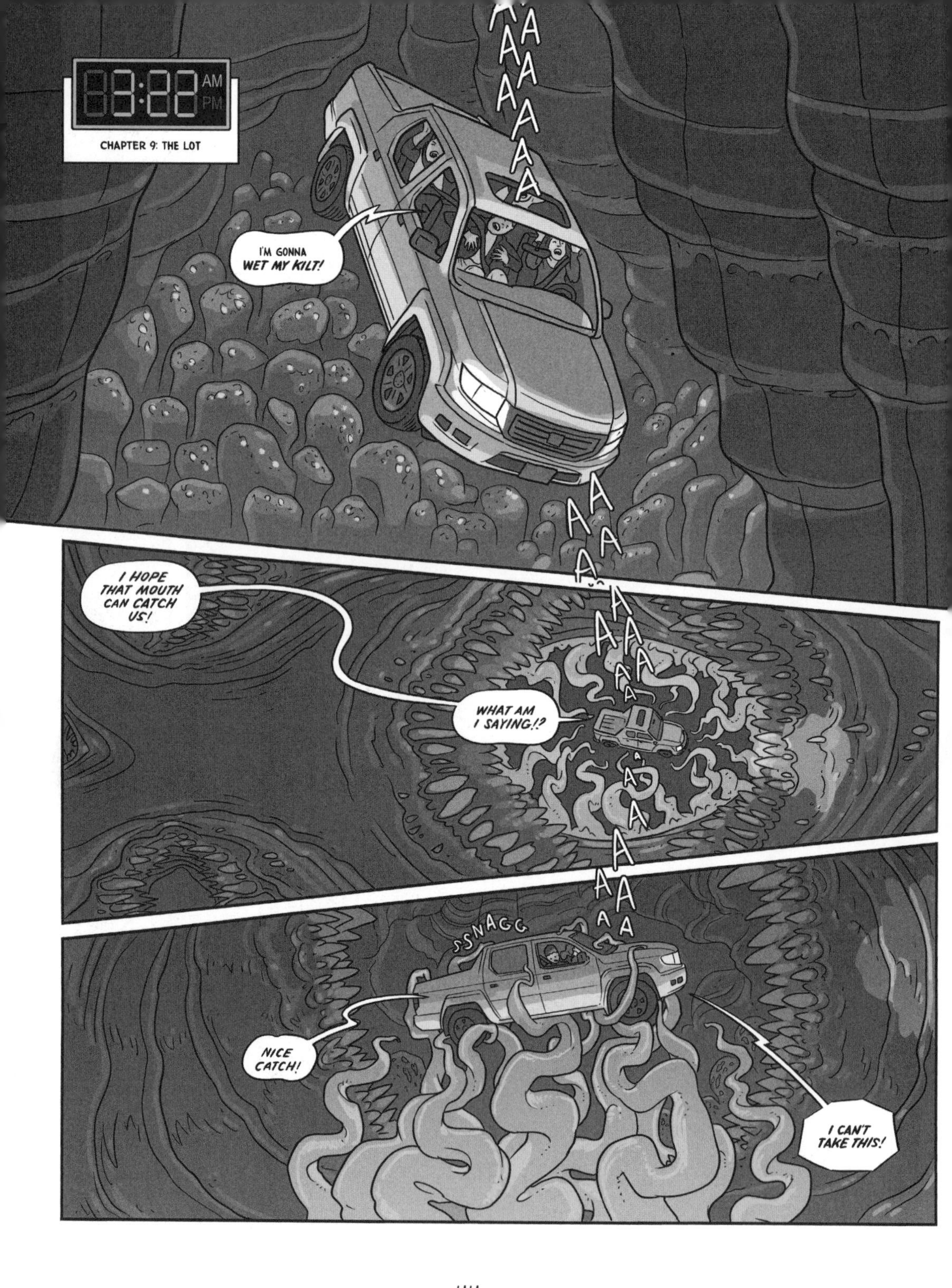

13:22 AM PM
CHAPTER 9: THE LOT
AAAAAAAAA
I'M GONNA WET MY KILT!
AAAAAAAAAAAAAAAA
I HOPE THAT MOUTH CAN CATCH US!
WHAT AM I SAYING!?
SNAGG
NICE CATCH!
I CAN'T TAKE THIS!

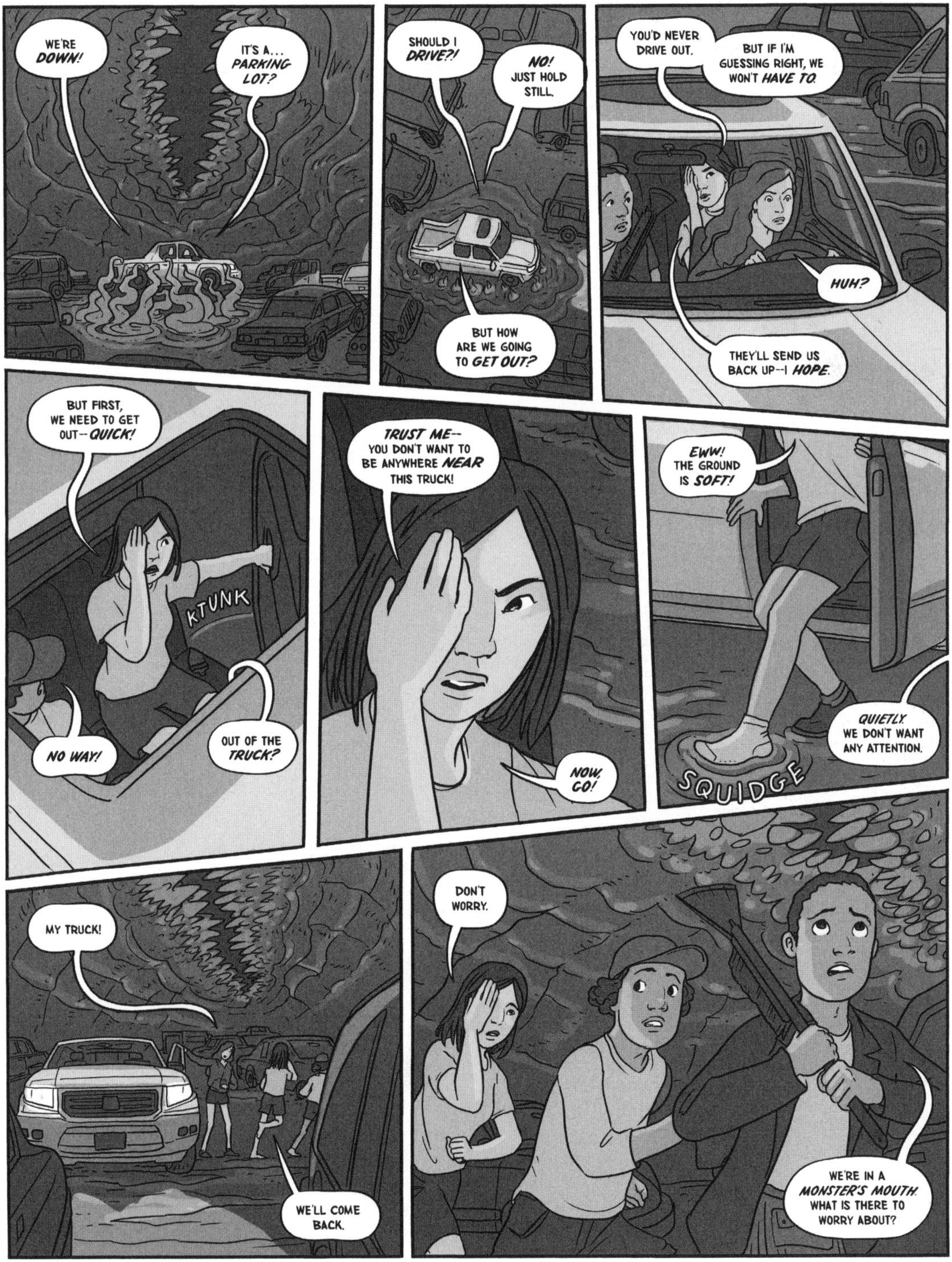
WE'RE DOWN!
IT'S A... PARKING LOT?
SHOULD I DRIVE?!
NO! JUST HOLD STILL.
BUT HOW ARE WE GOING TO GET OUT?
YOU'D NEVER DRIVE OUT.
BUT IF I'M GUESSING RIGHT, WE WON'T HAVE TO.
HUH?
THEY'LL SEND US BACK UP--I HOPE.
BUT FIRST, WE NEED TO GET OUT--QUICK!
KTUNK
NO WAY!
OUT OF THE TRUCK?
TRUST ME-- YOU DON'T WANT TO BE ANYWHERE NEAR THIS TRUCK!
NOW, GO!
EWW! THE GROUND IS SOFT!
QUIETLY. WE DON'T WANT ANY ATTENTION.
SQUIDGE
MY TRUCK!
WE'LL COME BACK.
DON'T WORRY.
WE'RE IN A MONSTER'S MOUTH. WHAT IS THERE TO WORRY ABOUT?

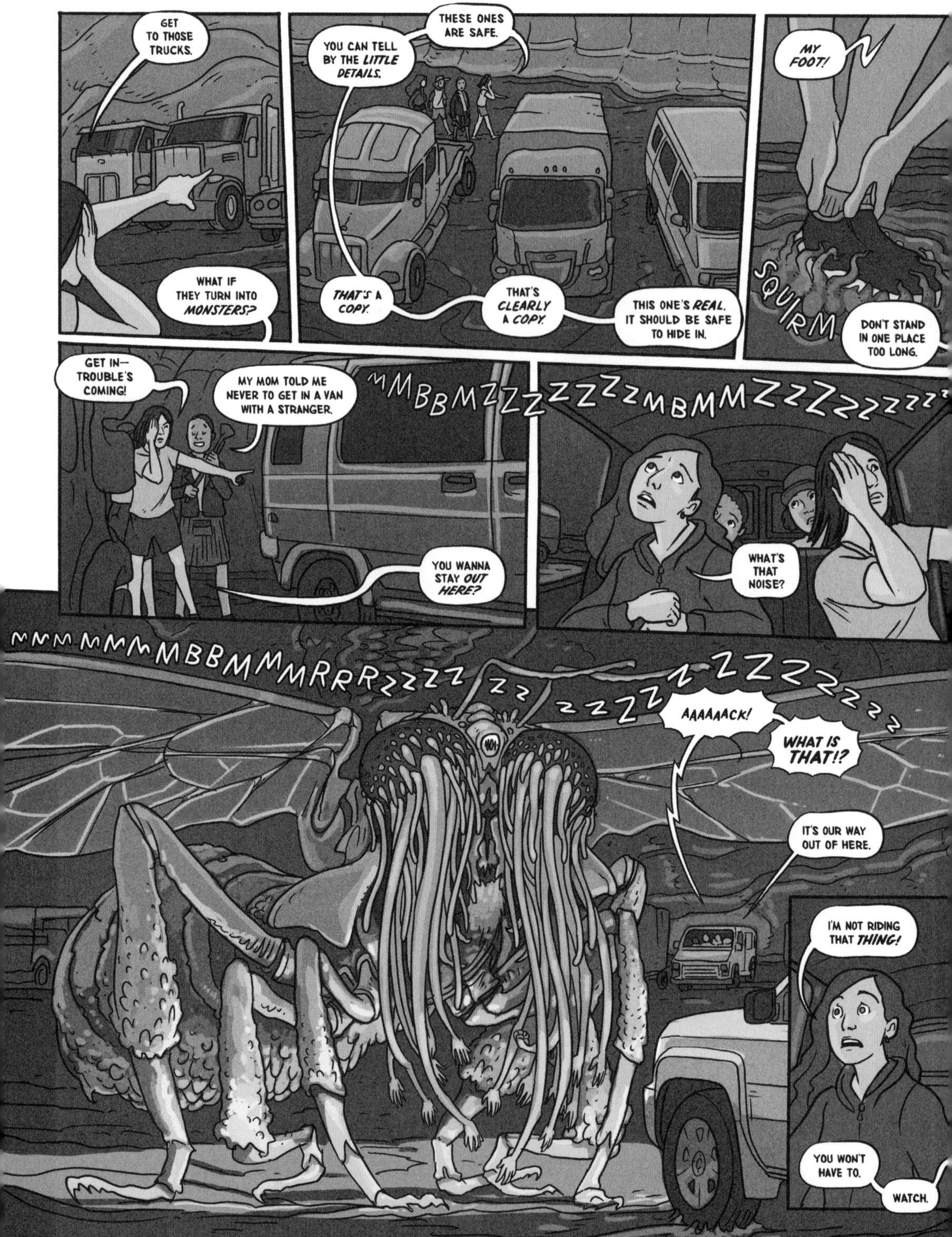
GET TO THOSE TRUCKS.
WHAT IF THEY TURN INTO *MONSTERS?*
THESE ONES ARE SAFE.
YOU CAN TELL BY THE *LITTLE DETAILS.*
THAT'S A *COPY.*
THAT'S *CLEARLY* A *COPY.*
THIS ONE'S *REAL.* IT SHOULD BE SAFE TO HIDE IN.
MY FOOT!
SQUIRM
DON'T STAND IN ONE PLACE TOO LONG.
GET IN— TROUBLE'S COMING!
MY MOM TOLD ME NEVER TO GET IN A VAN WITH A STRANGER.
YOU WANNA STAY *OUT HERE?*
MMBBMZZZZZZZZMBMMZZZZZZZZZ
WHAT'S THAT NOISE?
MMMMMMMMBBMMMRRRRZZZZ ZZ ZZZZZ ZZZZZZZZZ
AAAAAACK!
WHAT IS THAT!?
IT'S OUR WAY OUT OF HERE.
I'M NOT RIDING THAT *THING!*
YOU WON'T HAVE TO.
WATCH.

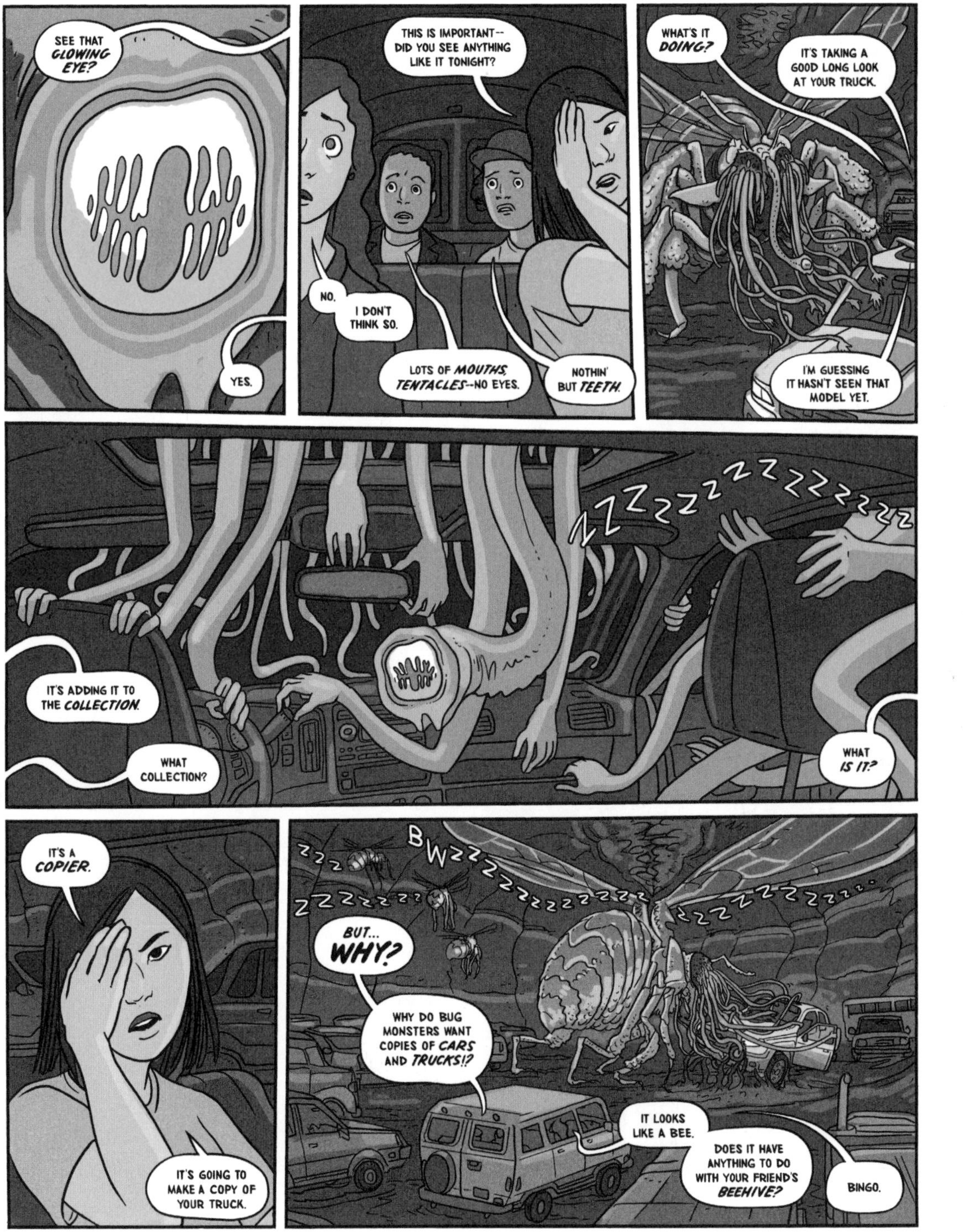
SEE THAT *GLOWING EYE?*
YES.
THIS IS IMPORTANT-- DID YOU SEE ANYTHING LIKE IT TONIGHT?
NO.
I DON'T THINK SO.
LOTS OF *MOUTHS, TENTACLES*--NO EYES.
NOTHIN' BUT *TEETH.*
WHAT'S IT *DOING?*
IT'S TAKING A GOOD LONG LOOK AT YOUR TRUCK.
I'M GUESSING IT HASN'T SEEN THAT MODEL YET.
ZZZZZZZZZZZZZZZZZZZ
IT'S ADDING IT TO THE *COLLECTION.*
WHAT COLLECTION?
WHAT *IS IT?*
IT'S A *COPIER.*
IT'S GOING TO MAKE A COPY OF YOUR TRUCK.
BWZZZZZZZZZZZZZZZZ
BUT... *WHY?*
WHY DO BUG MONSTERS WANT COPIES OF *CARS* AND *TRUCKS!?*
IT LOOKS LIKE A BEE.
DOES IT HAVE ANYTHING TO DO WITH YOUR FRIEND'S *BEEHIVE?*
BINGO.

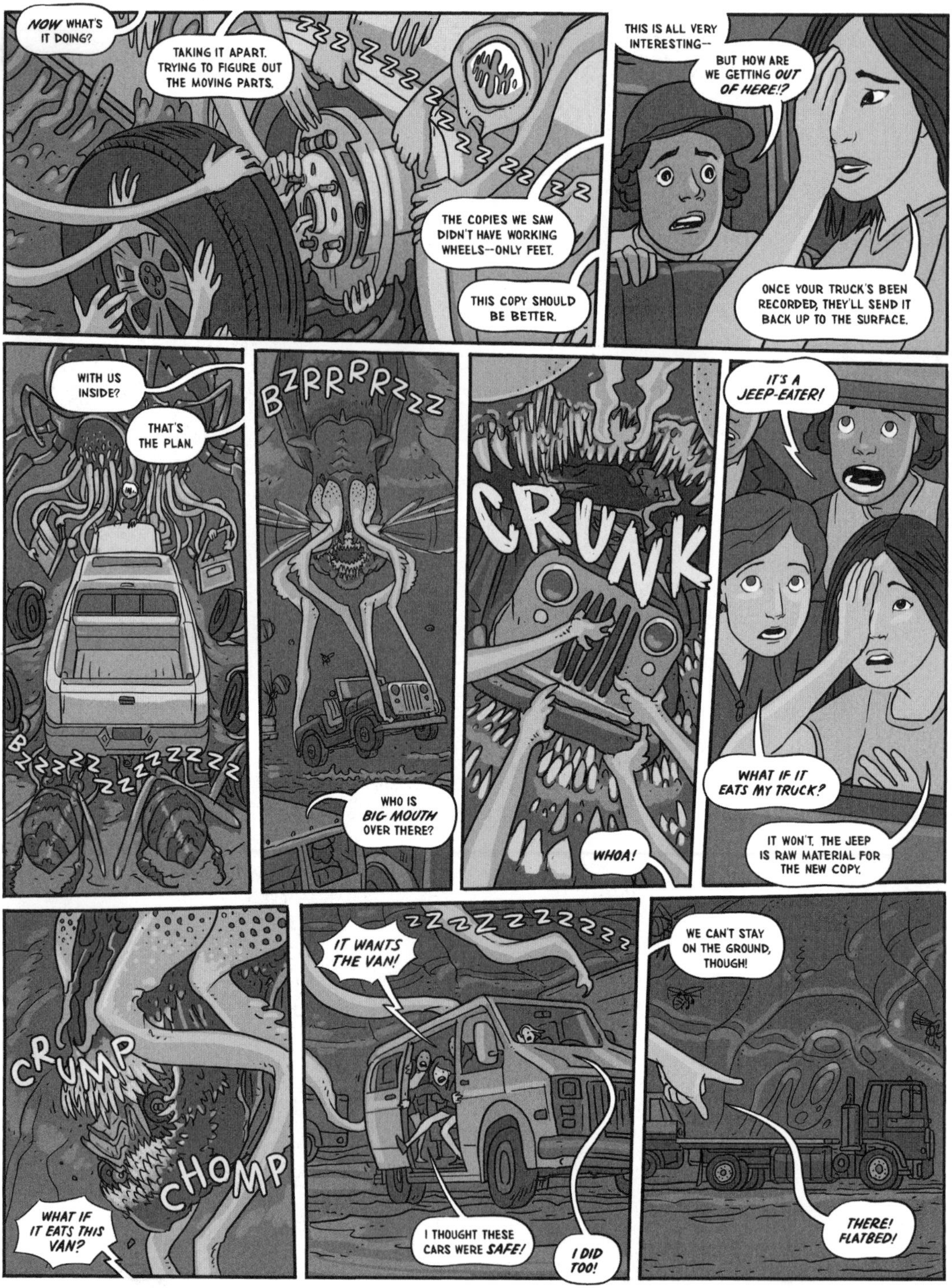
NOW WHAT'S IT DOING?
TAKING IT APART. TRYING TO FIGURE OUT THE MOVING PARTS.
ZZZZZZZZZZZZZZ
THE COPIES WE SAW DIDN'T HAVE WORKING WHEELS--ONLY FEET.
THIS COPY SHOULD BE BETTER.
THIS IS ALL VERY INTERESTING--
BUT HOW ARE WE GETTING OUT OF HERE!?
ONCE YOUR TRUCK'S BEEN RECORDED, THEY'LL SEND IT BACK UP TO THE SURFACE.
WITH US INSIDE?
THAT'S THE PLAN.
BZZZZZZZZZZZZ
BZRRRRRZZZ
WHO IS BIG MOUTH OVER THERE?
CRUNK
WHOA!
IT'S A JEEP-EATER!
WHAT IF IT EATS MY TRUCK?
IT WON'T. THE JEEP IS RAW MATERIAL FOR THE NEW COPY.
CRUMP
CHOMP
WHAT IF IT EATS THIS VAN?
ZZZZZZZZZZZZ
IT WANTS THE VAN!
I THOUGHT THESE CARS WERE SAFE!
I DID TOO!
WE CAN'T STAY ON THE GROUND, THOUGH!
THERE! FLATBED!

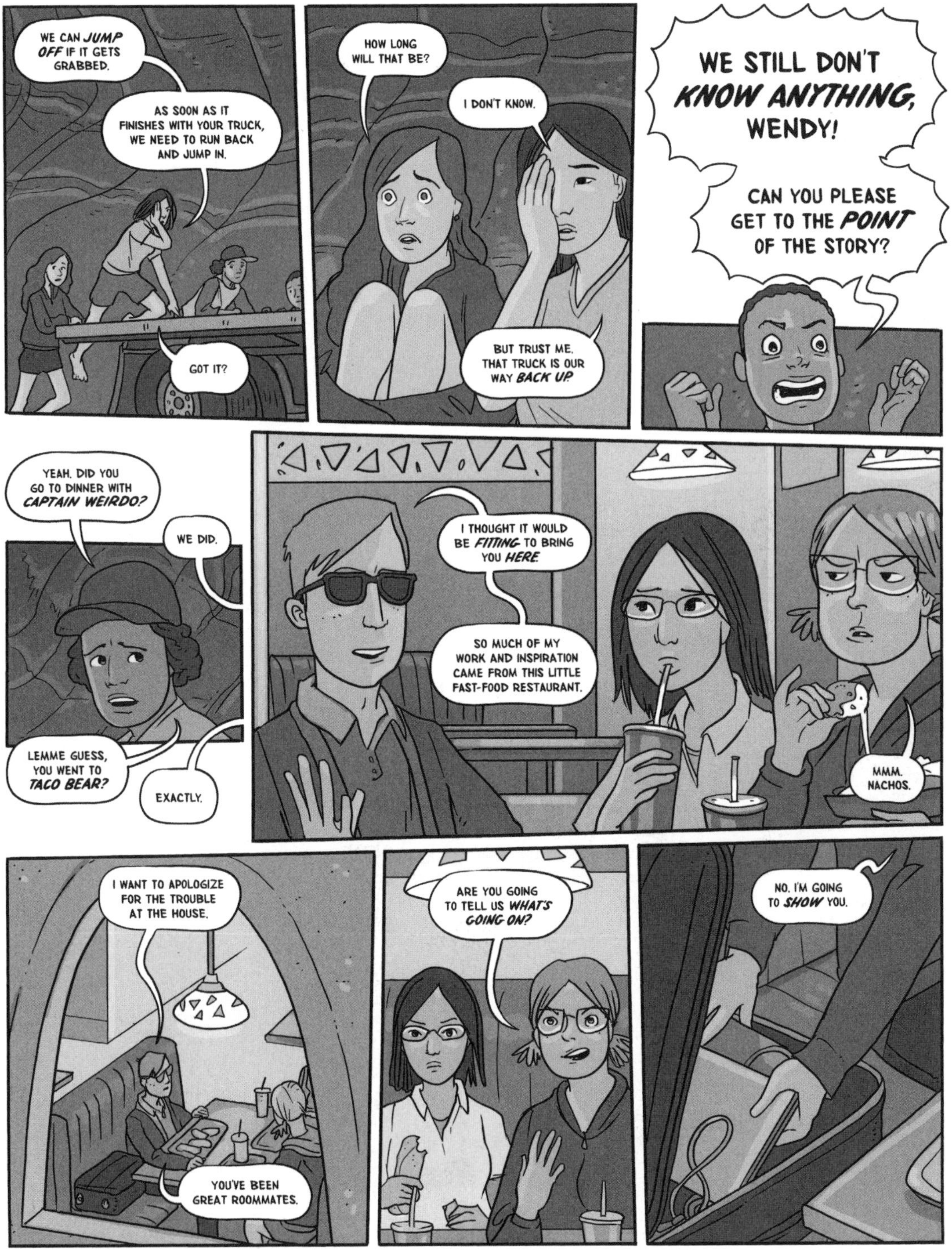

WE CAN JUMP OFF IF IT GETS GRABBED.
AS SOON AS IT FINISHES WITH YOUR TRUCK, WE NEED TO RUN BACK AND JUMP IN.
GOT IT?
HOW LONG WILL THAT BE?
I DON'T KNOW.
BUT TRUST ME. THAT TRUCK IS OUR WAY BACK UP.
WE STILL DON'T KNOW ANYTHING, WENDY!
CAN YOU PLEASE GET TO THE POINT OF THE STORY?
YEAH. DID YOU GO TO DINNER WITH CAPTAIN WEIRDO?
WE DID.
LEMME GUESS, YOU WENT TO TACO BEAR?
EXACTLY.
I THOUGHT IT WOULD BE FITTING TO BRING YOU HERE.
SO MUCH OF MY WORK AND INSPIRATION CAME FROM THIS LITTLE FAST-FOOD RESTAURANT.
MMM. NACHOS.
I WANT TO APOLOGIZE FOR THE TROUBLE AT THE HOUSE.
YOU'VE BEEN GREAT ROOMMATES.
ARE YOU GOING TO TELL US WHAT'S GOING ON?
NO. I'M GOING TO SHOW YOU.

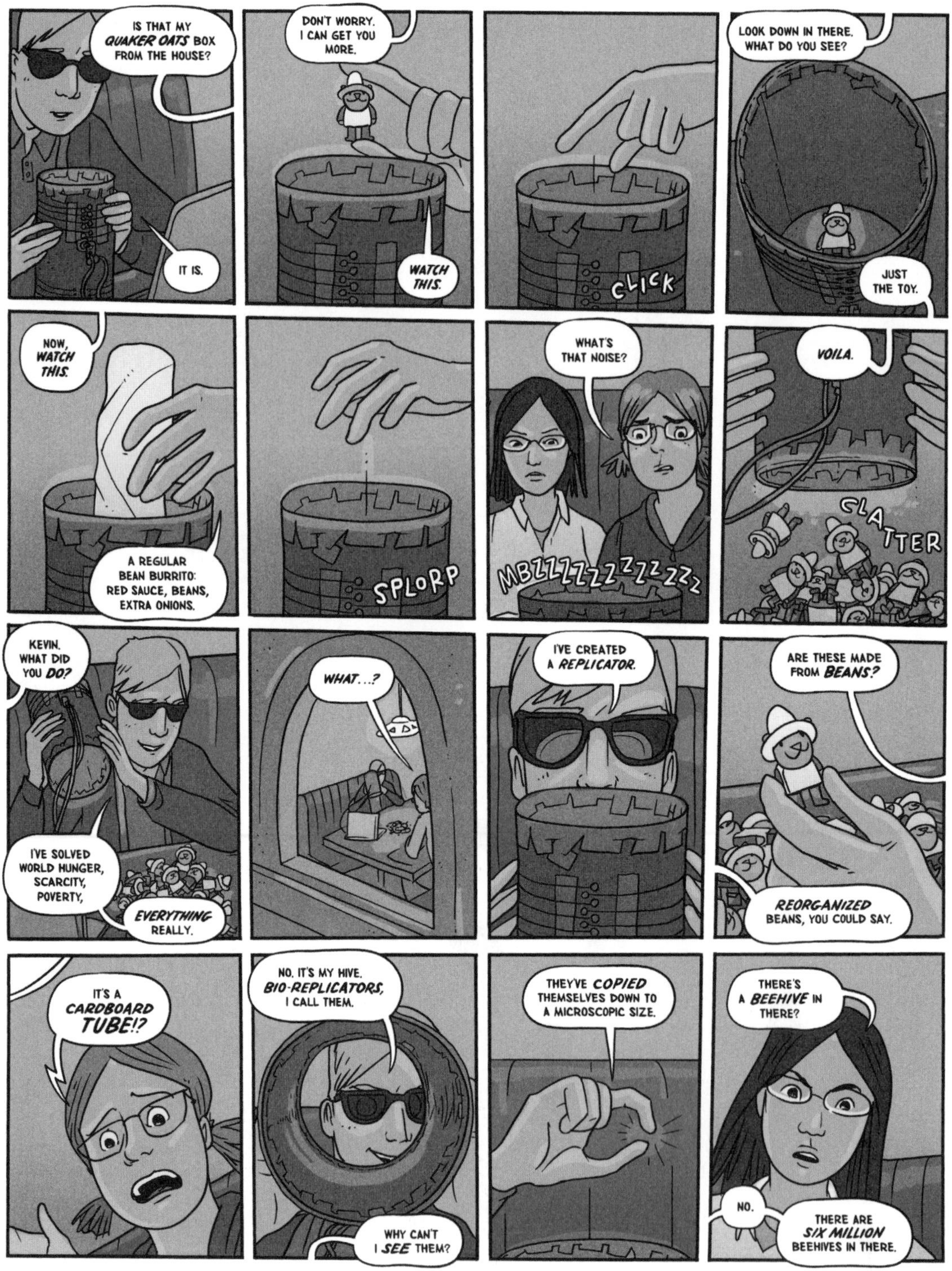
IS THAT MY QUAKER OATS BOX FROM THE HOUSE?
IT IS.
DON'T WORRY. I CAN GET YOU MORE.
WATCH THIS.
CLICK
LOOK DOWN IN THERE. WHAT DO YOU SEE?
JUST THE TOY.
NOW, WATCH THIS.
A REGULAR BEAN BURRITO: RED SAUCE, BEANS, EXTRA ONIONS.
SPLORP
WHAT'S THAT NOISE?
MBZZZZZZZZZZZZZ
VOILA.
CLATTER
KEVIN. WHAT DID YOU DO?
I'VE SOLVED WORLD HUNGER, SCARCITY, POVERTY,
EVERYTHING REALLY.
WHAT...?
I'VE CREATED A REPLICATOR.
ARE THESE MADE FROM BEANS?
REORGANIZED BEANS, YOU COULD SAY.
IT'S A CARDBOARD TUBE!?
NO, IT'S MY HIVE. BIO-REPLICATORS, I CALL THEM.
WHY CAN'T I SEE THEM?
THEY'VE COPIED THEMSELVES DOWN TO A MICROSCOPIC SIZE.
THERE'S A BEEHIVE IN THERE?
NO.
THERE ARE SIX MILLION BEEHIVES IN THERE.

AND THEY MAKE *TACO BEAR* TOYS?

THEY MAKE *ANYTHING* I WANT THEM TO.

LET ME SEE YOUR GLASSES.

IN GO THE GLASSES,

CL*INK* CL*INK* SPLORP

WITH ANOTHER BURRITO, AND SOME COINS.

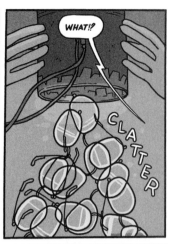

WHAT!?

C L A T T E R

I CAN'T BELIEVE IT!

DO MINE.

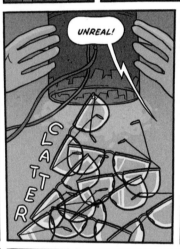

UNREAL!

C L A T T E R

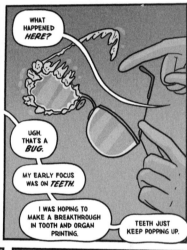

WHAT HAPPENED *HERE?*

UGH. THAT'S A *BUG.*

MY EARLY FOCUS WAS ON *TEETH.*

I WAS HOPING TO MAKE A BREAKTHROUGH IN TOOTH AND ORGAN PRINTING.

TEETH JUST KEEP POPPING UP.

ORGAN PRINTING IS *OLD NEWS*--THEY'VE BEEN DOING IT SINCE THE EARLY *2000S.*

I DIDN'T WANT TO CREATE A MECHANICAL 3D BIO-PRINTER.

I WANTED TO MAKE A *BIOLOGICAL 3D BIO-PRINTER.*

BEES BUILD THEIR HIVES WITH THEIR OWN WAX SECRETIONS.

I JUST CHANGED WHAT THEY SECRETE.

BEES MADE THESE?

HOW DO THEY *KNOW* WHAT TO *MAKE?*

I'M USING AN OLD *PRINTER* INTERFACE:

CUT, COPY, PASTE.

51

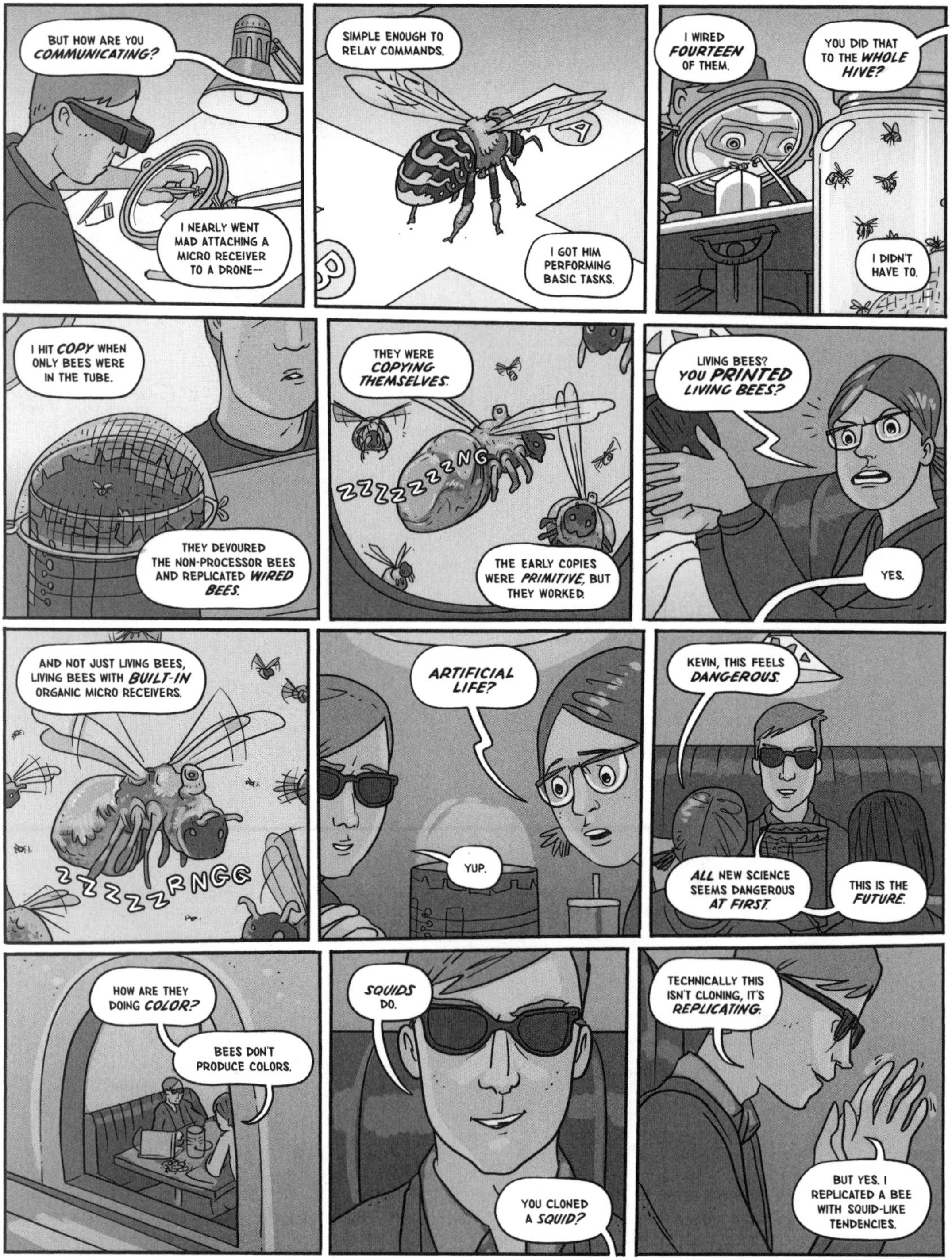

BUT HOW ARE YOU *COMMUNICATING?*
I NEARLY WENT MAD ATTACHING A MICRO RECEIVER TO A DRONE--
SIMPLE ENOUGH TO RELAY COMMANDS.
I GOT HIM PERFORMING BASIC TASKS.
I WIRED *FOURTEEN* OF THEM.
YOU DID THAT TO THE *WHOLE HIVE?*
I DIDN'T HAVE TO.
I HIT *COPY* WHEN ONLY BEES WERE IN THE TUBE.
THEY DEVOURED THE NON-PROCESSOR BEES AND REPLICATED *WIRED BEES.*
THEY WERE *COPYING THEMSELVES.*
ZZZZZZZZNG
THE EARLY COPIES WERE *PRIMITIVE,* BUT THEY WORKED.
LIVING BEES? *YOU PRINTED LIVING BEES?*
YES.
AND NOT JUST LIVING BEES, LIVING BEES WITH *BUILT-IN* ORGANIC MICRO RECEIVERS.
ZZZZZZRNGG
ARTIFICIAL LIFE?
YUP.
KEVIN, THIS FEELS *DANGEROUS.*
ALL NEW SCIENCE SEEMS DANGEROUS *AT FIRST.*
THIS IS THE *FUTURE.*
HOW ARE THEY DOING *COLOR?*
BEES DON'T PRODUCE COLORS.
SQUIDS DO.
YOU CLONED A *SQUID?*
TECHNICALLY THIS ISN'T CLONING, IT'S *REPLICATING.*
BUT YES. I REPLICATED A BEE WITH SQUID-LIKE TENDENCIES.

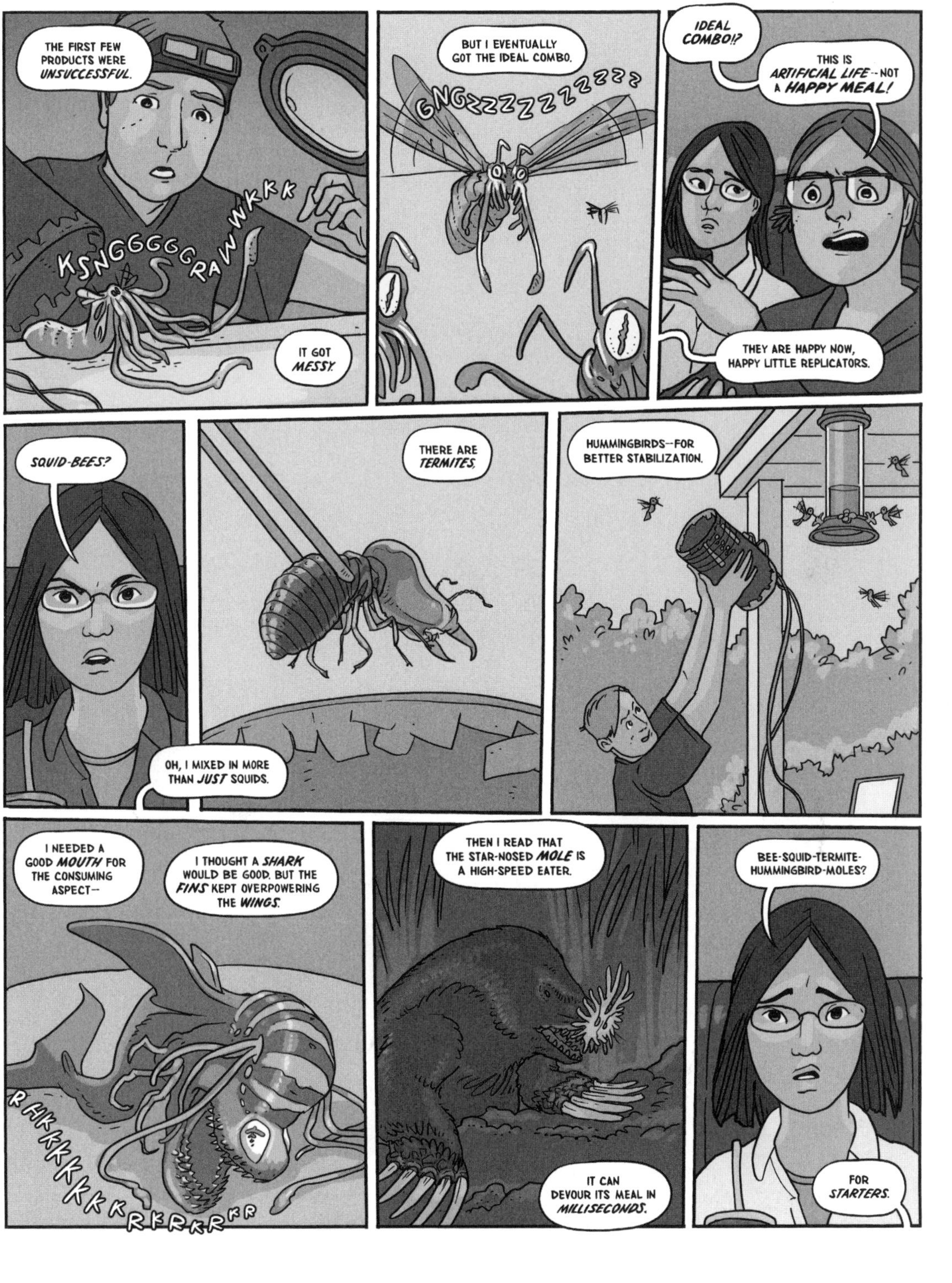
THE FIRST FEW PRODUCTS WERE *UNSUCCESSFUL.*
KSNGGGGGRAWKKK
IT GOT *MESSY.*
BUT I EVENTUALLY GOT THE IDEAL COMBO.
GNGZZZZZZZZZZ
IDEAL COMBO!?
THIS IS *ARTIFICIAL LIFE*--NOT A *HAPPY MEAL!*
THEY ARE HAPPY NOW, HAPPY LITTLE REPLICATORS.
SQUID-BEES?
OH, I MIXED IN MORE THAN *JUST* SQUIDS.
THERE ARE *TERMITES.*
HUMMINGBIRDS--FOR BETTER STABILIZATION.
I NEEDED A GOOD *MOUTH* FOR THE CONSUMING ASPECT--
I THOUGHT A *SHARK* WOULD BE GOOD, BUT THE *FINS* KEPT OVERPOWERING THE *WINGS.*
RHKKKKKKKRKRKRKR
THEN I READ THAT THE STAR-NOSED *MOLE* IS A HIGH-SPEED EATER.
IT CAN DEVOUR ITS MEAL IN *MILLISECONDS.*
BEE-SQUID-TERMITE-HUMMINGBIRD-MOLES?
FOR *STARTERS.*

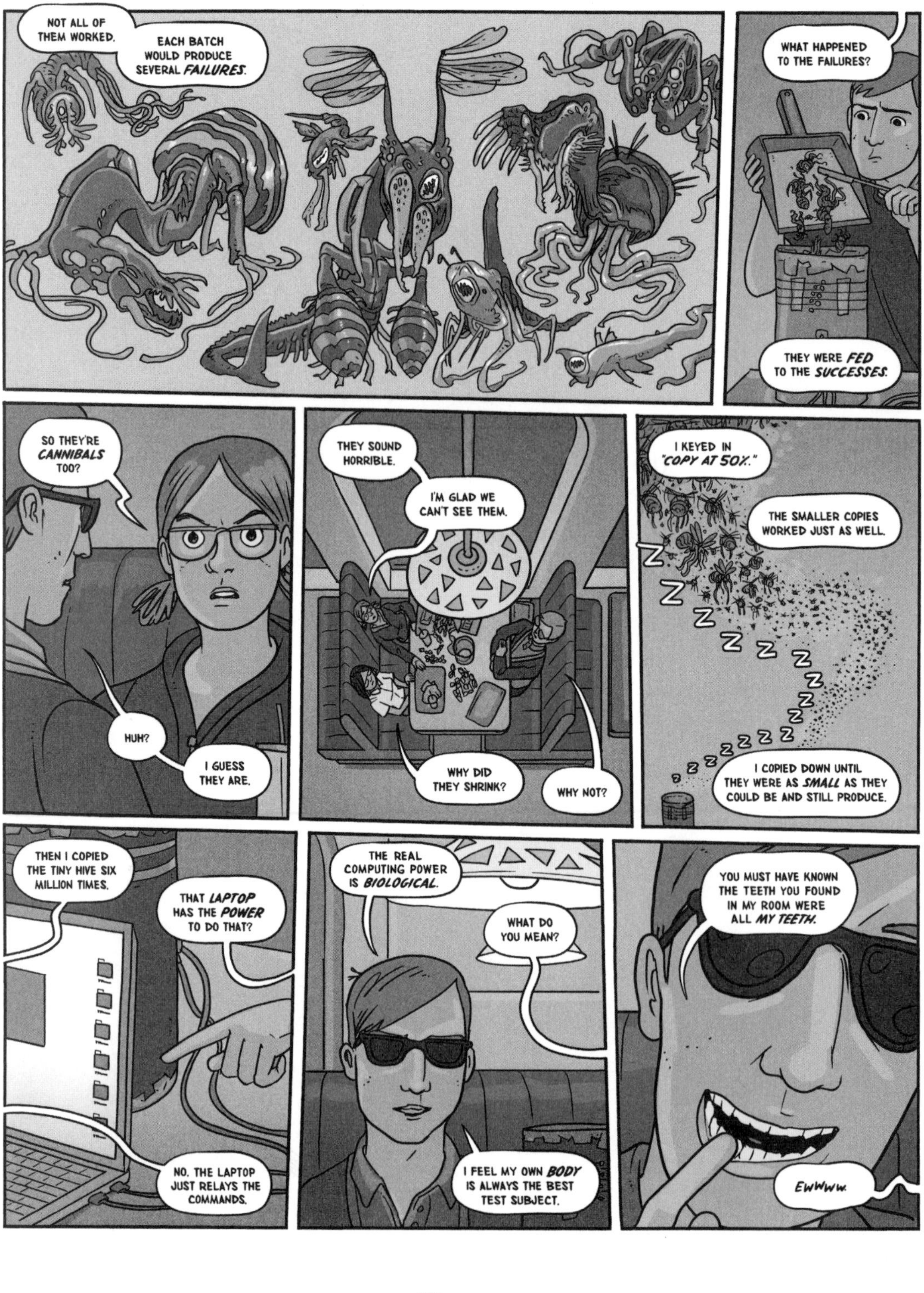
NOT ALL OF THEM WORKED.
EACH BATCH WOULD PRODUCE SEVERAL *FAILURES*.
WHAT HAPPENED TO THE FAILURES?
THEY WERE *FED* TO THE *SUCCESSES*.
SO THEY'RE *CANNIBALS* TOO?
HUH?
I GUESS THEY ARE.
THEY SOUND HORRIBLE.
I'M GLAD WE CAN'T SEE THEM.
WHY DID THEY SHRINK?
WHY NOT?
I KEYED IN *"COPY AT 50%."*
THE SMALLER COPIES WORKED JUST AS WELL.
I COPIED DOWN UNTIL THEY WERE AS *SMALL* AS THEY COULD BE AND STILL PRODUCE.
THEN I COPIED THE TINY HIVE SIX MILLION TIMES.
THAT *LAPTOP* HAS THE *POWER* TO DO THAT?
NO. THE LAPTOP JUST RELAYS THE COMMANDS.
THE REAL COMPUTING POWER IS *BIOLOGICAL*.
WHAT DO YOU MEAN?
I FEEL MY OWN *BODY* IS ALWAYS THE BEST TEST SUBJECT.
YOU MUST HAVE KNOWN THE TEETH YOU FOUND IN MY ROOM WERE ALL *MY TEETH.*
EWWWW.

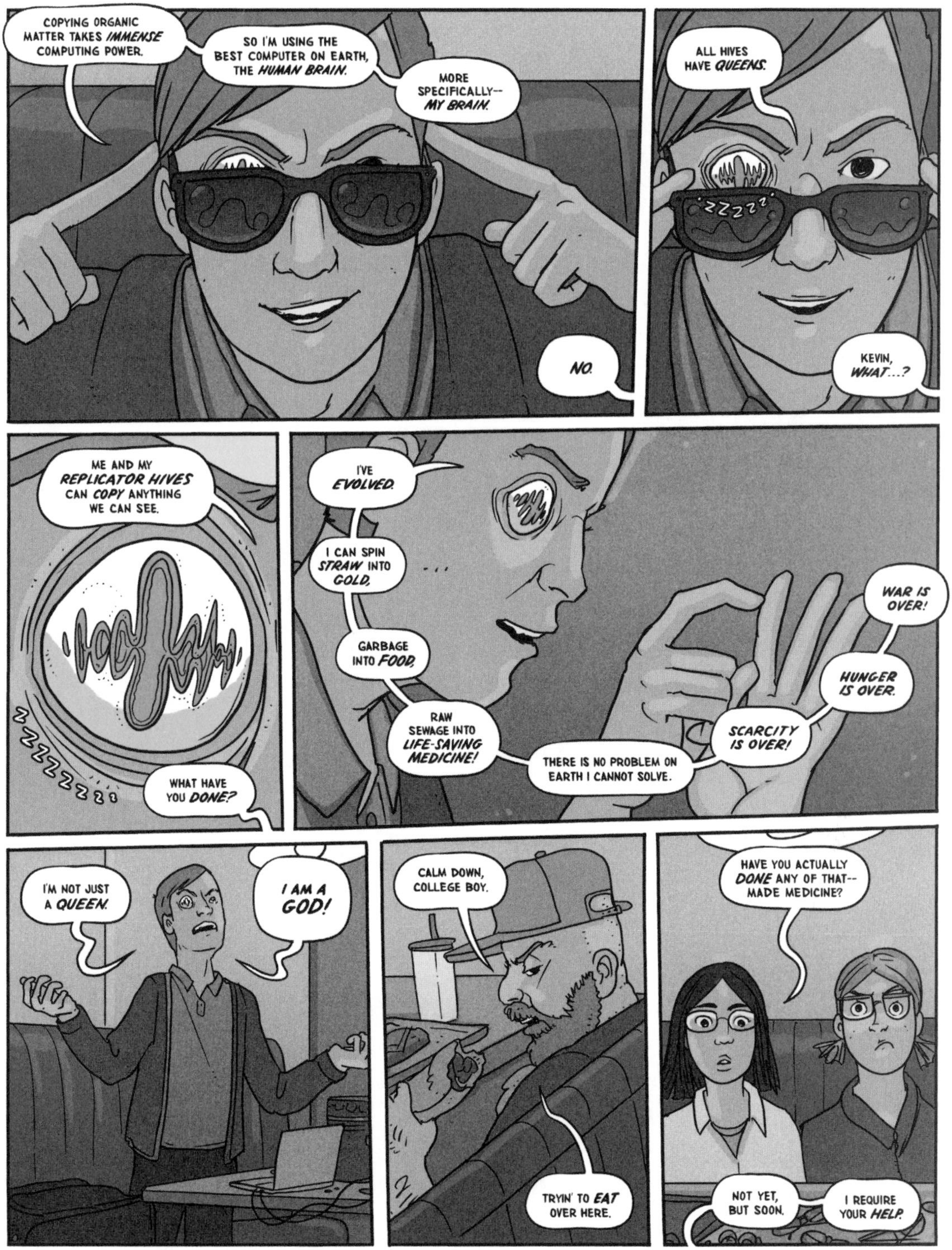

COPYING ORGANIC MATTER TAKES IMMENSE COMPUTING POWER.
SO I'M USING THE BEST COMPUTER ON EARTH, THE HUMAN BRAIN.
MORE SPECIFICALLY-- MY BRAIN.
NO.
ALL HIVES HAVE QUEENS.
ZZZZZ
KEVIN, WHAT...?
ME AND MY REPLICATOR HIVES CAN COPY ANYTHING WE CAN SEE.
ZZZZZZZZZ
WHAT HAVE YOU DONE?
I'VE EVOLVED.
I CAN SPIN STRAW INTO GOLD,
GARBAGE INTO FOOD,
RAW SEWAGE INTO LIFE-SAVING MEDICINE!
THERE IS NO PROBLEM ON EARTH I CANNOT SOLVE.
SCARCITY IS OVER!
HUNGER IS OVER.
WAR IS OVER!
I'M NOT JUST A QUEEN.
I AM A GOD!
CALM DOWN, COLLEGE BOY.
TRYIN' TO EAT OVER HERE.
HAVE YOU ACTUALLY DONE ANY OF THAT-- MADE MEDICINE?
NOT YET, BUT SOON.
I REQUIRE YOUR HELP.

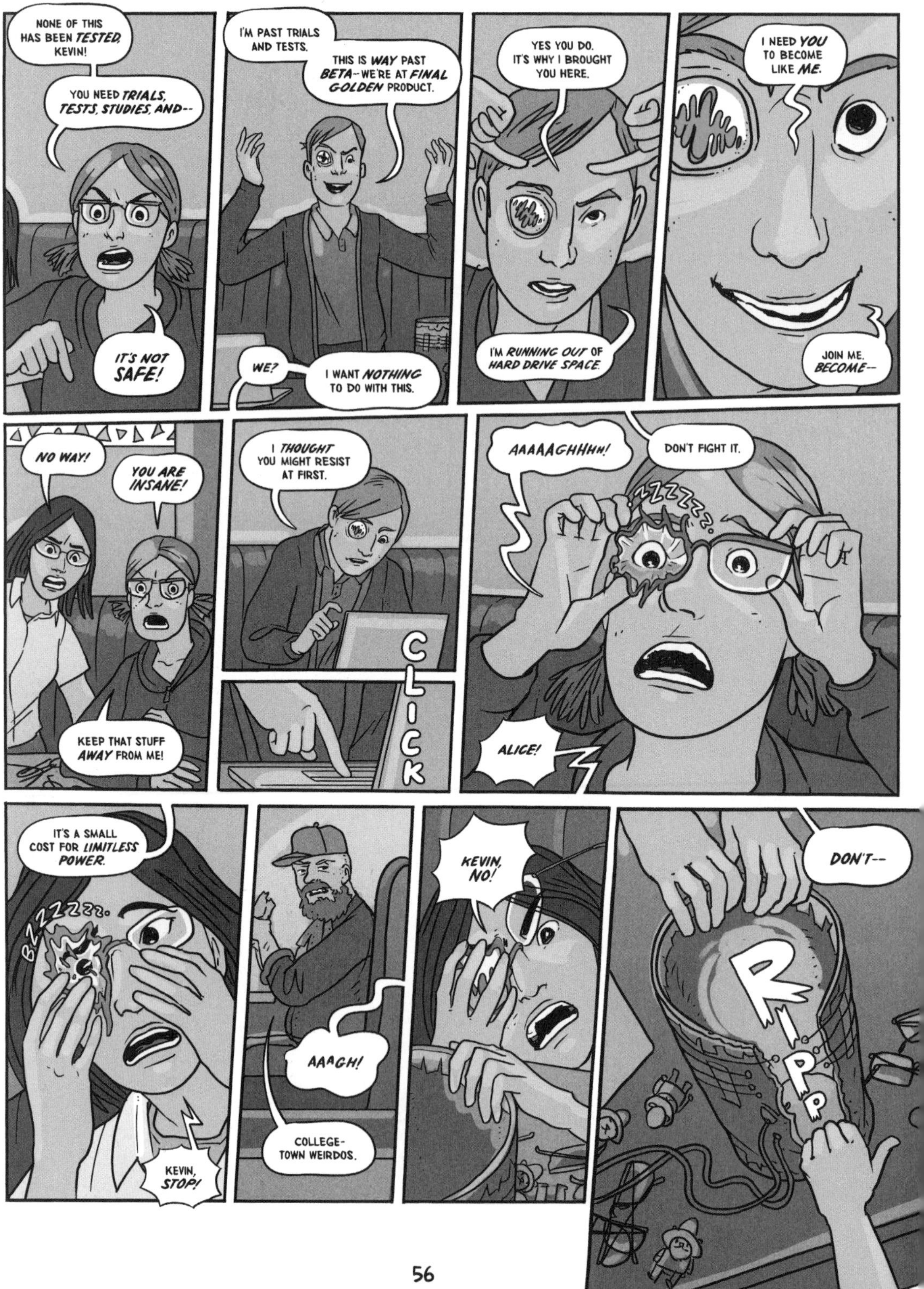
NONE OF THIS HAS BEEN TESTED, KEVIN!
YOU NEED TRIALS, TESTS, STUDIES, AND--
IT'S NOT SAFE!
I'M PAST TRIALS AND TESTS.
THIS IS WAY PAST BETA--WE'RE AT FINAL GOLDEN PRODUCT.
WE?
I WANT NOTHING TO DO WITH THIS.
YES YOU DO. IT'S WHY I BROUGHT YOU HERE.
I'M RUNNING OUT OF HARD DRIVE SPACE.
I NEED YOU TO BECOME LIKE ME.
JOIN ME. BECOME--
NO WAY!
YOU ARE INSANE!
KEEP THAT STUFF AWAY FROM ME!
I THOUGHT YOU MIGHT RESIST AT FIRST.
CLICK
AAAAAGHHHH!
DON'T FIGHT IT.
ZZZZZZ
ALICE!
IT'S A SMALL COST FOR LIMITLESS POWER.
BZZZZZzz
KEVIN, STOP!
AAAGH!
COLLEGE-TOWN WEIRDOS.
KEVIN, NO!
DON'T--
RIPP

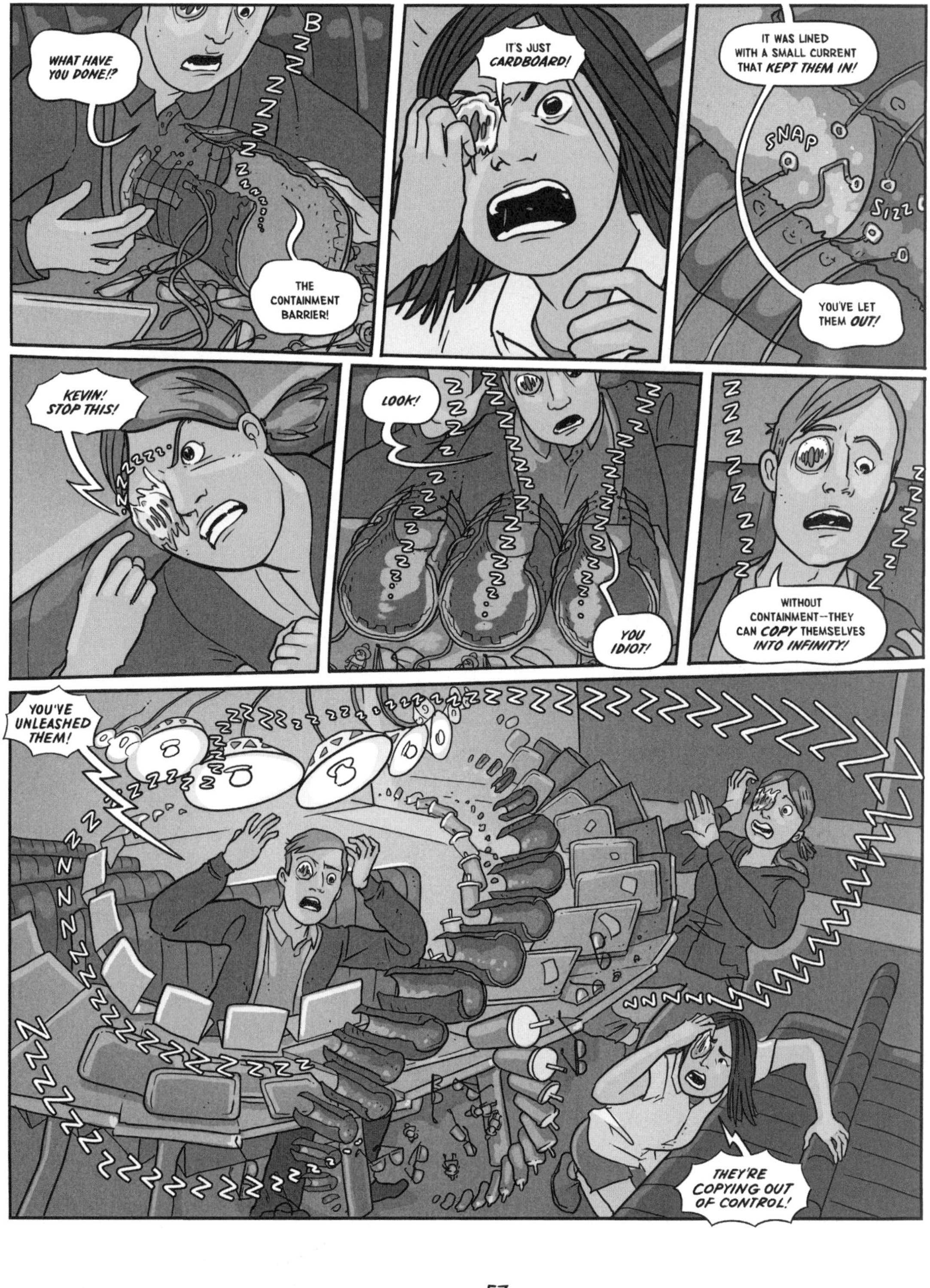
WHAT HAVE YOU DONE!?
BZZZZZZZZZZZ
THE CONTAINMENT BARRIER!
IT'S JUST CARDBOARD!
IT WAS LINED WITH A SMALL CURRENT THAT KEPT THEM IN!
SNAP
SIZZ
YOU'VE LET THEM OUT!
KEVIN! STOP THIS!
LOOK!
YOU IDIOT!
WITHOUT CONTAINMENT--THEY CAN COPY THEMSELVES INTO INFINITY!
YOU'VE UNLEASHED THEM!
THEY'RE COPYING OUT OF CONTROL!

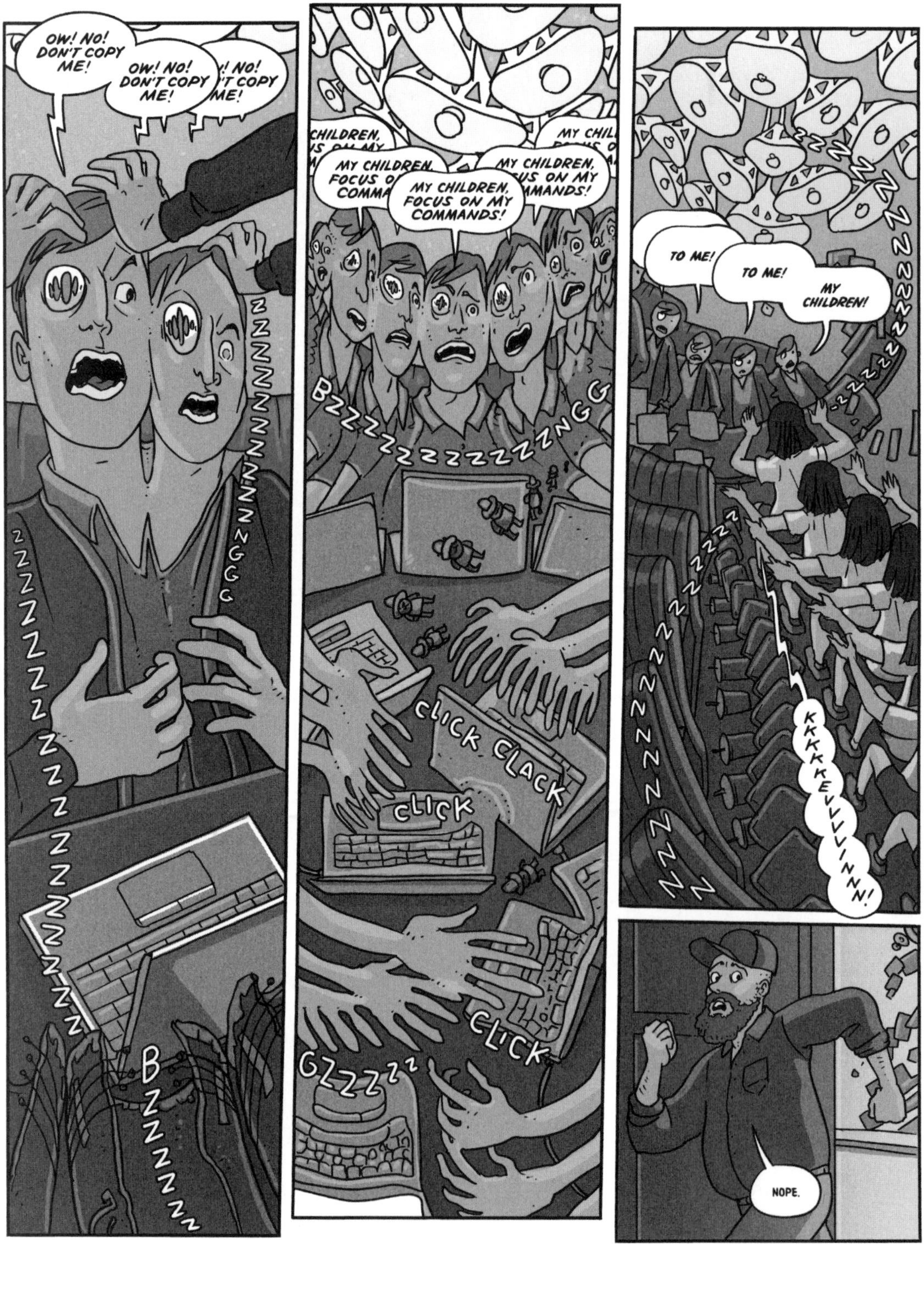

OW! NO! DON'T COPY ME!
OW! NO! DON'T COPY ME!
ZZZZZZZZZZZZNGGG
ZZZZZZZZZZZZZZZZZZZZZZ
BZZZZZZ
MY CHILDREN, FOCUS ON MY COMMANDS!
MY CHILDREN, FOCUS ON MY COMMANDS!
MY CHILDREN, FOCUS ON MY COMMANDS!
BZZZZZZZZZZZZZZZNGG
CLICK CLACK
CLICK
CLICK
GZZZZZZ
TO ME!
TO ME!
MY CHILDREN!
KKKKEVVVVINNN!
NOPE.

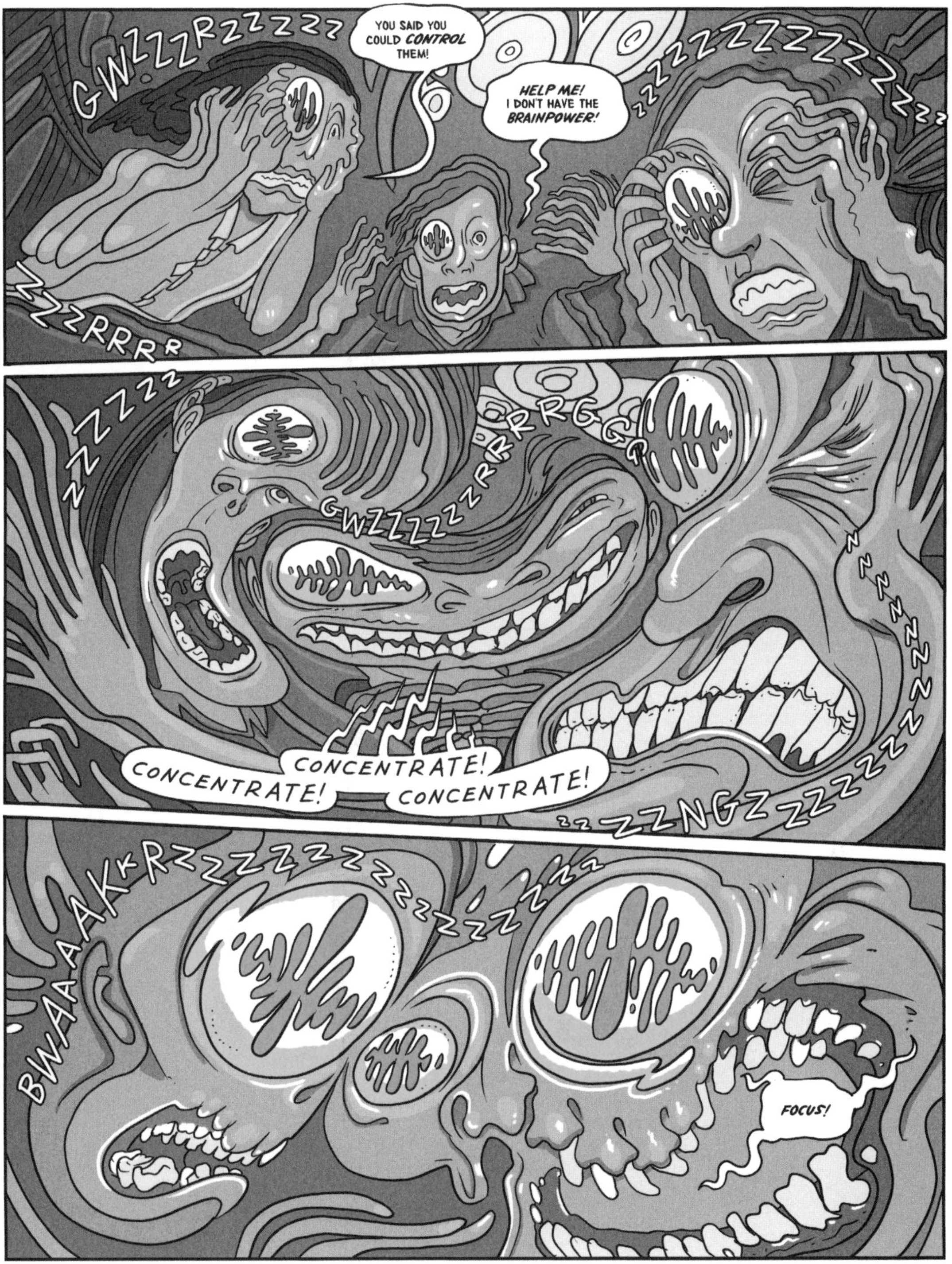
GWZZZRZZZZZZ
YOU SAID YOU COULD CONTROL THEM!
HELP ME! I DON'T HAVE THE BRAINPOWER!
ZZZZZZZZZZZZZZZZZZ
ZZZRRRRR
ZZZZZZZZ
GWZZZZZZZRRRRGGG
ZZZZZZZZZZZ
CONCENTRATE!
CONCENTRATE!
CONCENTRATE!
ZZZZNGZZZZZZZ
BWAAAAKKRZZZZZZZZZZZZZZZZZZ
FOCUS!

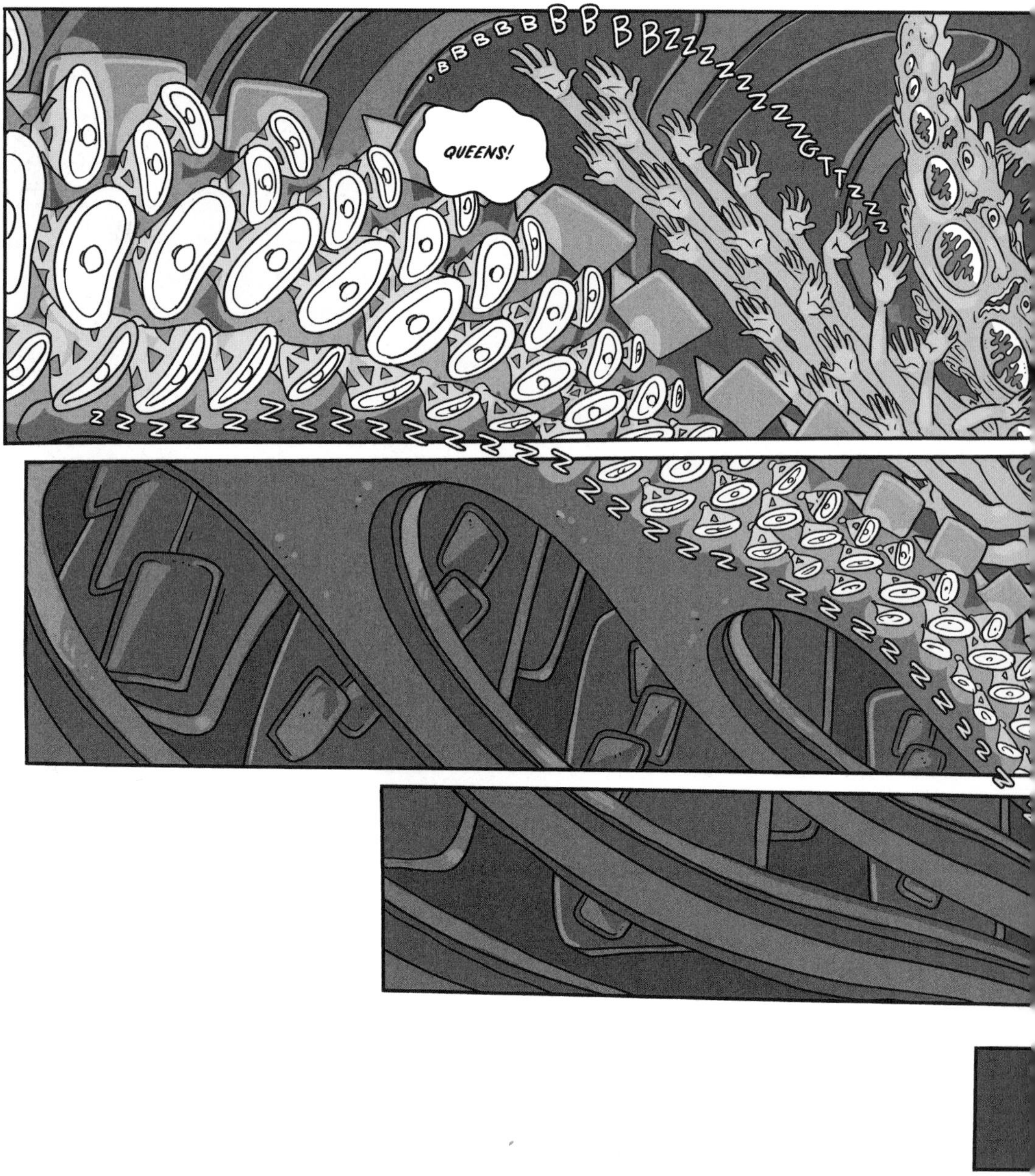
BBBBBBBBBZZZZZZZZNGTTZZZ
QUEENS!

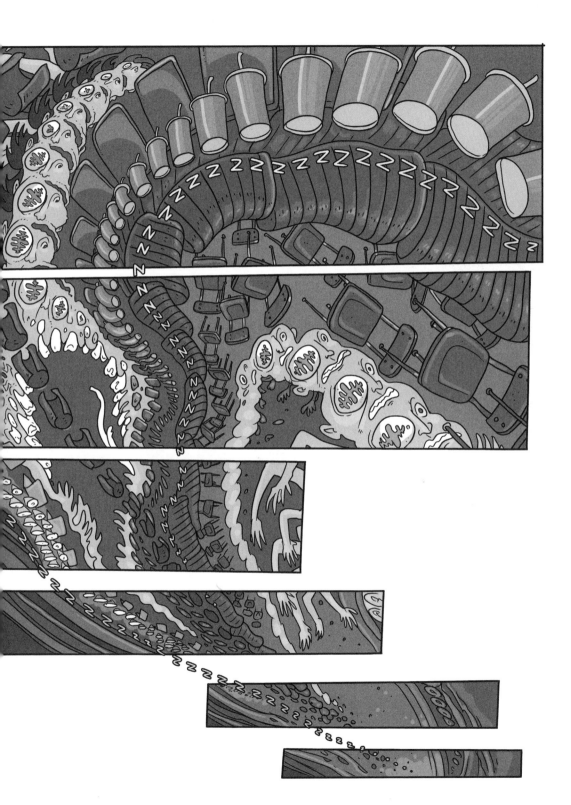

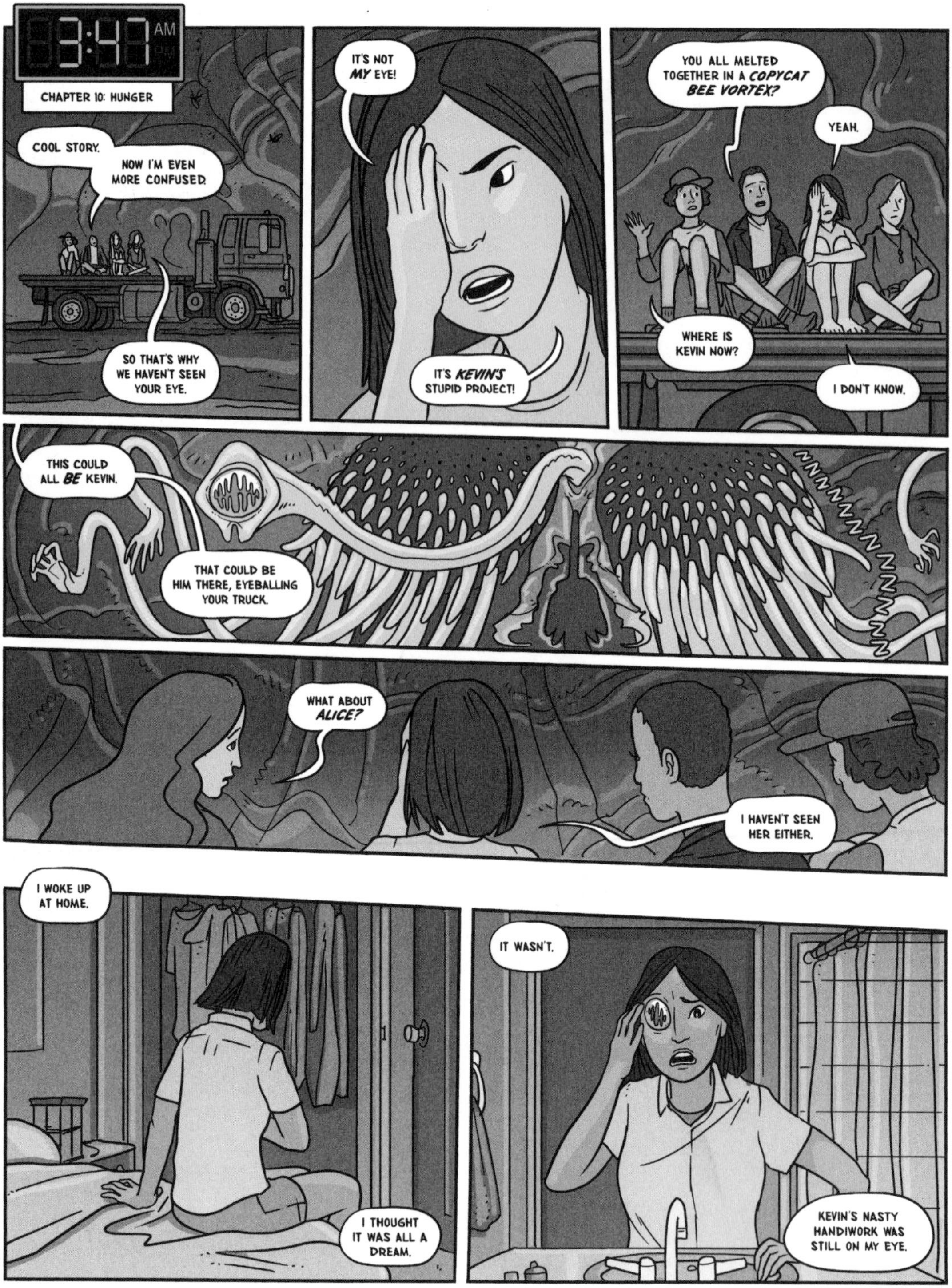
3:47 AM PM
CHAPTER 10: HUNGER
COOL STORY.
NOW I'M EVEN MORE CONFUSED.
SO THAT'S WHY WE HAVEN'T SEEN YOUR EYE.
IT'S NOT MY EYE!
IT'S KEVIN'S STUPID PROJECT!
YOU ALL MELTED TOGETHER IN A COPYCAT BEE VORTEX?
YEAH.
WHERE IS KEVIN NOW?
I DON'T KNOW.
THIS COULD ALL BE KEVIN.
THAT COULD BE HIM THERE, EYEBALLING YOUR TRUCK.
ZZZZZZZZZZZZZZZZ
WHAT ABOUT ALICE?
I HAVEN'T SEEN HER EITHER.
I WOKE UP AT HOME.
I THOUGHT IT WAS ALL A DREAM.
IT WASN'T.
KEVIN'S NASTY HANDIWORK WAS STILL ON MY EYE.

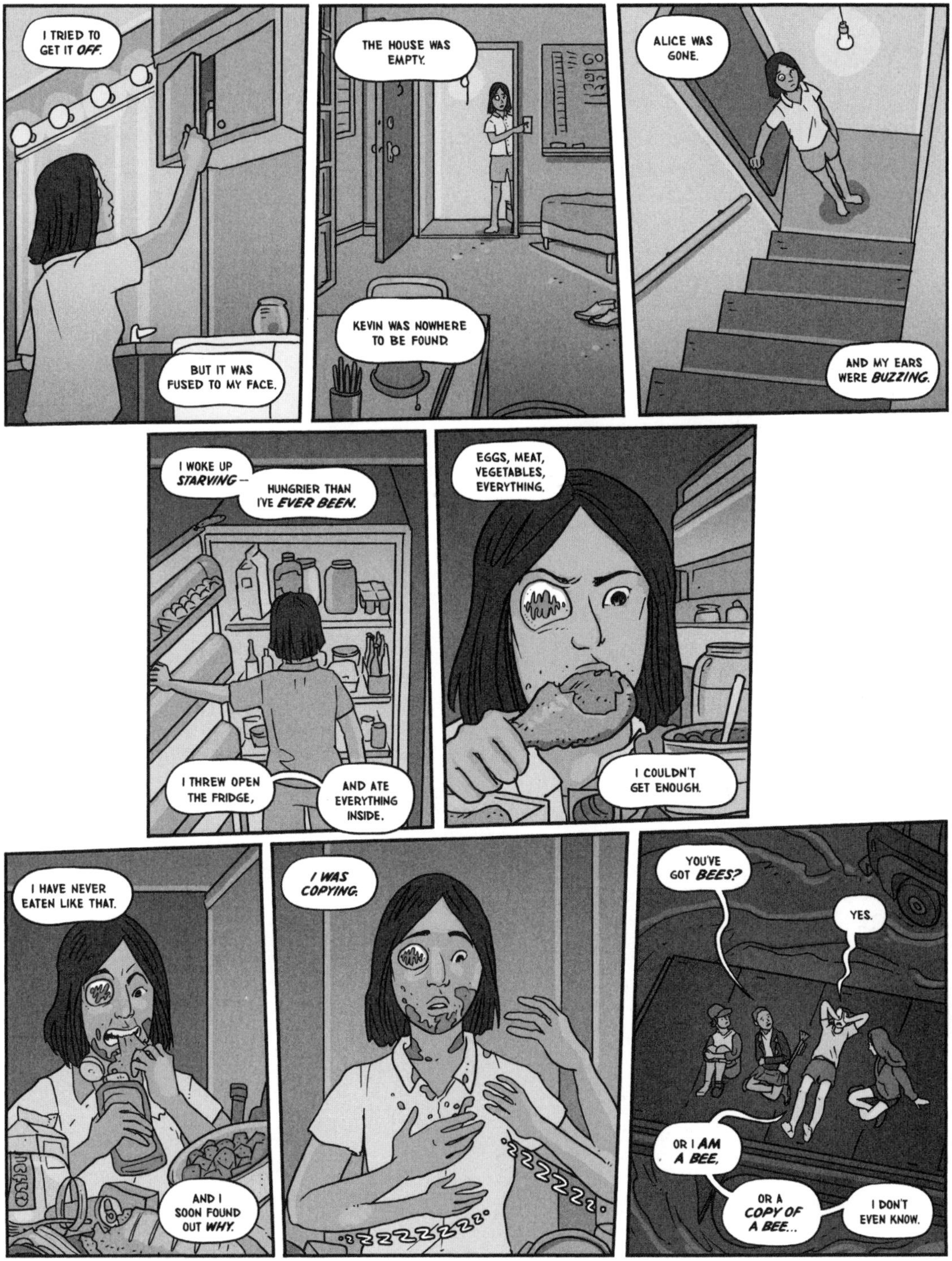

I TRIED TO GET IT *OFF.*
BUT IT WAS FUSED TO MY FACE.
THE HOUSE WAS EMPTY.
KEVIN WAS NOWHERE TO BE FOUND.
ALICE WAS GONE.
AND MY EARS WERE *BUZZING.*
I WOKE UP *STARVING*--
HUNGRIER THAN I'VE *EVER BEEN.*
I THREW OPEN THE FRIDGE,
AND ATE EVERYTHING INSIDE.
EGGS, MEAT, VEGETABLES, EVERYTHING.
I COULDN'T GET ENOUGH.
I HAVE NEVER EATEN LIKE THAT.
AND I SOON FOUND OUT *WHY.*
I WAS COPYING.
ZZZZZZ
ZZZZZZZZZ
YOU'VE GOT *BEES?*
YES.
OR I *AM A BEE,*
OR A *COPY OF A BEE...*
I DON'T EVEN KNOW.

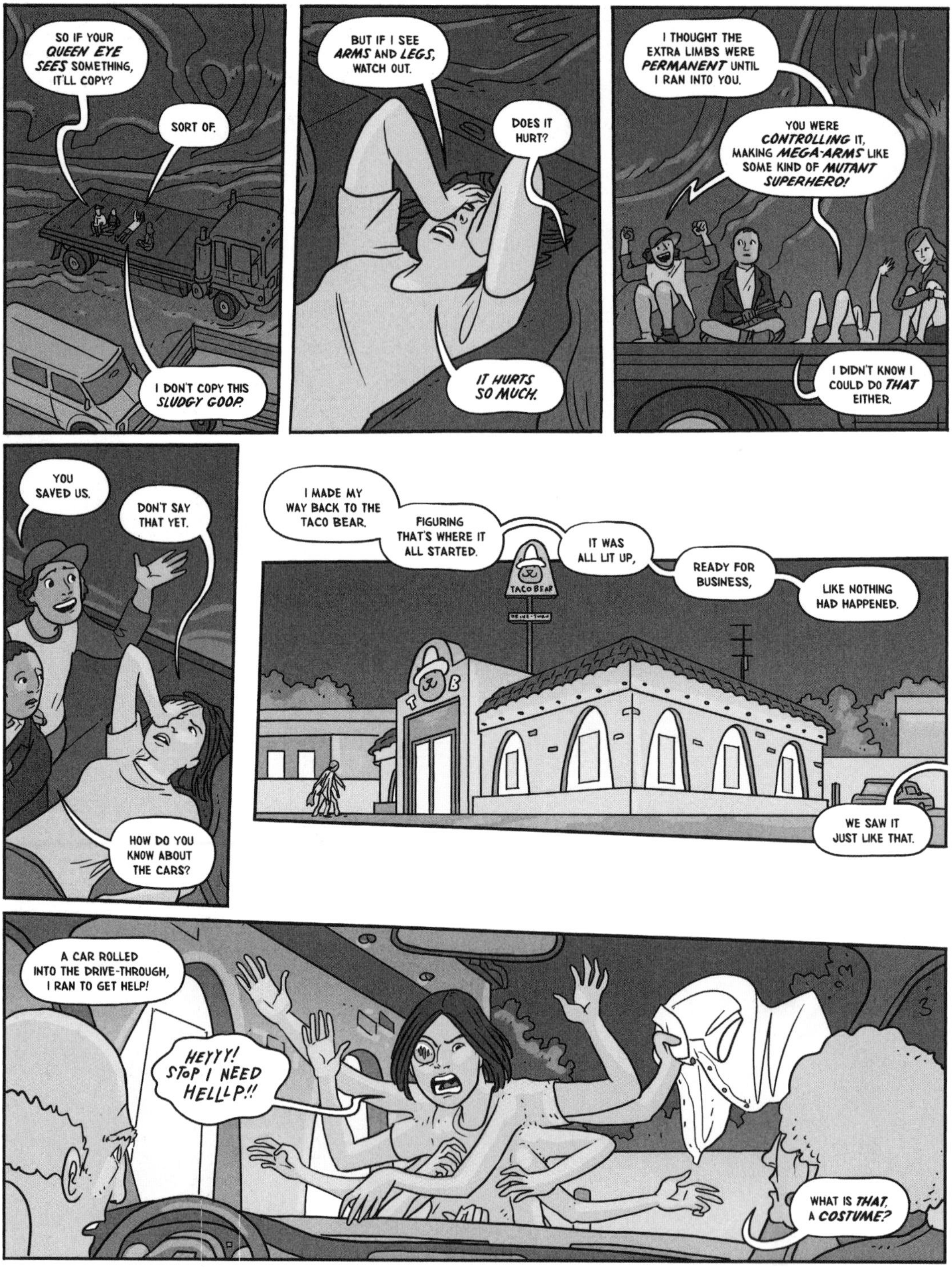
SO IF YOUR QUEEN EYE SEES SOMETHING, IT'LL COPY?
SORT OF.
I DON'T COPY THIS SLUDGY GOOP.
BUT IF I SEE ARMS AND LEGS, WATCH OUT.
DOES IT HURT?
IT HURTS SO MUCH.
I THOUGHT THE EXTRA LIMBS WERE PERMANENT UNTIL I RAN INTO YOU.
YOU WERE CONTROLLING IT, MAKING MEGA-ARMS LIKE SOME KIND OF MUTANT SUPERHERO!
I DIDN'T KNOW I COULD DO THAT EITHER.
YOU SAVED US.
DON'T SAY THAT YET.
HOW DO YOU KNOW ABOUT THE CARS?
I MADE MY WAY BACK TO THE TACO BEAR,
FIGURING THAT'S WHERE IT ALL STARTED.
IT WAS ALL LIT UP,
READY FOR BUSINESS,
LIKE NOTHING HAD HAPPENED.
TACO BEAR
WE SAW IT JUST LIKE THAT.
A CAR ROLLED INTO THE DRIVE-THROUGH, I RAN TO GET HELP!
HEYYY! STOP I NEED HELLLP!!
WHAT IS THAT, A COSTUME?

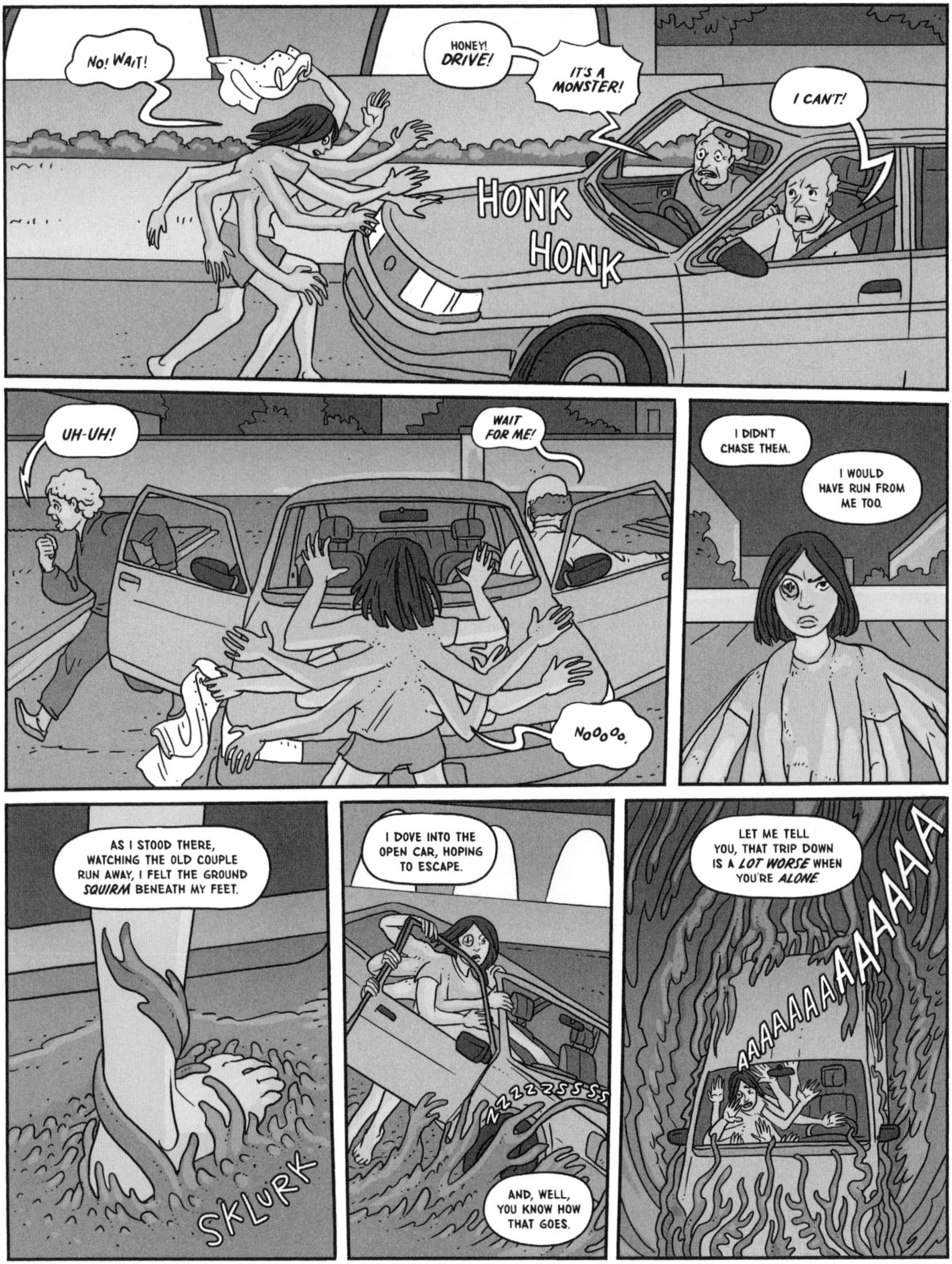
No! Wait!
Honey! DRIVE!
It's a MONSTER!
I CAN'T!
HONK
HONK
UH-UH!
WAIT FOR ME!
Noooo.
I DIDN'T CHASE THEM.
I WOULD HAVE RUN FROM ME TOO.
AS I STOOD THERE, WATCHING THE OLD COUPLE RUN AWAY, I FELT THE GROUND SQUIRM BENEATH MY FEET.
SKLURK
I DOVE INTO THE OPEN CAR, HOPING TO ESCAPE.
ZZZZZSSSSS
AND, WELL, YOU KNOW HOW THAT GOES.
LET ME TELL YOU, THAT TRIP DOWN IS A LOT WORSE WHEN YOU'RE ALONE.
AAAAAAAAAAAAAAA

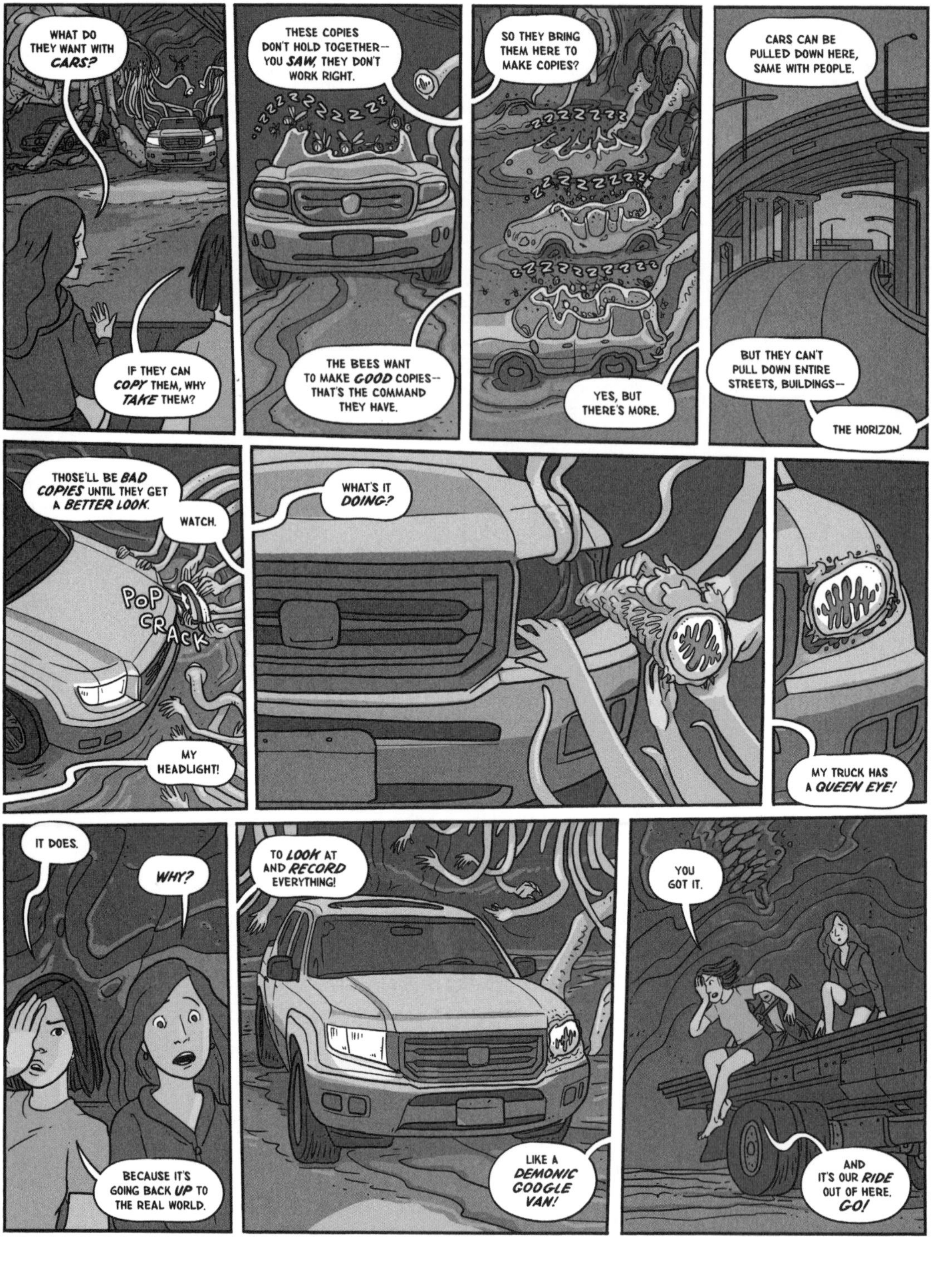
WHAT DO THEY WANT WITH CARS?
IF THEY CAN COPY THEM, WHY TAKE THEM?
THESE COPIES DON'T HOLD TOGETHER-- YOU SAW, THEY DON'T WORK RIGHT.
THE BEES WANT TO MAKE GOOD COPIES-- THAT'S THE COMMAND THEY HAVE.
SO THEY BRING THEM HERE TO MAKE COPIES?
YES, BUT THERE'S MORE.
CARS CAN BE PULLED DOWN HERE, SAME WITH PEOPLE.
BUT THEY CAN'T PULL DOWN ENTIRE STREETS, BUILDINGS--
THE HORIZON.
THOSE'LL BE BAD COPIES UNTIL THEY GET A BETTER LOOK.
WATCH.
POP
CRACK
MY HEADLIGHT!
WHAT'S IT DOING?
MY TRUCK HAS A QUEEN EYE!
IT DOES.
WHY?
BECAUSE IT'S GOING BACK UP TO THE REAL WORLD.
TO LOOK AT AND RECORD EVERYTHING!
LIKE A DEMONIC GOOGLE VAN!
YOU GOT IT.
AND IT'S OUR RIDE OUT OF HERE. GO!

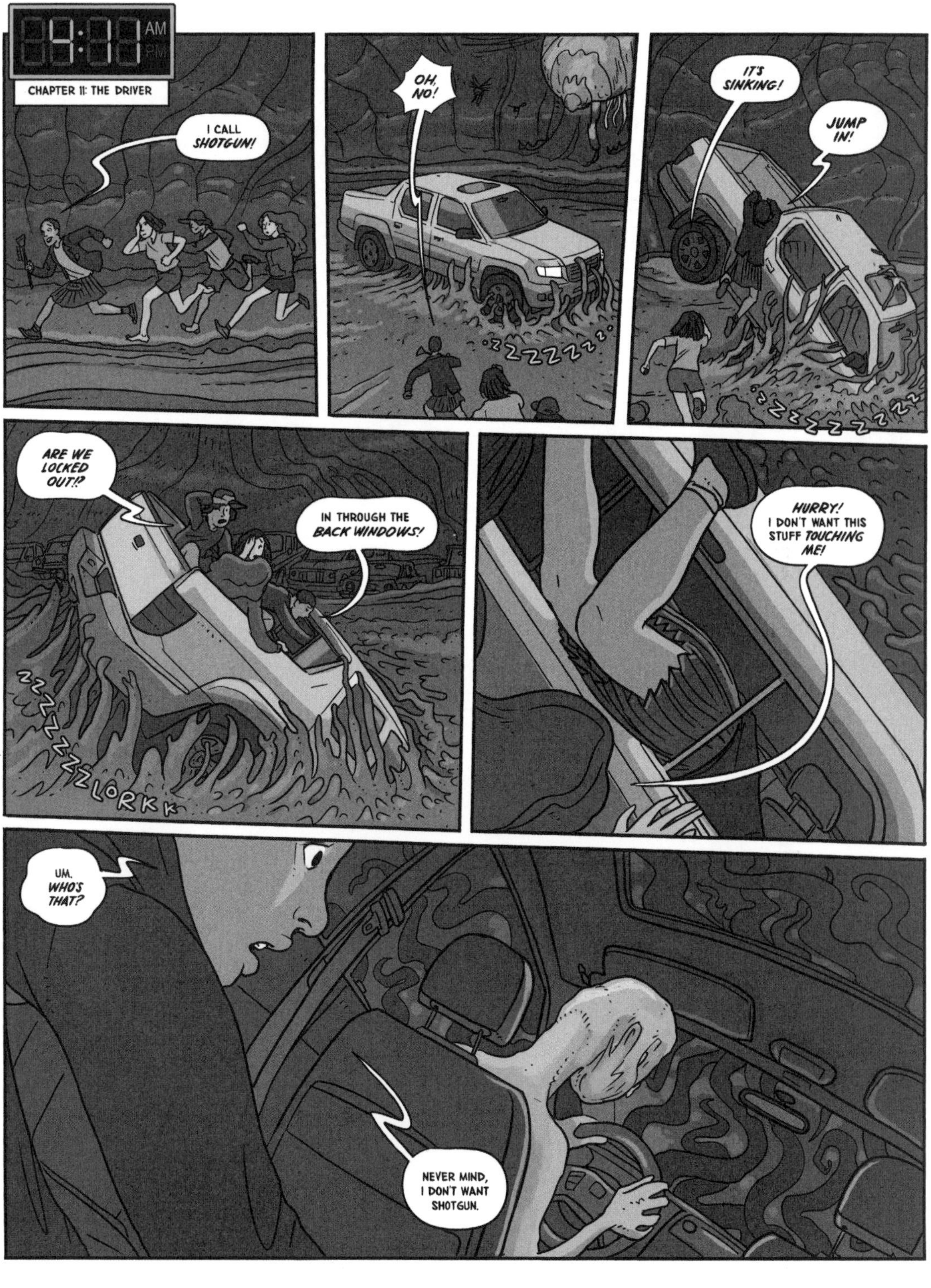
4:11 AM PM
CHAPTER 11: THE DRIVER
I CALL SHOTGUN!
OH, NO!
ZZZZZZZZ
IT'S SINKING!
JUMP IN!
ZZZZZZZZZZZ
ARE WE LOCKED OUT!?
IN THROUGH THE BACK WINDOWS!
ZZZZZZZZLORKK
HURRY! I DON'T WANT THIS STUFF TOUCHING ME!
UM. WHO'S THAT?
NEVER MIND, I DON'T WANT SHOTGUN.

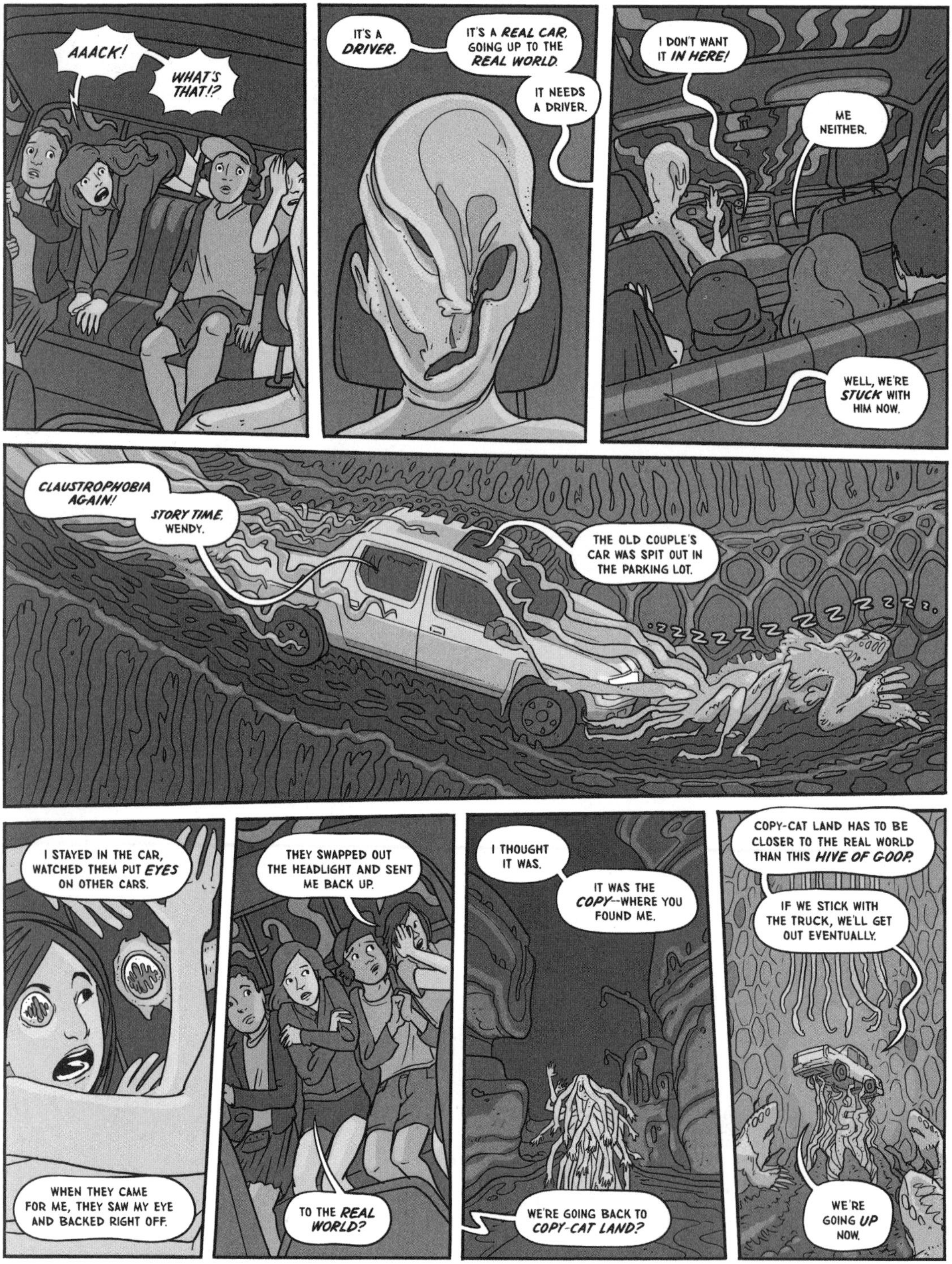
AAACK!
WHAT'S THAT!?
IT'S A DRIVER.
IT'S A REAL CAR, GOING UP TO THE REAL WORLD.
IT NEEDS A DRIVER.
I DON'T WANT IT IN HERE!
ME NEITHER.
WELL, WE'RE STUCK WITH HIM NOW.
CLAUSTROPHOBIA AGAIN!
STORY TIME, WENDY.
THE OLD COUPLE'S CAR WAS SPIT OUT IN THE PARKING LOT.
ZZZZZZZZZZZZZ...
I STAYED IN THE CAR, WATCHED THEM PUT EYES ON OTHER CARS.
WHEN THEY CAME FOR ME, THEY SAW MY EYE AND BACKED RIGHT OFF.
THEY SWAPPED OUT THE HEADLIGHT AND SENT ME BACK UP.
TO THE REAL WORLD?
I THOUGHT IT WAS.
IT WAS THE COPY--WHERE YOU FOUND ME.
WE'RE GOING BACK TO COPY-CAT LAND?
COPY-CAT LAND HAS TO BE CLOSER TO THE REAL WORLD THAN THIS HIVE OF GOOP.
IF WE STICK WITH THE TRUCK, WE'LL GET OUT EVENTUALLY.
WE'RE GOING UP NOW.

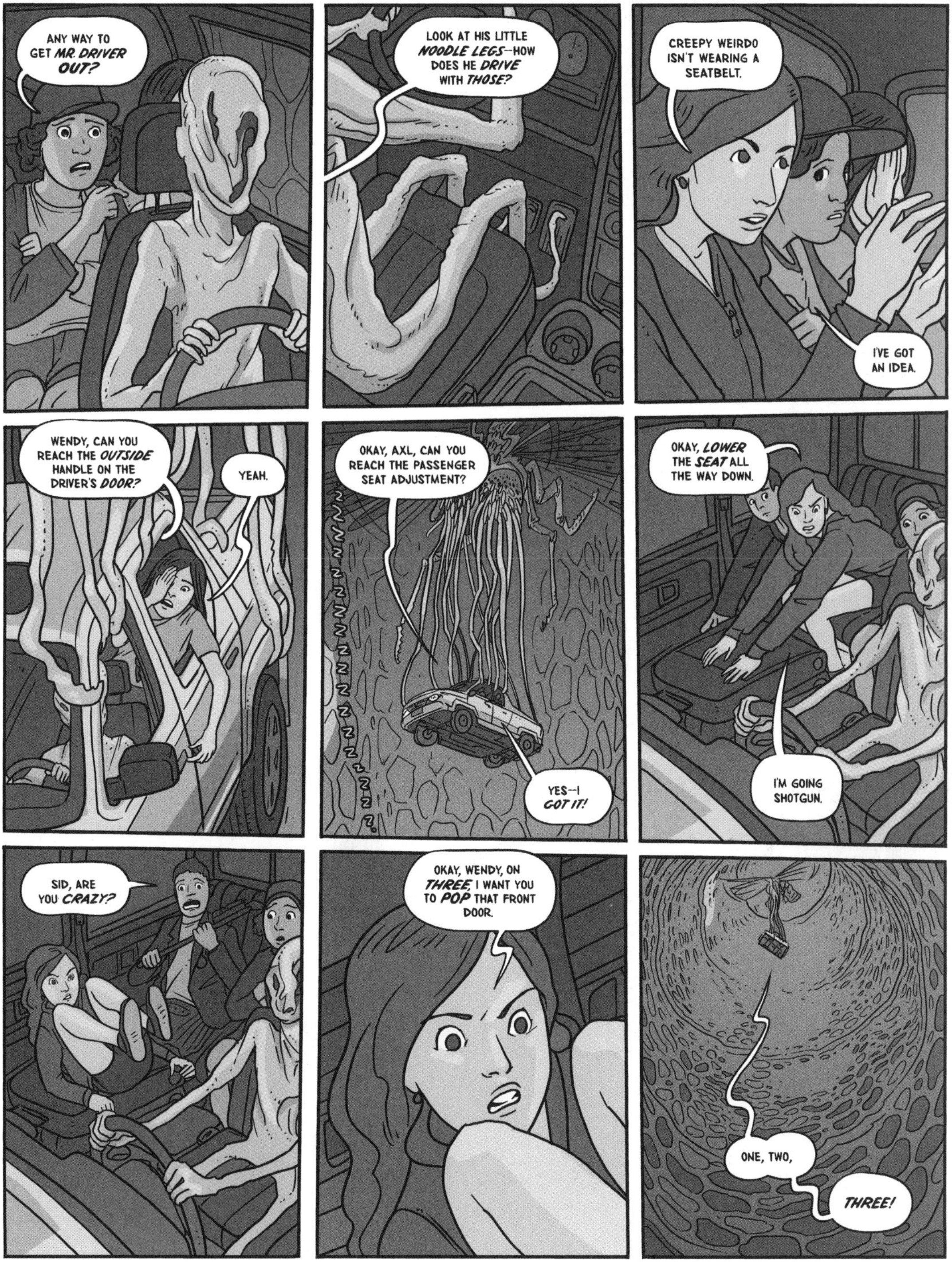
ANY WAY TO GET MR. DRIVER OUT?
LOOK AT HIS LITTLE NOODLE LEGS--HOW DOES HE DRIVE WITH THOSE?
CREEPY WEIRDO ISN'T WEARING A SEATBELT.
I'VE GOT AN IDEA.
WENDY, CAN YOU REACH THE OUTSIDE HANDLE ON THE DRIVER'S DOOR?
YEAH.
OKAY, AXL, CAN YOU REACH THE PASSENGER SEAT ADJUSTMENT?
YES--I GOT IT!
OKAY, LOWER THE SEAT ALL THE WAY DOWN.
I'M GOING SHOTGUN.
SID, ARE YOU CRAZY?
OKAY, WENDY, ON THREE, I WANT YOU TO POP THAT FRONT DOOR.
ONE, TWO,
THREE!

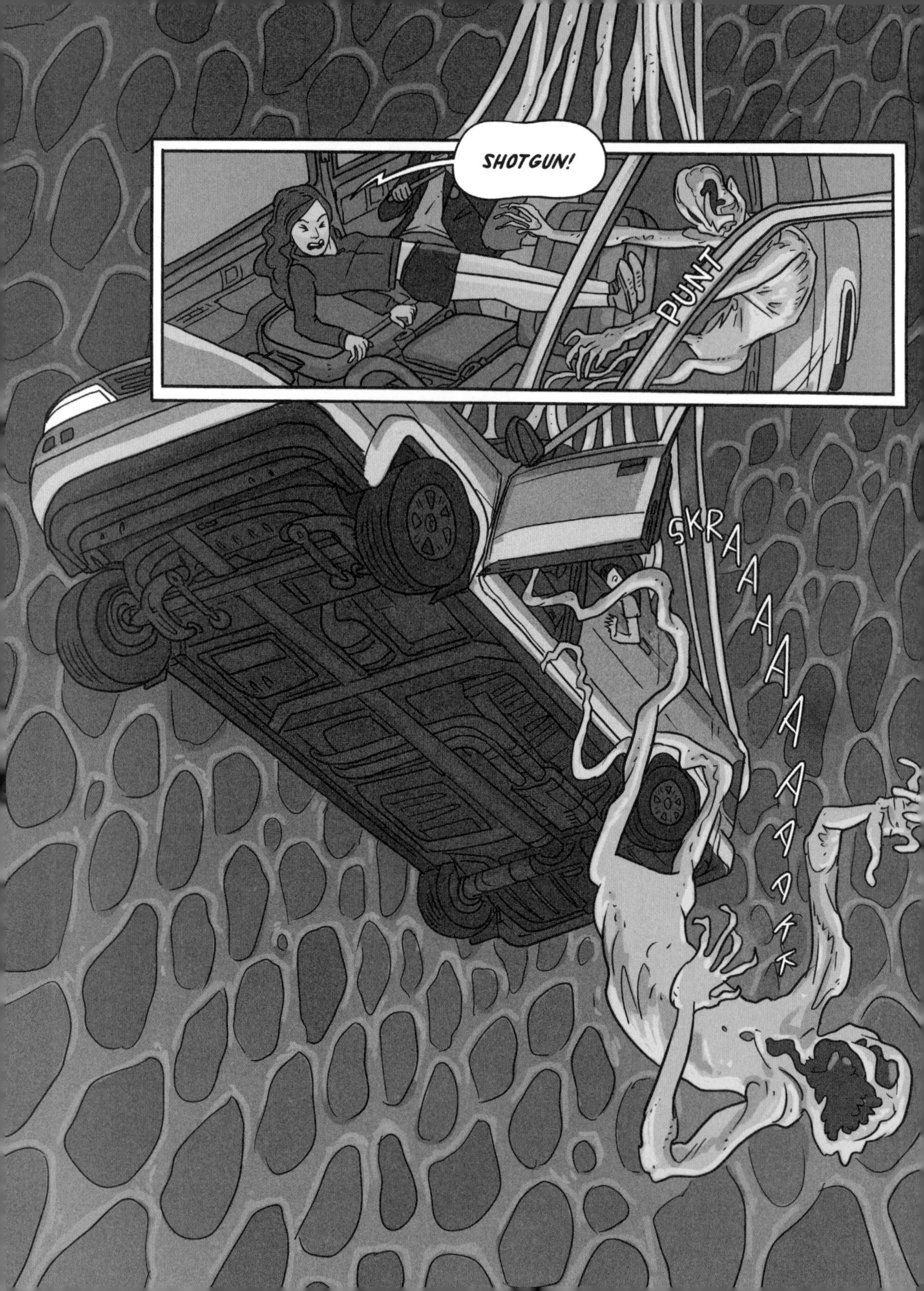
SHOTGUN!
PUNT
SKRAAAAAAAAAAKK

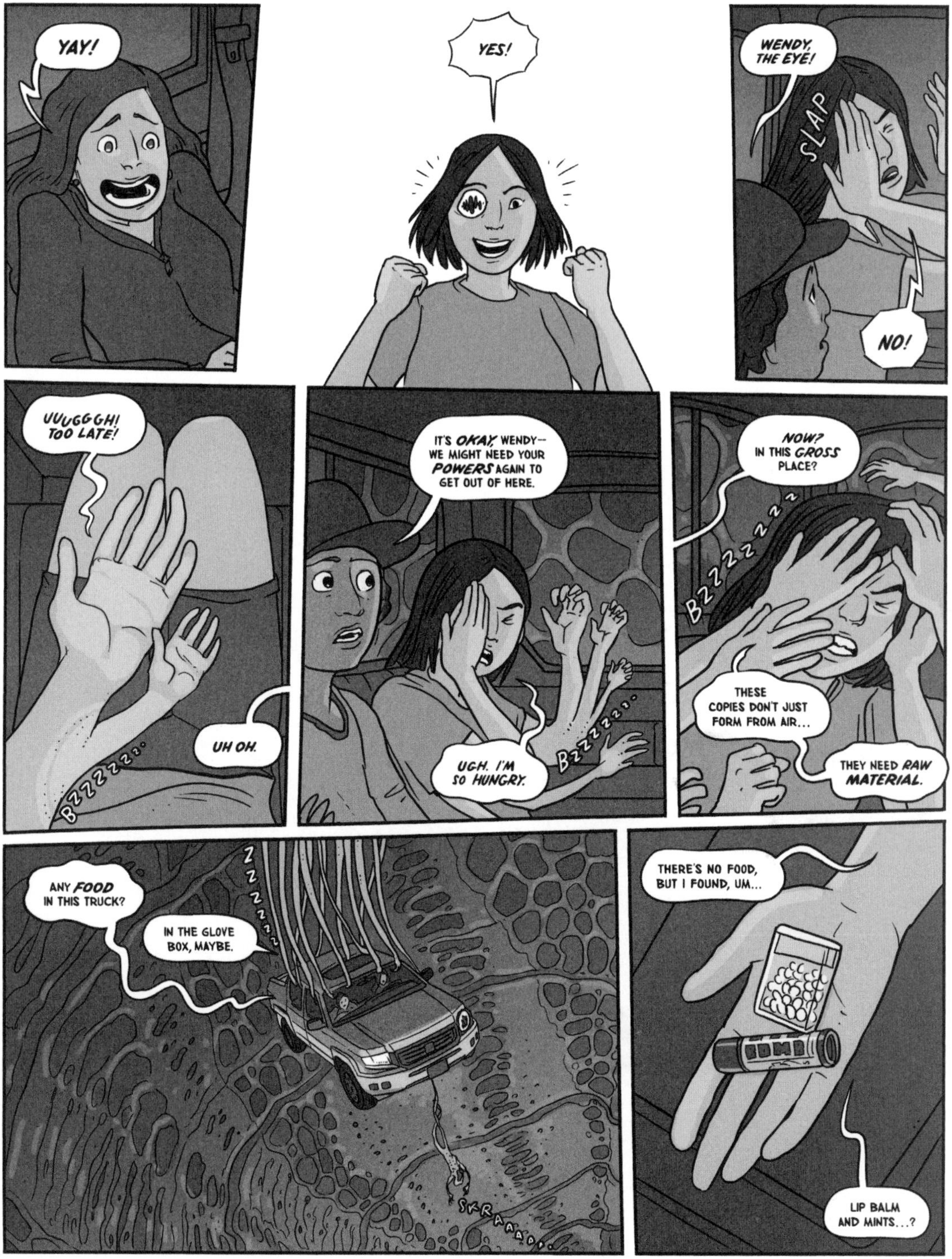
YAY!
YES!
WENDY, THE EYE!
SLAP
NO!
UUUGGGH! TOO LATE!
UH OH.
BZZZZZZZ...
IT'S OKAY, WENDY-- WE MIGHT NEED YOUR POWERS AGAIN TO GET OUT OF HERE.
UGH. I'M SO HUNGRY.
BZZZZZZZ...
NOW? IN THIS GROSS PLACE?
BZZZZZZZZZ
THESE COPIES DON'T JUST FORM FROM AIR...
THEY NEED RAW MATERIAL.
ANY FOOD IN THIS TRUCK?
IN THE GLOVE BOX, MAYBE.
SKRAAAAP...
THERE'S NO FOOD, BUT I FOUND, UM...
LIP BALM AND MINTS...?

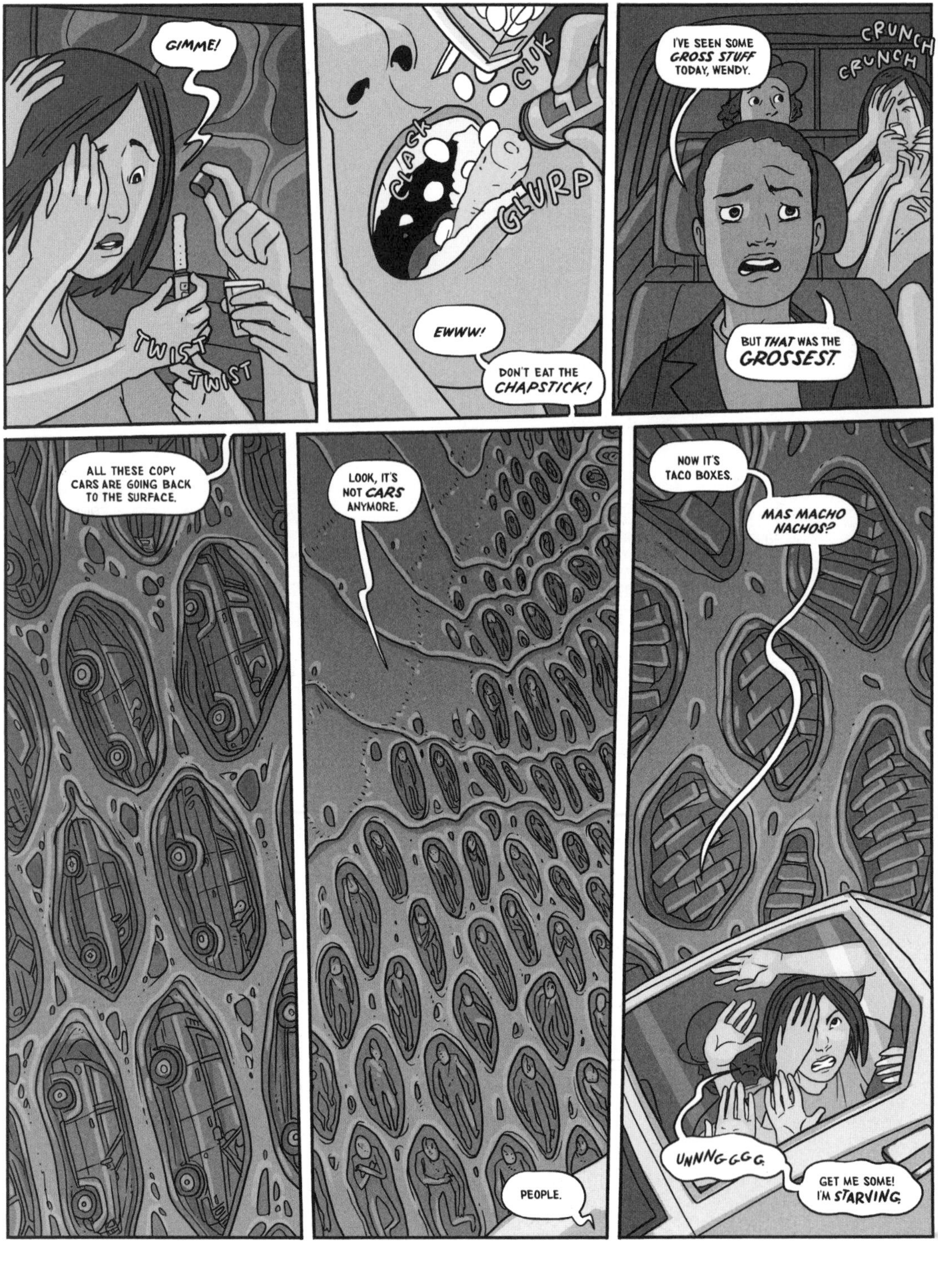
GIMME!
TWIST
TWIST
CLIK
CLACK
GLURP
EWWW!
DON'T EAT THE CHAPSTICK!
I'VE SEEN SOME GROSS STUFF TODAY, WENDY.
CRUNCH
CRUNCH
BUT THAT WAS THE GROSSEST.
ALL THESE COPY CARS ARE GOING BACK TO THE SURFACE.
LOOK, IT'S NOT CARS ANYMORE.
PEOPLE.
NOW IT'S TACO BOXES.
MAS MACHO NACHOS?
UNNNGGGG.
GET ME SOME! I'M STARVING.

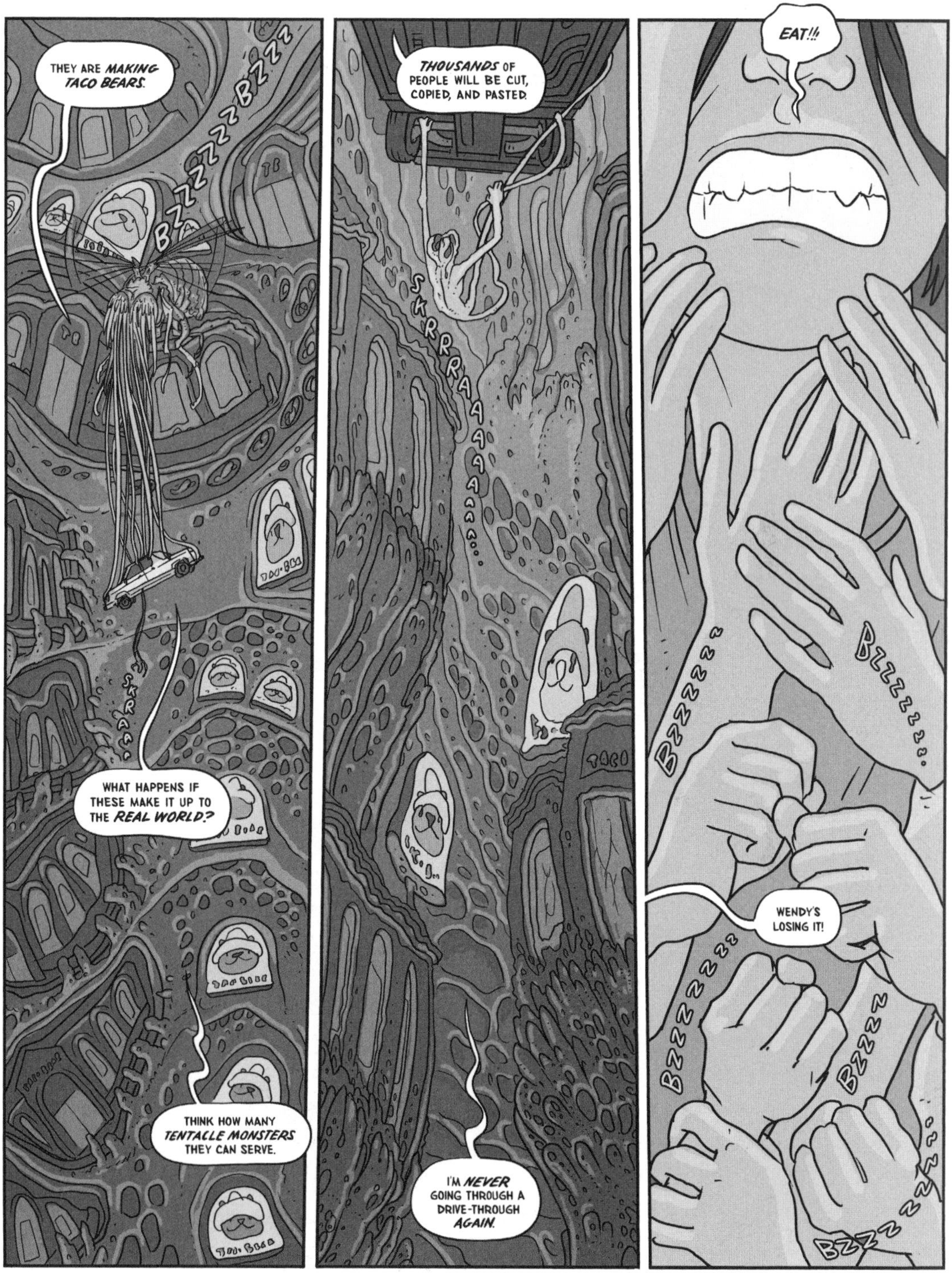
THEY ARE MAKING TACO BEARS.
BZZZZZZBZZZZ
SKRAAA
WHAT HAPPENS IF THESE MAKE IT UP TO THE REAL WORLD?
THINK HOW MANY TENTACLE MONSTERS THEY CAN SERVE.
THOUSANDS OF PEOPLE WILL BE CUT, COPIED, AND PASTED.
SKRRRAAAAAAAA...
I'M NEVER GOING THROUGH A DRIVE-THROUGH AGAIN.
EAT!!!
BZZZZZZZ...
BZZZZZZZ
WENDY'S LOSING IT!
BZZZZZZZZ
BZZZZZ
BZZZZZZZZ

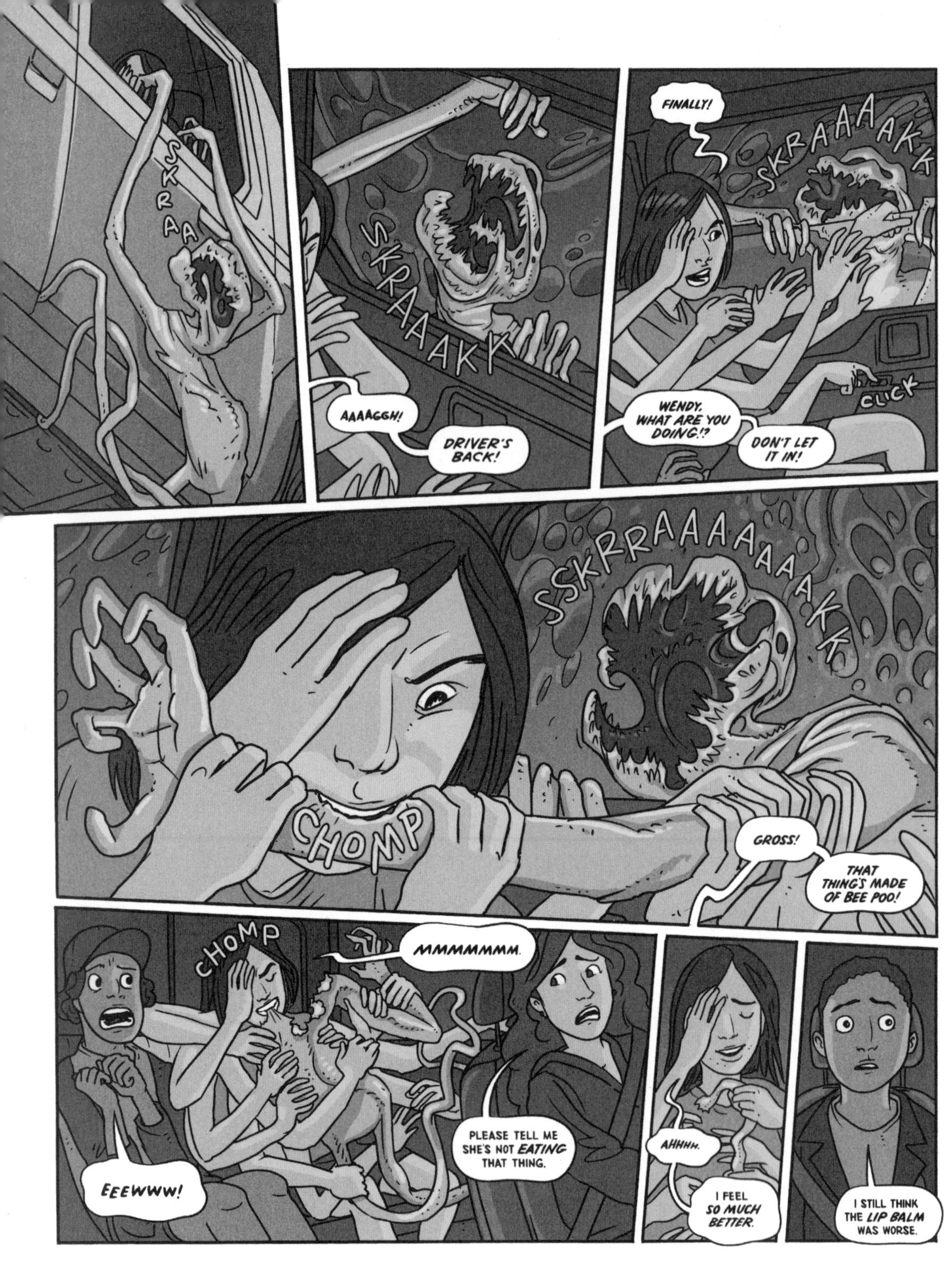
SKRAA
SKRAAAAKK
AAAAGGH!
DRIVER'S BACK!
FINALLY!
SKRAAAAAKK
CLICK
WENDY. WHAT ARE YOU DOING!?
DON'T LET IT IN!
SSKRRAAAAAAAAKK
CHOMP
GROSS!
THAT THING'S MADE OF BEE POO!
CHOMP
MMMMMMM.
EEEWWW!
PLEASE TELL ME SHE'S NOT EATING THAT THING.
AHHHH.
I FEEL SO MUCH BETTER.
I STILL THINK THE LIP BALM WAS WORSE.

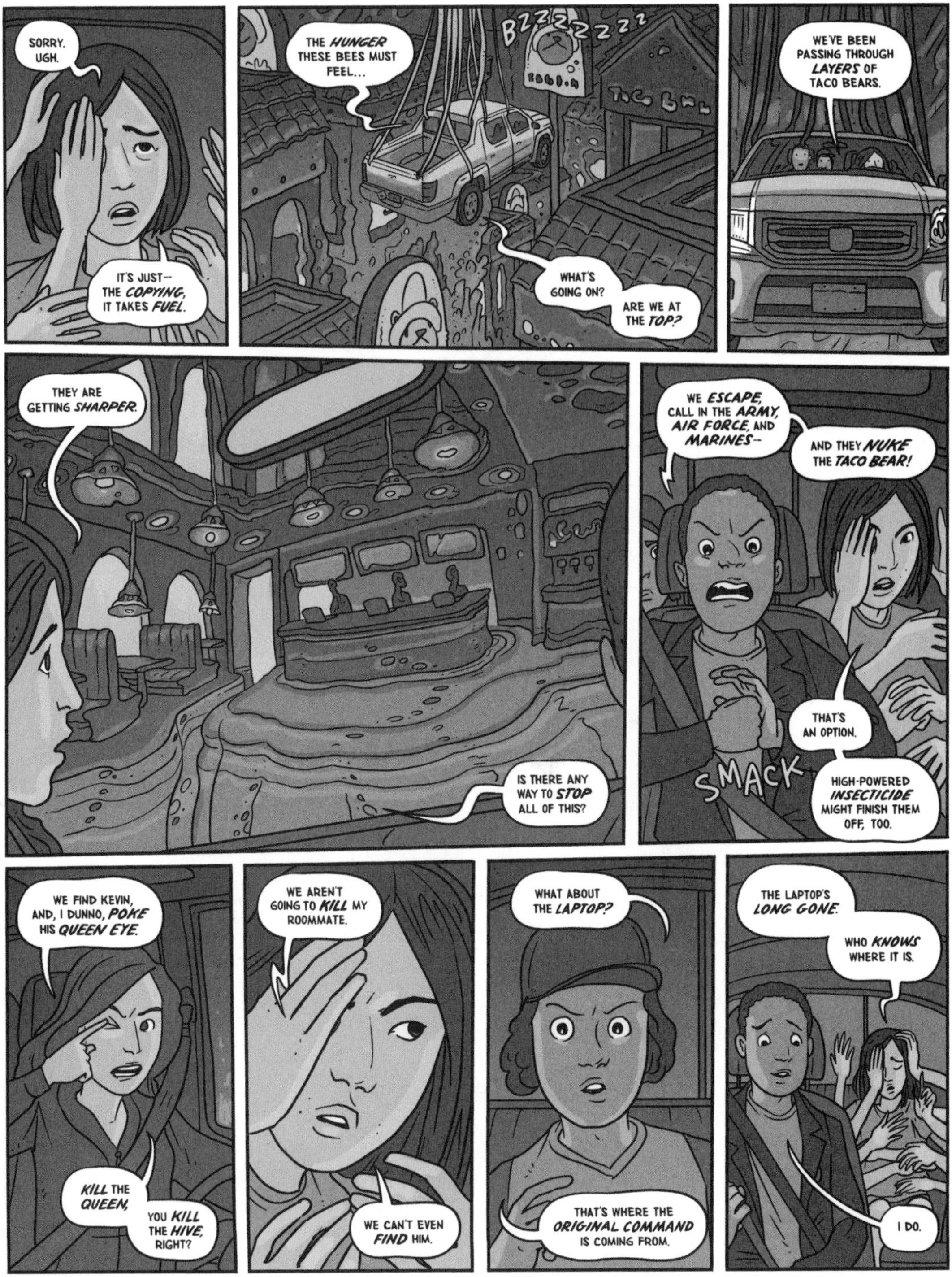
SORRY. UGH.
IT'S JUST-- THE COPYING, IT TAKES FUEL.
THE HUNGER THESE BEES MUST FEEL...
BZZZZZZZZ
WHAT'S GOING ON?
ARE WE AT THE TOP?
WE'VE BEEN PASSING THROUGH LAYERS OF TACO BEARS.
THEY ARE GETTING SHARPER.
IS THERE ANY WAY TO STOP ALL OF THIS?
WE ESCAPE, CALL IN THE ARMY, AIR FORCE, AND MARINES--
AND THEY NUKE THE TACO BEAR!
SMACK
THAT'S AN OPTION.
HIGH-POWERED INSECTICIDE MIGHT FINISH THEM OFF, TOO.
WE FIND KEVIN, AND, I DUNNO, POKE HIS QUEEN EYE.
KILL THE QUEEN,
YOU KILL THE HIVE, RIGHT?
WE AREN'T GOING TO KILL MY ROOMMATE.
WE CAN'T EVEN FIND HIM.
WHAT ABOUT THE LAPTOP?
THAT'S WHERE THE ORIGINAL COMMAND IS COMING FROM.
THE LAPTOP'S LONG GONE.
WHO KNOWS WHERE IT IS.
I DO.

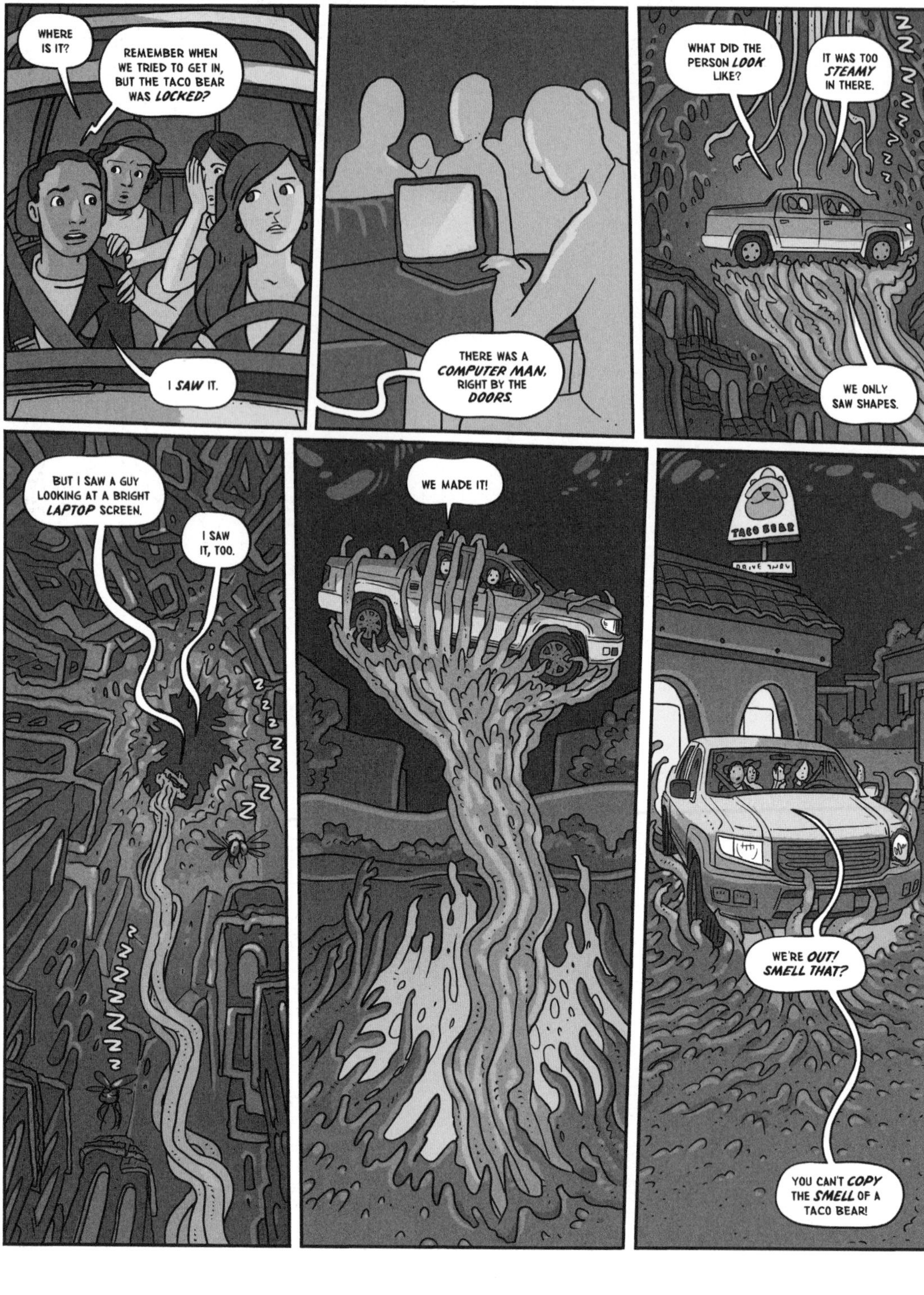
WHERE IS IT?
REMEMBER WHEN WE TRIED TO GET IN, BUT THE TACO BEAR WAS LOCKED?
I SAW IT.
THERE WAS A COMPUTER MAN, RIGHT BY THE DOORS.
WHAT DID THE PERSON LOOK LIKE?
IT WAS TOO STEAMY IN THERE.
WE ONLY SAW SHAPES.
BUT I SAW A GUY LOOKING AT A BRIGHT LAPTOP SCREEN.
I SAW IT, TOO.
WE MADE IT!
TACO BEAR
DRIVE THRU
WE'RE OUT! SMELL THAT?
YOU CAN'T COPY THE SMELL OF A TACO BEAR!

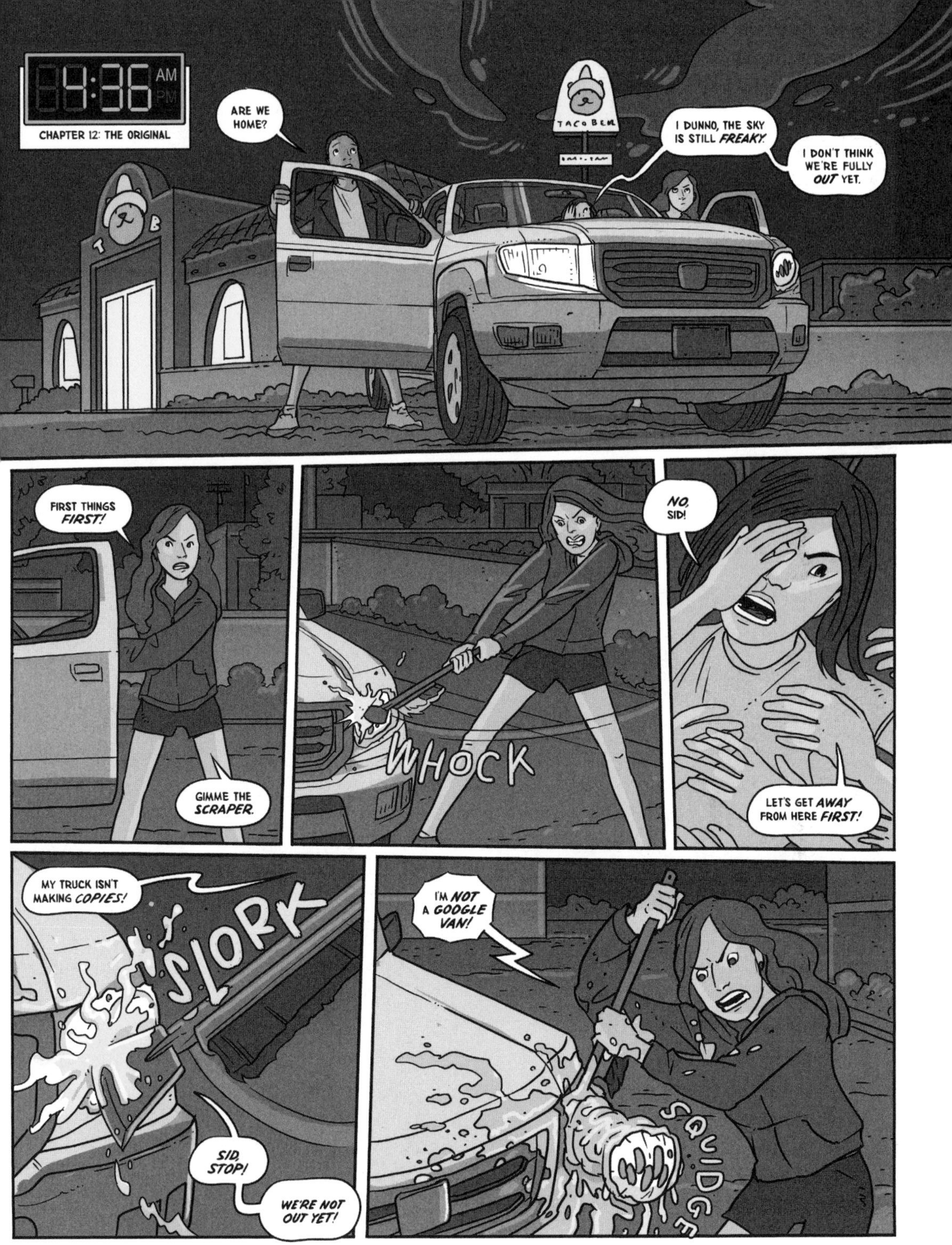
4:36 AM PM
CHAPTER 12: THE ORIGINAL
ARE WE HOME?
TACO BELL
I DUNNO, THE SKY IS STILL FREAKY.
I DON'T THINK WE'RE FULLY OUT YET.
FIRST THINGS FIRST!
GIMME THE SCRAPER.
WHOCK
NO, SID!
LET'S GET AWAY FROM HERE FIRST!
MY TRUCK ISN'T MAKING COPIES!
SLORK
SID, STOP!
WE'RE NOT OUT YET!
I'M NOT A GOOGLE VAN!
SQUIDGE

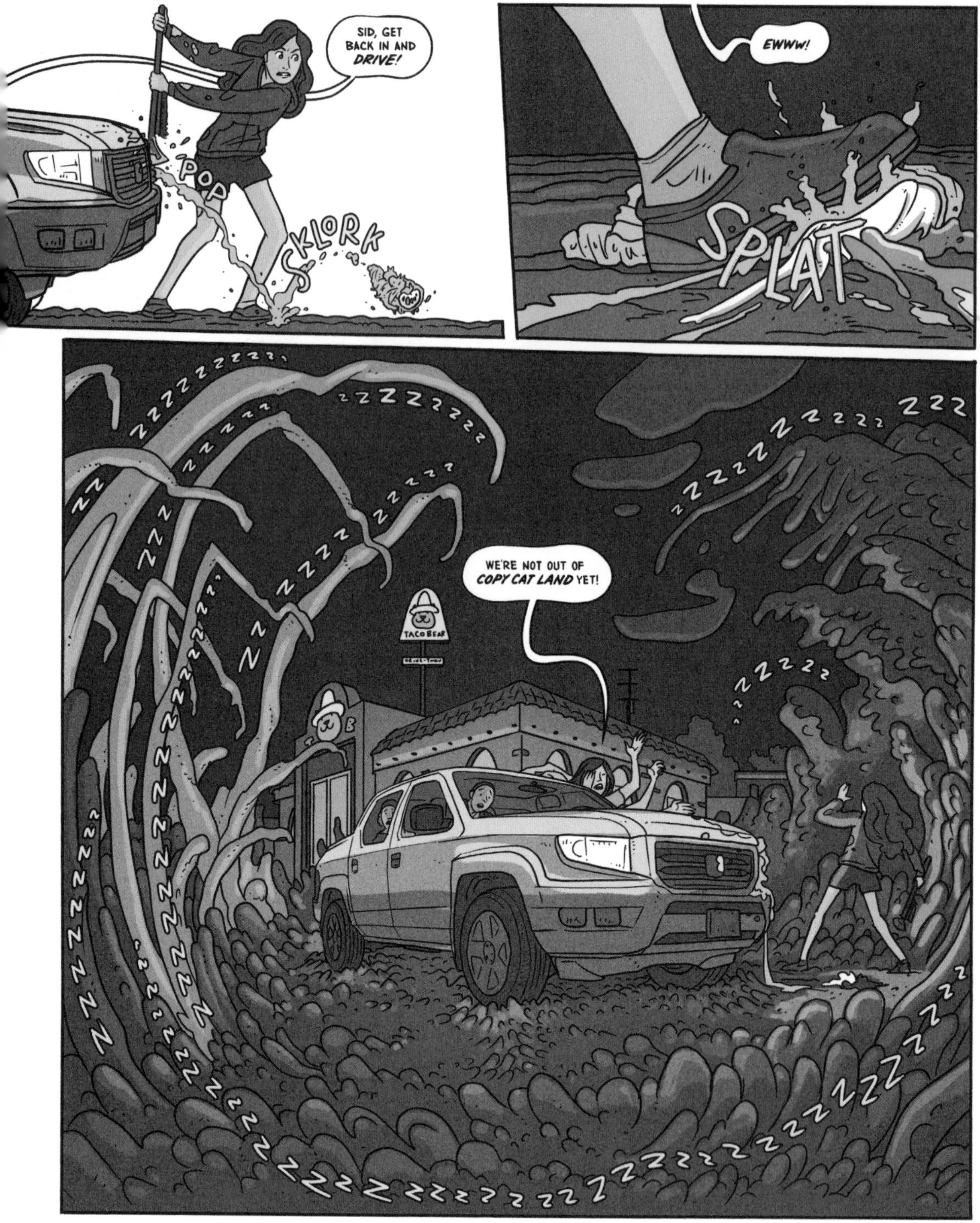
SID, GET BACK IN AND *DRIVE!*
POP
SKLORK
EWWW!
SPLAT
WE'RE NOT OUT OF *COPY CAT LAND* YET!
TACO BEAR

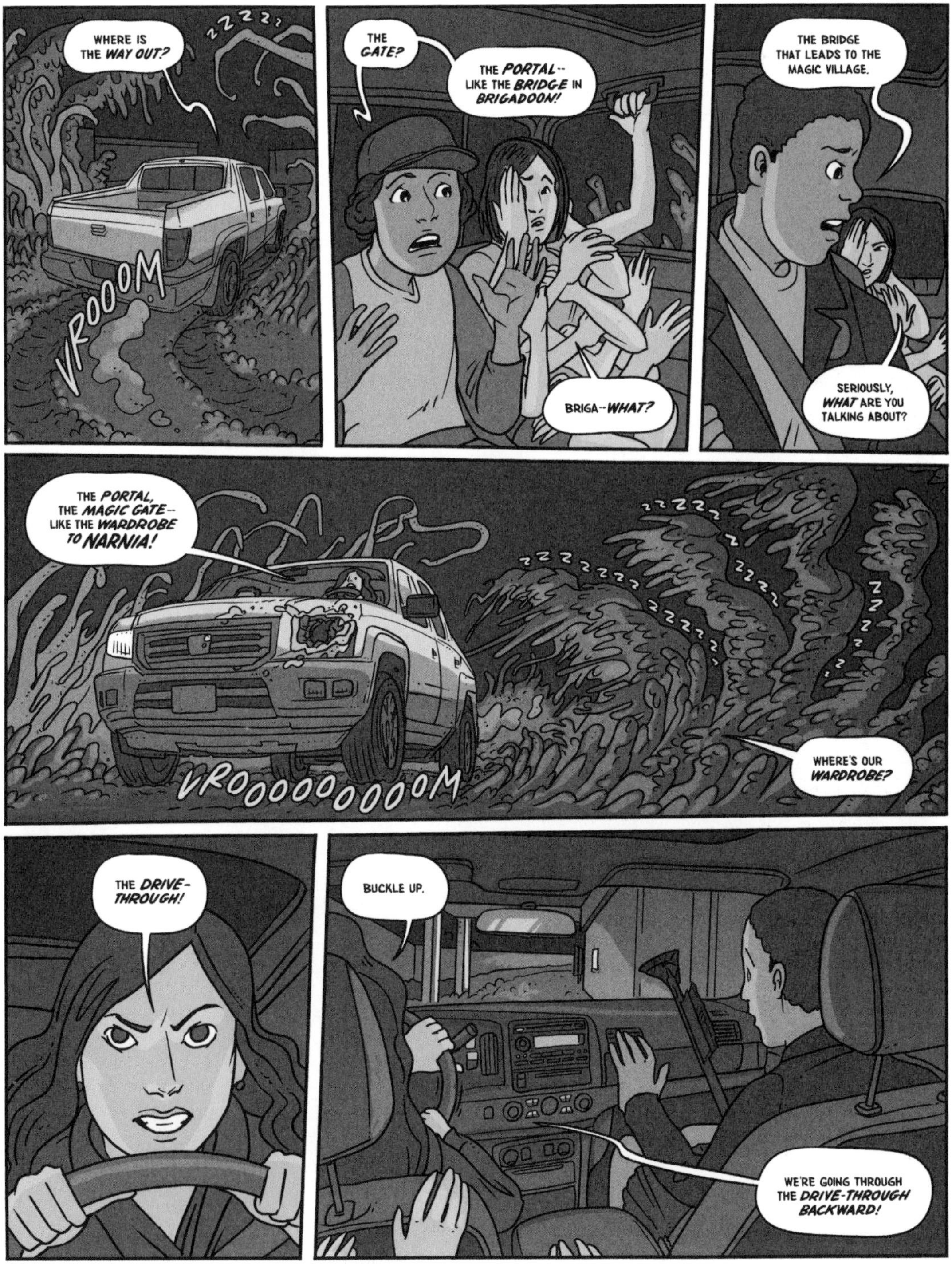
WHERE IS THE WAY OUT?
ZZZZZ
VROOOM
THE GATE?
THE PORTAL-- LIKE THE BRIDGE IN BRIGADOON!
BRIGA--WHAT?
THE BRIDGE THAT LEADS TO THE MAGIC VILLAGE.
SERIOUSLY, WHAT ARE YOU TALKING ABOUT?
THE PORTAL, THE MAGIC GATE-- LIKE THE WARDROBE TO NARNIA!
WHERE'S OUR WARDROBE?
VROOOOOOOOOOM
THE DRIVE-THROUGH!
BUCKLE UP.
WE'RE GOING THROUGH THE DRIVE-THROUGH BACKWARD!

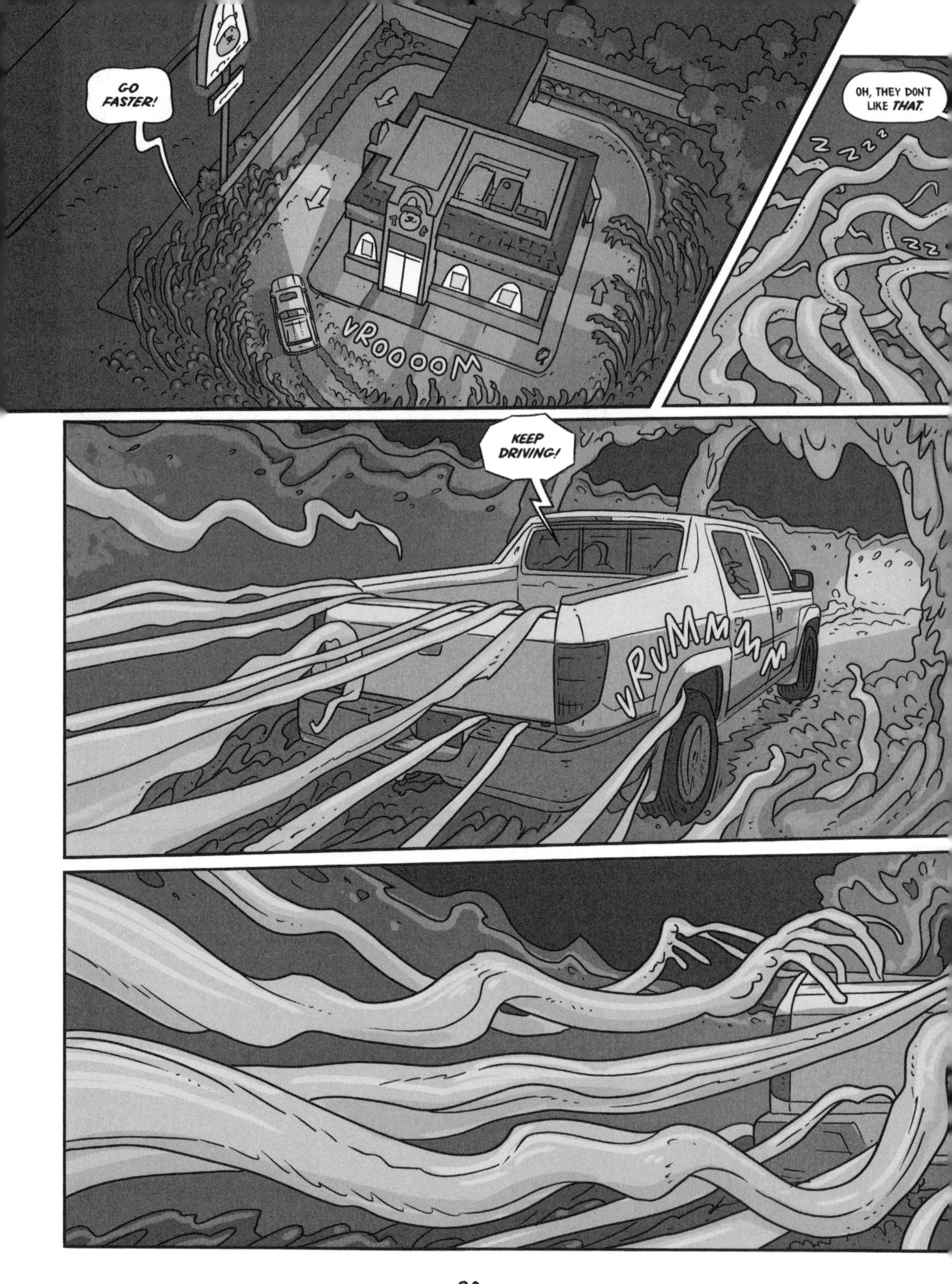
GO FASTER!
VROOOOM
OH, THEY DON'T LIKE THAT.
Z Z Z Z
Z Z Z
KEEP DRIVING!
VRUMMMMM

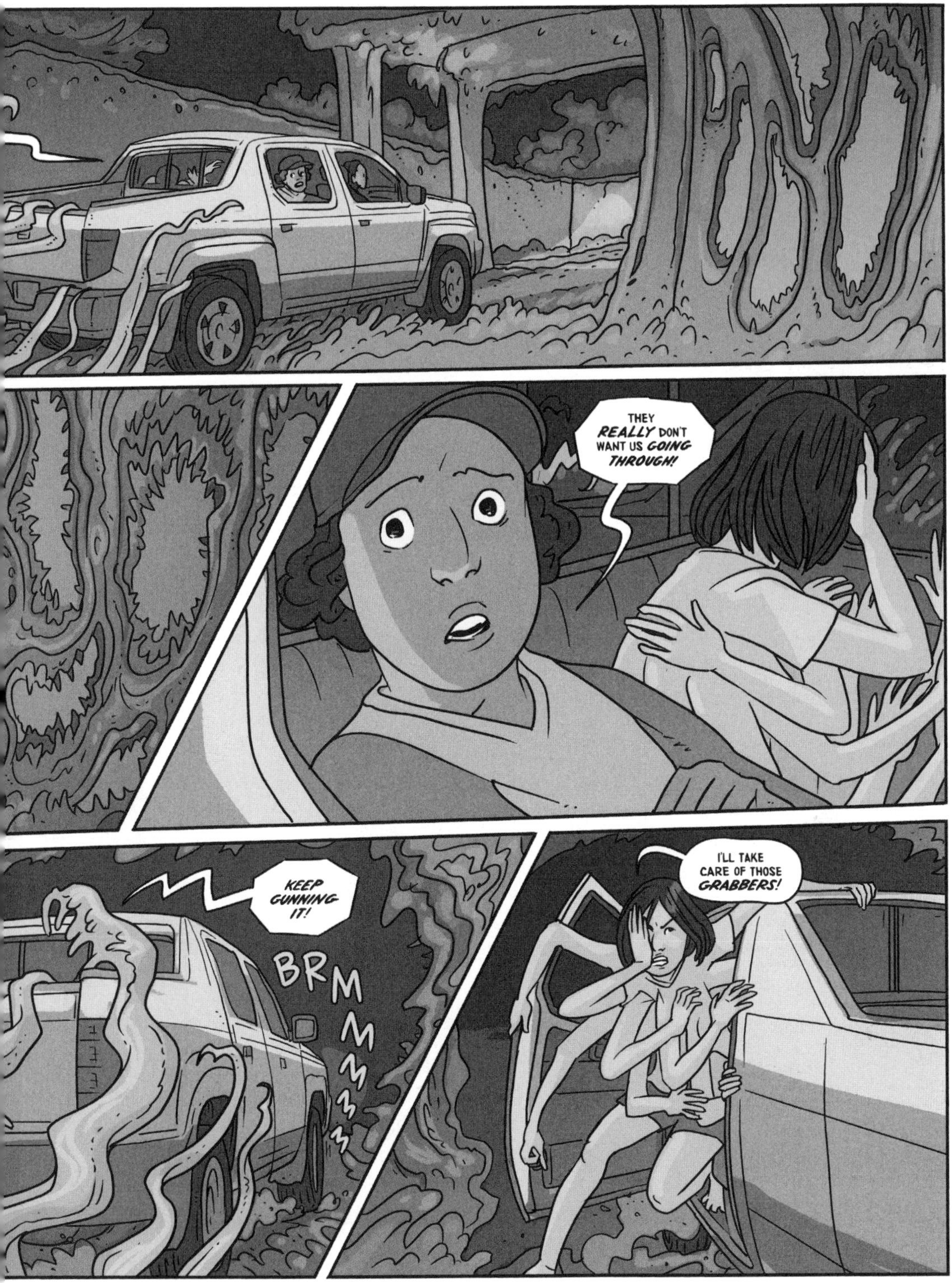
THEY REALLY DON'T WANT US GOING THROUGH!
KEEP GUNNING IT!
BRMMMMMMM
I'LL TAKE CARE OF THOSE GRABBERS!

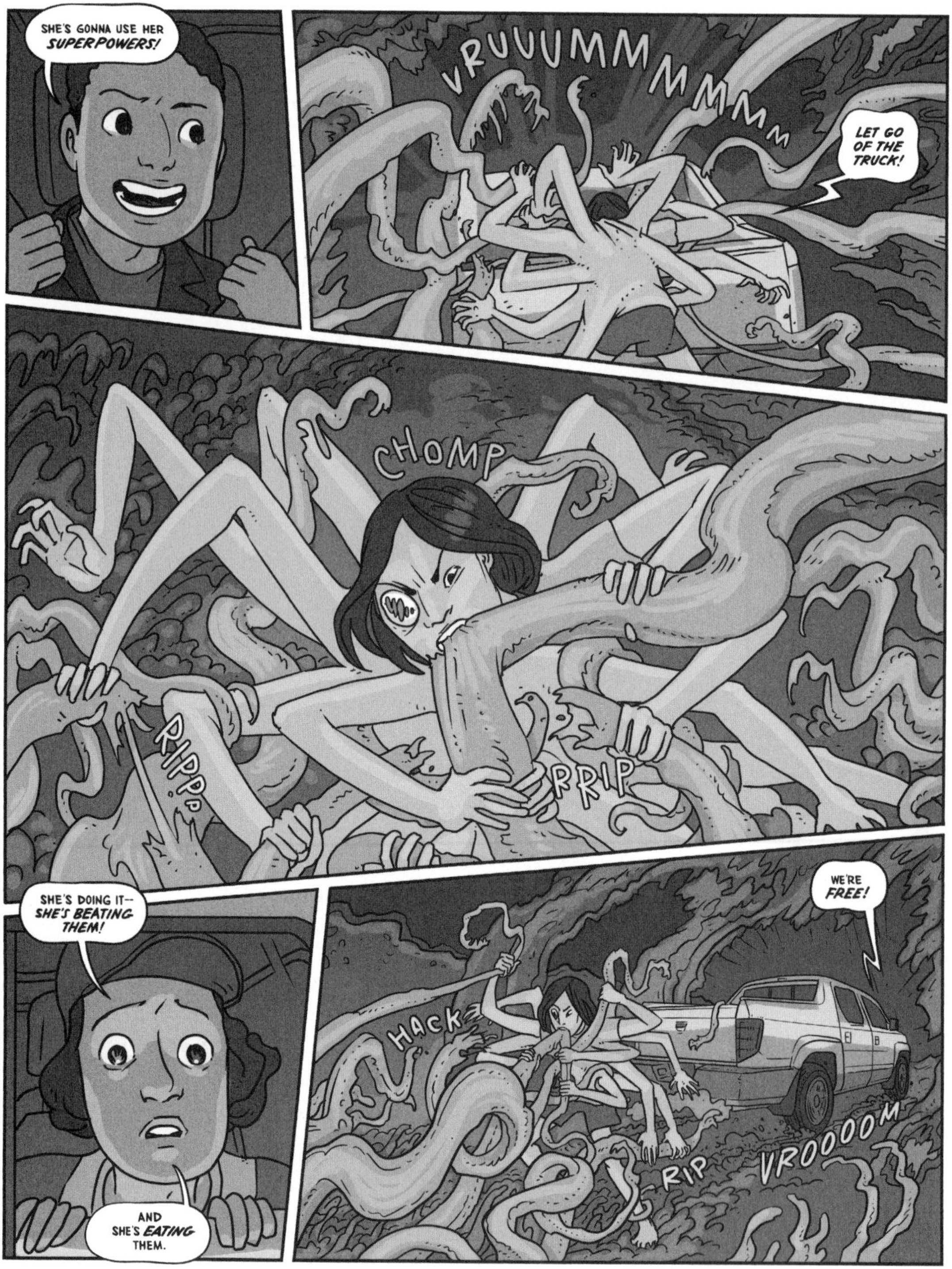

SHE'S GONNA USE HER SUPERPOWERS!
VRUUUMMMMMMMm
LET GO OF THE TRUCK!
CHOMP
RIPPP
RRIP
SHE'S DOING IT-- SHE'S BEATING THEM!
AND SHE'S EATING THEM.
WE'RE FREE!
HACK
RIP
VROOOOM

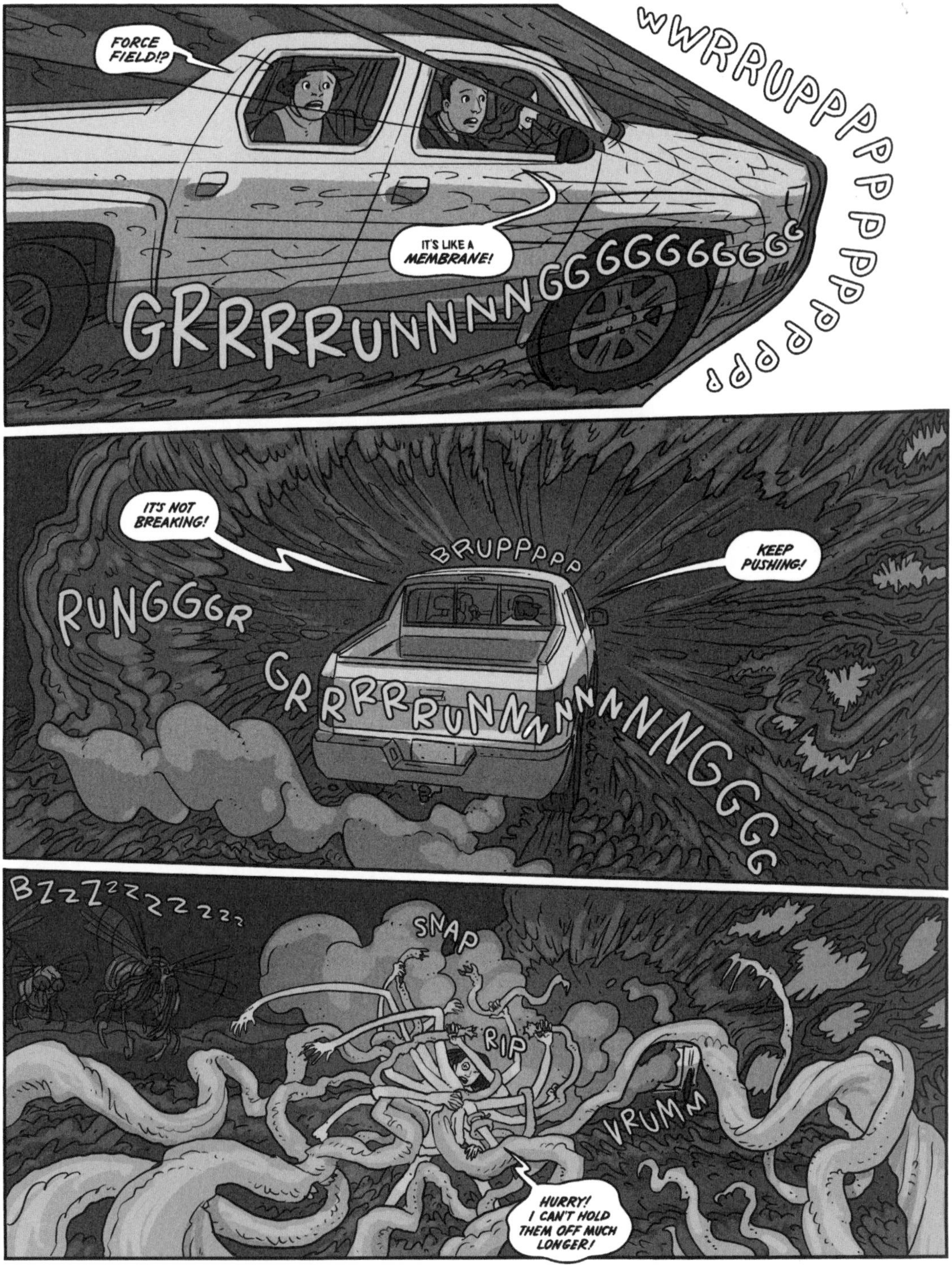
wWRRUPPPPPPPPPPPPPP
FORCE FIELD!?
IT'S LIKE A MEMBRANE!
GRRRRUNNNNNGGGGGGGGGG
IT'S NOT BREAKING!
BRUPPPPPP
KEEP PUSHING!
RUNGGGR
GRRRRRUNNNNNNNNGGGGG
BZZZZZZZZZZ
SNAP
RIP
VRUMM
HURRY! I CAN'T HOLD THEM OFF MUCH LONGER!

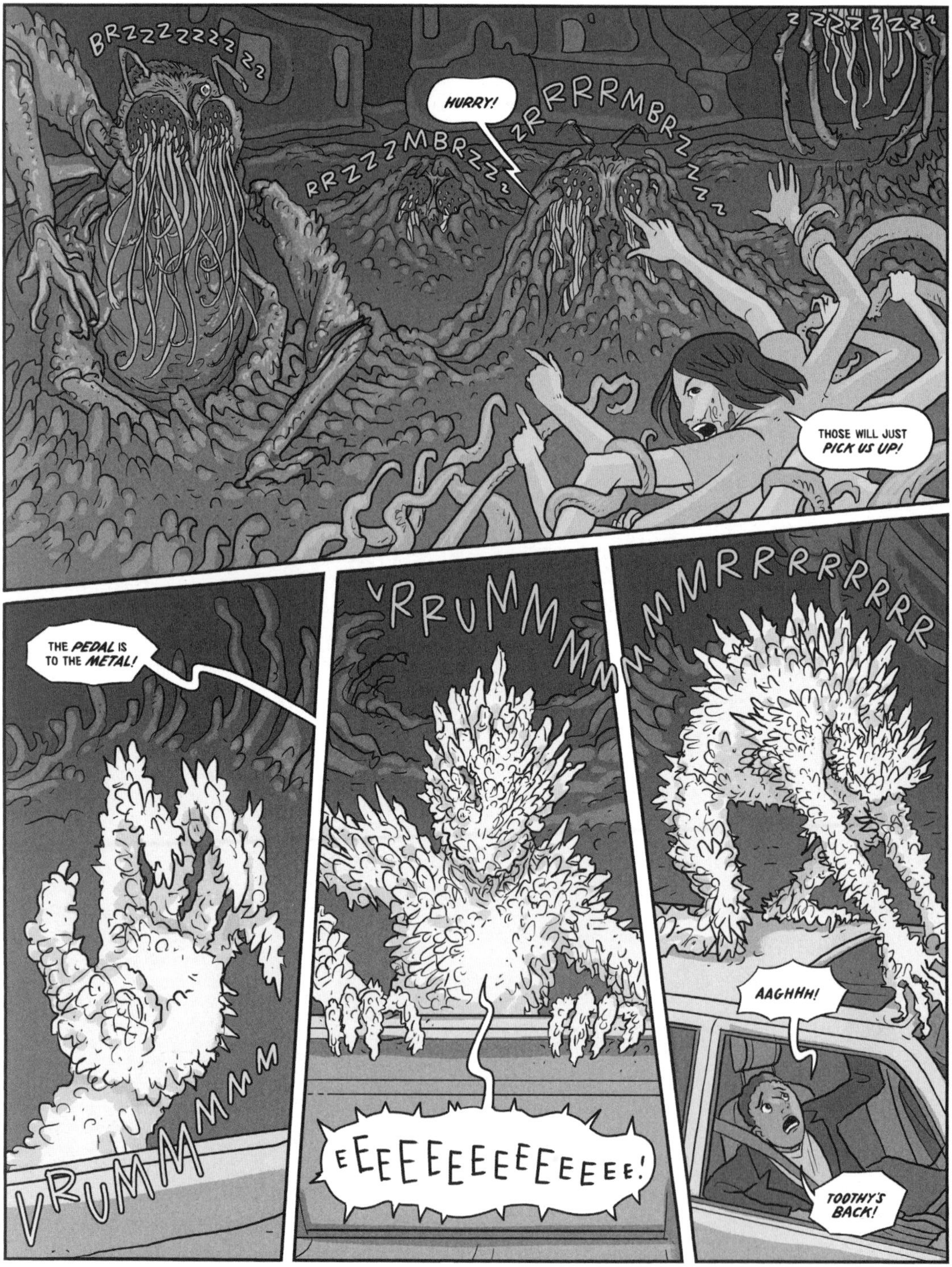
BRZZZZZZZZZ
HURRY!
RRZZZMBRZZZ
ZRRRRMBRZZZZZ
ZZZZZZZZZ
THOSE WILL JUST PICK US UP!
THE PEDAL IS TO THE METAL!
VRUMMMMMMM
VRRUMMMMMMMMMRRRRRRRRRR
EEEEEEEEEEEEEE!
AAGHHH!
TOOTHY'S BACK!

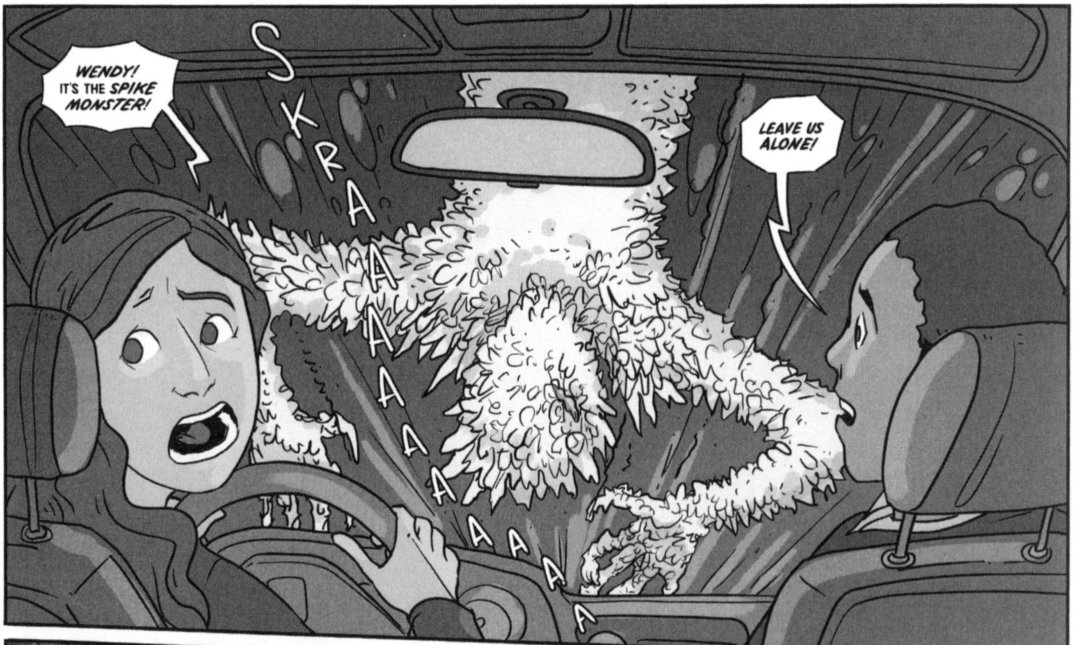
WENDY! IT'S THE SPIKE MONSTER!
SKRAAAAAAAAAAAA
LEAVE US ALONE!

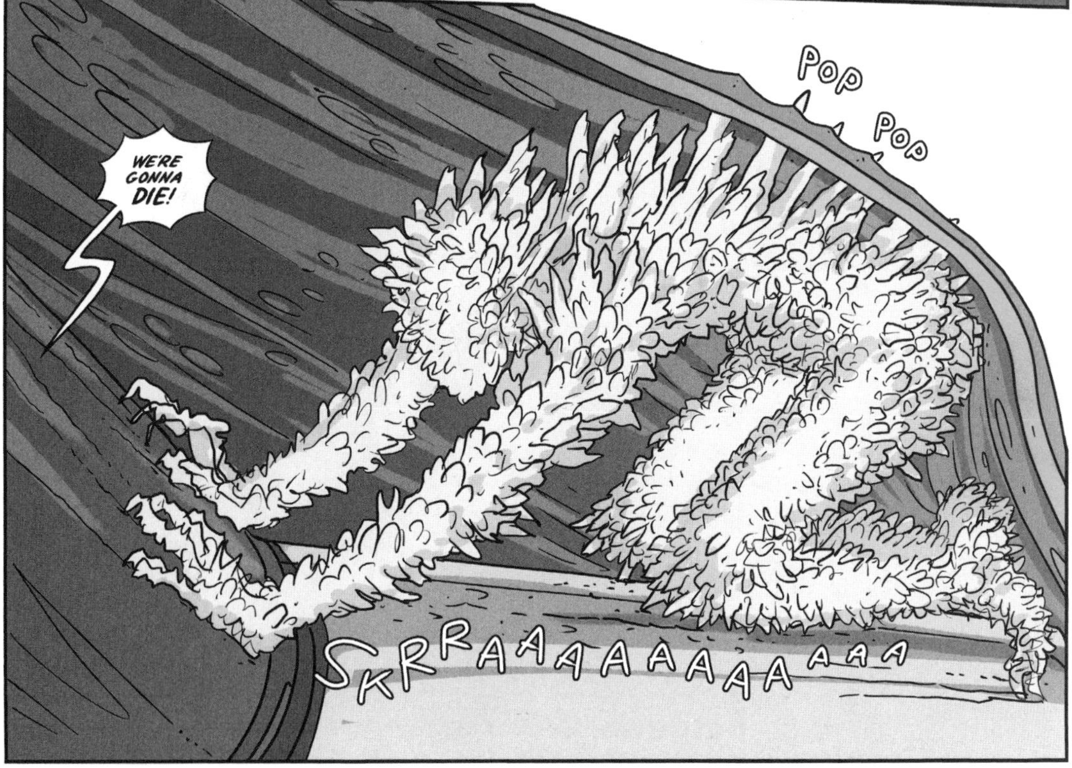
WE'RE GONNA DIE!
POP
POP
SKRRAAAAAAAAAAAA

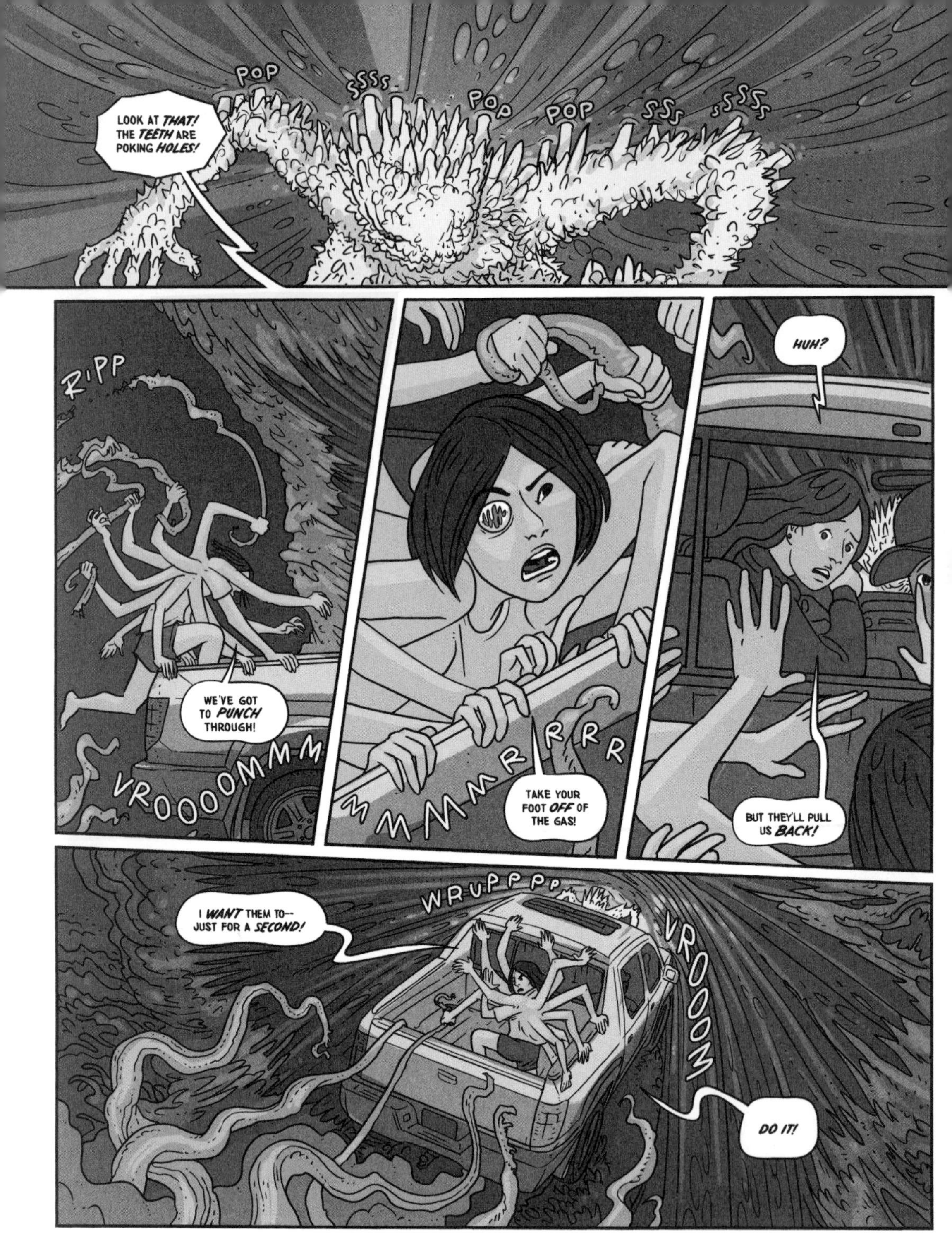
POP
SSSS
POP
POP
SSS
SSSS
LOOK AT THAT! THE TEETH ARE POKING HOLES!
RIPP
WE'VE GOT TO PUNCH THROUGH!
VROOOOOMMM
MMMMMRRRRR
TAKE YOUR FOOT OFF OF THE GAS!
HUH?
BUT THEY'LL PULL US BACK!
WRUPPPPP
I WANT THEM TO-- JUST FOR A SECOND!
VROOOM
DO IT!

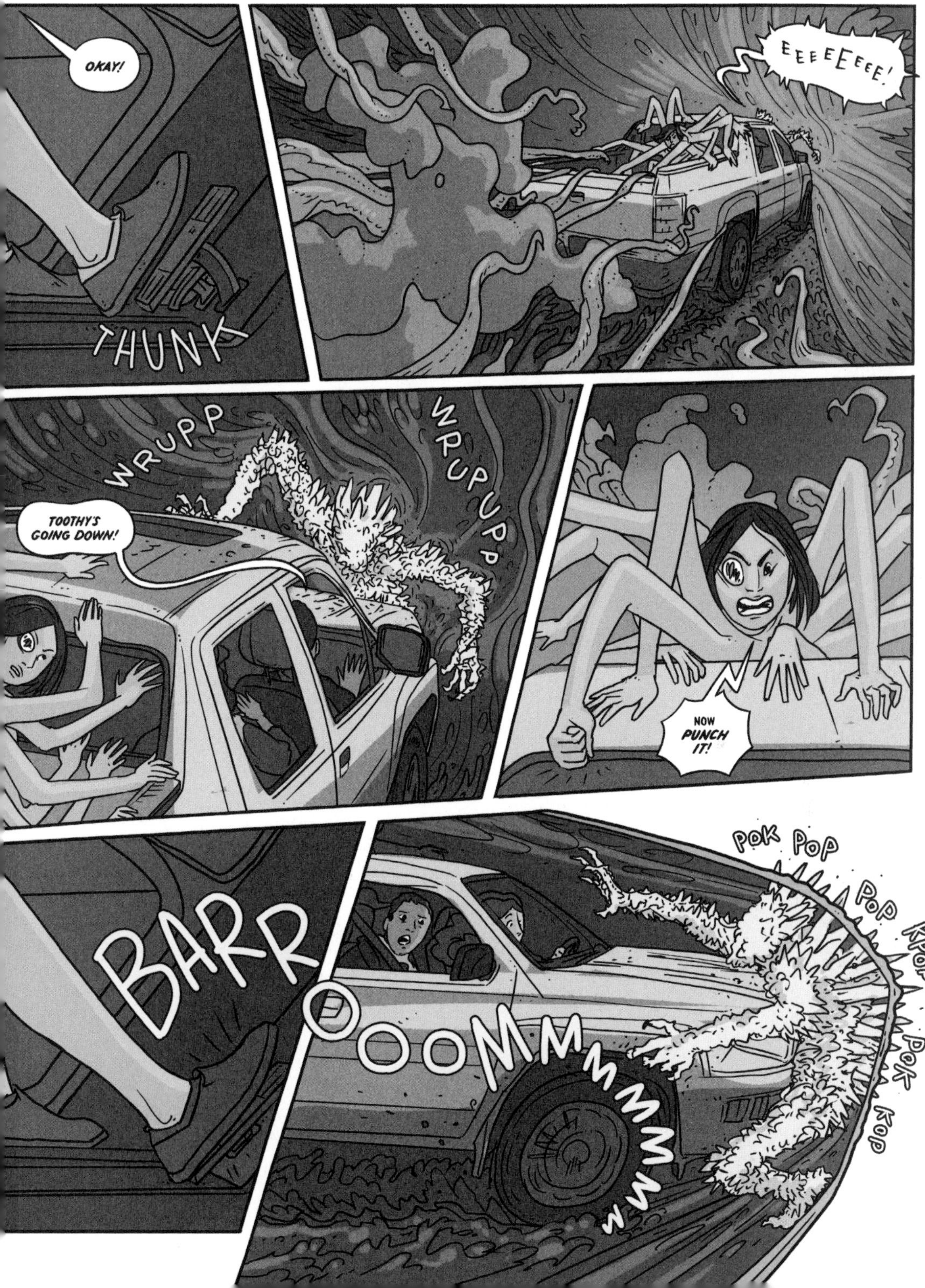
OKAY!
THUNK
EEEEEEEE!
WRUPP
WRUPUPP
TOOTHY'S GOING DOWN!
NOW PUNCH IT!
BARROOOMMMMMMMM
POK POP
POP
KPOP
POK
POK
KOP

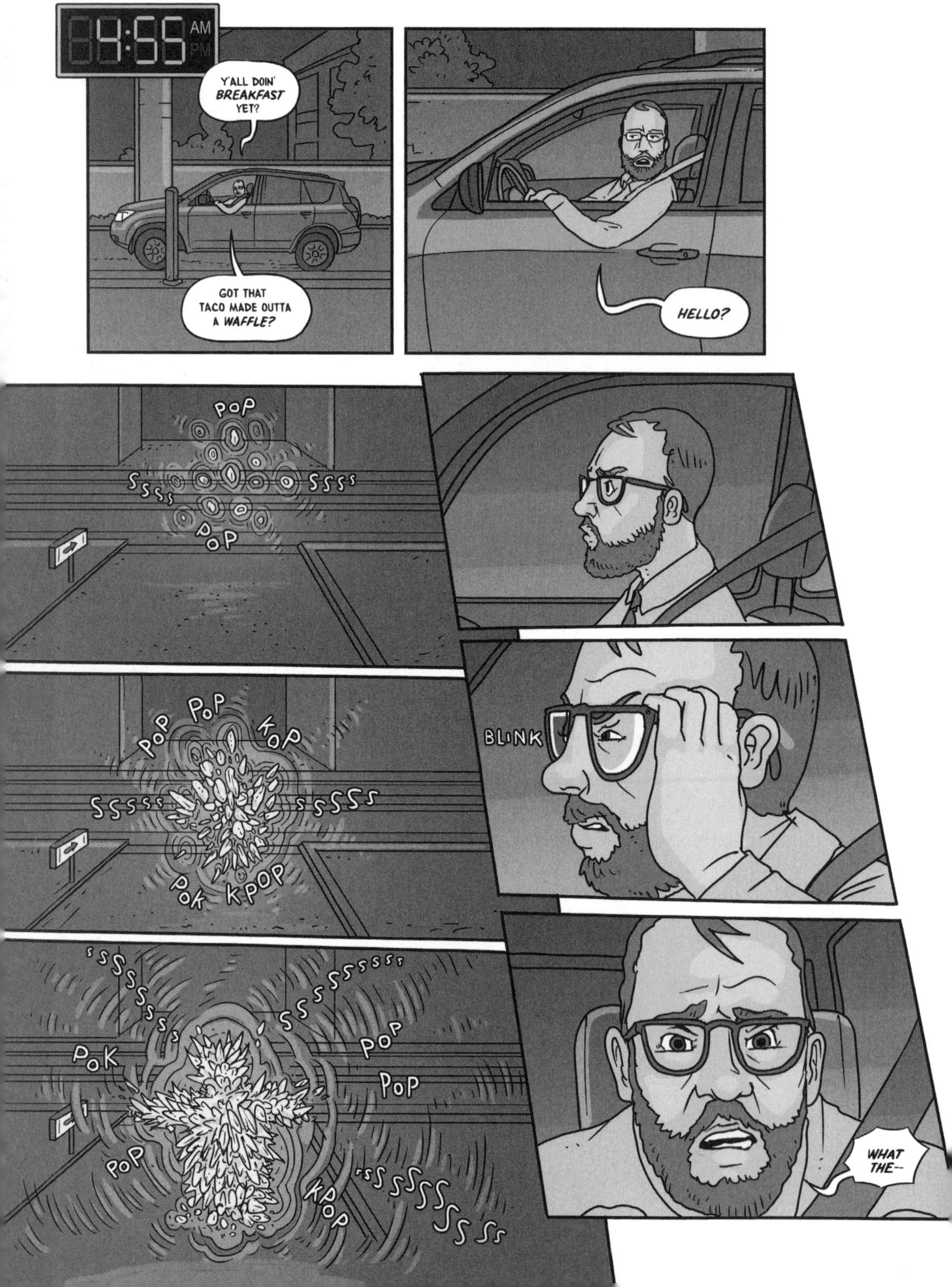

4:55 AM PM
Y'ALL DOIN' *BREAKFAST* YET?
GOT THAT TACO MADE OUTTA A *WAFFLE?*
HELLO?
POP
SSSSS
SSSS
POP
POP POP
KOP
SSSSS
SSSSS
POK KPOP
BLINK
SSSSSSSS
SSSSSSSSSS
POK
POP
POP
POP
KPOP
SSSSSSSSSS
WHAT THE--

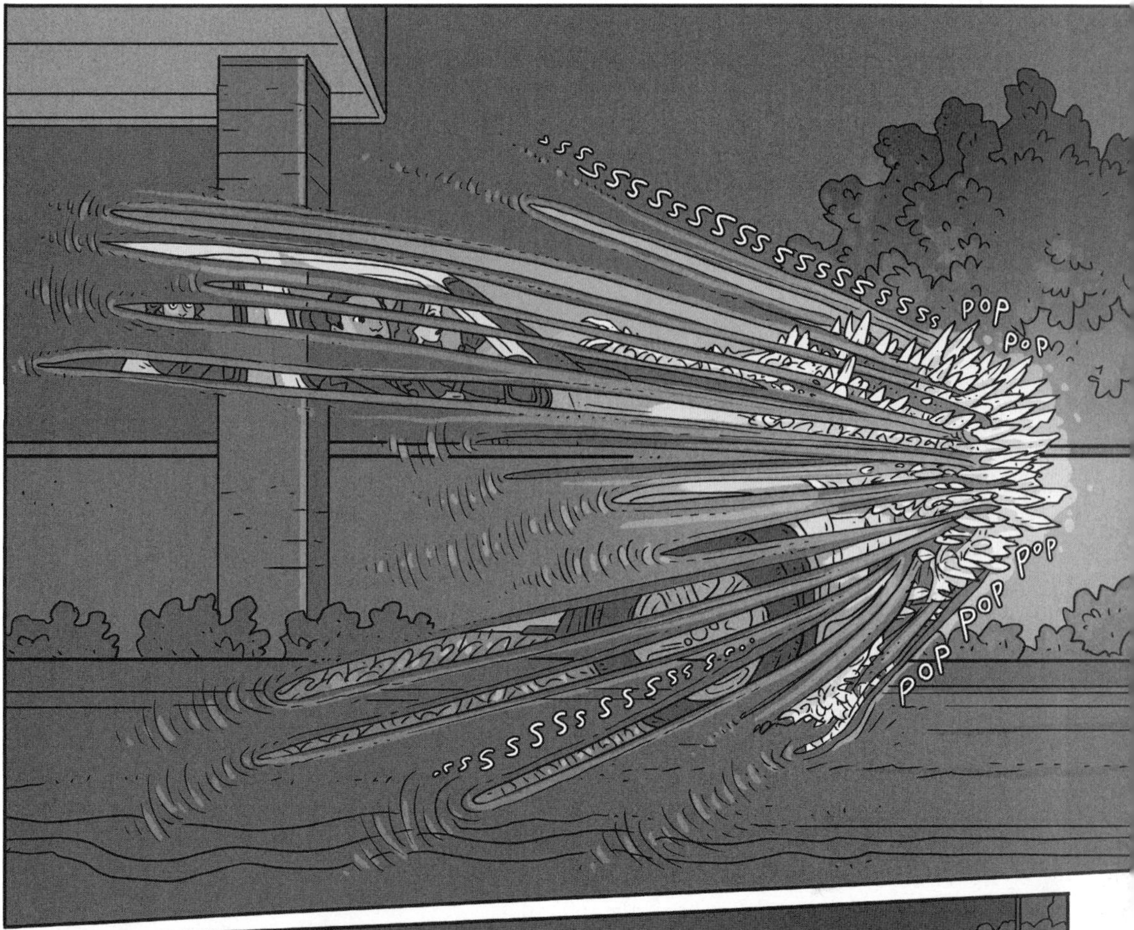
sssSSSSSSSSSSSSSSSSSSSSSsss
POP
POP
POP
POP
POP POP POP
sssSSSSSSSSSSsss

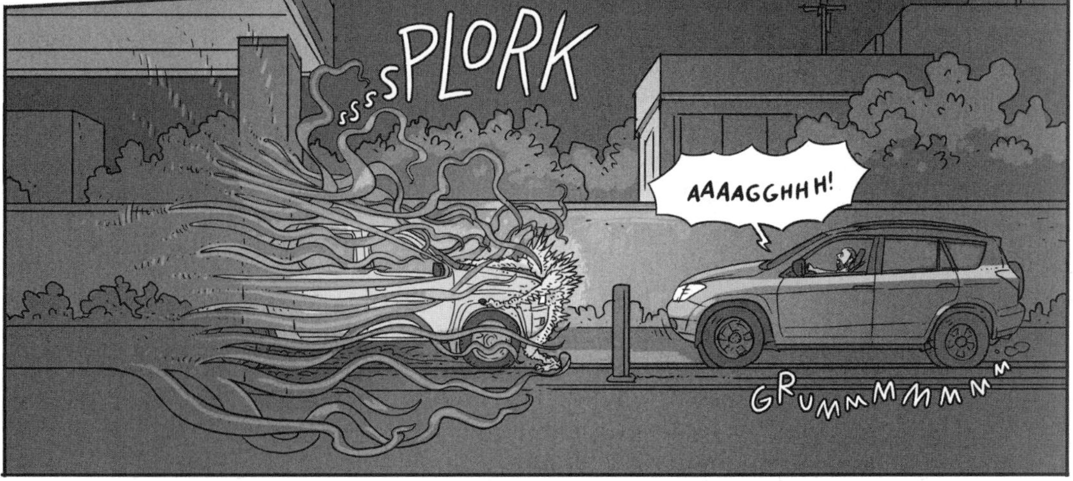
ssssPLORK
AAAAGGHHH!
GRUMMMMMMMM

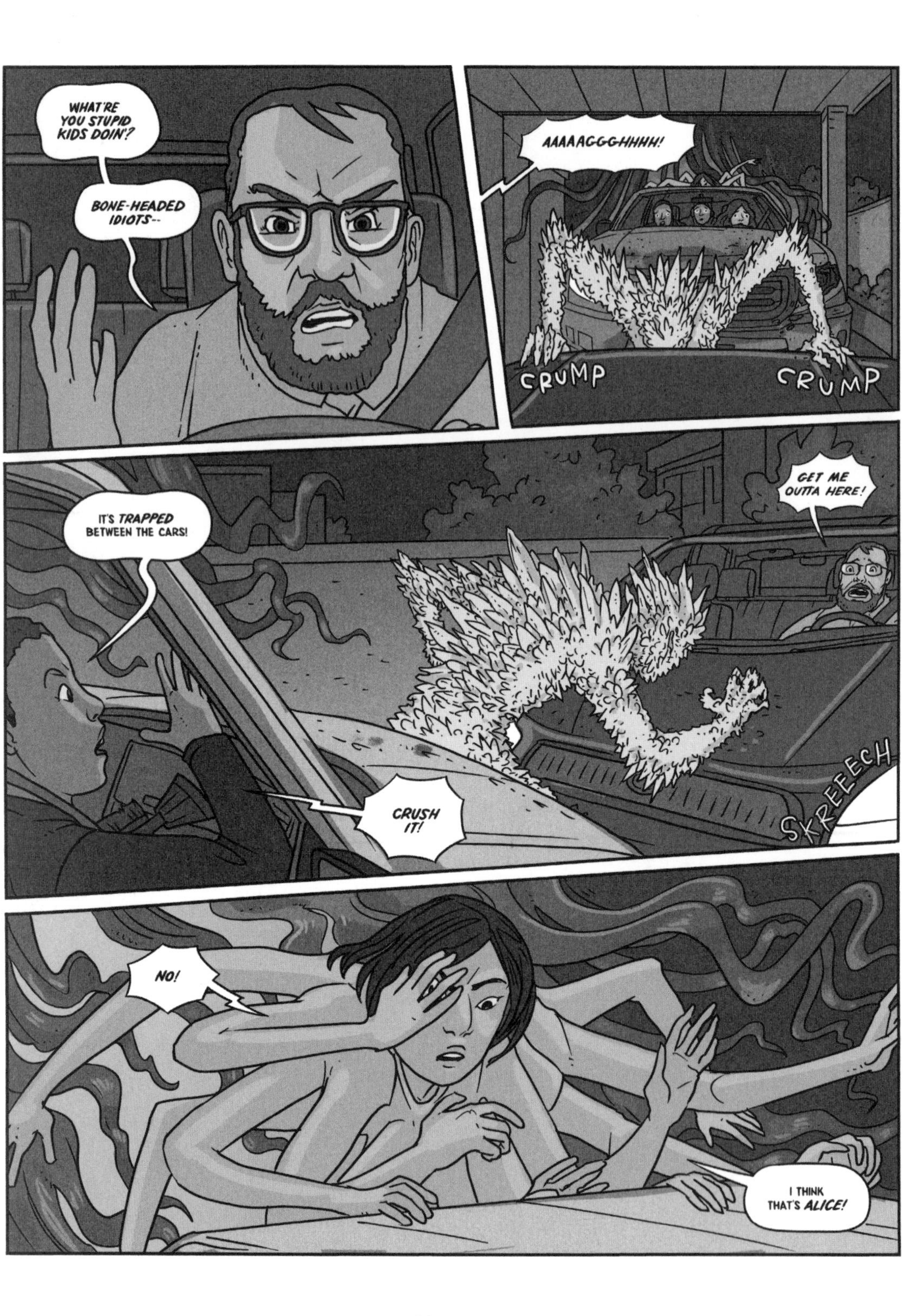

WHAT'RE YOU STUPID KIDS DOIN'?
BONE-HEADED IDIOTS--
AAAAAGGGHHHH!
CRUMP
CRUMP
IT'S TRAPPED BETWEEN THE CARS!
GET ME OUTTA HERE!
SKREEECH
CRUSH IT!
NO!
I THINK THAT'S ALICE!

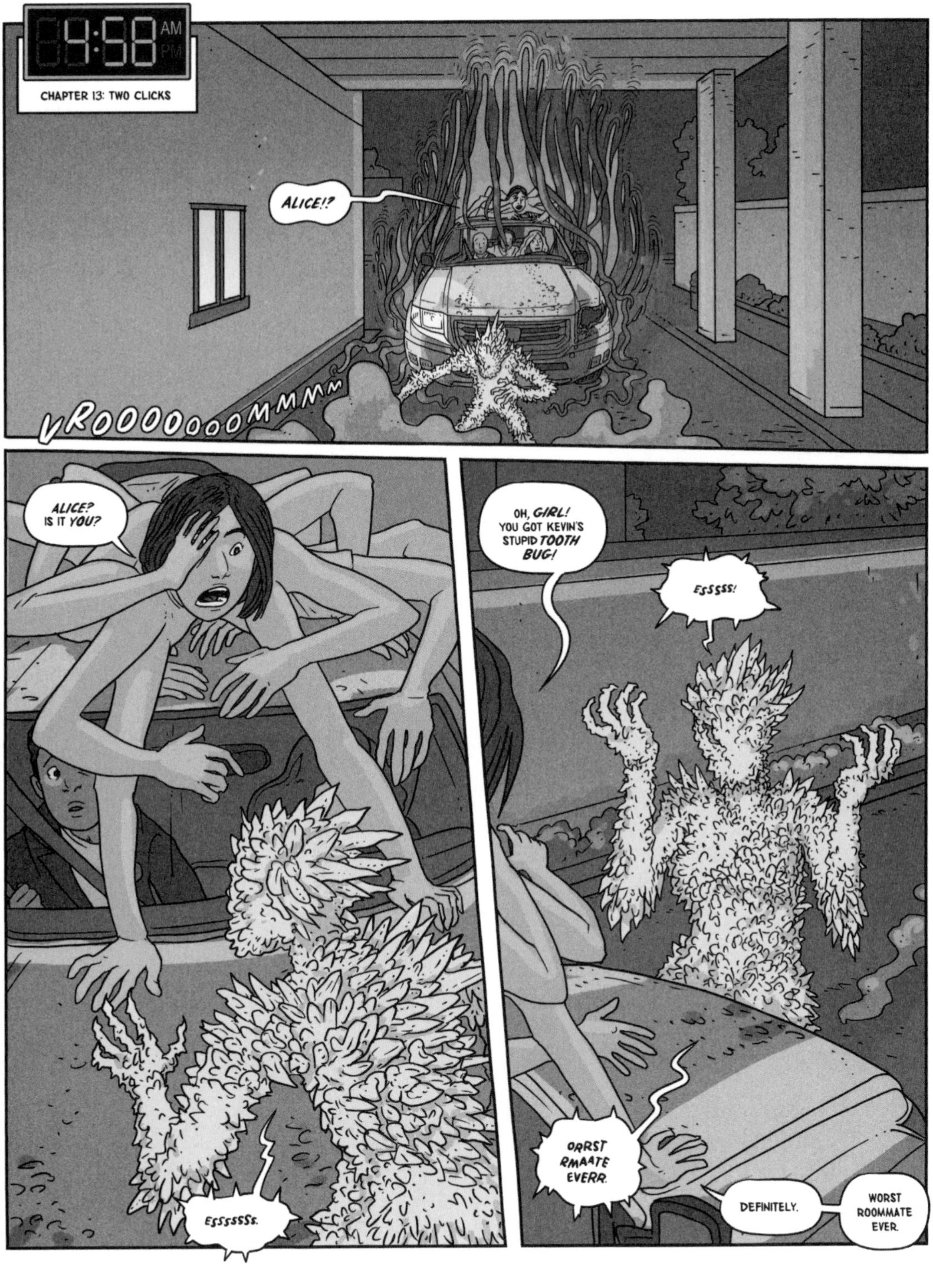
4:58 AM PM
CHAPTER 13: TWO CLICKS
ALICE!?
VROOOOOOOOMMMM
ALICE? IS IT YOU?
OH, GIRL! YOU GOT KEVIN'S STUPID TOOTH BUG!
ESSSSS!
ESSSSSSS.
ORRST RMAATE EVERR.
DEFINITELY.
WORST ROOMMATE EVER.

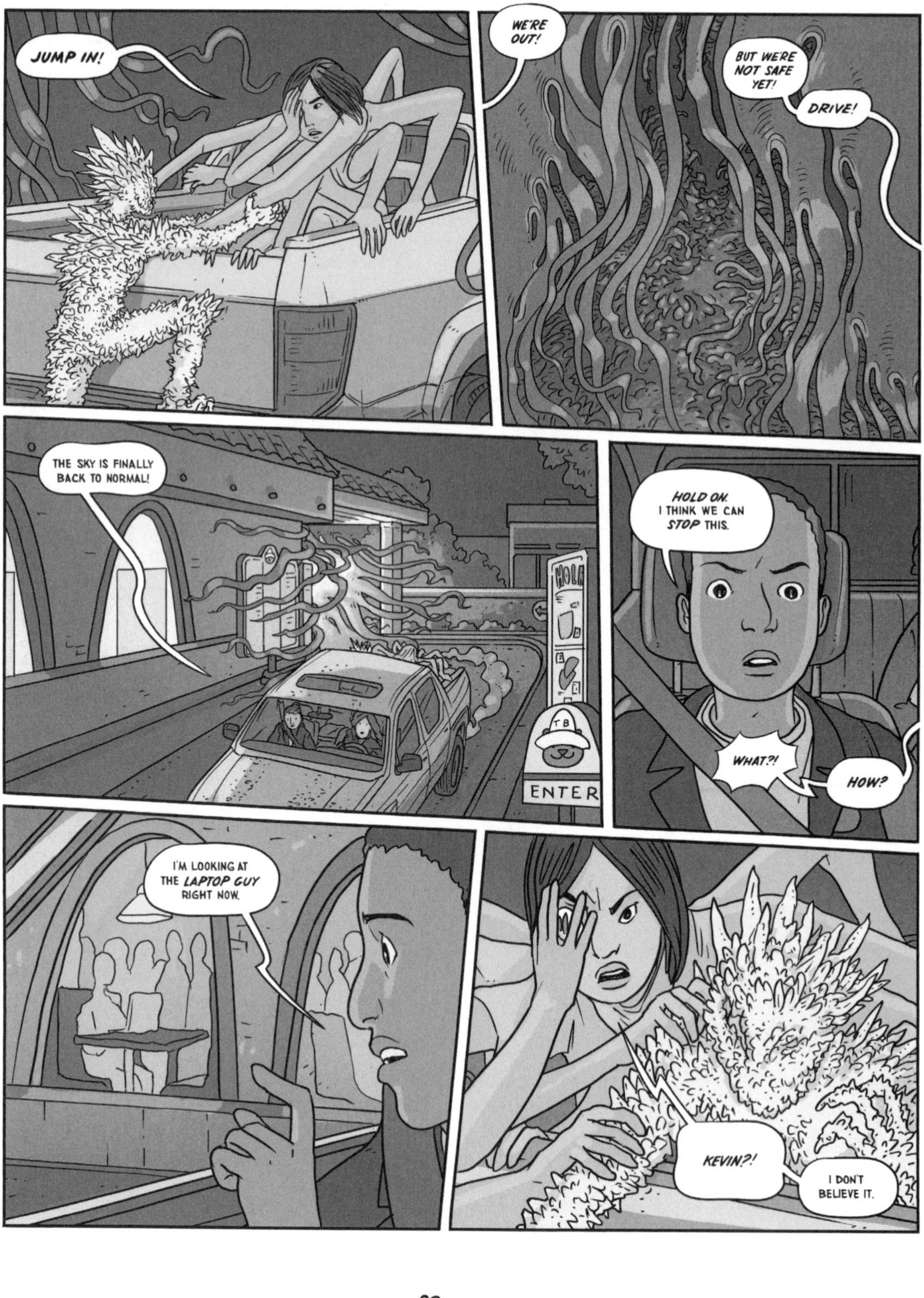
JUMP IN!
WE'RE OUT!
BUT WE'RE NOT SAFE YET!
DRIVE!
THE SKY IS FINALLY BACK TO NORMAL!
ENTER
HOLD ON. I THINK WE CAN STOP THIS.
WHAT?!
HOW?
I'M LOOKING AT THE LAPTOP GUY RIGHT NOW.
KEVIN?!
I DON'T BELIEVE IT.

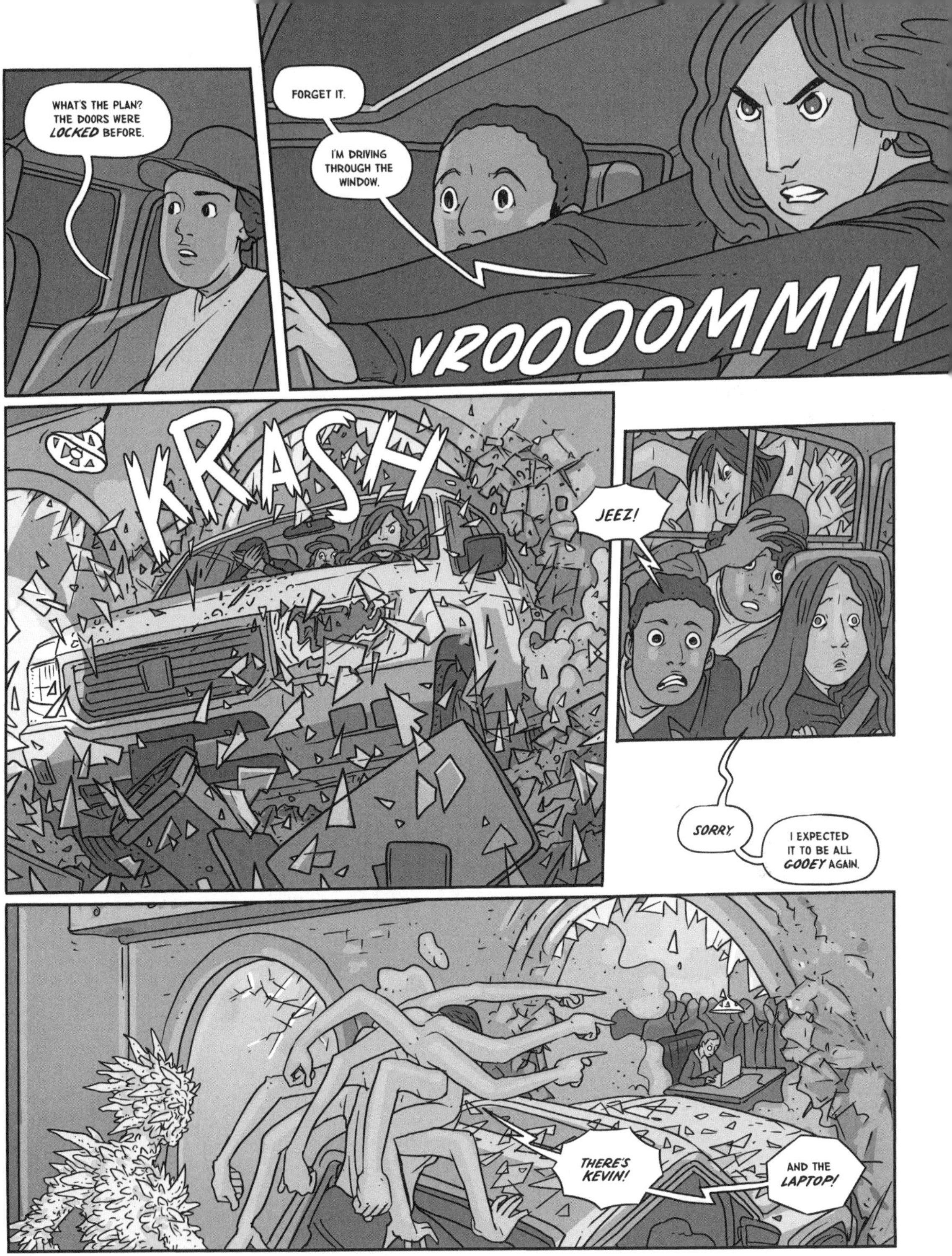
WHAT'S THE PLAN? THE DOORS WERE LOCKED BEFORE.
FORGET IT.
I'M DRIVING THROUGH THE WINDOW.
VROOOOMMM
KRASH
JEEZ!
SORRY.
I EXPECTED IT TO BE ALL GOOEY AGAIN.
THERE'S KEVIN!
AND THE LAPTOP!

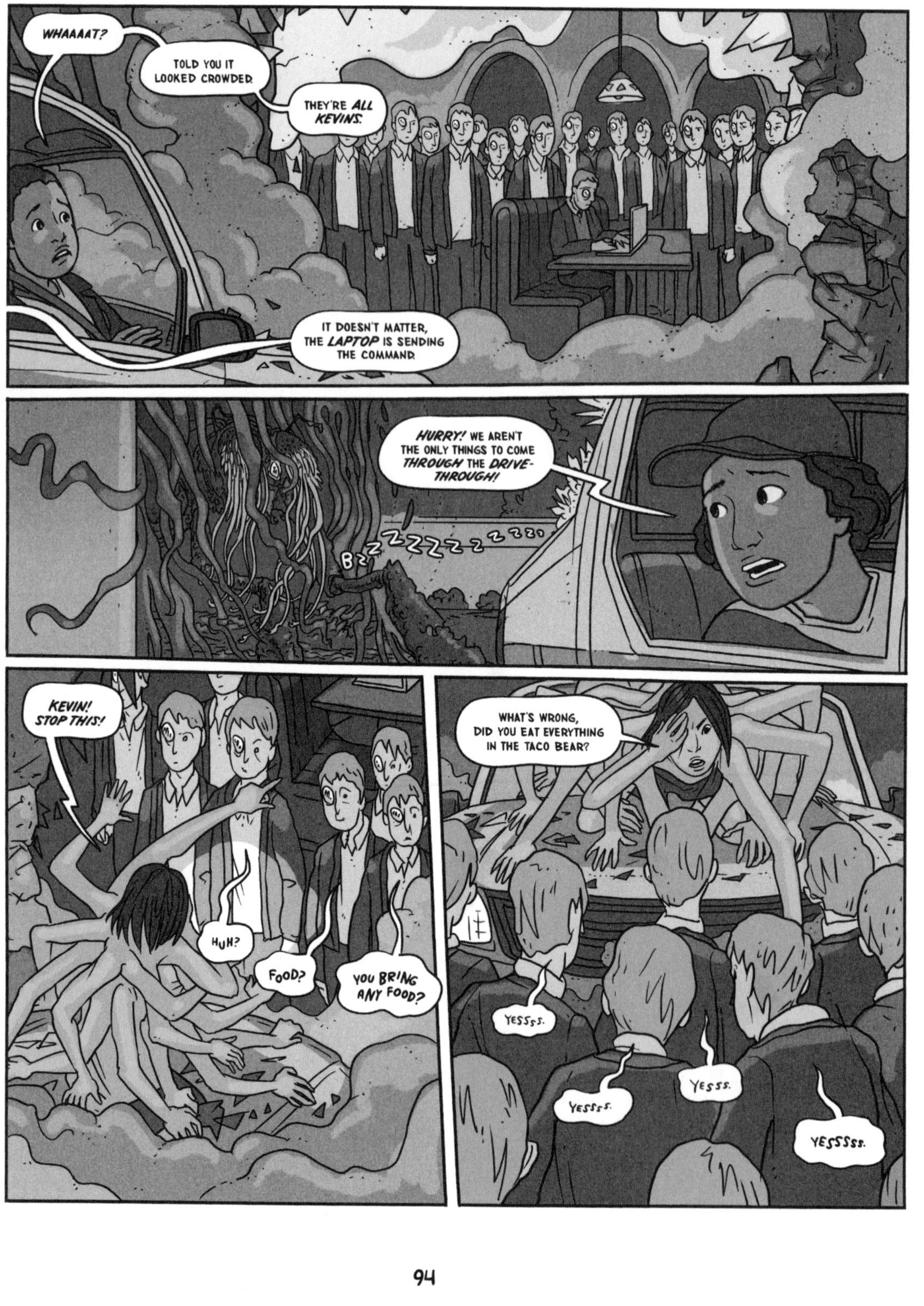
WHAAAAT?
TOLD YOU IT LOOKED CROWDED.
THEY'RE ALL KEVINS.
IT DOESN'T MATTER, THE LAPTOP IS SENDING THE COMMAND.
HURRY! WE AREN'T THE ONLY THINGS TO COME THROUGH THE DRIVE-THROUGH!
BZZZZZZZZZZZZ
KEVIN! STOP THIS!
HUH?
FOOD?
YOU BRING ANY FOOD?
WHAT'S WRONG, DID YOU EAT EVERYTHING IN THE TACO BEAR?
YESSss.
YESSss.
YESSS.
YESSSSss.

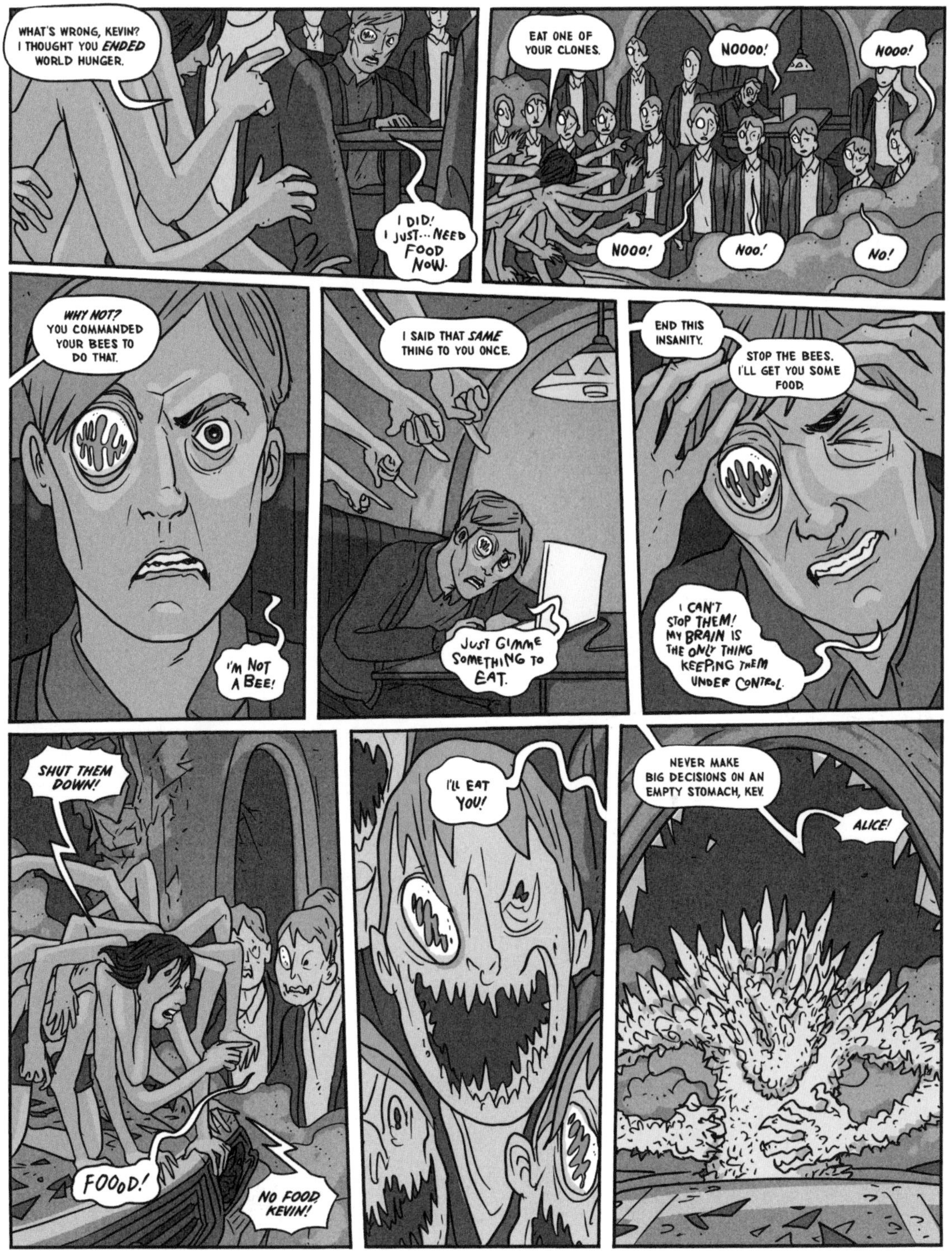
WHAT'S WRONG, KEVIN? I THOUGHT YOU ENDED WORLD HUNGER.
I DID! I JUST... NEED FOOD NOW.
EAT ONE OF YOUR CLONES.
NOOOO!
NOOO!
NOOO!
NOO!
NO!
WHY NOT? YOU COMMANDED YOUR BEES TO DO THAT.
I'M NOT A BEE!
I SAID THAT SAME THING TO YOU ONCE.
JUST GIMME SOMETHING TO EAT.
END THIS INSANITY.
STOP THE BEES. I'LL GET YOU SOME FOOD.
I CAN'T STOP THEM! MY BRAIN IS THE ONLY THING KEEPING THEM UNDER CONTROL.
SHUT THEM DOWN!
FOOOD!
NO FOOD, KEVIN!
I'LL EAT YOU!
NEVER MAKE BIG DECISIONS ON AN EMPTY STOMACH, KEV.
ALICE!

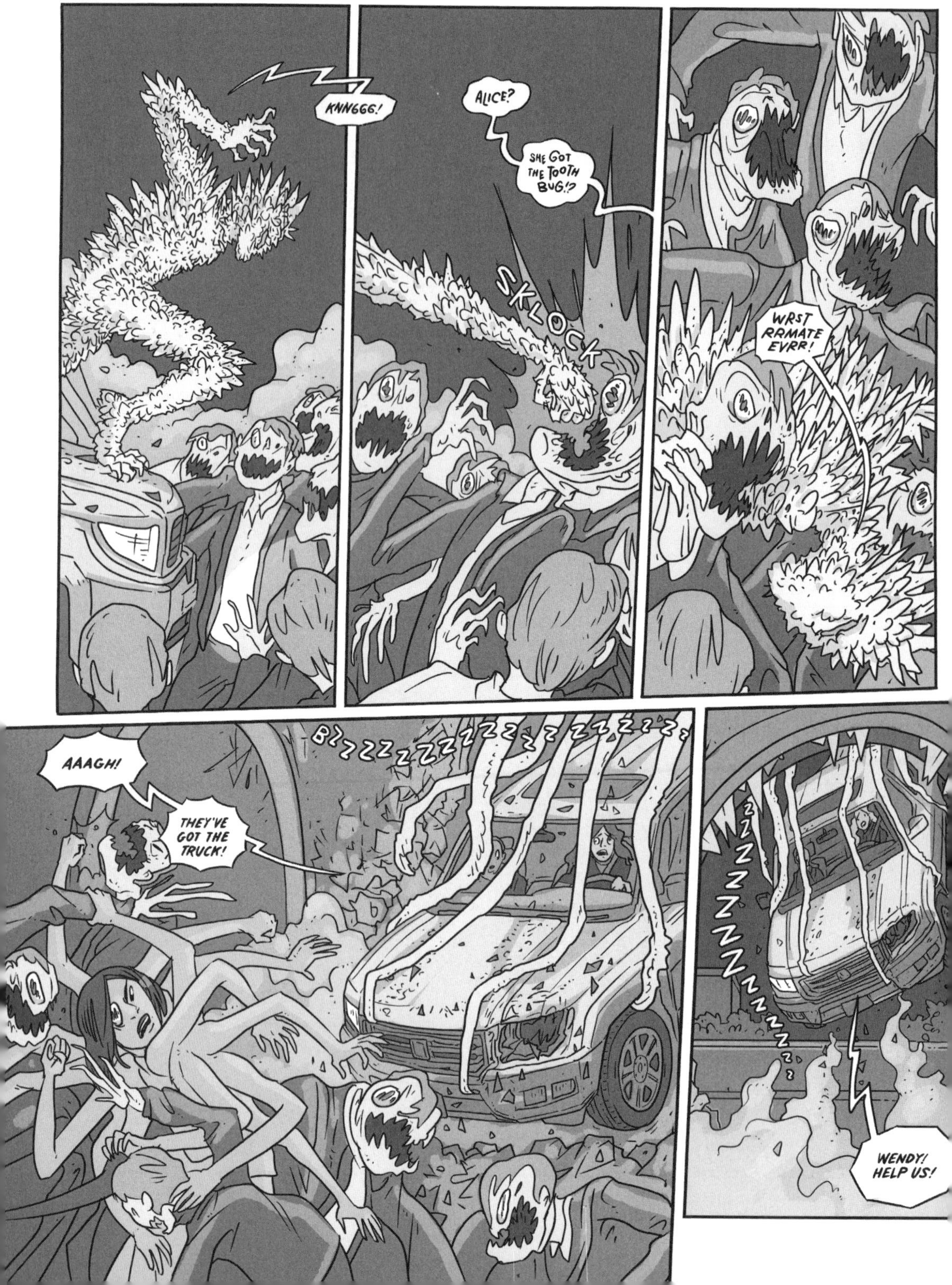
KNNGGG!
ALICE?
SHE GOT THE TOOTH BUG!?
SKLOCK
WRST RRMATE EVRR!
AAAGH!
THEY'VE GOT THE TRUCK!
BZZZZZZZZZZZZZZZZZZZ
ZZZZZZZZZZZZZ
WENDY! HELP US!

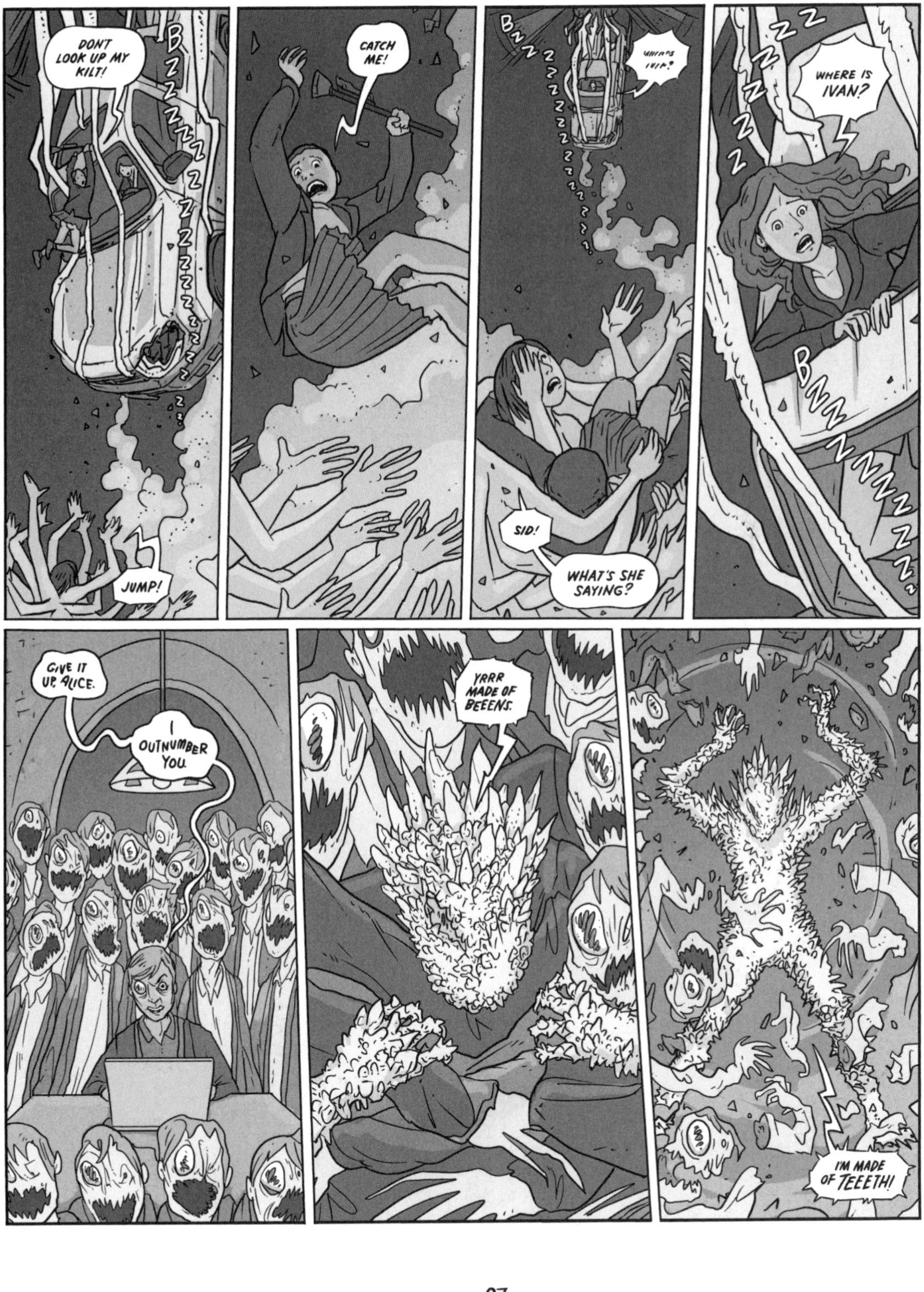
DON'T LOOK UP MY KILT!
JUMP!
CATCH ME!
SID!
WHAT'S SHE SAYING?
WHERE IS IVAN?
GIVE IT UP, ALICE.
I OUTNUMBER YOU.
YRRR MADE OF BEEENS.
I'M MADE OF TEEETH!

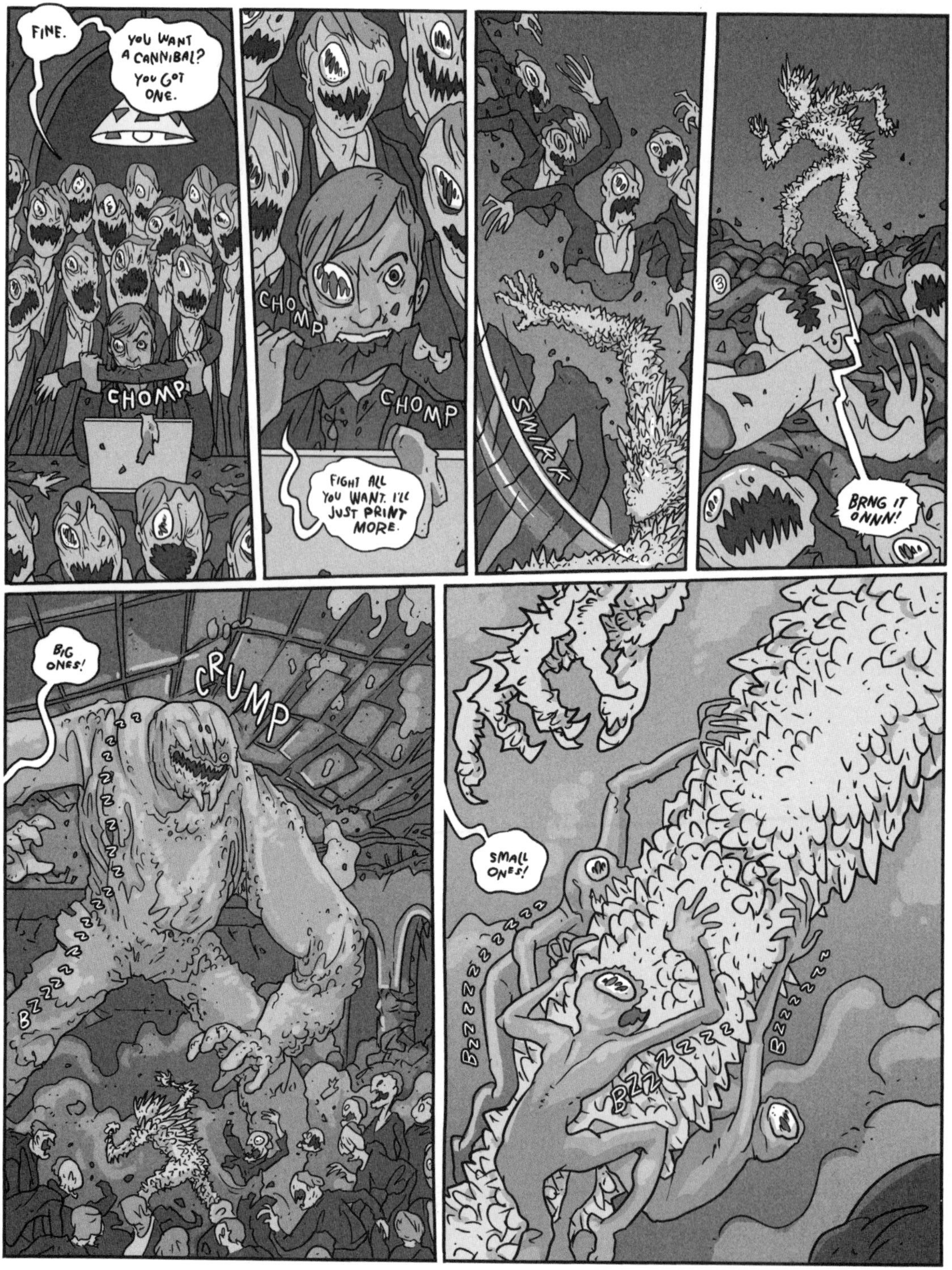
FINE.
YOU WANT A CANNIBAL? YOU GOT ONE.
CHOMP
CHOMP
CHOMP
FIGHT ALL YOU WANT. I'LL JUST PRINT MORE.
SWIKK
BRNG IT ONNN!
BIG ONES!
CRUMP
BZZZZ
SMALL ONES!
BZZZZ
BZZZ

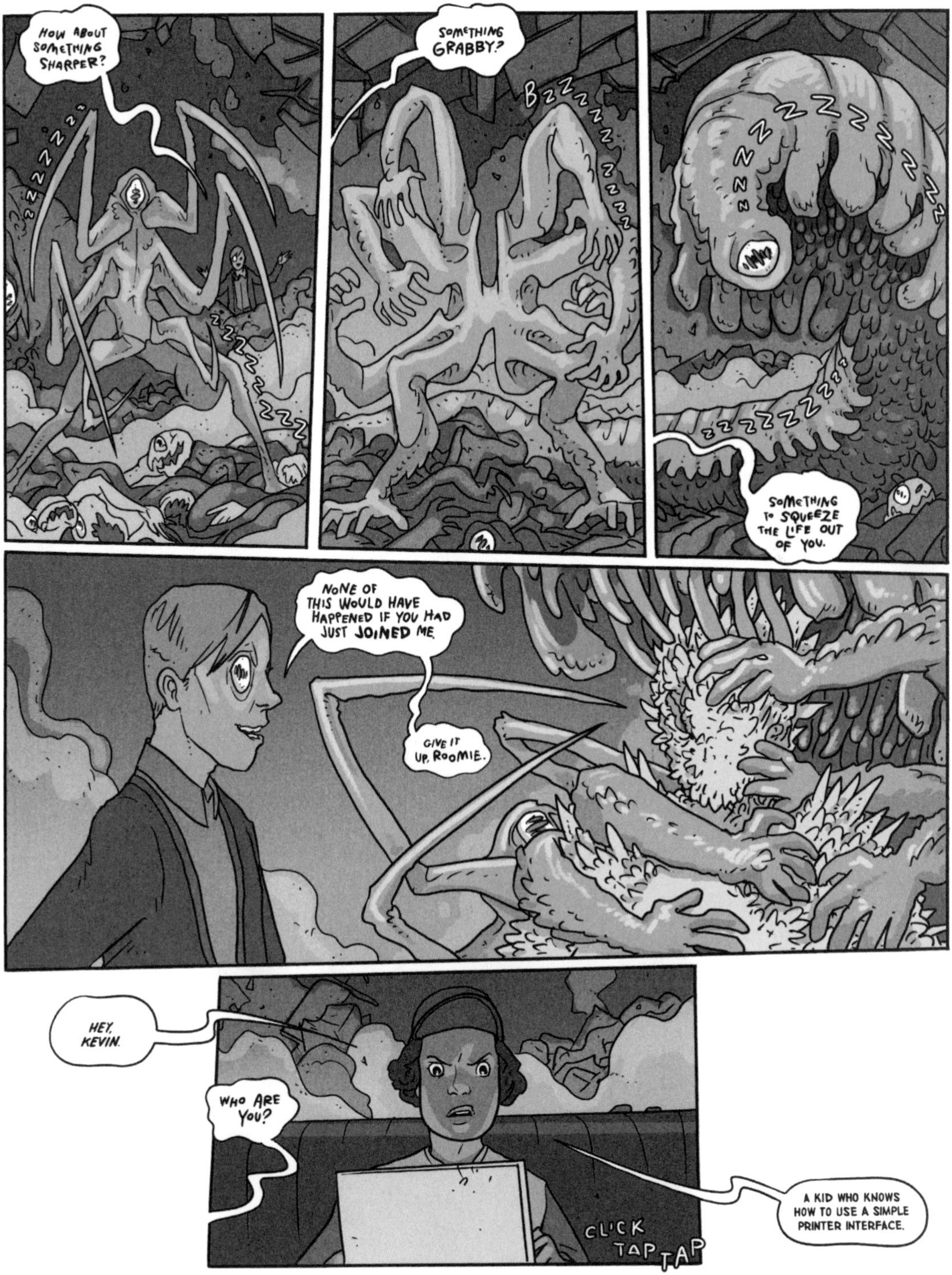
HOW ABOUT SOMETHING SHARPER?
ZZZZZZZ
ZZZZZZ
SOMETHING GRABBY?
BZZZZZZZZZ
ZZZZZZZZZ
SOMETHING TO SQUEEZE THE LIFE OUT OF YOU.
NONE OF THIS WOULD HAVE HAPPENED IF YOU HAD JUST JOINED ME.
GIVE IT UP, ROOMIE.
HEY, KEVIN.
WHO ARE YOU?
A KID WHO KNOWS HOW TO USE A SIMPLE PRINTER INTERFACE.
CLICK
TAP TAP

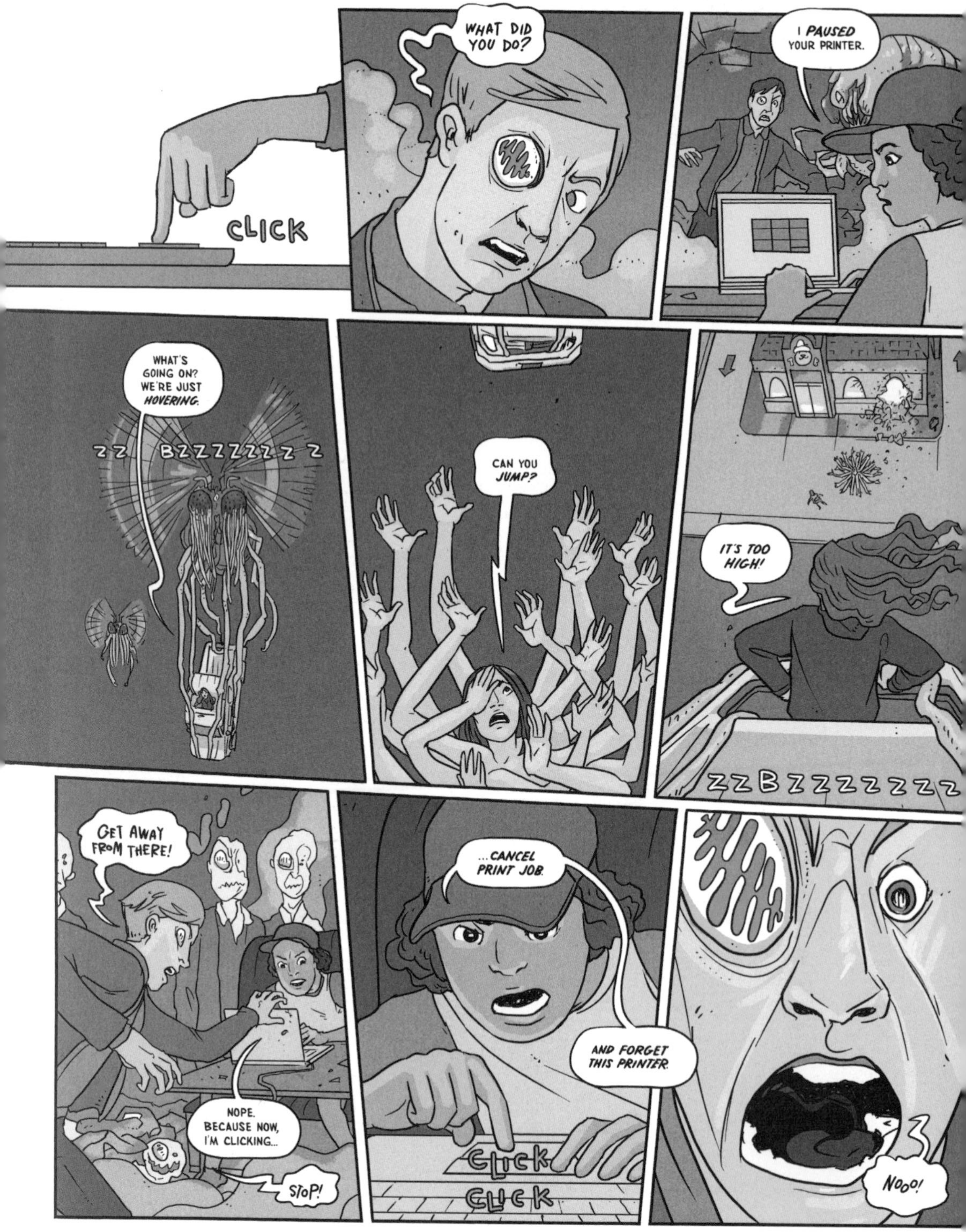
CLICK
WHAT DID YOU DO?
I PAUSED YOUR PRINTER.
WHAT'S GOING ON? WE'RE JUST HOVERING.
ZZ BZZZZZZZZ Z
CAN YOU JUMP?
IT'S TOO HIGH!
ZZBZZZZZZZZ
GET AWAY FROM THERE!
NOPE. BECAUSE NOW, I'M CLICKING...
STOP!
...CANCEL PRINT JOB.
AND FORGET THIS PRINTER.
CLICK
CLICK
NOOO!

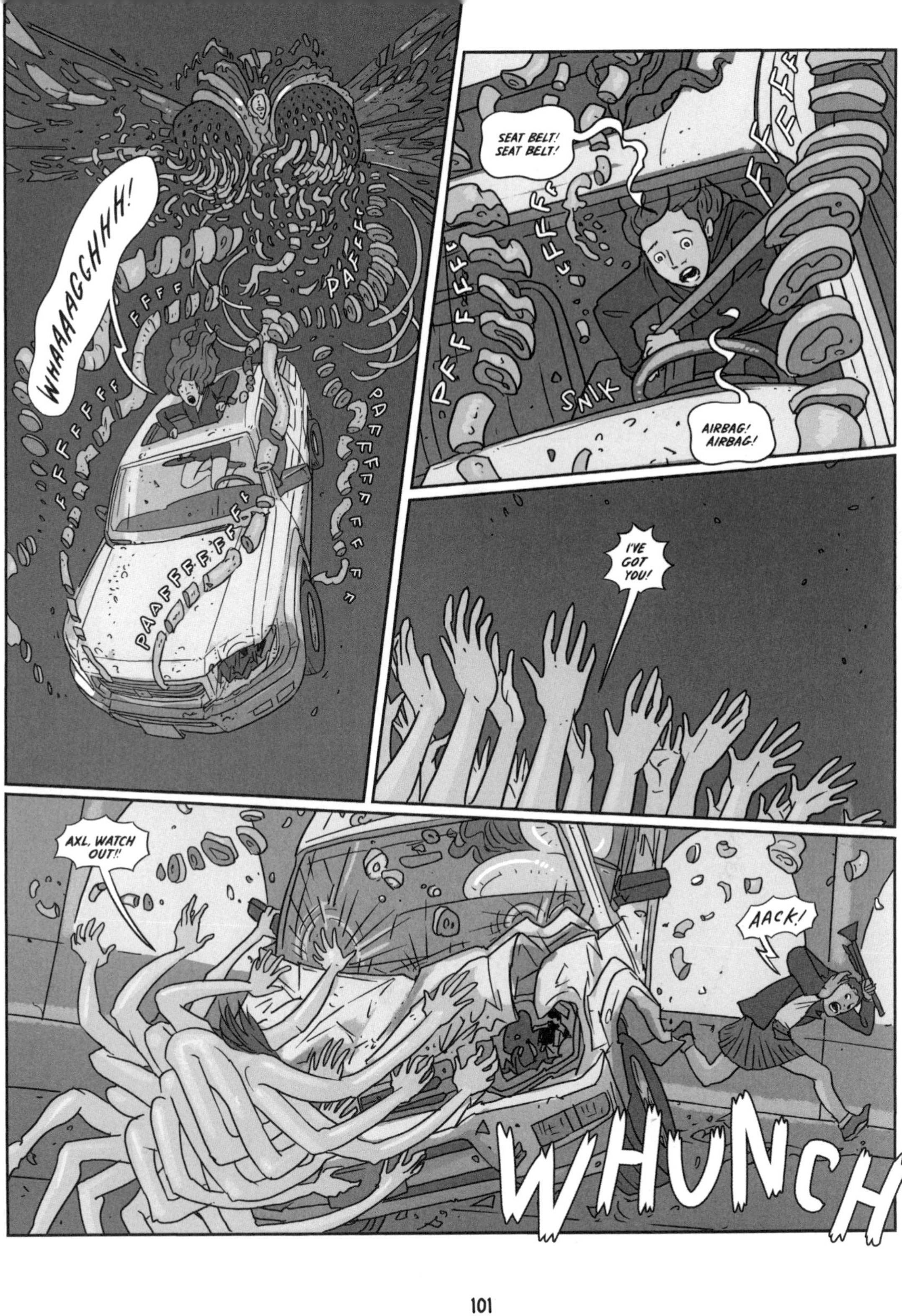
WHAAAAGGHHH!
FFFF
PAFFFF
PAFFFFFFFF
PAAFFFFFFFF
SEAT BELT! SEAT BELT!
PFFFFFF
SNIK
AIRBAG! AIRBAG!
I'VE GOT YOU!
AXL, WATCH OUT!!
AACK!
WHUNCH

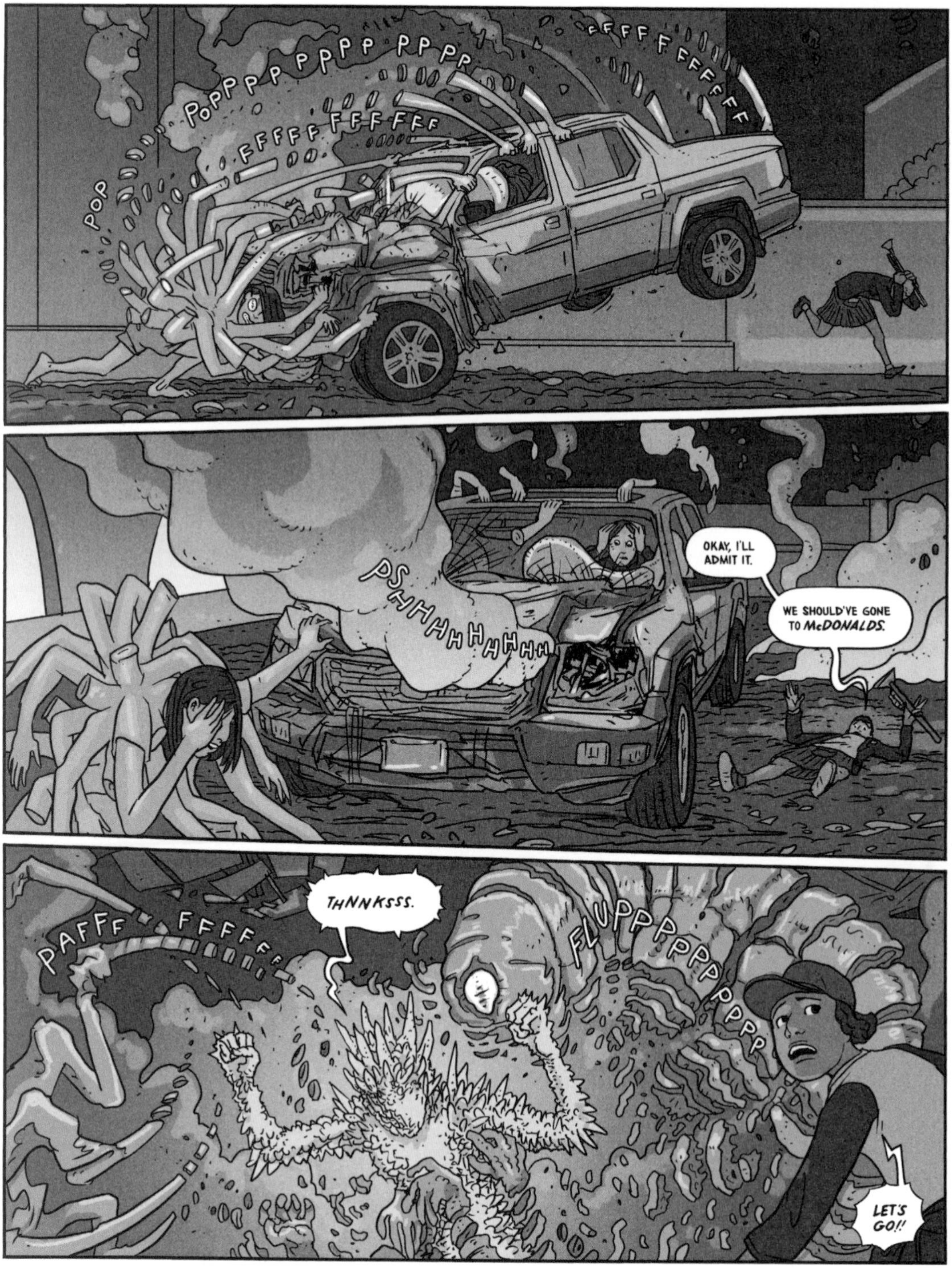
POP
POPPPPP PPPPP PPPP
FFFFF FFFFFFF
FFFFF FFFFFFF
PSHHHHHHHHHHH
OKAY, I'LL ADMIT IT.
WE SHOULD'VE GONE TO McDONALDS.
PAFFF FFFFFF
THNNKSSS.
FLUPPPPPPPPPPP
LET'S GO!!

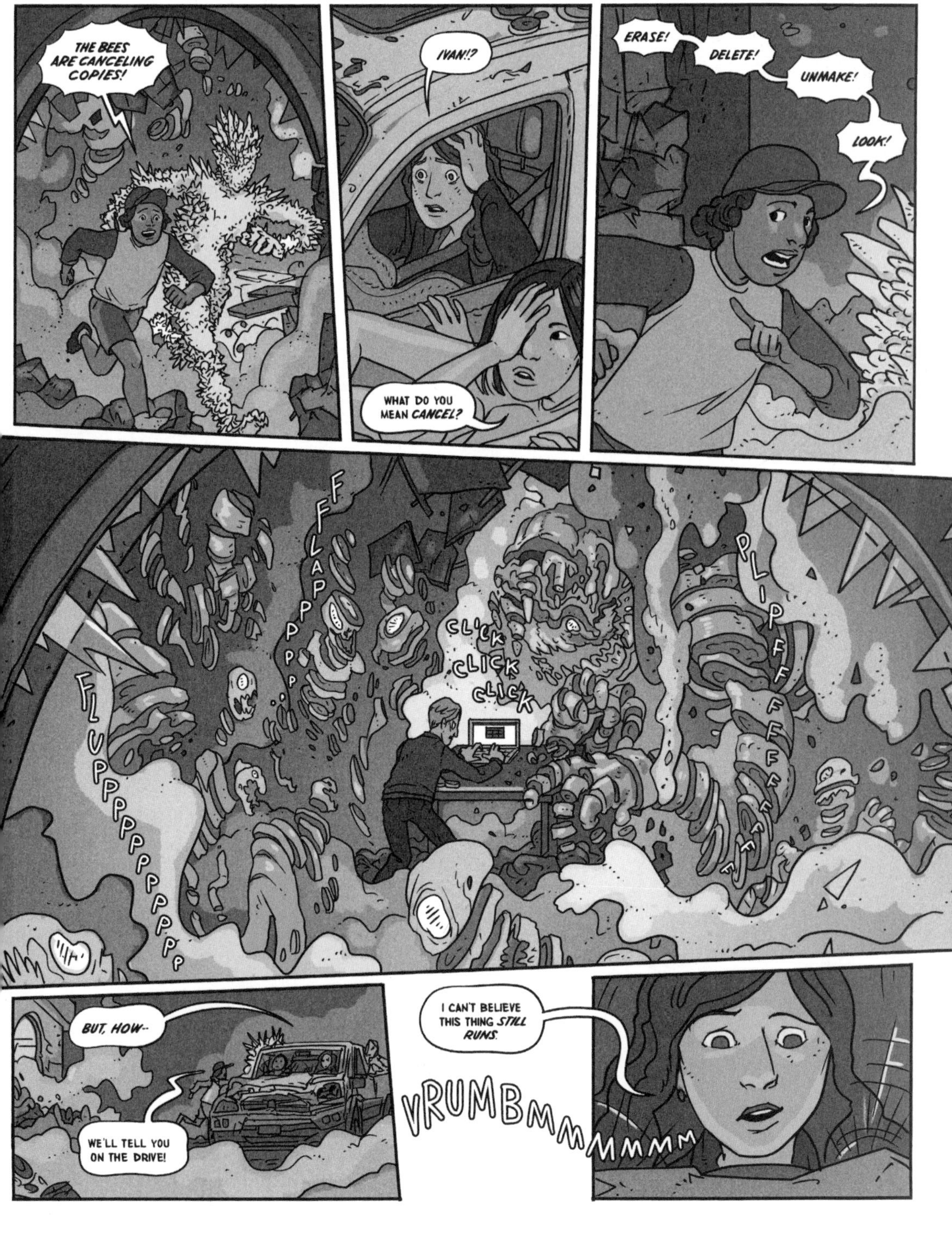
THE BEES ARE CANCELING COPIES!
IVAN!?
WHAT DO YOU MEAN CANCEL?
ERASE!
DELETE!
UNMAKE!
LOOK!
FFLAPPPPPP
CLICK CLICK CLICK
PLIPFFFFFFFFF
FLUPPPPPPPPPPPPP
BUT, HOW--
WE'LL TELL YOU ON THE DRIVE!
VRUMBMMMMMMM
I CAN'T BELIEVE THIS THING STILL RUNS.

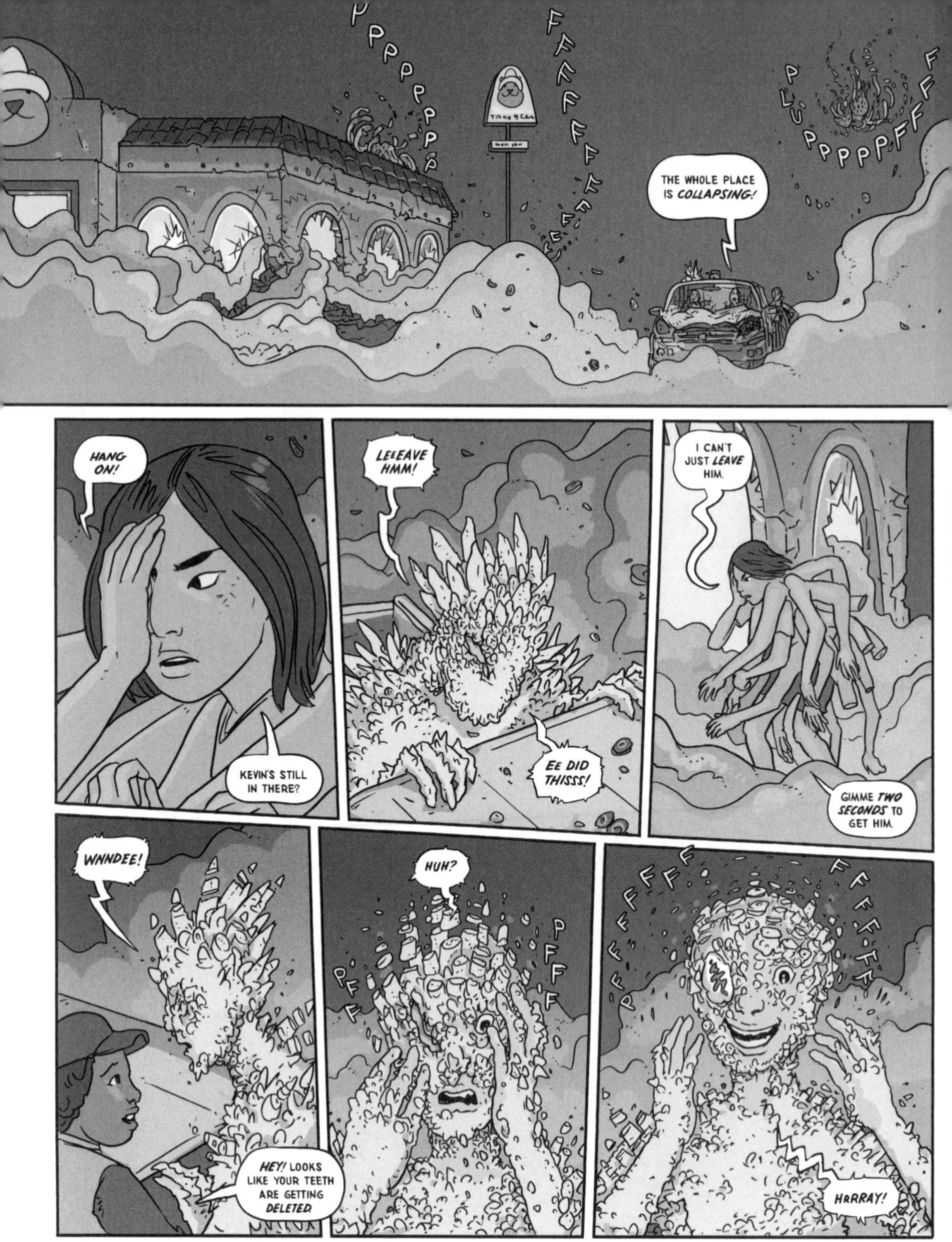
PPPPPPPP
FFFFFFFFFF
PLUPPPPPPFFFF
THE WHOLE PLACE IS COLLAPSING!
HANG ON!
KEVIN'S STILL IN THERE?
LE-LEAVE HMM!
EE DID THISSS!
I CAN'T JUST LEAVE HIM.
GIMME TWO SECONDS TO GET HIM.
WNNDEE!
HEY! LOOKS LIKE YOUR TEETH ARE GETTING DELETED.
HUH?
PFF
PFFFF
FFFFFF
FFFFF
HRRRAY!

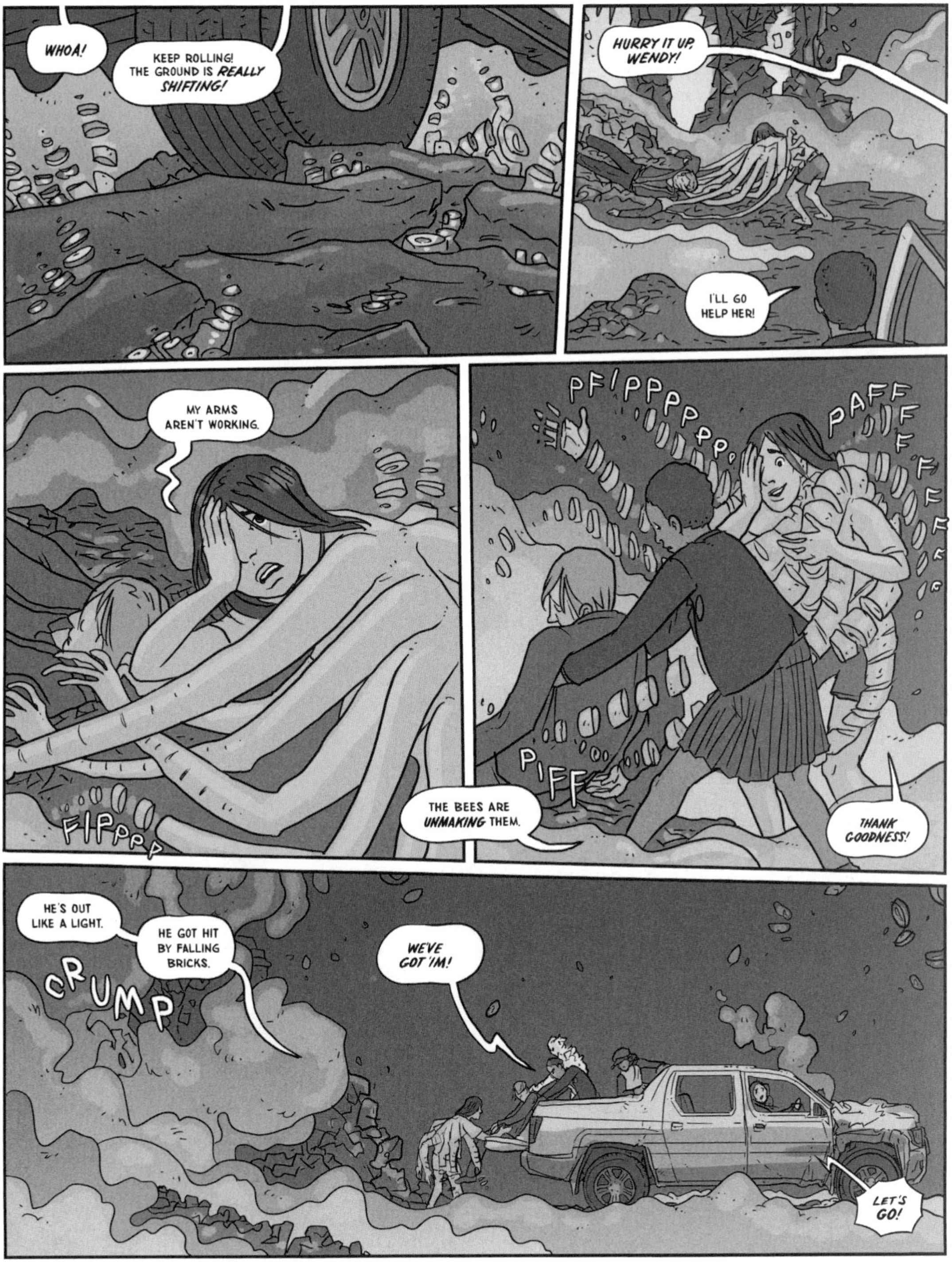
WHOA!
KEEP ROLLING! THE GROUND IS REALLY SHIFTING!
HURRY IT UP, WENDY!
I'LL GO HELP HER!
MY ARMS AREN'T WORKING.
FIPPPP
PF/PPPPPPP
PAFFFFFFF
PIFF
THE BEES ARE UNMAKING THEM.
THANK GOODNESS!
HE'S OUT LIKE A LIGHT.
HE GOT HIT BY FALLING BRICKS.
CRUMP
WE'VE GOT 'IM!
LET'S GO!

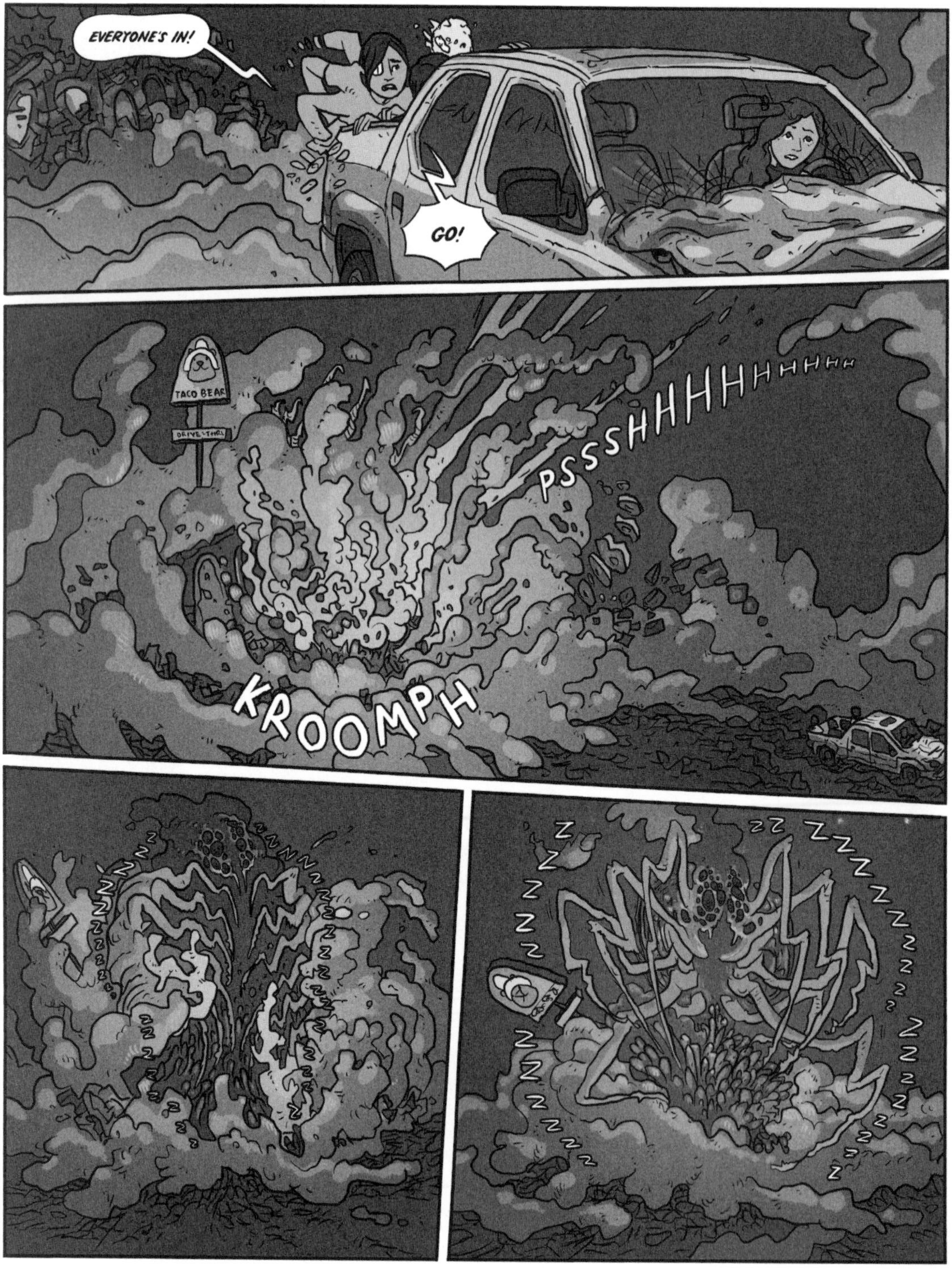
EVERYONE'S IN!
GO!
TACO BEAR
DRIVE-THRU
PSSSHHHHHHHHHH
KROOMPH
ZZZ
ZZZZZ

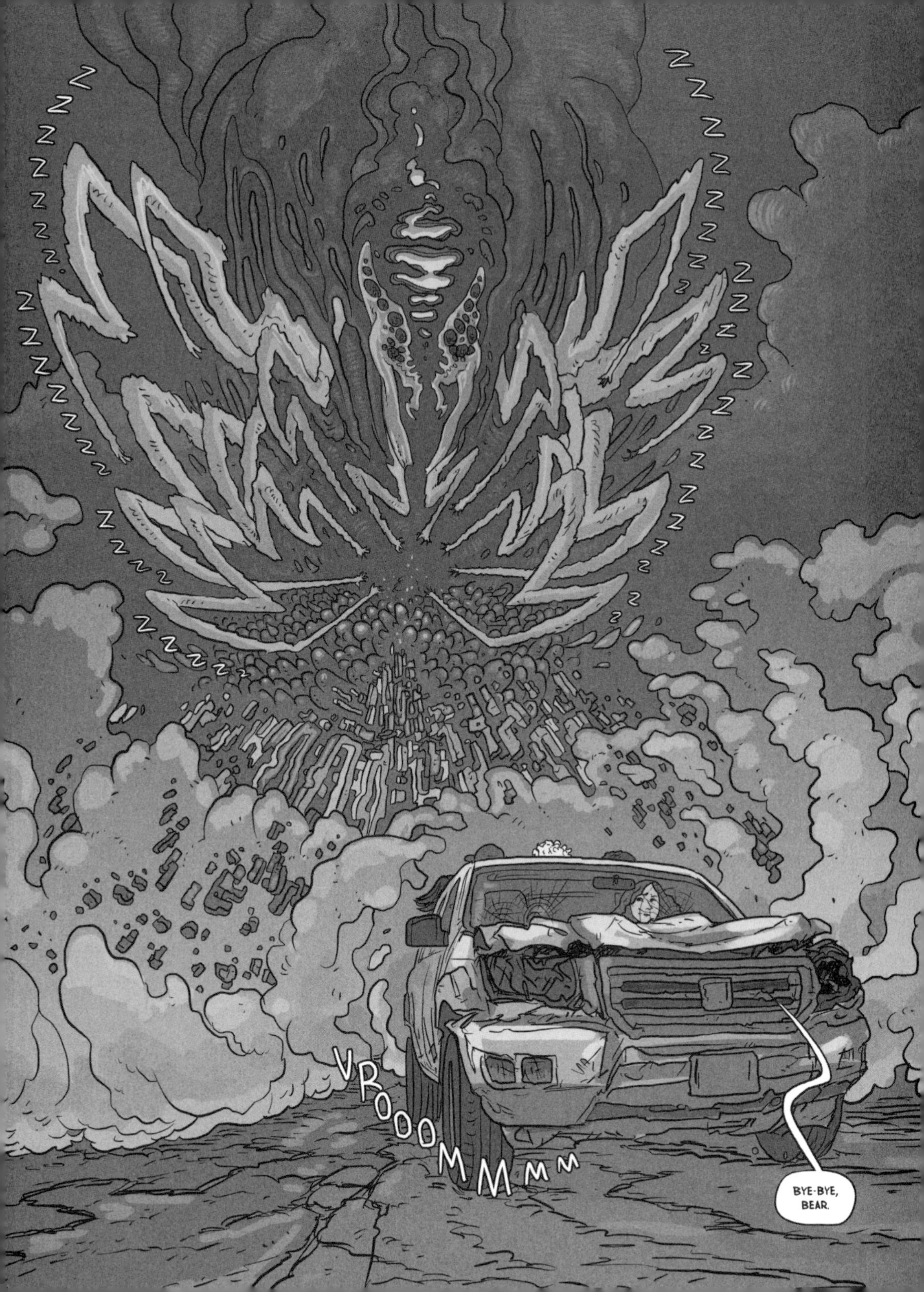

VROOOMMMMM
BYE-BYE, BEAR.

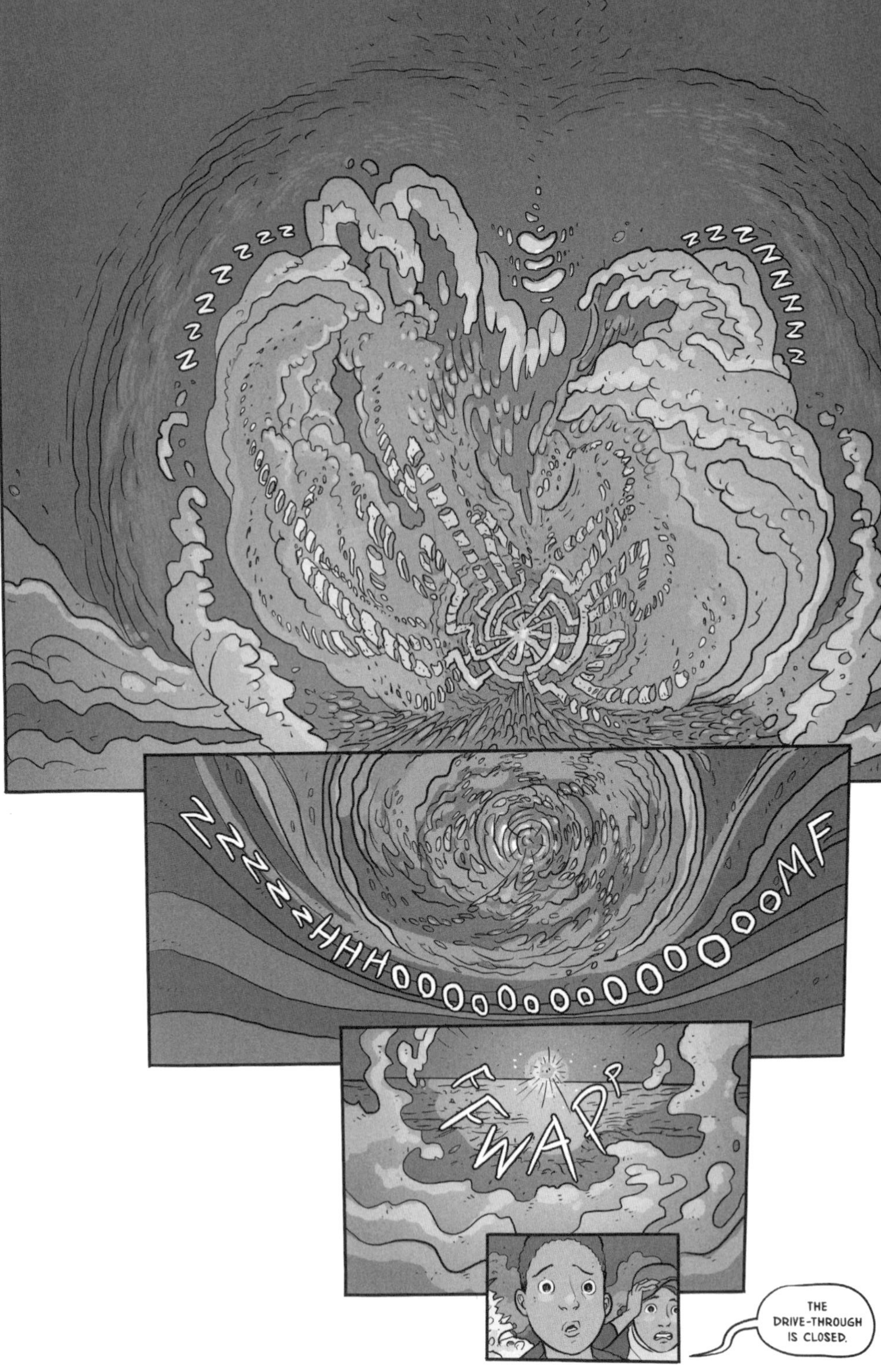
ZZZZZZZZZZ
ZZZZZZZZZZ
ZZZZZzHHHooOOoOooOoOOOOooMF
FWAPP
THE DRIVE-THROUGH IS CLOSED.

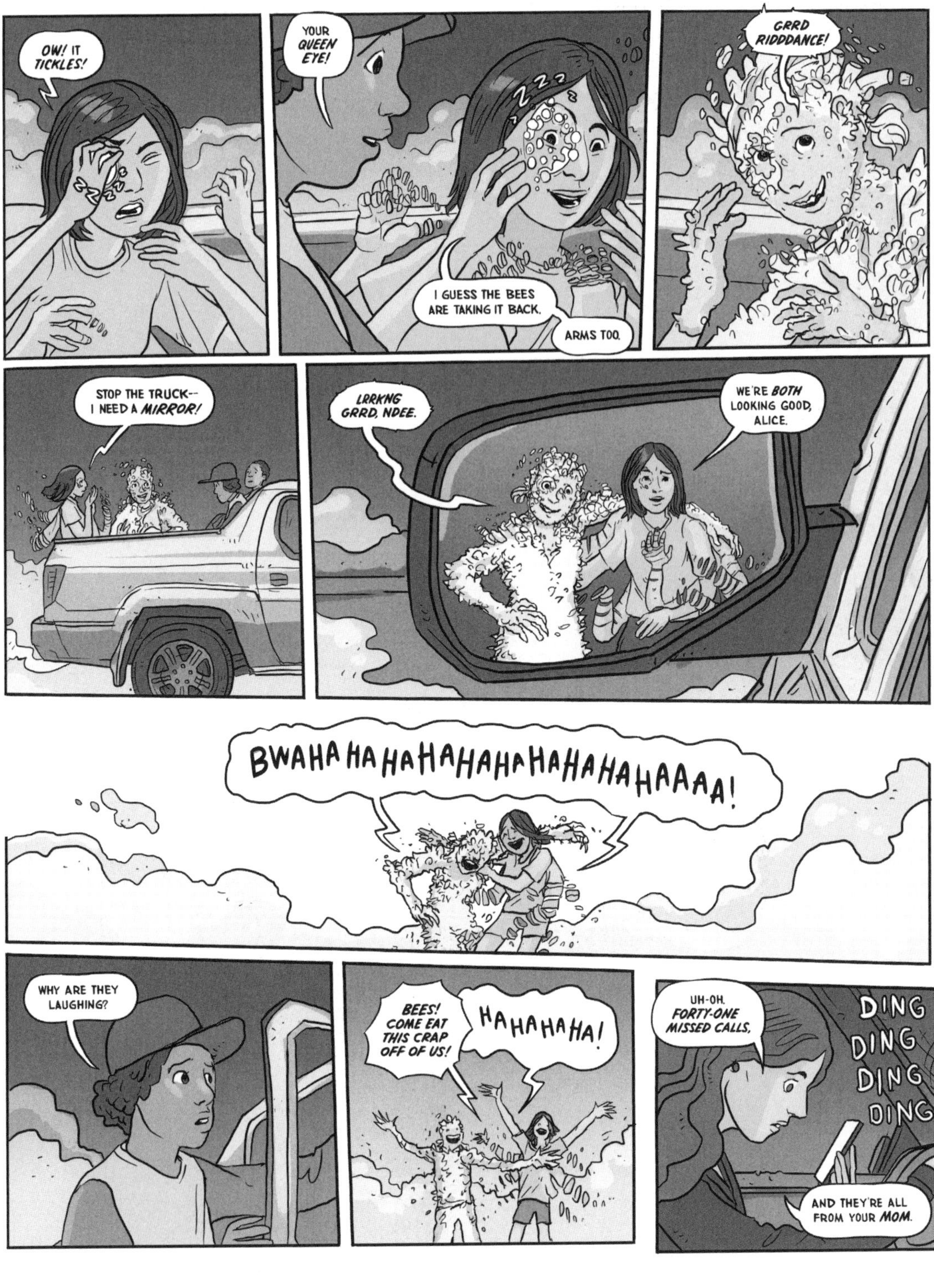
OW! IT TICKLES!
YOUR QUEEN EYE!
I GUESS THE BEES ARE TAKING IT BACK.
ARMS TOO.
GRRD RIDDDANCE!
STOP THE TRUCK-- I NEED A MIRROR!
LRRKNG GRRD, NDEE.
WE'RE BOTH LOOKING GOOD, ALICE.
BWAHAHAHAHAHAHAHAHAHAHAHAHAAAAA!
WHY ARE THEY LAUGHING?
BEES! COME EAT THIS CRAP OFF OF US!
HAHAHAHAHA!
UH-OH. FORTY-ONE MISSED CALLS.
DING DING DING DING
AND THEY'RE ALL FROM YOUR MOM.

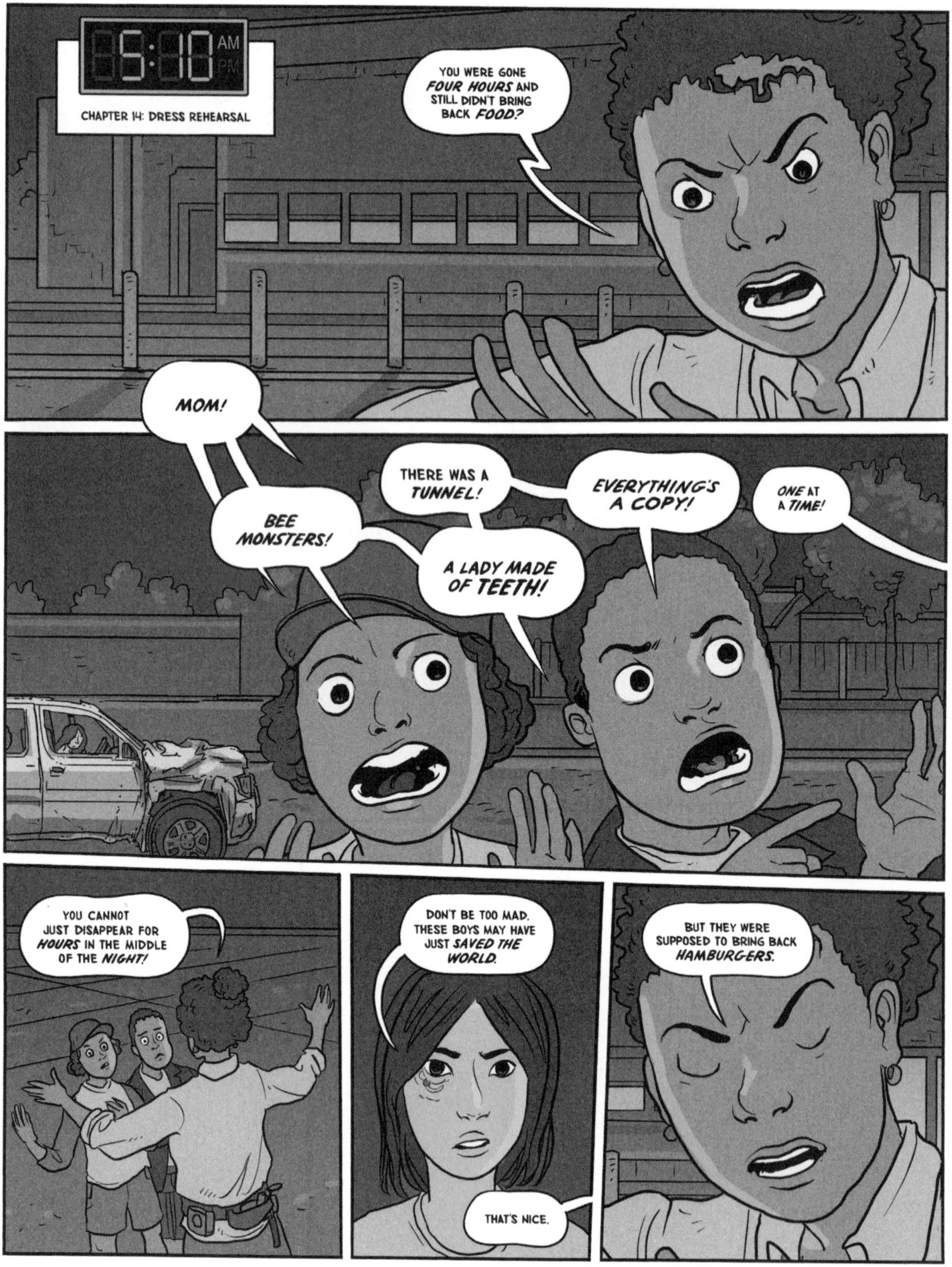

5:10 AM PM
CHAPTER 14: DRESS REHEARSAL
YOU WERE GONE FOUR HOURS AND STILL DIDN'T BRING BACK FOOD?
MOM!
BEE MONSTERS!
THERE WAS A TUNNEL!
A LADY MADE OF TEETH!
EVERYTHING'S A COPY!
ONE AT A TIME!
YOU CANNOT JUST DISAPPEAR FOR HOURS IN THE MIDDLE OF THE NIGHT!
DON'T BE TOO MAD. THESE BOYS MAY HAVE JUST SAVED THE WORLD.
THAT'S NICE.
BUT THEY WERE SUPPOSED TO BRING BACK HAMBURGERS.

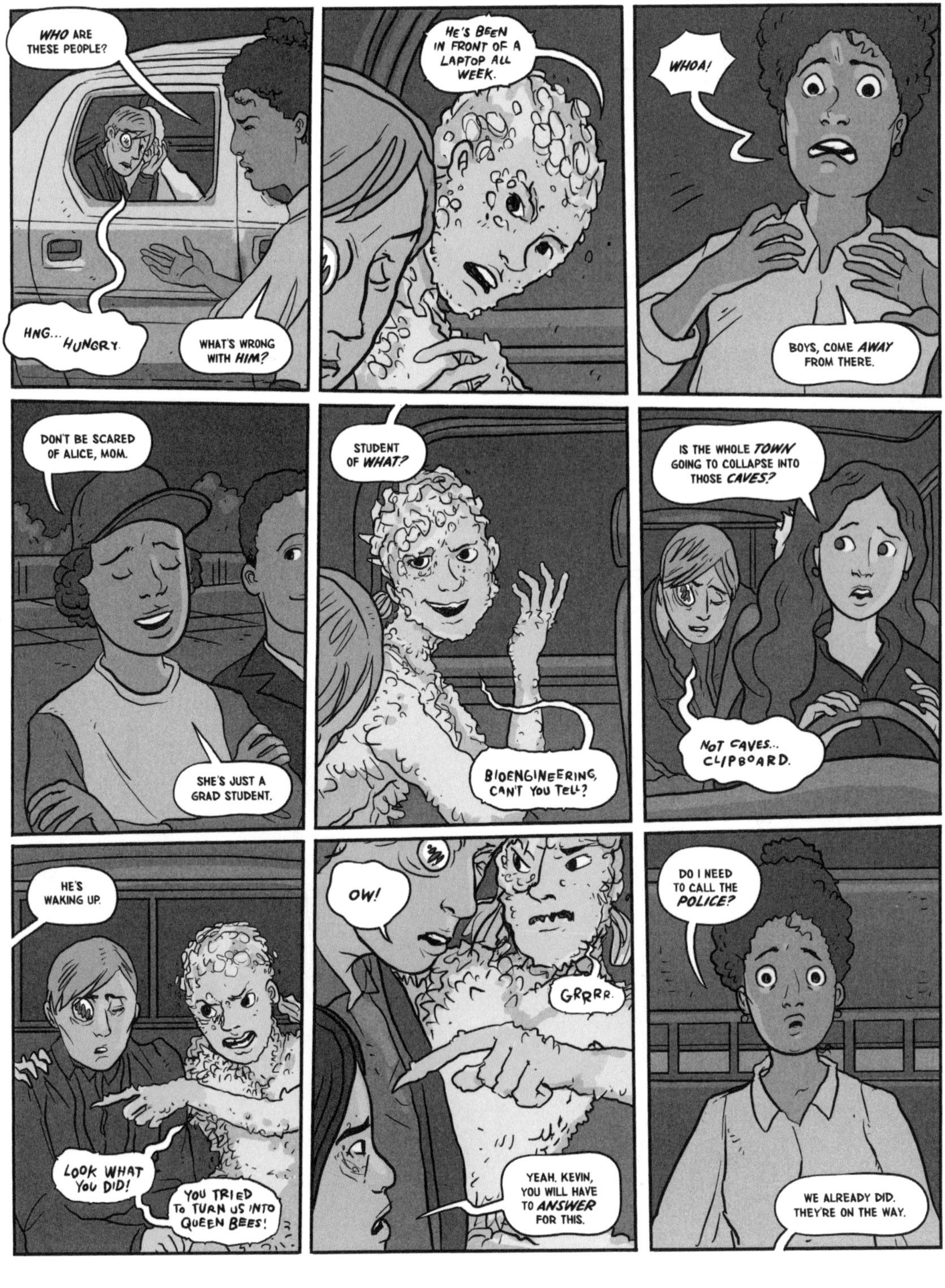
WHO ARE THESE PEOPLE?
HNG... HUNGRY.
WHAT'S WRONG WITH HIM?
HE'S BEEN IN FRONT OF A LAPTOP ALL WEEK.
WHOA!
BOYS, COME AWAY FROM THERE.
DON'T BE SCARED OF ALICE, MOM.
SHE'S JUST A GRAD STUDENT.
STUDENT OF WHAT?
BIOENGINEERING, CAN'T YOU TELL?
IS THE WHOLE TOWN GOING TO COLLAPSE INTO THOSE CAVES?
NOT CAVES... CLIPBOARD.
HE'S WAKING UP.
LOOK WHAT YOU DID!
YOU TRIED TO TURN US INTO QUEEN BEES!
OW!
GRRRR.
YEAH, KEVIN, YOU WILL HAVE TO ANSWER FOR THIS.
DO I NEED TO CALL THE POLICE?
WE ALREADY DID. THEY'RE ON THE WAY.

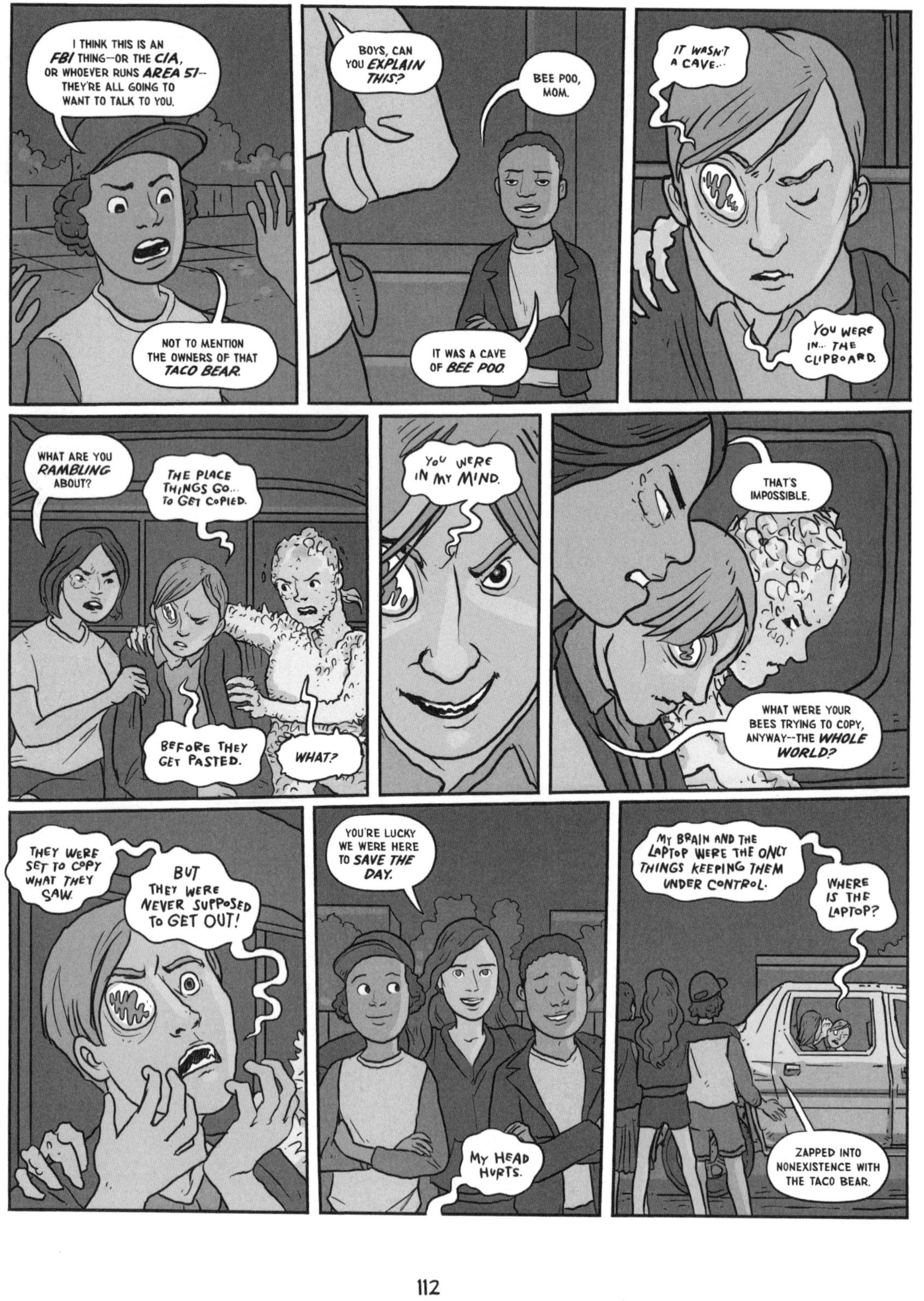
I THINK THIS IS AN FBI THING--OR THE CIA, OR WHOEVER RUNS AREA 51--THEY'RE ALL GOING TO WANT TO TALK TO YOU.
NOT TO MENTION THE OWNERS OF THAT TACO BEAR.
BOYS, CAN YOU EXPLAIN THIS?
BEE POO, MOM.
IT WAS A CAVE OF BEE POO.
IT WASN'T A CAVE...
YOU WERE IN... THE CLIPBOARD.
WHAT ARE YOU RAMBLING ABOUT?
THE PLACE THINGS GO... TO GET COPIED.
BEFORE THEY GET PASTED.
WHAT?
YOU WERE IN MY MIND.
THAT'S IMPOSSIBLE.
WHAT WERE YOUR BEES TRYING TO COPY, ANYWAY--THE WHOLE WORLD?
THEY WERE SET TO COPY WHAT THEY SAW.
BUT THEY WERE NEVER SUPPOSED TO GET OUT!
YOU'RE LUCKY WE WERE HERE TO SAVE THE DAY.
MY HEAD HURTS.
MY BRAIN AND THE LAPTOP WERE THE ONLY THINGS KEEPING THEM UNDER CONTROL.
WHERE IS THE LAPTOP?
ZAPPED INTO NONEXISTENCE WITH THE TACO BEAR.

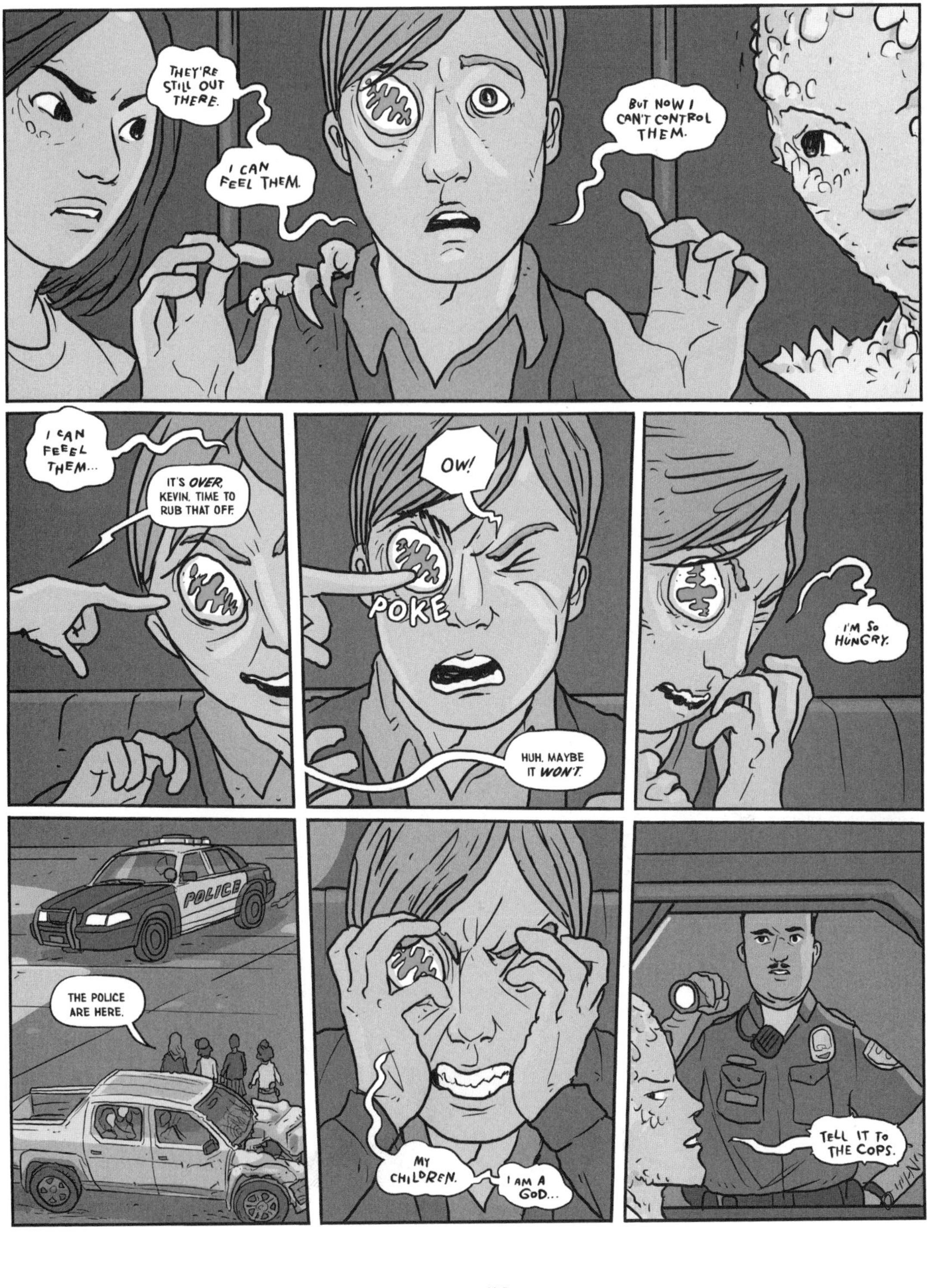
THEY'RE STILL OUT THERE.
I CAN FEEL THEM.
BUT NOW I CAN'T CONTROL THEM.
I CAN FEEEL THEM...
IT'S *OVER*, KEVIN. TIME TO RUB THAT OFF.
OW!
POKE
HUH. MAYBE IT *WON'T*.
I'M SO HUNGRY.
THE POLICE ARE HERE.
POLICE
MY CHILDREN.
I AM A GOD...
TELL IT TO THE COPS.

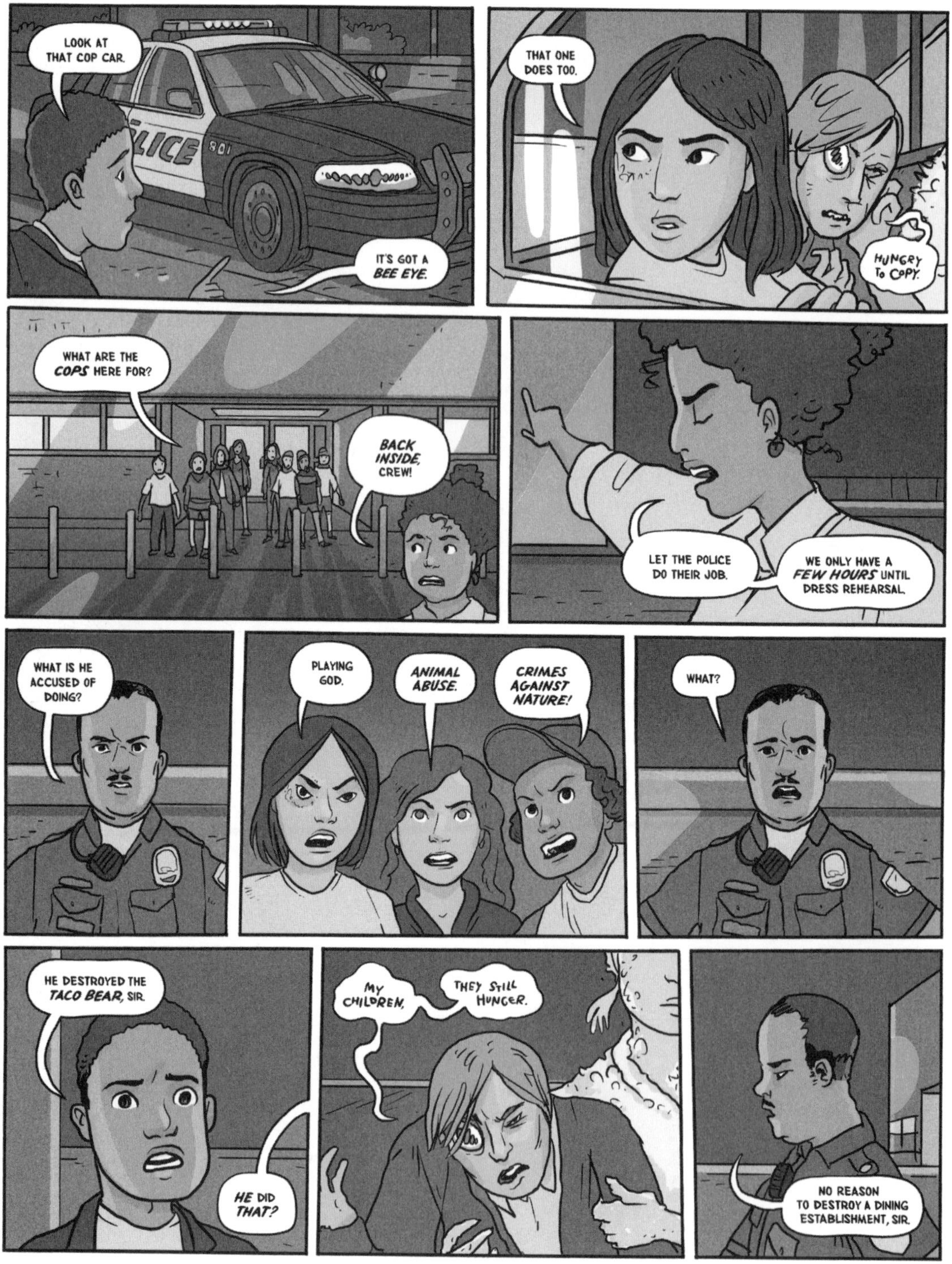
LOOK AT THAT COP CAR.
POLICE 801
IT'S GOT A BEE EYE.
THAT ONE DOES TOO.
HUNGRY TO COPY.
WHAT ARE THE COPS HERE FOR?
BACK INSIDE, CREW!
LET THE POLICE DO THEIR JOB.
WE ONLY HAVE A FEW HOURS UNTIL DRESS REHEARSAL.
WHAT IS HE ACCUSED OF DOING?
PLAYING GOD.
ANIMAL ABUSE.
CRIMES AGAINST NATURE!
WHAT?
HE DESTROYED THE TACO BEAR, SIR.
HE DID THAT?
MY CHILDREN,
THEY STILL HUNGER.
NO REASON TO DESTROY A DINING ESTABLISHMENT, SIR.

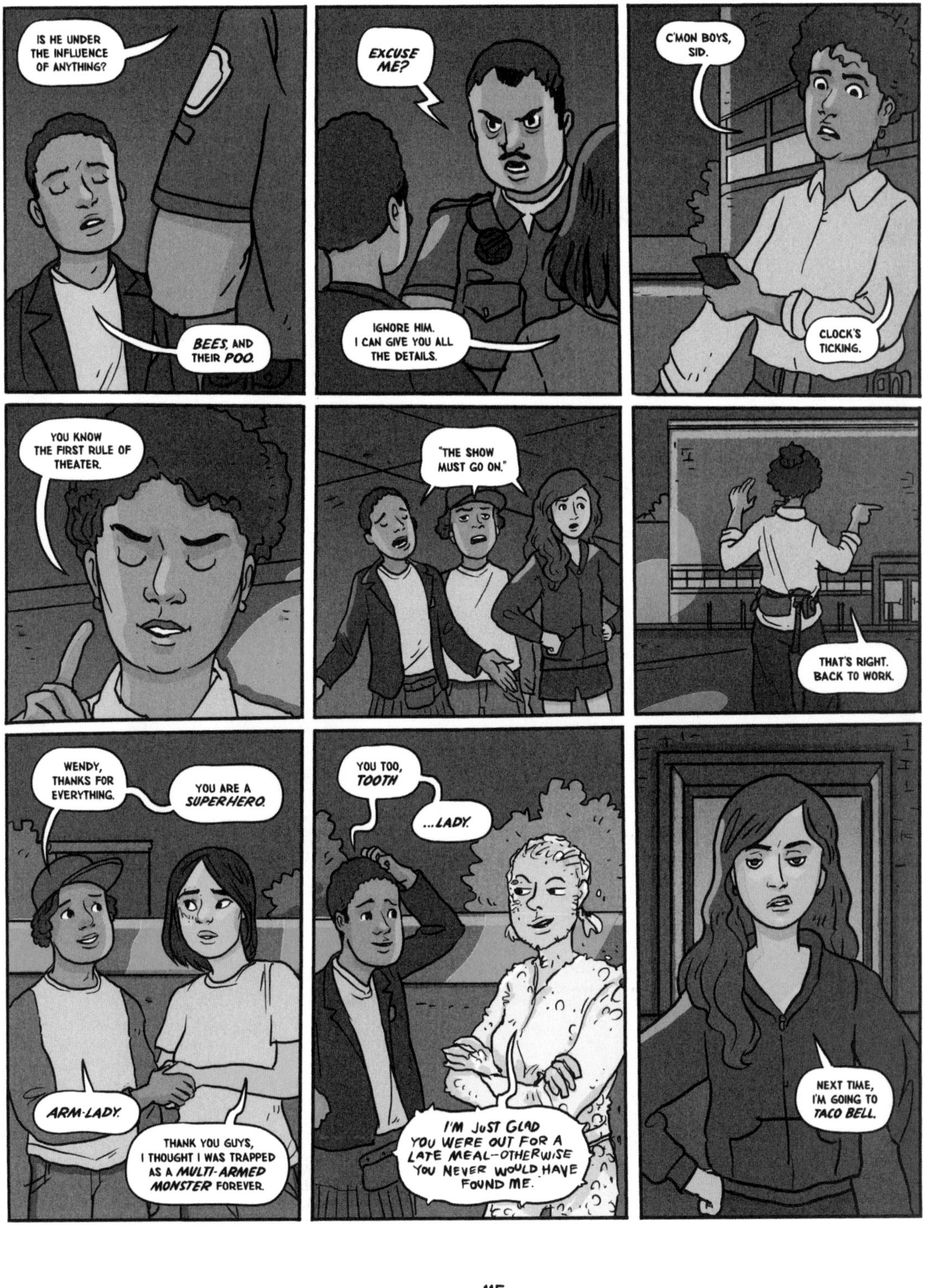
IS HE UNDER THE INFLUENCE OF ANYTHING?
BEES, AND THEIR POO.
EXCUSE ME?
IGNORE HIM. I CAN GIVE YOU ALL THE DETAILS.
C'MON BOYS, SID.
CLOCK'S TICKING.
YOU KNOW THE FIRST RULE OF THEATER.
"THE SHOW MUST GO ON."
THAT'S RIGHT. BACK TO WORK.
WENDY, THANKS FOR EVERYTHING.
YOU ARE A SUPERHERO.
ARM-LADY.
THANK YOU GUYS, I THOUGHT I WAS TRAPPED AS A MULTI-ARMED MONSTER FOREVER.
YOU TOO, TOOTH
...LADY.
I'M JUST GLAD YOU WERE OUT FOR A LATE MEAL--OTHERWISE YOU NEVER WOULD HAVE FOUND ME.
NEXT TIME, I'M GOING TO TACO BELL.

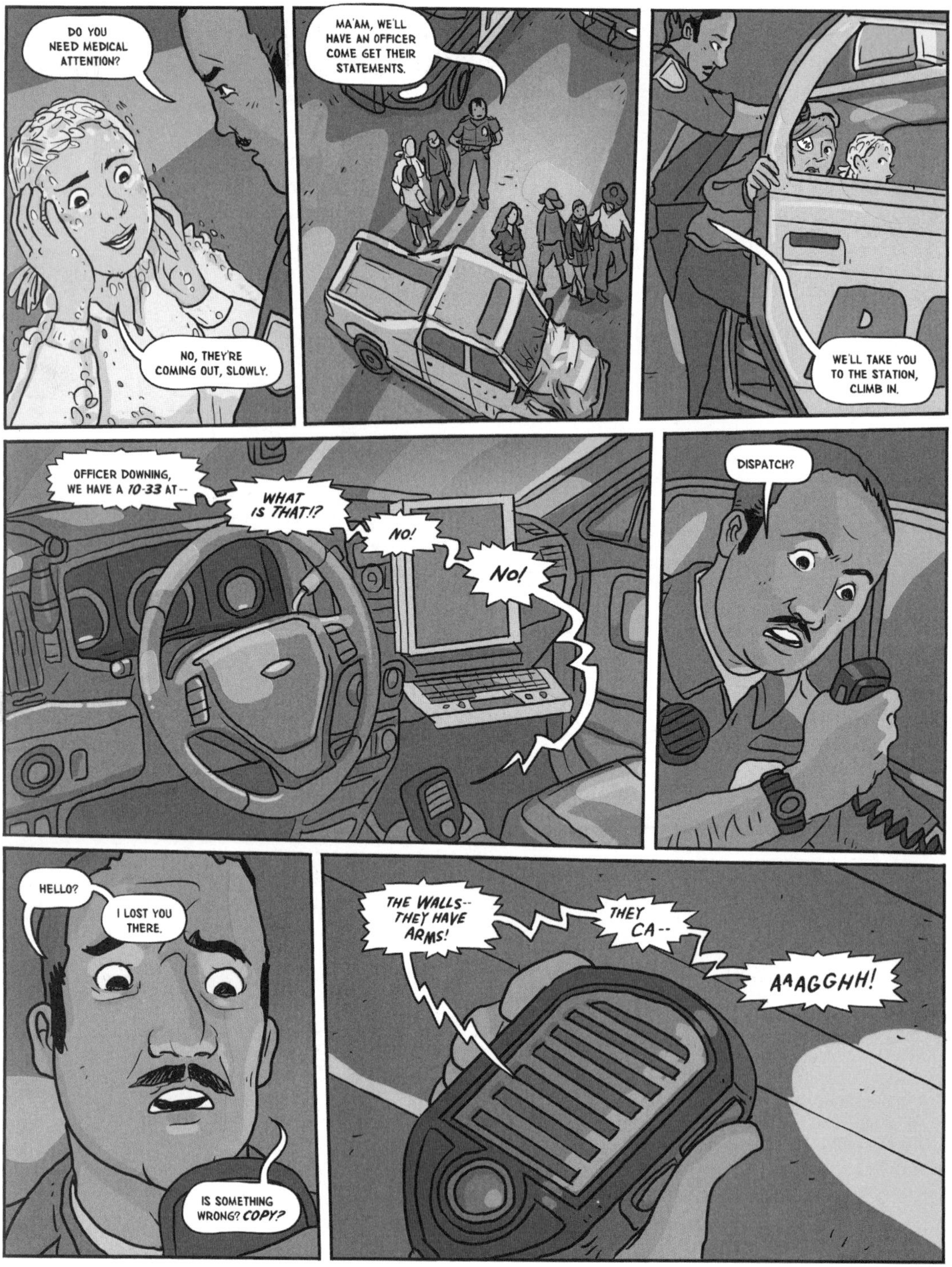
DO YOU NEED MEDICAL ATTENTION?
NO, THEY'RE COMING OUT, SLOWLY.
MA'AM, WE'LL HAVE AN OFFICER COME GET THEIR STATEMENTS.
WE'LL TAKE YOU TO THE STATION, CLIMB IN.
OFFICER DOWNING, WE HAVE A 10-33 AT--
WHAT IS THAT!?
NO!
NO!
DISPATCH?
HELLO?
I LOST YOU THERE.
IS SOMETHING WRONG? COPY?
THE WALLS-- THEY HAVE ARMS!
THEY CA--
AAAGGHH!

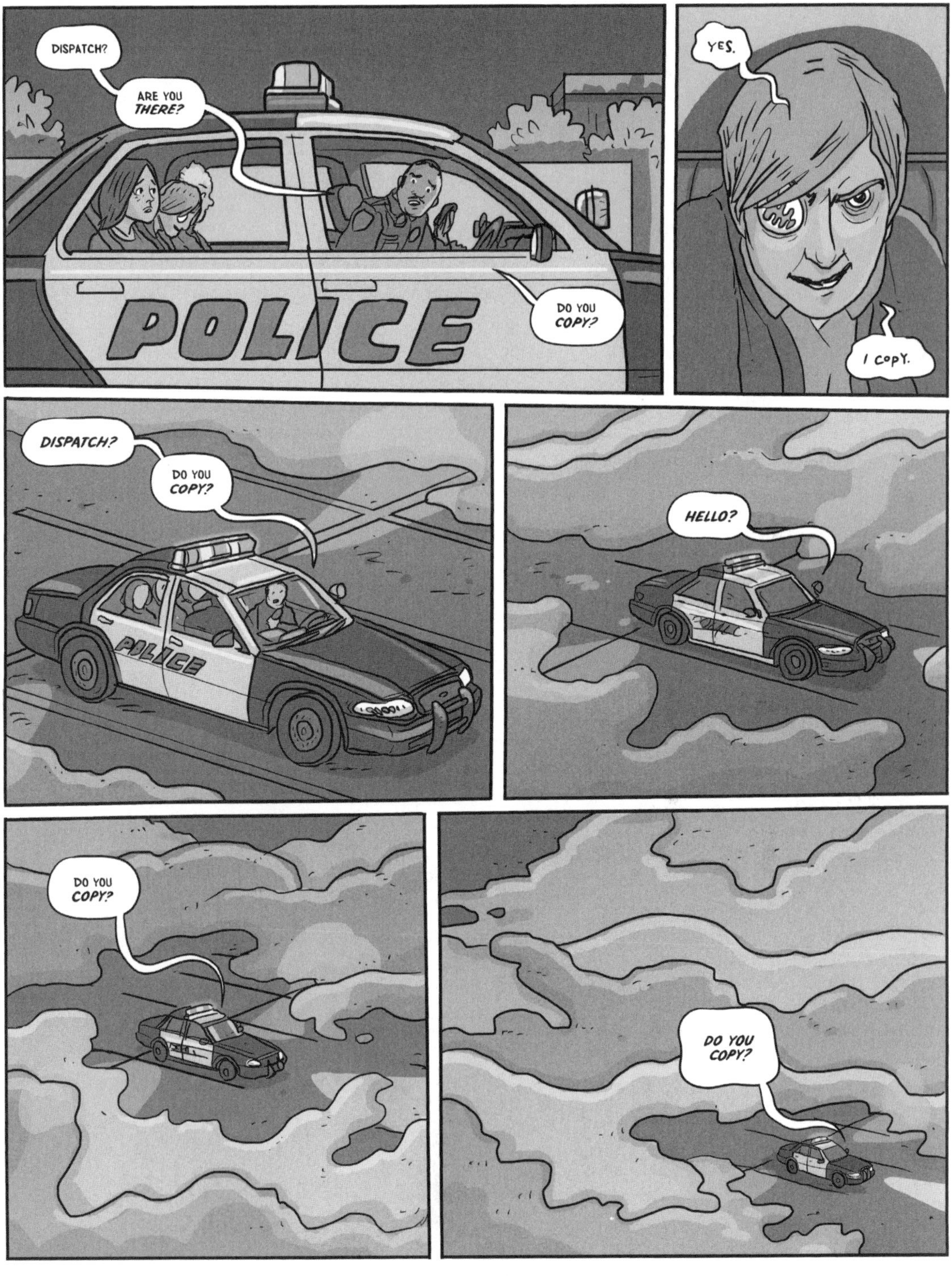
DISPATCH?
ARE YOU THERE?
POLICE
DO YOU COPY?
YES.
I COPY.
DISPATCH?
DO YOU COPY?
POLICE
HELLO?
DO YOU COPY?
DO YOU COPY?

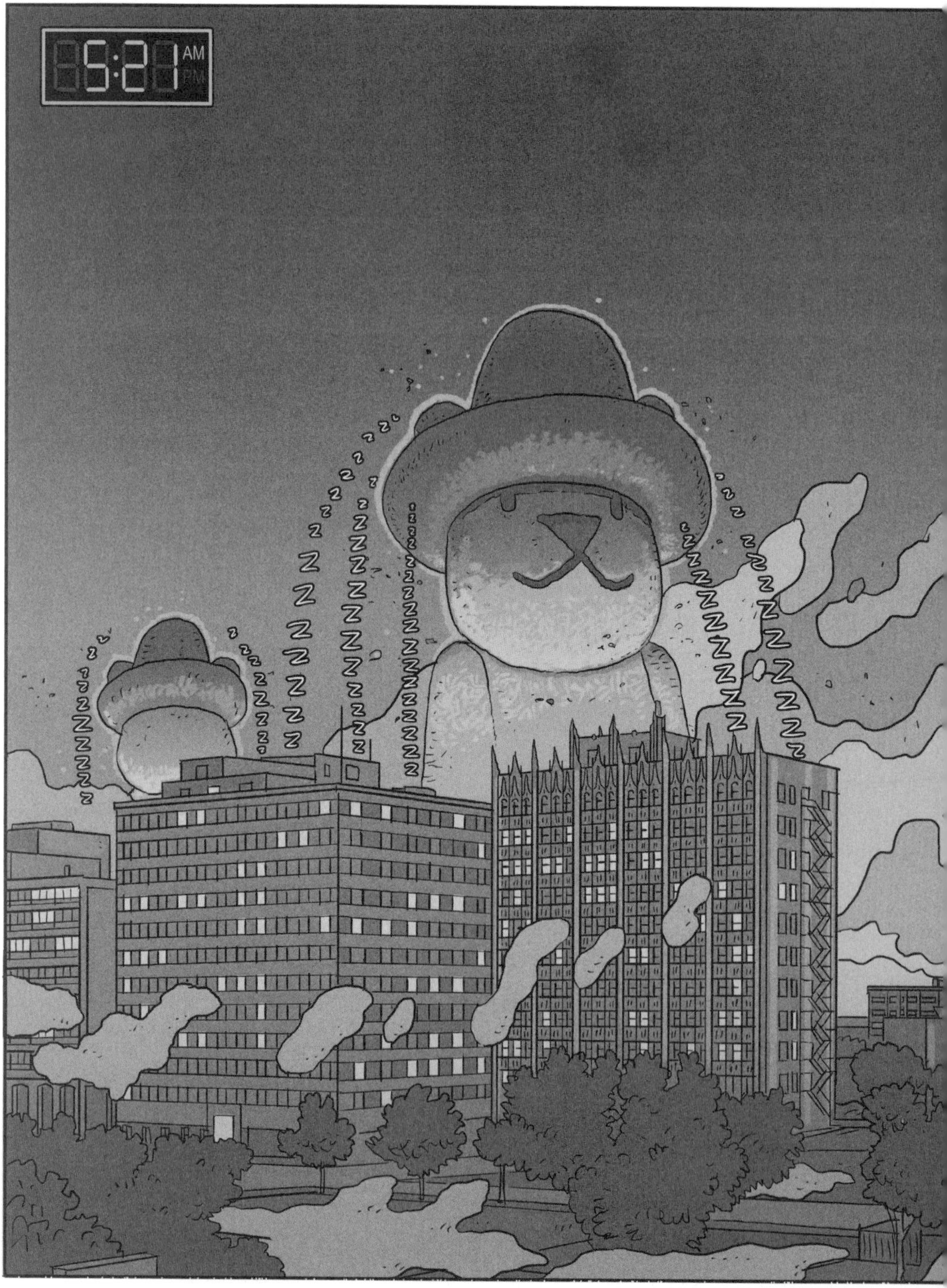
5:21 AM PM

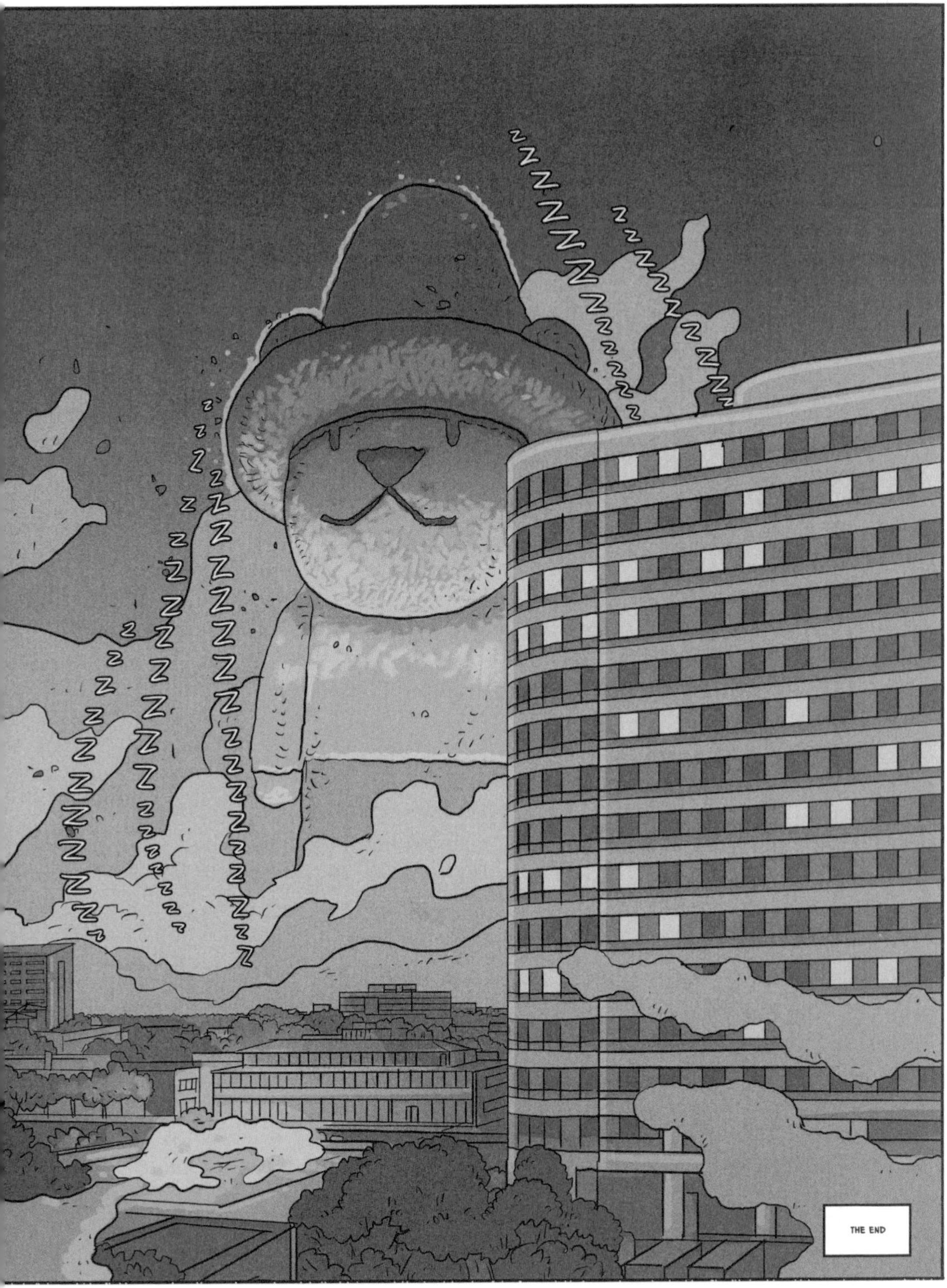

THE END

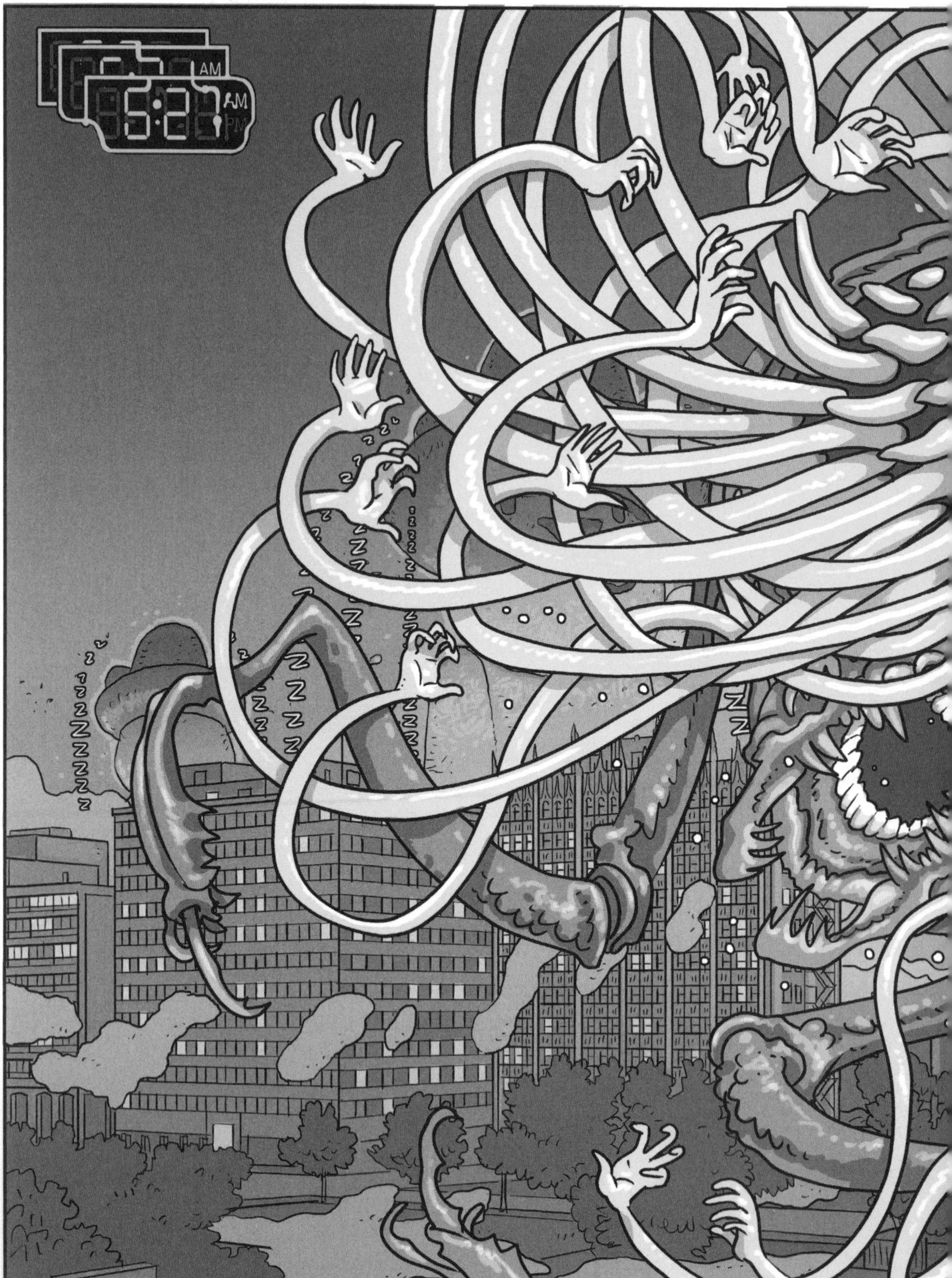
AM
AM
PM

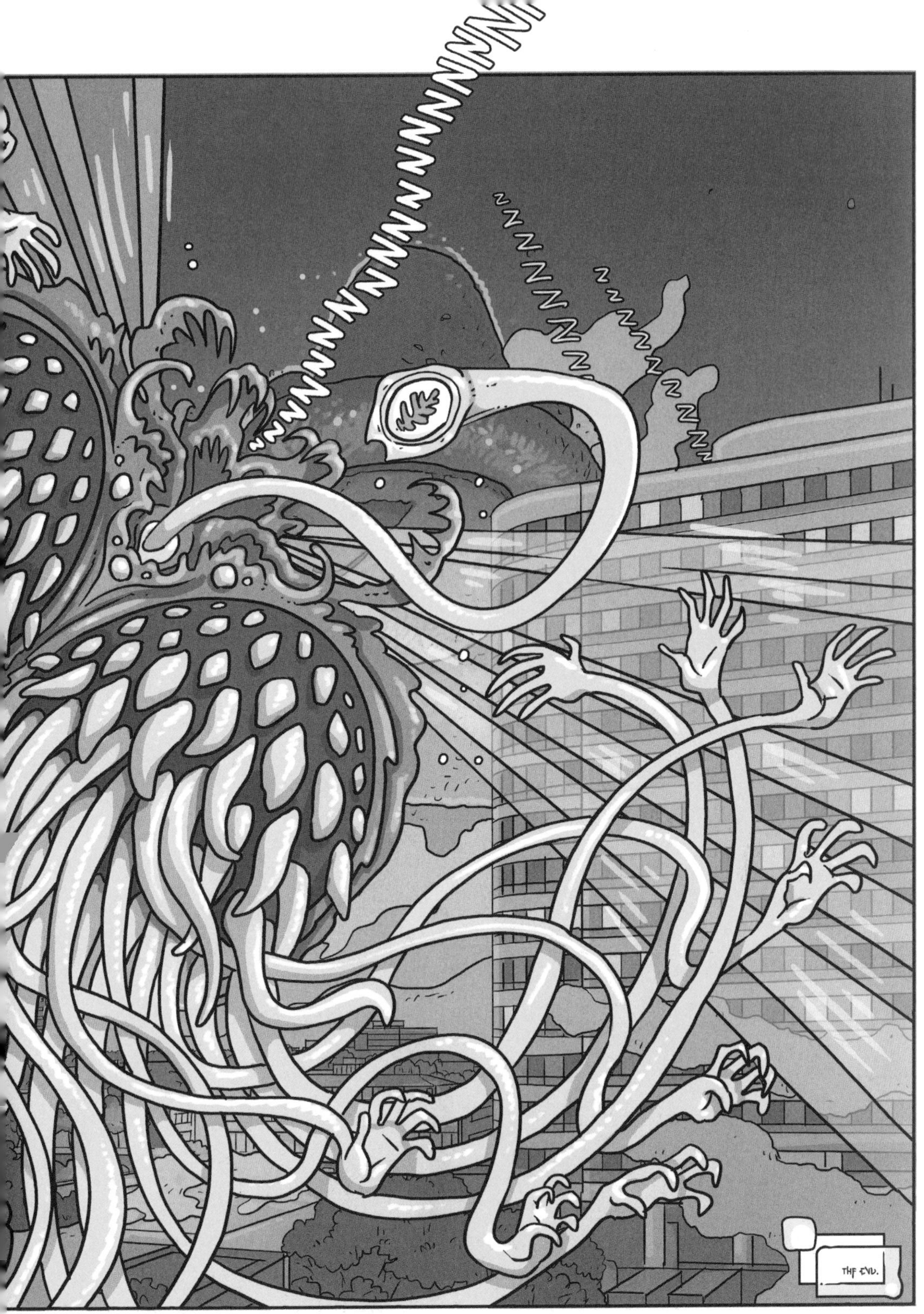
THE END.

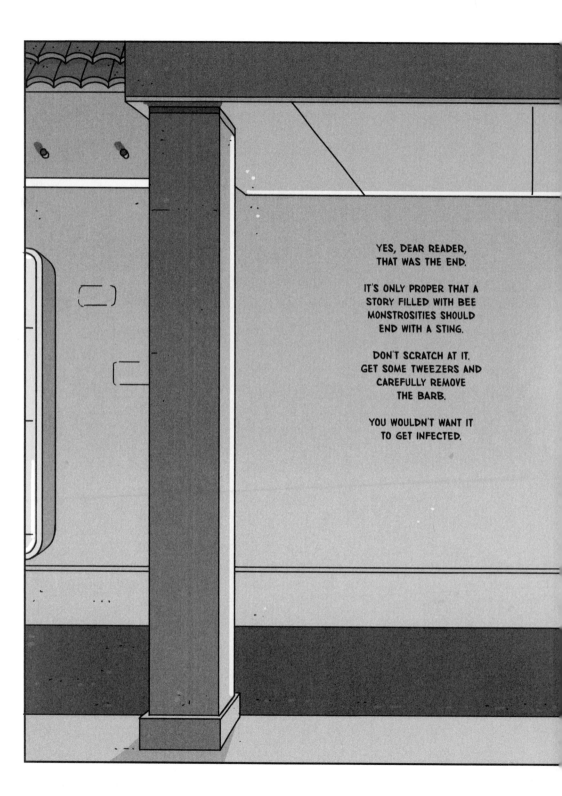

YES, DEAR READER,
THAT WAS THE END.

IT'S ONLY PROPER THAT A
STORY FILLED WITH BEE
MONSTROSITIES SHOULD
END WITH A STING.

DON'T SCRATCH AT IT.
GET SOME TWEEZERS AND
CAREFULLY REMOVE
THE BARB.

YOU WOULDN'T WANT IT
TO GET INFECTED.

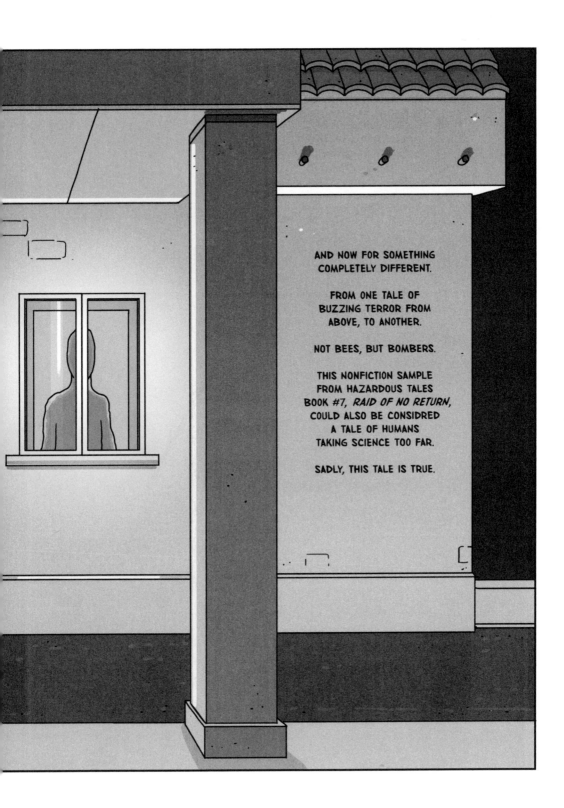

AND NOW FOR SOMETHING
COMPLETELY DIFFERENT.

FROM ONE TALE OF
BUZZING TERROR FROM
ABOVE, TO ANOTHER.

NOT BEES, BUT BOMBERS.

THIS NONFICTION SAMPLE
FROM HAZARDOUS TALES
BOOK #7, *RAID OF NO RETURN*,
COULD ALSO BE CONSIDRED
A TALE OF HUMANS
TAKING SCIENCE TOO FAR.

SADLY, THIS TALE IS TRUE.

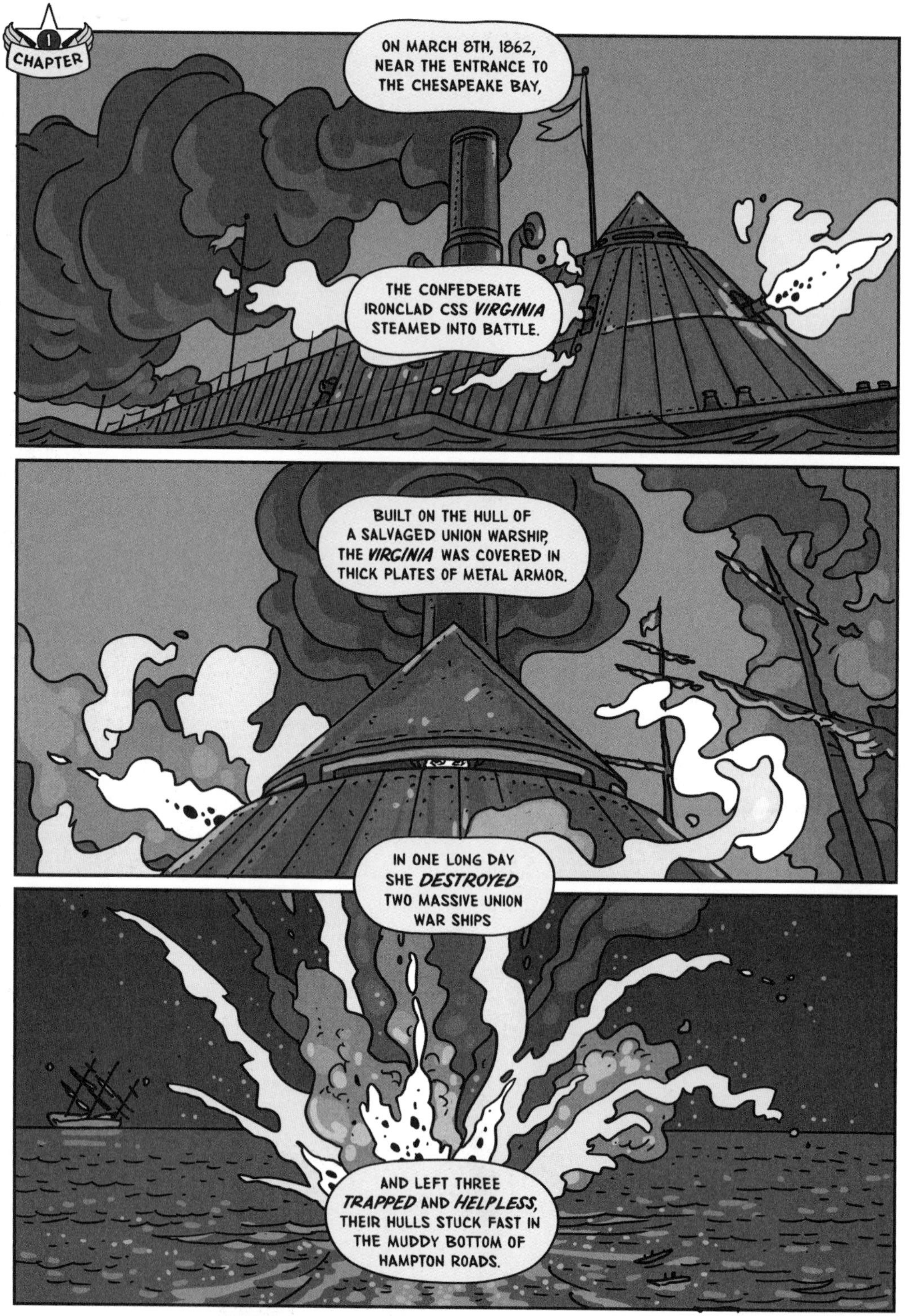
CHAPTER 1
ON MARCH 8TH, 1862, NEAR THE ENTRANCE TO THE CHESAPEAKE BAY,
THE CONFEDERATE IRONCLAD CSS VIRGINIA STEAMED INTO BATTLE.
BUILT ON THE HULL OF A SALVAGED UNION WARSHIP, THE VIRGINIA WAS COVERED IN THICK PLATES OF METAL ARMOR.
IN ONE LONG DAY SHE DESTROYED TWO MASSIVE UNION WAR SHIPS
AND LEFT THREE TRAPPED AND HELPLESS, THEIR HULLS STUCK FAST IN THE MUDDY BOTTOM OF HAMPTON ROADS.

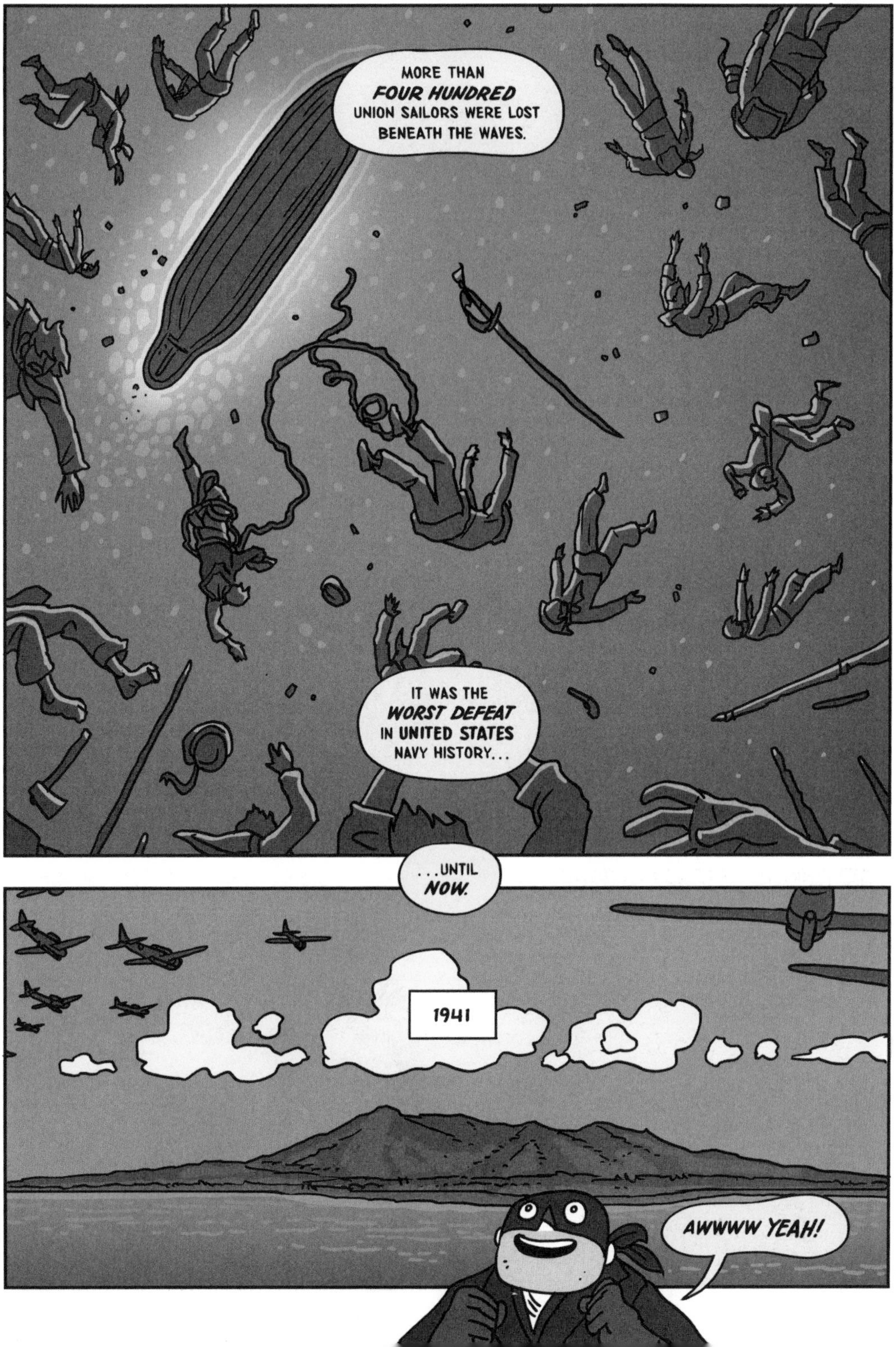
MORE THAN FOUR HUNDRED UNION SAILORS WERE LOST BENEATH THE WAVES.
IT WAS THE WORST DEFEAT IN UNITED STATES NAVY HISTORY...
...UNTIL NOW.
1941
AWWWW YEAH!

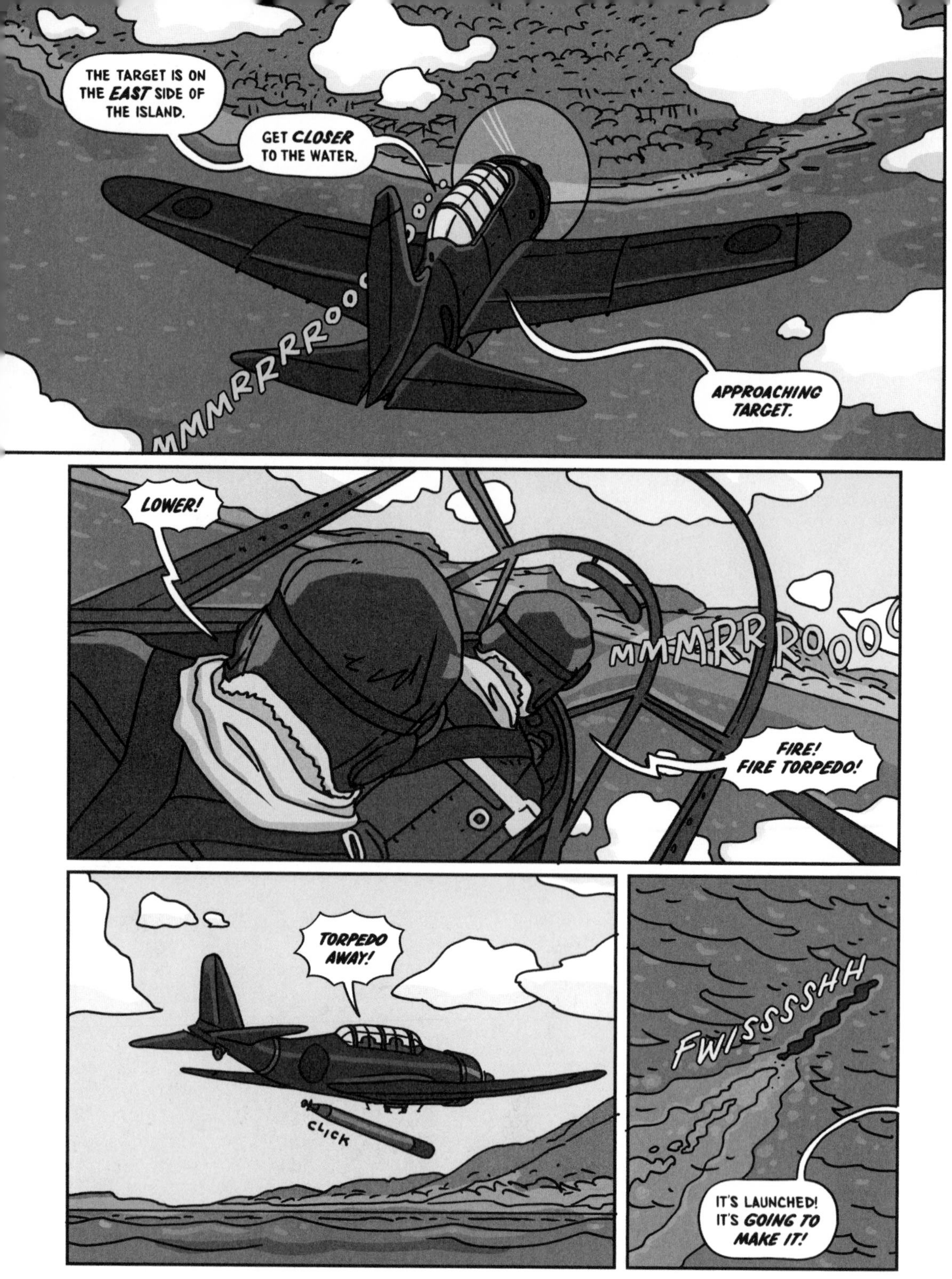
THE TARGET IS ON THE *EAST* SIDE OF THE ISLAND.
GET *CLOSER* TO THE WATER.
MMMRRRROOO
APPROACHING TARGET.
LOWER!
MMMRRROOOO
FIRE! FIRE TORPEDO!
TORPEDO AWAY!
CLICK
FWISSSSHH
IT'S LAUNCHED! IT'S *GOING TO MAKE IT!*

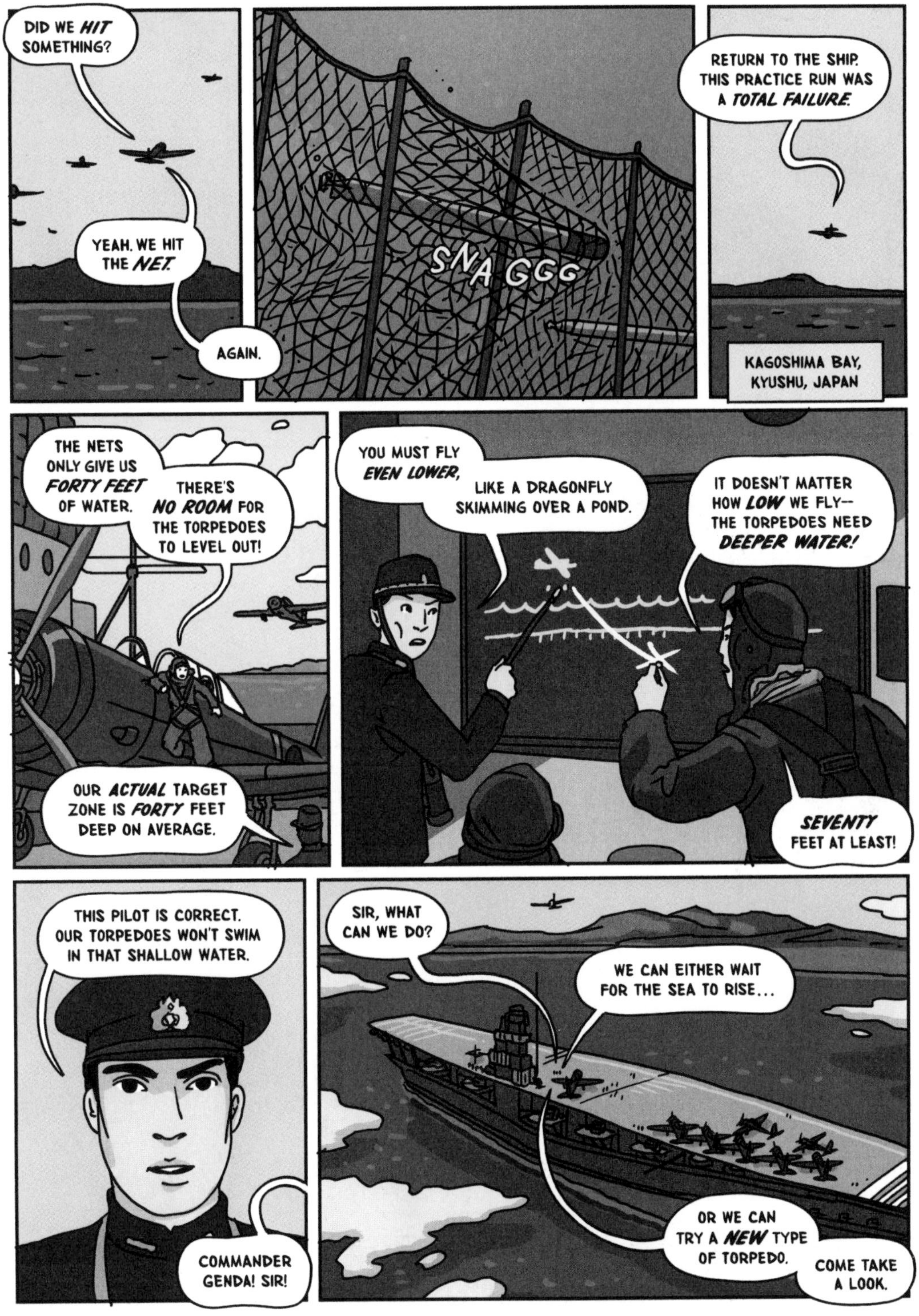
DID WE HIT SOMETHING?
YEAH. WE HIT THE NET.
AGAIN.
SNAGGG
RETURN TO THE SHIP. THIS PRACTICE RUN WAS A TOTAL FAILURE.
KAGOSHIMA BAY, KYUSHU, JAPAN
THE NETS ONLY GIVE US FORTY FEET OF WATER.
THERE'S NO ROOM FOR THE TORPEDOES TO LEVEL OUT!
OUR ACTUAL TARGET ZONE IS FORTY FEET DEEP ON AVERAGE.
YOU MUST FLY EVEN LOWER,
LIKE A DRAGONFLY SKIMMING OVER A POND.
IT DOESN'T MATTER HOW LOW WE FLY-- THE TORPEDOES NEED DEEPER WATER!
SEVENTY FEET AT LEAST!
THIS PILOT IS CORRECT. OUR TORPEDOES WON'T SWIM IN THAT SHALLOW WATER.
COMMANDER GENDA! SIR!
SIR, WHAT CAN WE DO?
WE CAN EITHER WAIT FOR THE SEA TO RISE...
OR WE CAN TRY A NEW TYPE OF TORPEDO.
COME TAKE A LOOK.

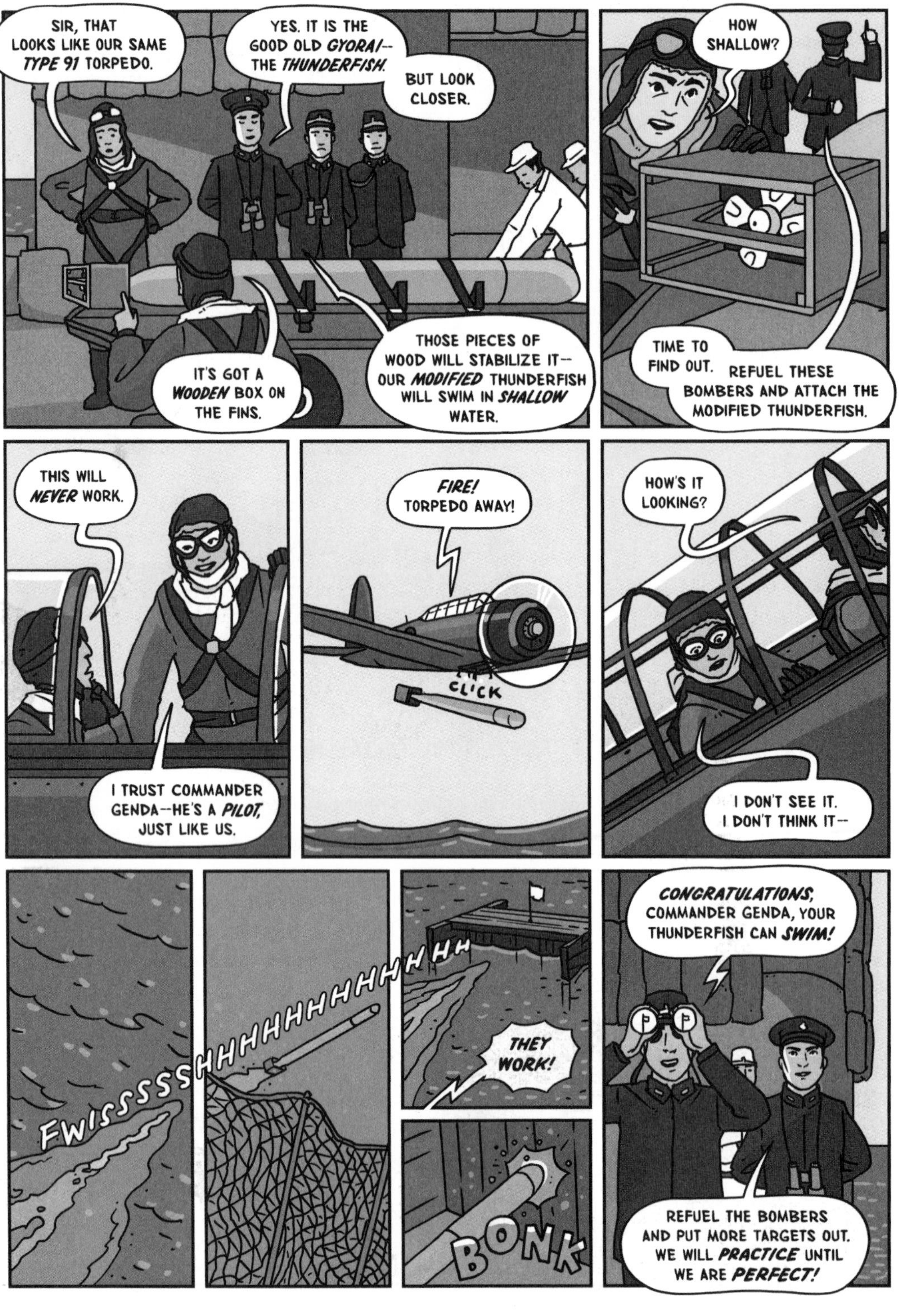

SIR, THAT LOOKS LIKE OUR SAME TYPE 91 TORPEDO.
YES. IT IS THE GOOD OLD GYORAI-- THE THUNDERFISH.
BUT LOOK CLOSER.
IT'S GOT A WOODEN BOX ON THE FINS.
THOSE PIECES OF WOOD WILL STABILIZE IT-- OUR MODIFIED THUNDERFISH WILL SWIM IN SHALLOW WATER.
HOW SHALLOW?
TIME TO FIND OUT.
REFUEL THESE BOMBERS AND ATTACH THE MODIFIED THUNDERFISH.
THIS WILL NEVER WORK.
I TRUST COMMANDER GENDA--HE'S A PILOT, JUST LIKE US.
FIRE! TORPEDO AWAY!
CLICK
HOW'S IT LOOKING?
I DON'T SEE IT. I DON'T THINK IT--
FWISSSSSHHHHHHHHHHHHHH
THEY WORK!
BONK
CONGRATULATIONS, COMMANDER GENDA, YOUR THUNDERFISH CAN SWIM!
REFUEL THE BOMBERS AND PUT MORE TARGETS OUT. WE WILL PRACTICE UNTIL WE ARE PERFECT!

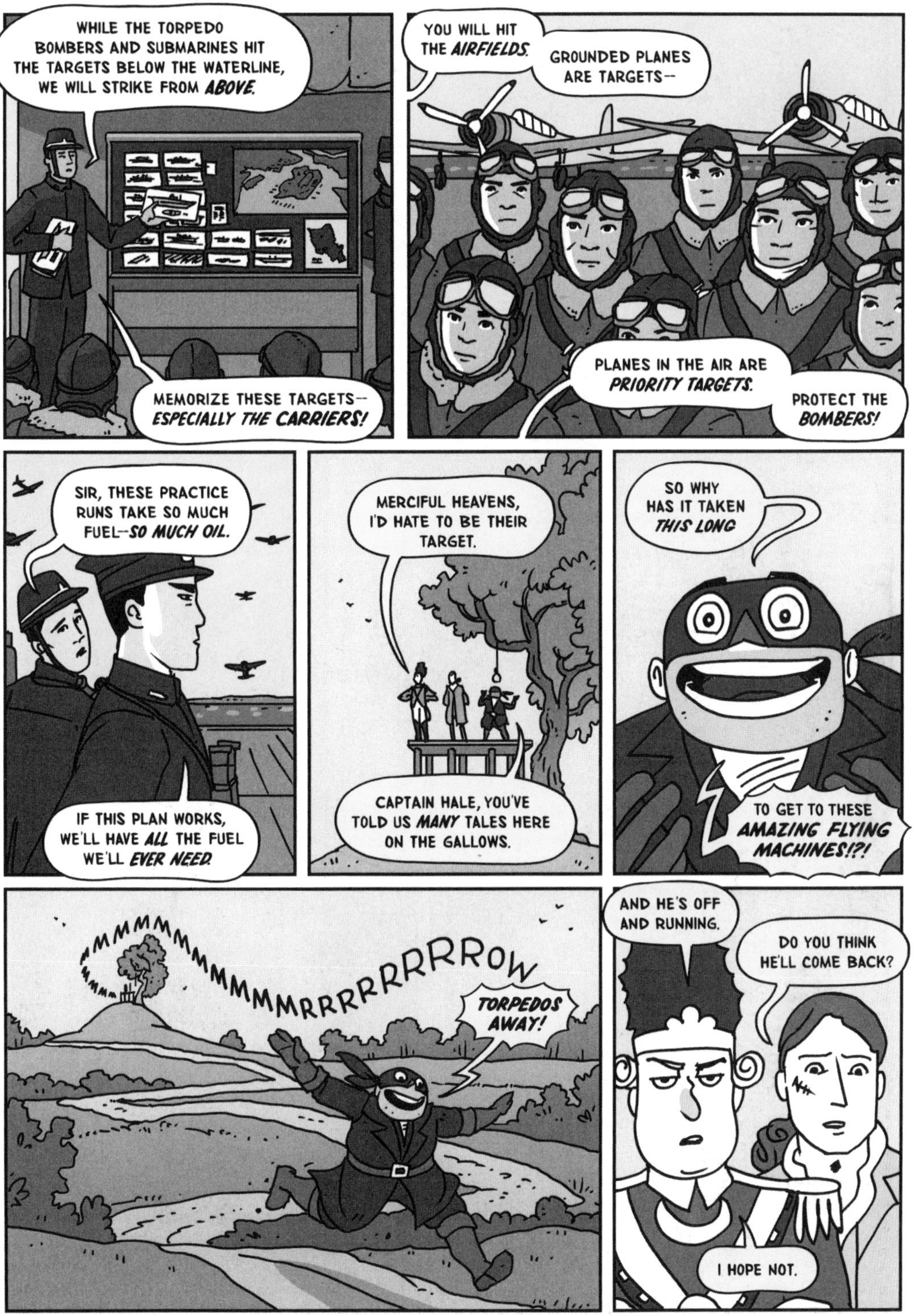
WHILE THE TORPEDO BOMBERS AND SUBMARINES HIT THE TARGETS BELOW THE WATERLINE, WE WILL STRIKE FROM *ABOVE.*
MEMORIZE THESE TARGETS-- *ESPECIALLY THE CARRIERS!*
YOU WILL HIT THE *AIRFIELDS.*
GROUNDED PLANES ARE TARGETS--
PLANES IN THE AIR ARE *PRIORITY TARGETS.*
PROTECT THE *BOMBERS!*
SIR, THESE PRACTICE RUNS TAKE SO MUCH FUEL--*SO MUCH OIL.*
IF THIS PLAN WORKS, WE'LL HAVE *ALL* THE FUEL WE'LL *EVER NEED.*
MERCIFUL HEAVENS, I'D HATE TO BE THEIR TARGET.
CAPTAIN HALE, YOU'VE TOLD US *MANY* TALES HERE ON THE GALLOWS.
SO WHY HAS IT TAKEN *THIS LONG*
TO GET TO THESE *AMAZING FLYING MACHINES!?!*
MMMMMMMMMMMMMMMMRRRRRRRROW
TORPEDOS AWAY!
AND HE'S OFF AND RUNNING.
DO YOU THINK HE'LL COME BACK?
I HOPE NOT.

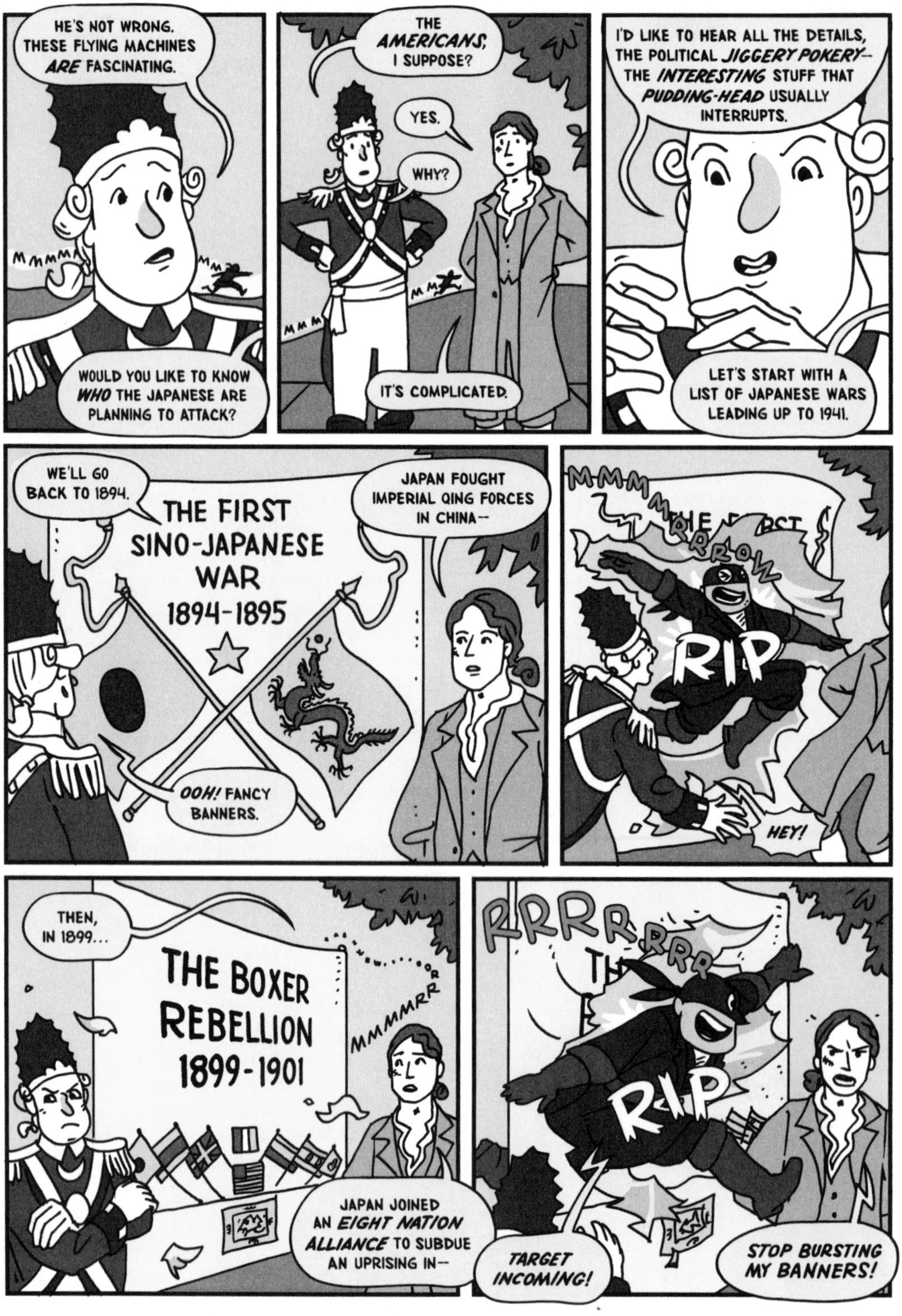

HE'S NOT WRONG. THESE FLYING MACHINES ARE FASCINATING.
MMMMM
MMM
WOULD YOU LIKE TO KNOW WHO THE JAPANESE ARE PLANNING TO ATTACK?
THE AMERICANS, I SUPPOSE?
YES.
WHY?
MMM
MMM
IT'S COMPLICATED.
I'D LIKE TO HEAR ALL THE DETAILS, THE POLITICAL JIGGERY POKERY-- THE INTERESTING STUFF THAT PUDDING-HEAD USUALLY INTERRUPTS.
LET'S START WITH A LIST OF JAPANESE WARS LEADING UP TO 1941.
WE'LL GO BACK TO 1894.
THE FIRST SINO-JAPANESE WAR 1894-1895
JAPAN FOUGHT IMPERIAL QING FORCES IN CHINA--
OOH! FANCY BANNERS.
MMMMRRROW
RIP
HEY!
THEN, IN 1899...
THE BOXER REBELLION 1899-1901
MMMMRR
JAPAN JOINED AN EIGHT NATION ALLIANCE TO SUBDUE AN UPRISING IN--
RRRRRRR
RIP
TARGET INCOMING!
STOP BURSTING MY BANNERS!

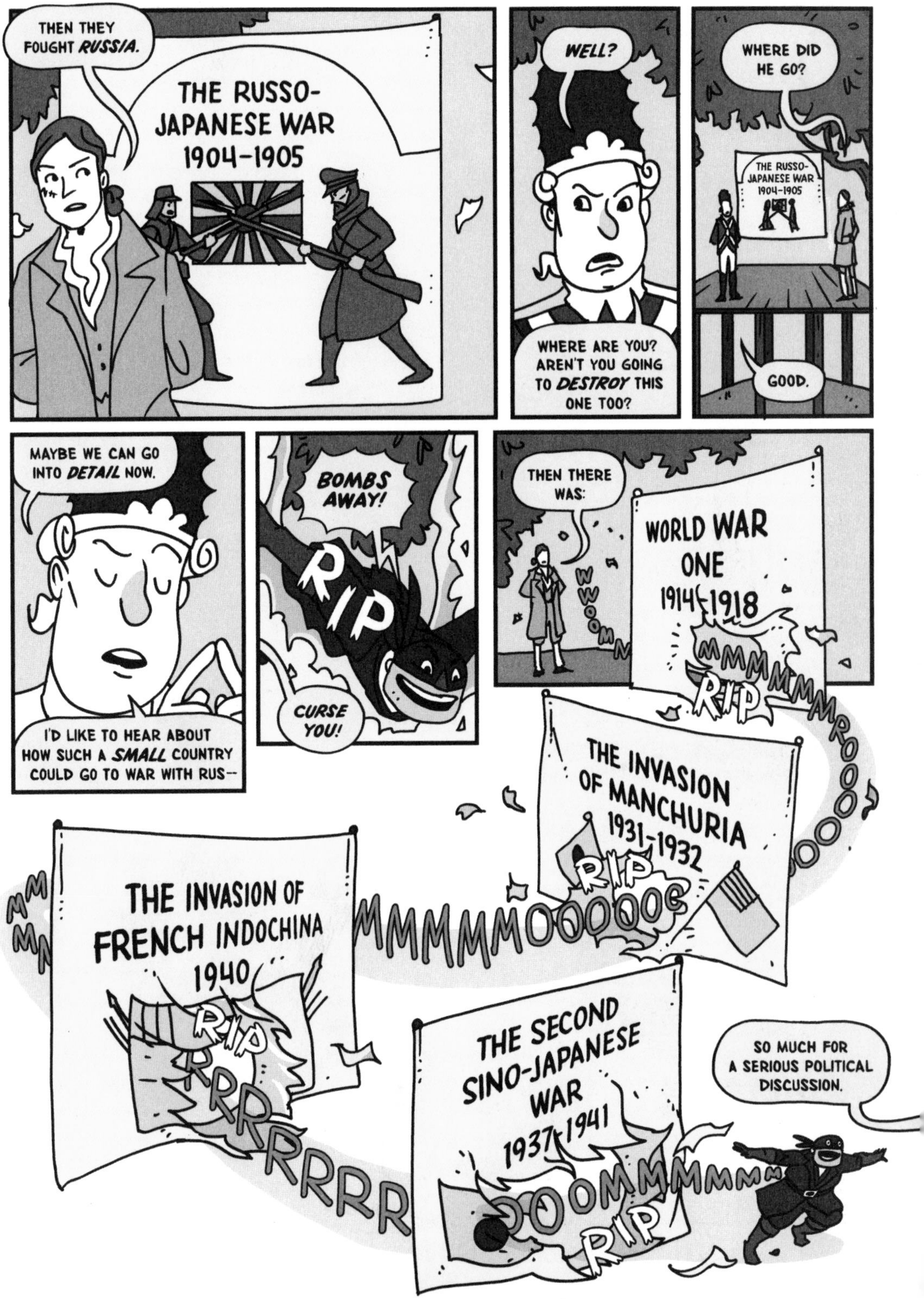
THEN THEY FOUGHT RUSSIA.
THE RUSSO-JAPANESE WAR 1904–1905
WELL?
WHERE ARE YOU? AREN'T YOU GOING TO DESTROY THIS ONE TOO?
WHERE DID HE GO?
THE RUSSO-JAPANESE WAR 1904–1905
GOOD.
MAYBE WE CAN GO INTO DETAIL NOW.
I'D LIKE TO HEAR ABOUT HOW SUCH A SMALL COUNTRY COULD GO TO WAR WITH RUS--
BOMBS AWAY!
RIP
CURSE YOU!
THEN THERE WAS:
WORLD WAR ONE 1914–1918
RIP
THE INVASION OF MANCHURIA 1931–1932
RIP
THE INVASION OF FRENCH INDOCHINA 1940
RIP
THE SECOND SINO-JAPANESE WAR 1937–1941
RIP
SO MUCH FOR A SERIOUS POLITICAL DISCUSSION.

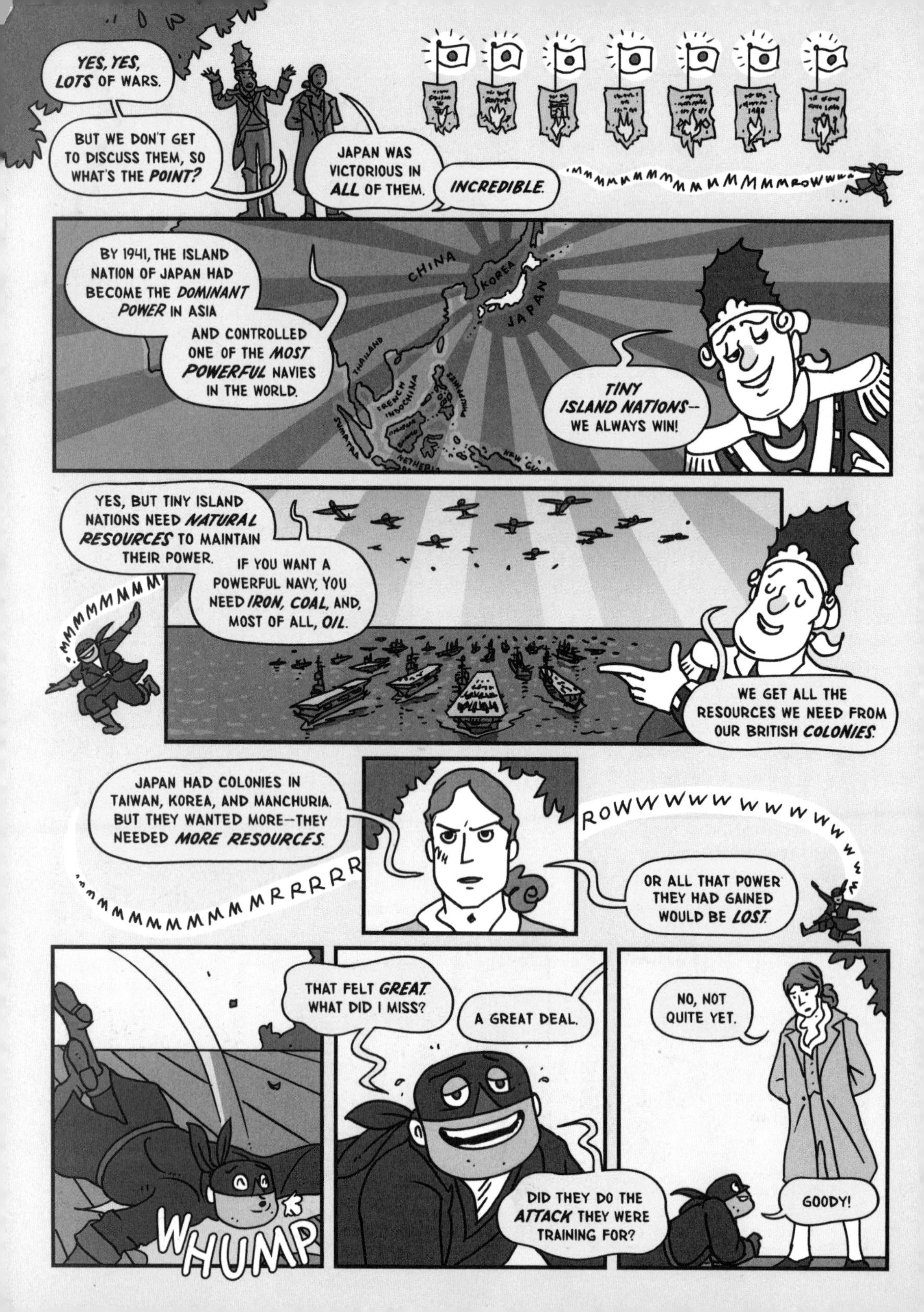
YES, YES, LOTS OF WARS.
BUT WE DON'T GET TO DISCUSS THEM, SO WHAT'S THE POINT?
JAPAN WAS VICTORIOUS IN ALL OF THEM.
INCREDIBLE.
MMMMMMMMMMMMMMMMMROWWW
BY 1941, THE ISLAND NATION OF JAPAN HAD BECOME THE DOMINANT POWER IN ASIA
AND CONTROLLED ONE OF THE MOST POWERFUL NAVIES IN THE WORLD.
CHINA
KOREA
JAPAN
THAILAND
FRENCH INDOCHINA
SUMATRA
TINY ISLAND NATIONS-- WE ALWAYS WIN!
YES, BUT TINY ISLAND NATIONS NEED NATURAL RESOURCES TO MAINTAIN THEIR POWER.
IF YOU WANT A POWERFUL NAVY, YOU NEED IRON, COAL, AND, MOST OF ALL, OIL.
MMMMMMMMMMM
WE GET ALL THE RESOURCES WE NEED FROM OUR BRITISH COLONIES.
JAPAN HAD COLONIES IN TAIWAN, KOREA, AND MANCHURIA. BUT THEY WANTED MORE--THEY NEEDED MORE RESOURCES.
ROWWWWWWWWWWWWWW
MMMMMMMMMMMMMRRRRR
OR ALL THAT POWER THEY HAD GAINED WOULD BE LOST.
WHUMP
THAT FELT GREAT. WHAT DID I MISS?
A GREAT DEAL.
DID THEY DO THE ATTACK THEY WERE TRAINING FOR?
NO, NOT QUITE YET.
GOODY!

WASHINGTON, D.C.

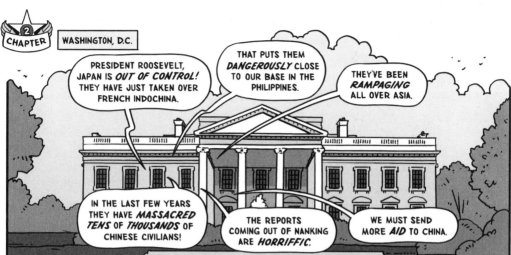

PRESIDENT ROOSEVELT, JAPAN IS *OUT OF CONTROL!* THEY HAVE JUST TAKEN OVER FRENCH INDOCHINA.

THAT PUTS THEM *DANGEROUSLY* CLOSE TO OUR BASE IN THE PHILIPPINES.

THEY'VE BEEN *RAMPAGING* ALL OVER ASIA.

IN THE LAST FEW YEARS THEY HAVE *MASSACRED TENS* OF *THOUSANDS* OF CHINESE CIVILIANS!

THE REPORTS COMING OUT OF NANKING ARE *HORRIFFIC.*

WE MUST SEND MORE *AID* TO CHINA.

I SAY WE PUT OUR PACIFIC FLEET TO WORK.

IF WE *DECLARE WAR,* OUR NAVY CAN *BLAST* THEM OUT OF CHINA, INDOCHINA, AND *ANYWHERE ELSE* THEY'VE INVADED!

JAPAN HAS JUST SIGNED AN *ALLIANCE* WITH GERMANY AND ITALY.

IF WE ATTACK *THEM,* WE OPEN OURSELVES TO WAR ON *ALL SIDES.*

ARE YOU READY TO DO THE *GREAT WAR* ALL OVER AGAIN?

WHAT IS THE ALTERNATIVE? SIT BY AND WAIT FOR THEM TO *ATTACK US?*

PRESIDENT FRANKLIN DELANO ROOSEVELT

SPEAKING OF THE GREAT WAR, I WAS WOODROW WILSON'S ASSISTANT SECRETARY OF THE NAVY DURING THAT CONFLICT.

I KNOW WHAT NAVIES RUN ON: *OIL.*

DO YOU KNOW *WHERE* THE JAPANESE GET THEIR OIL?

FROM US!

EIGHTY PERCENT OF THEIR GASOLINE AND OIL COMES FROM *AMERICA.*

THE REST COMES FROM GREAT BRITAIN AND THE DUTCH EAST INDIES.

WE SHUT OFF THEIR ACCESS TO OIL, AND THAT NAVY *CAN'T SWIM.*

WHAM

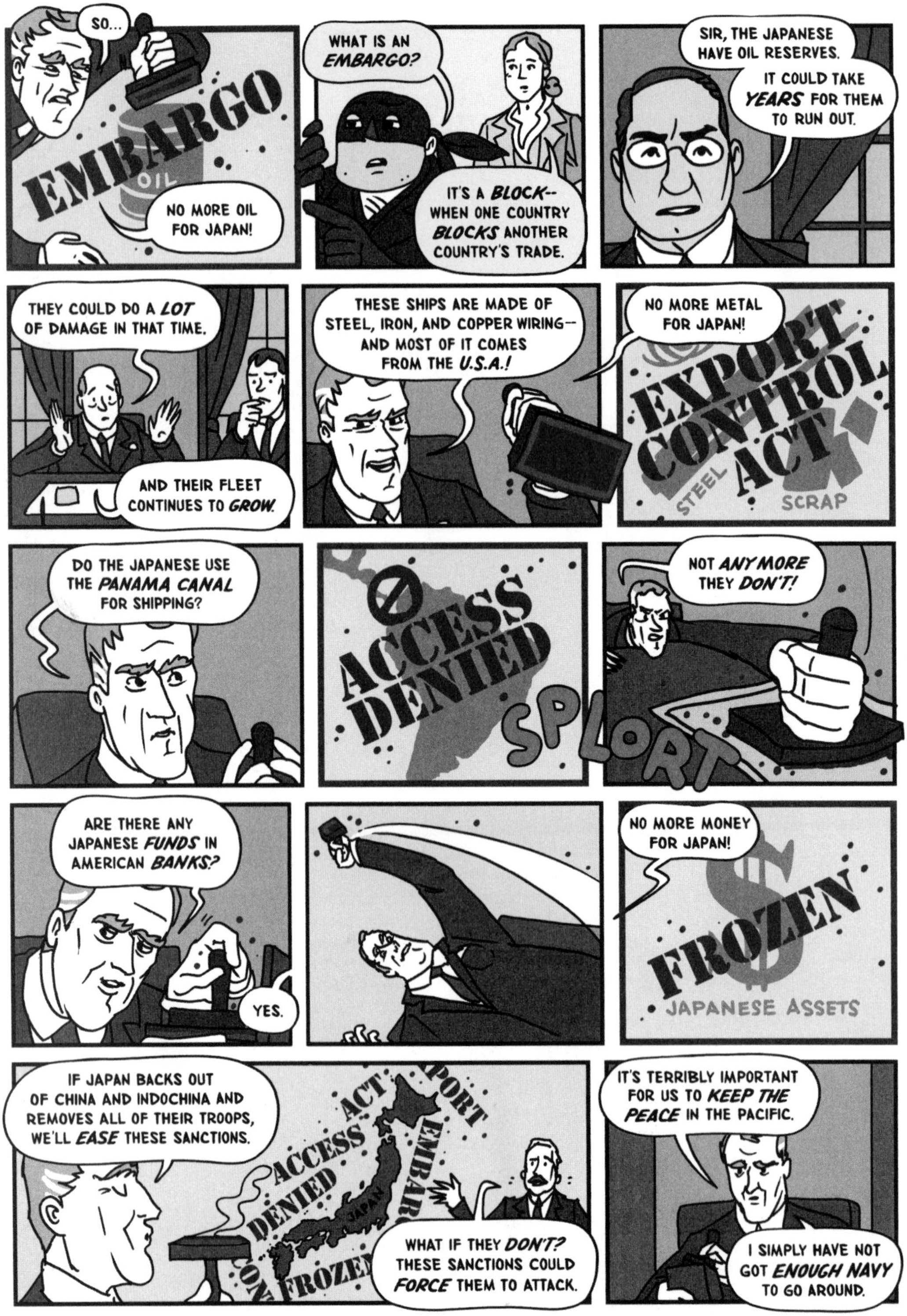
SO...
EMBARGO
OIL
NO MORE OIL FOR JAPAN!
WHAT IS AN EMBARGO?
IT'S A BLOCK-- WHEN ONE COUNTRY BLOCKS ANOTHER COUNTRY'S TRADE.
SIR, THE JAPANESE HAVE OIL RESERVES.
IT COULD TAKE YEARS FOR THEM TO RUN OUT.
THEY COULD DO A LOT OF DAMAGE IN THAT TIME.
AND THEIR FLEET CONTINUES TO GROW.
THESE SHIPS ARE MADE OF STEEL, IRON, AND COPPER WIRING-- AND MOST OF IT COMES FROM THE U.S.A.!
NO MORE METAL FOR JAPAN!
EXPORT CONTROL ACT
STEEL
SCRAP
DO THE JAPANESE USE THE PANAMA CANAL FOR SHIPPING?
ACCESS DENIED
NOT ANY MORE THEY DON'T!
SPLORT
ARE THERE ANY JAPANESE FUNDS IN AMERICAN BANKS?
YES.
NO MORE MONEY FOR JAPAN!
FROZEN
JAPANESE ASSETS
IF JAPAN BACKS OUT OF CHINA AND INDOCHINA AND REMOVES ALL OF THEIR TROOPS, WE'LL EASE THESE SANCTIONS.
ACCESS DENIED
ACT
JAPAN
FROZEN
WHAT IF THEY DON'T? THESE SANCTIONS COULD FORCE THEM TO ATTACK.
IT'S TERRIBLY IMPORTANT FOR US TO KEEP THE PEACE IN THE PACIFIC.
I SIMPLY HAVE NOT GOT ENOUGH NAVY TO GO AROUND.

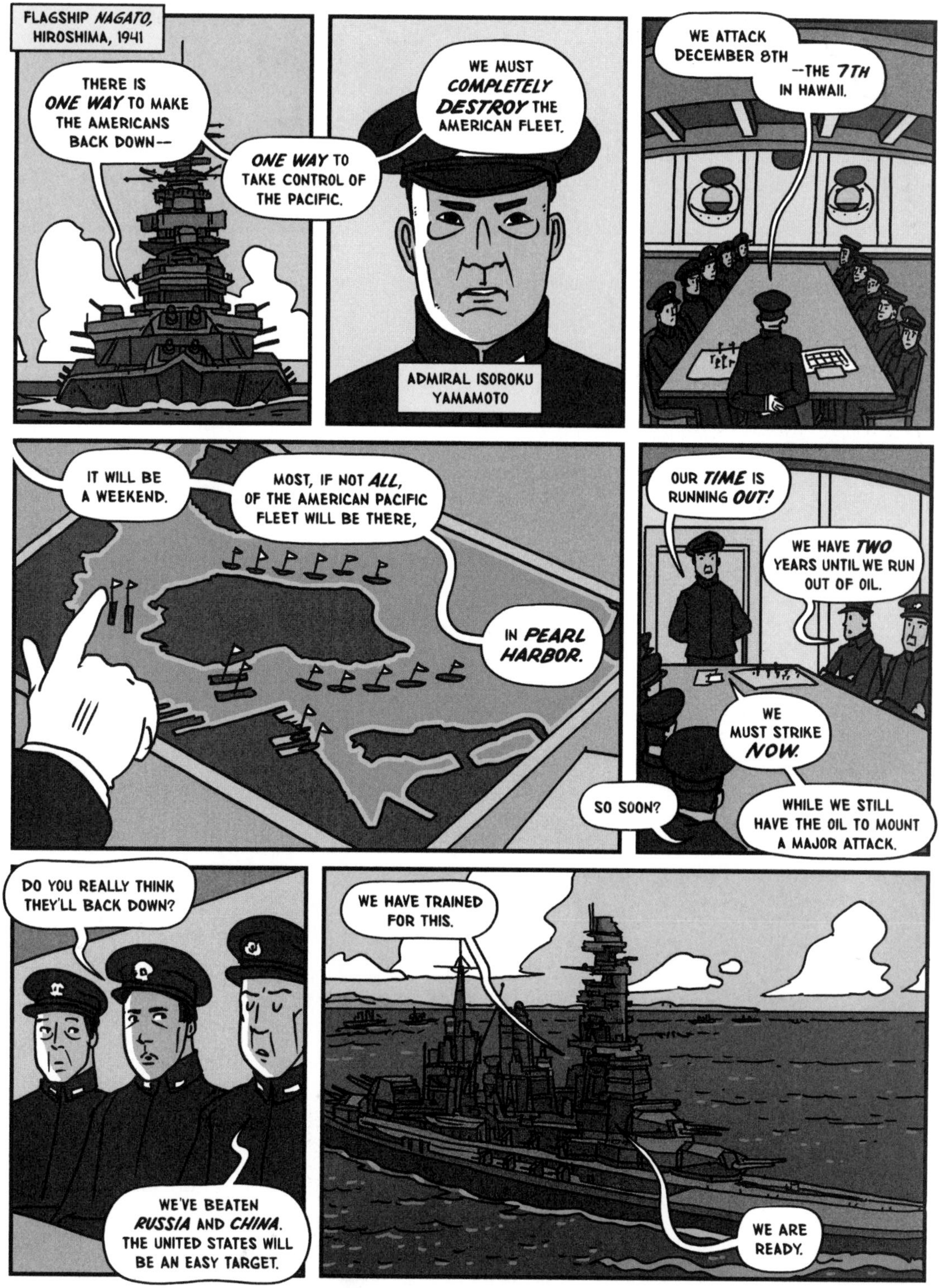
FLAGSHIP NAGATO, HIROSHIMA, 1941
THERE IS ONE WAY TO MAKE THE AMERICANS BACK DOWN--
ONE WAY TO TAKE CONTROL OF THE PACIFIC.
WE MUST COMPLETELY DESTROY THE AMERICAN FLEET.
ADMIRAL ISOROKU YAMAMOTO
WE ATTACK DECEMBER 8TH
--THE 7TH IN HAWAII.
IT WILL BE A WEEKEND.
MOST, IF NOT ALL, OF THE AMERICAN PACIFIC FLEET WILL BE THERE,
IN PEARL HARBOR.
OUR TIME IS RUNNING OUT!
WE HAVE TWO YEARS UNTIL WE RUN OUT OF OIL.
WE MUST STRIKE NOW.
SO SOON?
WHILE WE STILL HAVE THE OIL TO MOUNT A MAJOR ATTACK.
DO YOU REALLY THINK THEY'LL BACK DOWN?
WE'VE BEATEN RUSSIA AND CHINA. THE UNITED STATES WILL BE AN EASY TARGET.
WE HAVE TRAINED FOR THIS.
WE ARE READY.

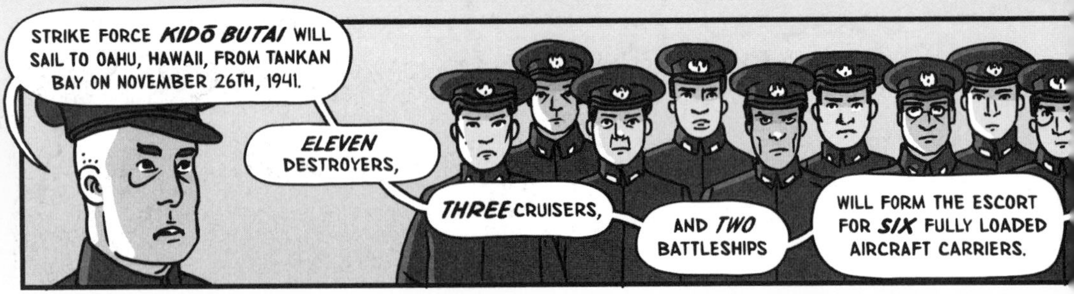
STRIKE FORCE KIDŌ BUTAI WILL SAIL TO OAHU, HAWAII, FROM TANKAN BAY ON NOVEMBER 26TH, 1941.
ELEVEN DESTROYERS,
THREE CRUISERS,
AND TWO BATTLESHIPS
WILL FORM THE ESCORT FOR SIX FULLY LOADED AIRCRAFT CARRIERS.

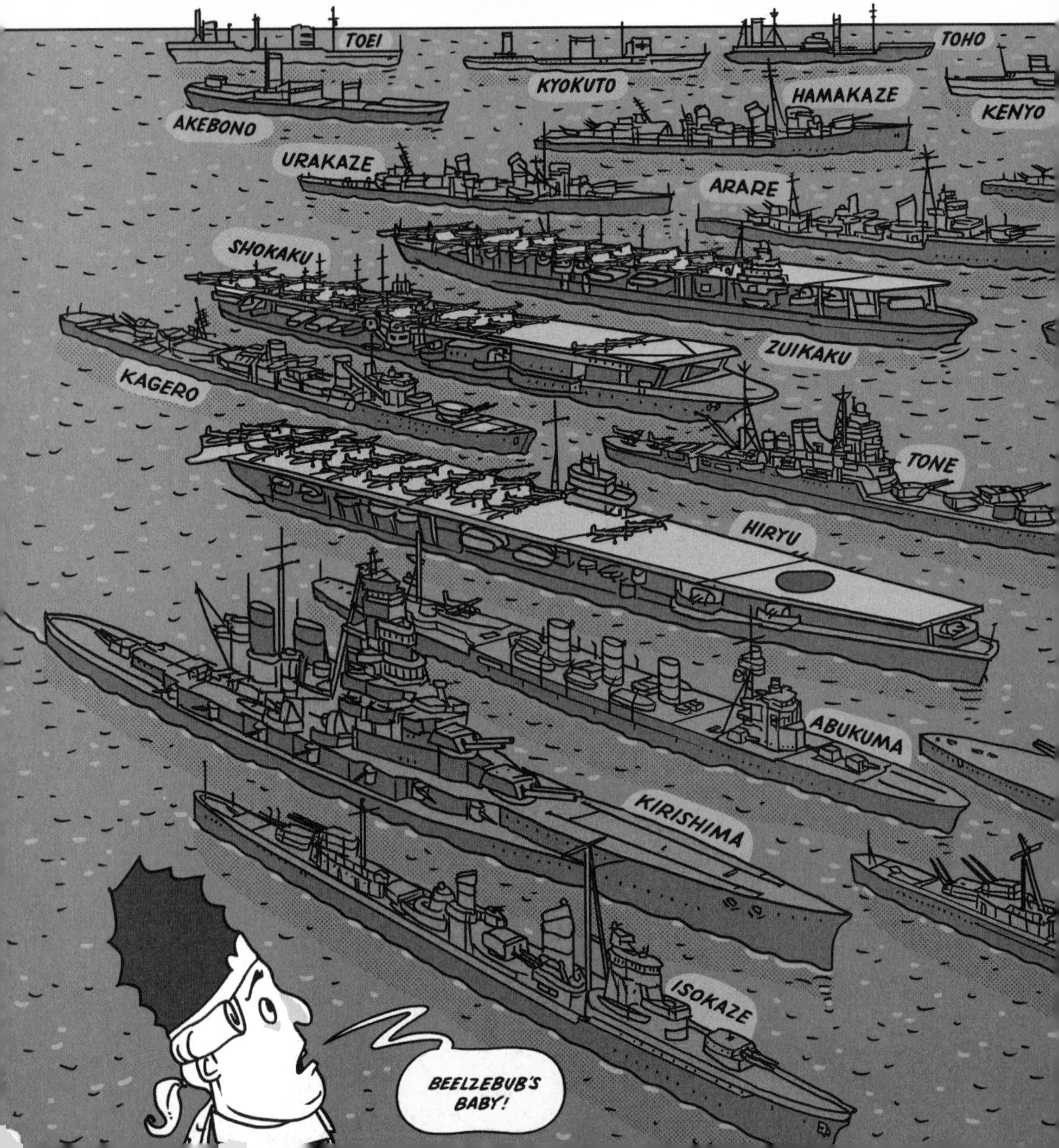
TOEI
TOHO
KYOKUTO
HAMAKAZE
AKEBONO
KENYO
URAKAZE
ARARE
SHOKAKU
ZUIKAKU
KAGERO
TONE
HIRYU
ABUKUMA
KIRISHIMA
ISOKAZE
BEELZEBUB'S BABY!

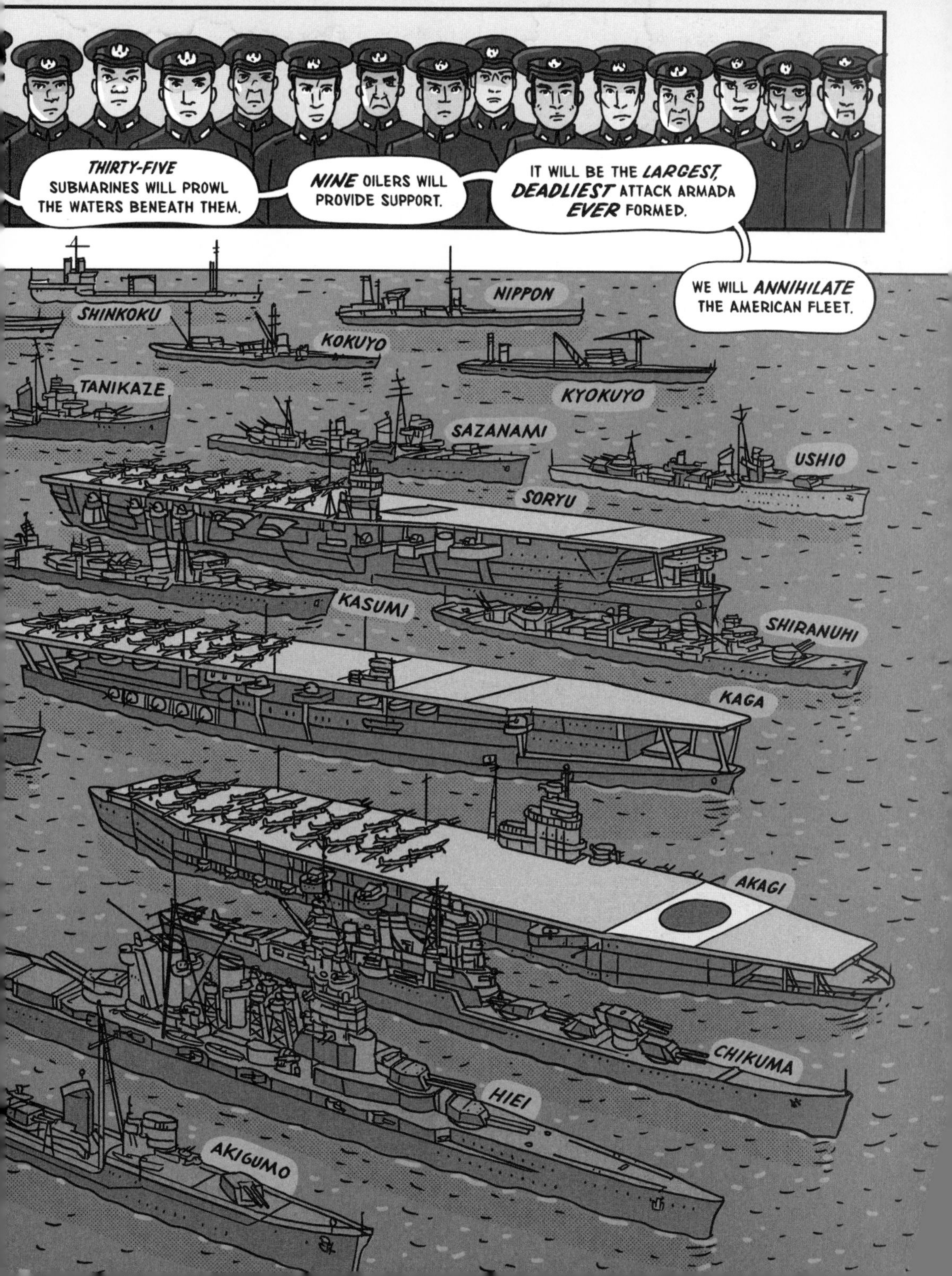
THIRTY-FIVE SUBMARINES WILL PROWL THE WATERS BENEATH THEM.
NINE OILERS WILL PROVIDE SUPPORT.
IT WILL BE THE LARGEST, DEADLIEST ATTACK ARMADA EVER FORMED.
WE WILL ANNIHILATE THE AMERICAN FLEET.
NIPPON
SHINKOKU
KOKUYO
TANIKAZE
KYOKUYO
SAZANAMI
USHIO
SORYU
KASUMI
SHIRANUHI
KAGA
AKAGI
CHIKUMA
HIEI
AKIGUMO

THANK YOU FOR
READING *APOCALYPSE TACO*
BY NATHAN HALE.

WE HOPE YOU HAVE ENJOYED THIS TALE OF
HUNGRY INVADERS.

FOR MORE
SCIENCE FICTION TERROR, PLEASE READ
ONE TRICK PONY.

AND FOR NONFICTION THRILLS AND CHILLS,
SEE THE ONGOING AMERICAN HISTORY SERIES
NATHAN HALE'S HAZARDOUS TALES.

FOR MORE, VISIT:
NATHANHALEAUTHOR.COM

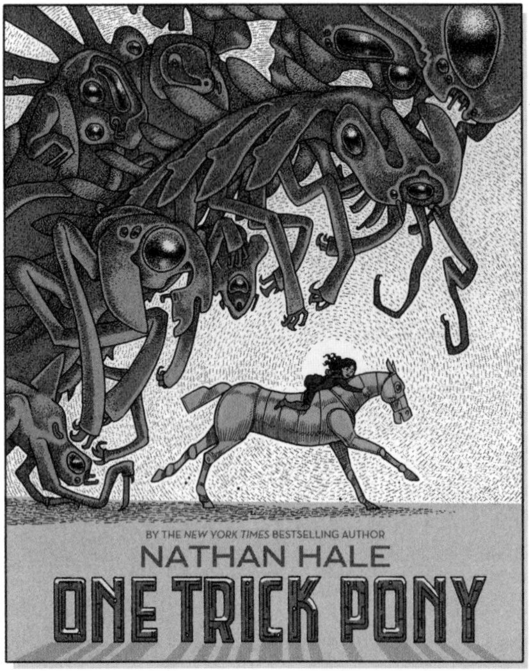

BY THE NEW YORK TIMES BESTSELLING AUTHOR
NATHAN HALE
ONE TRICK PONY

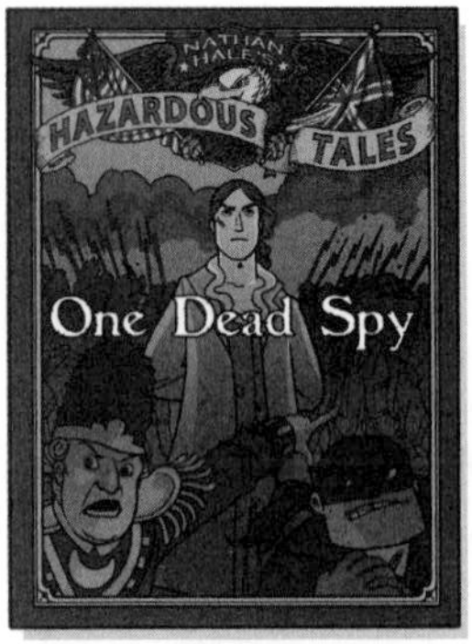

NATHAN HALE'S
HAZARDOUS
TALES
One Dead Spy

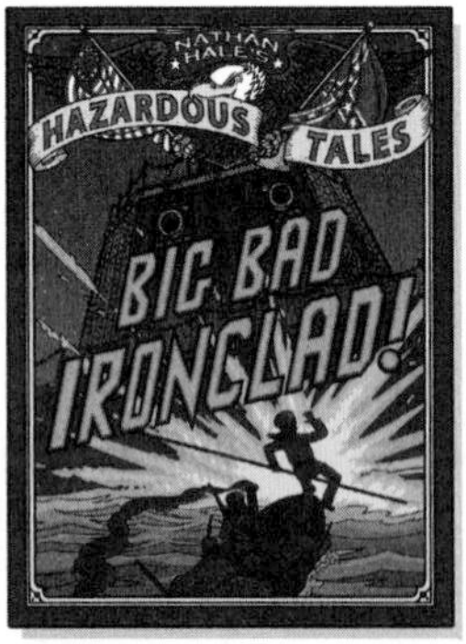

NATHAN HALE'S
HAZARDOUS
TALES
BIG BAD IRONCLAD!

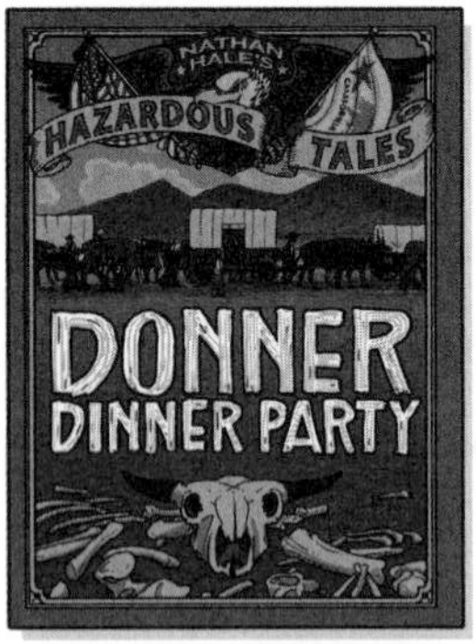

NATHAN HALE'S
HAZARDOUS
TALES
DONNER DINNER PARTY

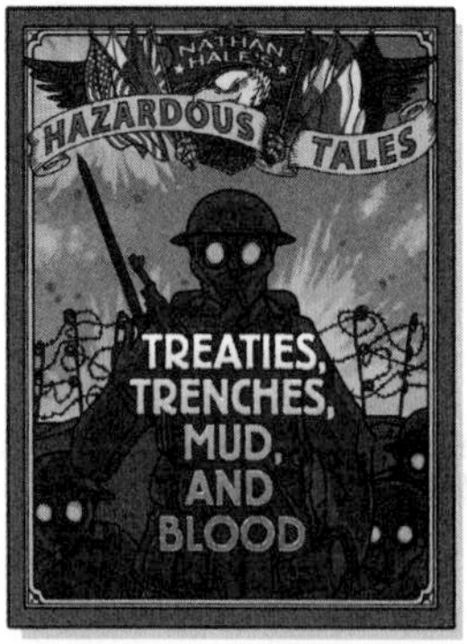

NATHAN HALE'S
HAZARDOUS
TALES
TREATIES, TRENCHES, MUD, AND BLOOD

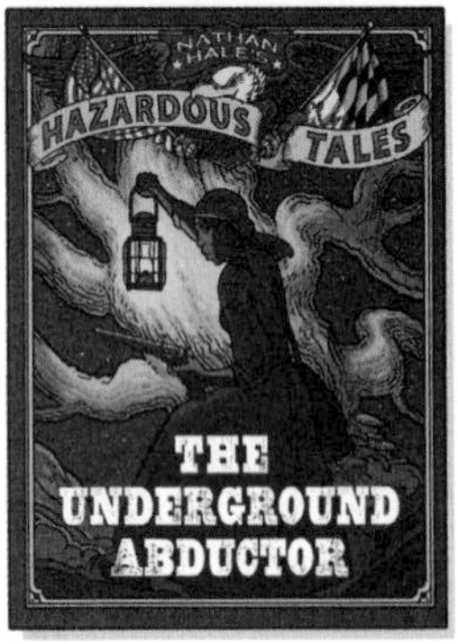

NATHAN HALE'S
HAZARDOUS
TALES
THE UNDERGROUND ABDUCTOR

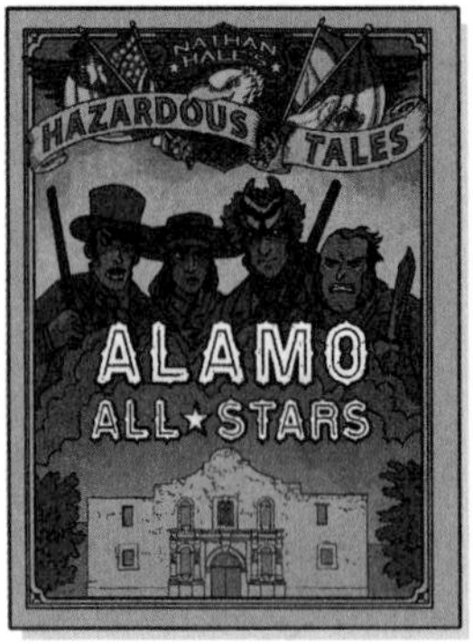

NATHAN HALE'S
HAZARDOUS
TALES
ALAMO ALL★STARS

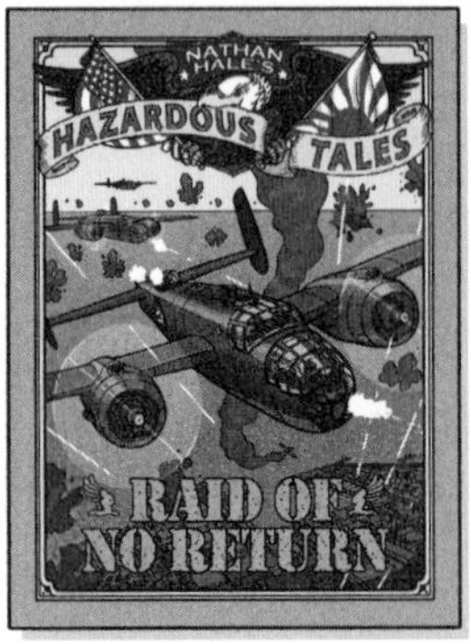

NATHAN HALE'S
HAZARDOUS
TALES
RAID OF NO RETURN

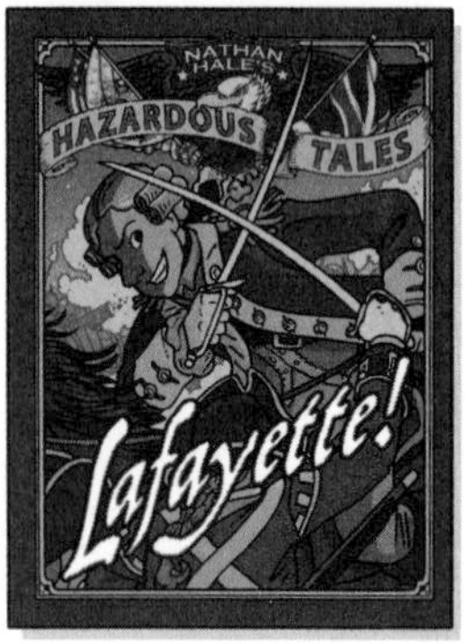

NATHAN HALE'S
HAZARDOUS
TALES
Lafayette!